SPIRITED

Berkley Sensation titles by Mary Behre

SPIRITED
GUARDED

GUARDED

Mary Behre

B

BERKLEY SENSATION, NEW YORK

THE BERKLEY PUBLISHING GROUP
Published by the Penguin Group
Penguin Group (USA) LLC
375 Hudson Street, New York, New York 10014

USA • Canada • UK • Ireland • Australia • New Zealand • India • South Africa • China

penguin.com

A Penguin Random House Company

GUARDED

A Berkley Sensation Book / published by arrangement with the author

For information, address: The Berkley Publishing Group,
a division of Penguin Group (USA) LLC,
375 Hudson Street, New York, New York 10014.

ISBN: 978-0-425-26862-9

PUBLISHING HISTORY
Berkley Sensation mass-market edition / August 2014

PRINTED IN THE UNITED STATES OF AMERICA

10 9 8 7 6 5 4 3 2 1

Cover illustration by Tony Mauro.
Cover design by Sarah Oberrender.

*For my children, who really wanted
me to write a story about talking animals.*

ACKNOWLEDGMENTS

Leis Pederson and Nalini Akolekar, thank you for believing in this series. Working with both of you is an honor.

The Berry Best Betas: Chris Behre Jr., Chris Behre Sr., Valerie Bowman, Kim Kenealy, Tara Kingston, Yvonne Richard, you patiently read whatever I put in front of you and the feedback is amazing. I simply cannot thank you enough.

Dianna Love, thank you for reading my first book in the airport and sending a cover quote that made me squeal with delight.

Kim, thank you. You are truly my best friend.

Thank you, Chief Scott Silverii, for patiently answering all of my questions about the various roles and responsibilities of police officers. Any mistakes made in this book were completely my own and sometimes intentional.

And as always, thank you, Sparky, Indy, and The Captain. You three make every day special. I love you.

PROLOGUE

THE COFFEE SUCKED. Why had he agreed to meet at this out-of-the way diner? Adam toyed with the stained mug in his hand, waiting impatiently for his client to arrive.

Client.

His lips twitched. No, the prick was Adam's mark. On the very short list of men Adam would make suffer and bleed for their crimes. The men would finally face the retribution they should have seen long ago.

The front door opened. Light shafted through briefly, out-lining the balding man's large frame. And he was a beast. Well over six feet tall, he filled the doorway or would have had he paused there long enough to cast more than a quick shadow. Instead, the client had spotted the table and loped into the room. Dressed in pressed blue jeans and a starched-collar, white button-down shirt, he gripped the strap of his messenger bag. He probably thought his semicasual look, despite the man-purse he clutched, made him blend in with the regulars of this establishment. He couldn't have stuck out worse had he shown up wearing Armani and suddenly broken into a rousing rendition of "The Eye of the Tiger."

Still, Adam nodded his greeting, gesturing to the open, faded maroon seat opposite him.

"Hi, hon. Welcome." The too-friendly, two-pack-a-day waitress nearly beat the behemoth to the table. She lifted a smudged glass pot and shook it gently, sloshing around the brown liquid. "Coffee, Mister?"

"Smythe. Jake Smythe," the client said, as if she'd been asking for his name. Given the addition of the many wrinkles on her forehead, it was clear she hadn't wanted anything other than his order.

"He'll have a cup of your *unbelievable* coffee too, Essie," Adam answered with a smile, reading her yellowed name tag.

She poured the vile liquid into a chipped white ceramic mug, then pointed to the milk cow and sugar container on the table. "If y'all need anythin' else, just give a yell."

Smythe watched the woman walk away. *Smythe, right, 'cause that didn't sound at all like Smith.*

"Mr. Smythe, do you have my money?"

Smythe's eyes widened and he glanced around before slouching in his seat.

No one looked at them. The four people in the diner, including the cook and the lone waitress, Essie, were on the opposite side of the room. Adam had selected that booth, in the corner farthest from the rest of the patrons at Café and Gas, to insure privacy.

Smythe didn't appear convinced. He fingered his coffee cup without taking a sip, frowned and darted nervous glances around the restaurant. Finally appearing reassured, he pushed the cup away from him and withdrew a thick white envelope from his murse. He flirted with dropping it on the table, twice letting the crisp edges brush the cracked laminate before twice pulling back. Finally, he dropped it into his lap.

Adam ground his back teeth, but said nothing and waited.

"How do I know you can deliver? I don't want some government busybody knocking on my door with a search warrant. It's imperative that the *thing*," he emphasized the word in a whisper, "I'm purchasing is free and clear."

Adam curled his lips into his best "you can trust me" smile. "*He's* all yours, free and clear. I've got the paperwork showing the transfer of ownership from a fictitious private collector to you. No one will come after you. Just make sure you don't pull an Ohio stunt, and the government boys will leave you alone."

Ohio. The site of the worst private zoo disaster in recent history. Revulsion crossed Smythe's face. "Right. When do I get it?"

"Tonight," Adam said and waited for Smythe to smile. Which he did. Predictable shit. "Provided you pay me. In full. Right. Now."

Smythe squirmed. Again, that fat envelope came into view. Like an overfed snake, sneaking up from beneath Smythe's side of the table. Smythe pushed it across the chipped laminate toward him.

Adam waited to see if the asshole would snatch it back again. When it remained there untouched for a full thirty seconds, he picked it up and glanced inside. While the envelope was thick, it wasn't filled with Benjamins. No, those were fifties in there. He shifted in the booth to relieve the sudden ache in his too-straight back. "Where's the rest of it?"

"Half now. Half upon delivery," the client beast said with a smug expression, then sipped his coffee. Smythe's eyes widened, smugness gave way to disgust, and he swallowed audibly.

Coughing into his fist, Smythe wheezed, "Take it or leave it."

"That wasn't the deal."

"What are you going to do? Sue me?" The Smythe asshole grinned.

Adam didn't curl his hands into fists. He didn't smash Smythe's face into the table hard enough to shatter his nose. He didn't jam the coffee spoon into the self-righteous shit's eye.

Instead, he shifted in his seat again trying to alleviate the strain on his spine. "I'll take it," Adam said, adding a heavy amount of aggravated surrender to his voice.

"Good." Smythe fished a business card out of his back pocket, then pushed it across the table. Pointing to it with one beefy finger he added, "Meet me at nine. I'll have the rest of your money."

Adam didn't answer. No need. Smythe was already heading out into the August afternoon sunshine.

One down. Four to go.

He'd go to the meet, show off the rare white tiger, and collect his money.

Then he'd feed Smythe to the hungry cat.

Or maybe not.

No sense giving the tiger indigestion before transferring him to his new home.

But Smythe would pay. Tonight.

Adam stood, dropped a couple of bills on the table, and headed toward the door. All the while envisioning how many pieces he could slice off Smythe before the bastard finally died.

CHAPTER 1

"SOMETHING'S WRONG WITH Mr. Fuzzbutt." Beau's angelic voice rang out seconds before the backside of his long-haired black guinea pig bounced before Dr. Shelley Morgan's eyes. At almost the same moment, a cry went up from the back room of the small veterinary clinic.

"Shelley, I need you!" Feet pounded quickly down the short hall before Jacob, the veterinary clinic's too-excitable intern, burst into the room yelling, "Lucy is trying to turn Hercules into her Thanksgiving dinner. And this time I think she might just chew his balls off."

"Language! And Thanksgiving's four weeks away. At most, she wants a light snack," Shelley said, pushing to her feet and sweeping the fur ball known as Mr. Fuzzbutt into her hands.

But Jacob hadn't heard her attempt to lighten the moment. The intern/groomer/assistant had already spun around and disappeared into the back room. His cries of, "Stop that, Lucy. Get up, Herc," were nearly drowned out by the cacophony of dogs barking.

Ah, it *was* a Wednesday. Most people hated Mondays because they believed the first day of the workweek was full of insanity, but Shelley knew otherwise. In her twenty-four years of life, every major catastrophe occurred on the day most folks referred to as "hump day." Today was shaping up to be as invariably crazy as every other weekday that started with the letter *W*.

"Doc, can you help him?" Beau's voice, still high-pitched from youth, wobbled as he spoke.

She turned to the worried ten-year-old who was small for his age. His large luminous brown eyes were framed by thick black glasses. His clothes, although threadbare and clearly hand-me-downs, were clean as were his faded blue sneakers.

"Don't worry, Beau. I'm sure he'll be fine. Just have a seat in the waiting area and I'll be back shortly. I'll bring Mr. . . ." she couldn't bring herself to say the word *Fuzzbutt* to the child, and settled with "your little buddy back after I've examined him."

"Okay, Doc. I trust you." Beau nodded. His words so mature for one so young. "But I can't just sit and wait. How about I bring in the bags of dog food from outside?"

"That would be a big help, Beau. You remember where the storeroom is? Just stack the ones you can carry in there. And don't try to lift the big ones."

Not that the little guy would be able to do much. The last time the clinic received donations, the dog food had come in fifty-pound bags. Beau likely didn't weigh more than sixty-five pounds himself. Plus, it had rained late last night and the town handyman she'd hired hadn't had a chance to fix the hole in the shed's roof. So chances were good several of the bags were sodden and useless.

Still, he beamed as if she'd just handed him a hundred-dollar bill. "You know it! I'll have the bags all put away before you can bring Mr. Fuzzbutt back. Just you wait and see."

Then Beau was out the front door. The length of bells hanging from the handle jangled and banged against the glass as he took off around the corner to the storage shed.

Gotta love small towns. Shelley couldn't suppress the grin, even as good ole Mr. F made a soft *whoop, whoop* noise in her hands. She glanced into his little black eyes and asked, "So are you really sick?"

The eye contact formed an instant telepathic connection. Shelley's world swirled to gray. Still vaguely aware of her surroundings, she focused her attention inward on the movie-like scenes sent from the little boar in her hands.

An image of Beau's anxious face peering between the bars of the cage, filling and refilling the bowl with pellets sprang into her mind. At first she thought the guinea pig was repeating the same image over and over, but quickly she realized what was happening.

"Oh, so you've been eating," she said. "But Beau doesn't realize it because he's been topping off the food bowl."

Mr. F. *whooped* again.

She chuckled. "Well, you're a pretty wise pig not to eat everything you've been given. Many others wouldn't have such restraint. I'm not sure I would. You sure you don't feel sick?"

The little pig winged an image of Beau snuggling him close and occasionally kissing him on the head as they watched *Scooby-Doo*. The image was so sweet she let herself get lost in the moment and almost forgot she was at the clinic.

"*Shell-ley,*" Jacob wailed.

She jumped and turned in time to see Jacob burst through the swinging door separating the back hallway from the reception area of the clinic. "Jeez! Jacob. You'll freak out the animals."

"Come *on*. I can't stop her and he's just lying there!" Jacob gestured wildly with both hands.

Right. Lucy attacking Hercules. Although Lucy was all of three pounds and a *ferret,* to Hercules, a ninety-pound dog. How much damage could she do?

"It's Wednesday," Shelley said on a sigh. "Although, at least if it started out like this, it can't get any crazier."

Mr. Fuzzbutt whooped again. *I swear, the little pig's laughing at me.*

"Jacob, take Mr. F and put him in examination room one." She hurried through the swinging white door, which led to the back, stopping briefly to hand Beau's pet to her intern. "There's a small cage in the cabinet under the sink. Pull it out and put him in it, then meet me in the doggie spa."

Without waiting for a response, she hustled to the back room. She usually avoided this area. She'd spent a weekend painting murals of fields, dog bones, blue skies, and fire hydrants on the walls to give dogs and their owners the impression of luxury accommodations. According to Jacob and their boss, Dr. Kessler, her hard work paid off. Unless she was in the room with the canines.

Today, six dogs were there for the Thanksgiving Special, a deluxe grooming, complete with a complimentary toy turkey. Metal cages lined one wall, each with a plush foam bed. The occupants waited in doggy paradise for their turn at the day's scheduled deluxe treatment by Jacob. Soft strains of Bach filtered through the air, barely audible over the ruckus of barks, yips, and howls as the canines commented on the show in the middle of the floor.

That was, until one of them caught her scent. Mrs. Hoffstedder's beagle noticed her first. He let out a single high-pitched yowl, then lowered his head and covered his eyes with his paws. One by one, the other five dogs did the same.

Shelley didn't bother to wonder why they feared her. She'd given up asking that question years ago. It's not as if she'd ever beaten an animal. Jeez, she didn't even raise her voice. But almost every dog she'd come into contact with for the past seven years either hid from her or tried to attack her.

Thank God, Jacob had remembered to lock their cages before he called for her, or it would have been dog-maggedon as the pooches ran for freedom.

She had to be the world's weirdest vet. Telepathic, she could talk to any animal alive, including snakes, hedgehogs, and naked mole rats. Any animal, that is, except for the canine variety. She hadn't spoken to a single dog since Barty, her Bay retriever, died in the car crash with her parents all those years ago. Just the thought of them made her chest tight. She shoved away the memories and focused on the clinic's current crisis.

Dr. Kessler's extremely valuable St. Bernard, Hercules, lay stretched out in the middle of the floor. The six-month-old puppy remained still. No small feat, considering Lucy, her beautiful cinnamon-colored sable ferret, was steadily chewing on his upper thigh, incredibly close to his testicles.

"You okay, Hercules?" she asked, gingerly kneeling down beside the pair and making eye contact with the dog.

Lifting only his head, he looked at her.

The telepathic connection zapped into place. An image of her prying her ferret off his body followed by him licking his dangly bits in relief flashed through her mind. She had to put her hand to her mouth to stifle a chuckle. Herc let out a loud sigh and dropped his head back to the floor.

Unlike every other dog in the world, Hercules neither feared nor loathed her. He didn't love her either. Usually he ignored her completely. But today he seemed to recognize if anyone could save his balls—*literally*—it was her.

"Lucy," she asked, focusing on her pet. "Why are you doing that?"

The ferret managed to glare briefly at Shelley and continue her assault at the same time.

In that momentary bit of eye contact, another collage of images soared into Shelley's head. It took a moment for Shelley to assemble them into an order she could understand.

"Ah, Hercules, *the gaseous*, accidentally sat on you, again, after eating his breakfast. Now you want to put 'that upstart pup' in his place?" Shelley sighed. "All right, you had your revenge. It's not like he wants to be gassy. Next time, try to avoid him after he eats. Let's go." The ferret didn't budge. Shelley prayed for patience and for no blood to be drawn. "Lucy, let go right now. You can't gnaw off his leg. And if you could, he'd be three-legged, wobbly, and end up squashing you anyway. Then you'd be trapped and forced to breathe his stench all day."

Hercules let out a rumbling *woof* of assent and shifted his weight, as if threatening to fulfill Shelley's prediction.

Lucy leapt away from Hercules with a shriek. She raced up Shelley's arm and wrapped herself around Shelley's neck for comfort. "You're all right, girl. Why don't you snuggle with me for a bit, hmmm?"

She patted the ferret on the head and rose to her feet. Hercules immediately began intimately examining his body, reassuring himself that he was still fully intact.

"Wow, how do you do that?" Jacob appeared behind her. She turned to find his brown eyes rounded and his mouth agape. "Ferrets are more like cats than dogs. But yours actually seems to understand you. Oh! They could make a reality show out of you. It could be called 'The Ferret Whisperer'."

Shelley swallowed a chuckle; no sense encouraging him. Instead, she spoke directly to the brown-and-white puppy behemoth still at her feet. "You're okay now, Hercules. It's safe to move again. Thanks for not eating her."

Hercules sprang to his paws and raced out of the room without so much as a backward glance.

And we're back to ignoring me. World order has returned.

She chuckled and didn't try to disguise it this time.

"Don't laugh. I'm serious," Jacob said. "We could make some real money if Hollywood ever heard about you." He stood, arms akimbo, in the doorway. His shaggy black hair hung in his face. He jerked his head to the right, throwing the sideways bangs out of his eyes. "I swear, I went near her and that rat tried to munch on my fingers. But *you* . . . you walked in and talked to her like Dr. Freaking Dolittle. And don't think I haven't seen you do it before. Mr. Fuzzbutt, for example. Yep, your parents misnamed you. You should have been called John Dolittle."

"I'm a woman."

"Jane then."

She shook her head at him. Little did Jacob know, she was more like the fictional character than Hugh Lofting had ever dreamed possible. Except she didn't speak to animals in their own languages. Shelley simply communicated with them telepathically. All creatures were connected. Well, mostly.

Humans were an entirely different story. She often felt like an outsider. And she was a member of the species.

"Lucy's a ferret, not a rat. If you're going to be a vet, you should know that. And as for what happened in the spa, it wasn't hard to figure out what was going on. Look, she's a good ferret who normally gets along with everyone, animals and people alike. I figured she must have been upset with Hercules. You saw him sit on her last week. And let's face it; he hasn't adjusted to the new dog food well. It didn't take much of a mental leap to figure something like that might have happened again," Shelley said, leaving the back room and heading toward her office.

"Yeah, I suppose so." Jacob sounded disappointed, but he rallied. Hurrying down the hall, he reiterated his previous comment. "Still, I've seen you do that with other animals too. It's like you know what they're thinking. Is that how you skipped ahead in vet school? You read the minds of the animal patients. Hey, would that be cheating? Can I learn how to do it?"

"What are you talking about?" Shelley stopped and faced him. His dizzying barrage of questions too much to absorb. She instead focused on the first one. "You can't skip ahead in veterinary school. I graduated last year."

"You're not old enough to have gone all the way through." Jacob waved at her. "Hello, you're my age, and I'm just getting started. Next semester anyway."

"First, you're barely old enough to be carded, but I'm twenty-four. Second, I graduated from high school with my associate's degree."

"Seriously? You took college classes in high school?"

Something about the tone of his voice set her teeth on edge, but still she kept her voice light. "Yes, and you could have done it too. I went from there to the university, where I finished up my bachelor's in twenty-four months because I didn't take summers off. Then I enrolled in veterinary school. I didn't *skip* anything."

Jacob frowned at her, then gave her a very obvious once-over. "You're . . . you're a *nerd*? But you're . . . hot. For a vet who dresses like my grandmother."

Shelley glanced at her four-inch heels. "Did you just compare me to your *grandmother*? Does she walk around in ankle-breaking high heels too?"

Jacob just grinned.

Shelley's eyes were going to pop out of her head if she listened to this guy another second. Without responding, she spun on her heel and closed the distance to her office door. Once inside the tiny space, she propped up the wooden and plastic-mesh baby gate across her doorway, designed to keep Hercules from wandering in while she was out. Setting Lucy on the floor, Shelley gave her pet a stern frown, then added aloud for good measure, "Behave. I mean it."

Lucy shook her head, sneezed indignantly, and pranced beneath Shelley's desk where her small travel cage rested. After climbing inside, she curled up into a tight ball and did what ferrets do best. She went to sleep.

"What do you want me to do with the guinea pig?" Jacob

asked. All questions about her age, her clothing, and her career seemingly forgotten. He leaned over the mesh gate rather than crossing into her sanctuary. Not that she could take refuge in it. The computer work she had to file needed to be done on the main computer out front. Her desktop had been crashing all week, and the repairman hadn't come yet.

"Leave him in the examination room until Beau's ready to take him home. I've already examined him. He's fine," she said, gathering her supplies and carefully stepping over the gate. "Look, I've got plenty of paperwork to finish before Dr. Kessler returns. So if you want to get started on Mrs. Hoff-stedder's beagle, that'd be great."

"No problem," Jacob said and disappeared into the back.

The smell of cinnamon and pinecones permeated the receptionist area. The scent was an instant soother for her nerves. Now that the dogs in the spa had calmed down, all was quiet. Peaceful.

Settling into the chair, she pulled up the afternoon schedule on the computer. The muscles in her shoulders eased. At barely noon, she had an hour before the next animal . . . er, guest, was set to arrive. Fifty guaranteed, crazy-free minutes.

She exhaled a relieved sigh. A little more tension slipped away.

Breathe, relax. This Wednesday isn't that bad.

"Uh, excuse me . . . Dr. Morgan?" Jacob's voice sounded a little too tentative. A little too respectful.

She glanced up to find the young intern standing before her. His gaze bounced around the room. He looked everywhere but at her.

An icy sensation slithered into her stomach, making it shrink. "What did you do?"

"It wasn't my fault," he said, quickly. "I didn't realize you'd left the front door open. I certainly wouldn't have let Hercules wander through the clinic unattended if you'd told me that the place was open for business. Or that you had some kid carrying bags of food inside from the shed. I would have locked him up."

"Him, who?" The words were out of her mouth nanoseconds before the answer slammed into her.

Hercules. The dog. *The* dog.

"Are you telling me that Hercules, Dr. Kessler's prized St.

Bernard . . ." Her voice pitched higher with each word. "The one he calls his *only true baby* is *missing*?"

"Not my fault." Jacob held up his hands.

From behind him came a sound of someone sniffing back tears. "I'm so sorry, Doc. I didn't see him by the door until after I'd opened it. I tried to stop him. I had him real good for about a minute."

Beau stepped out from behind Jacob. His blue shirt was torn from the shoulder to the wrist down one sleeve. Worse, he had an ugly patch of road rash on his upper left arm that disappeared up the ripped shirt. His glasses were askew and hanging by an arm.

She raced around Jacob and checked Beau's injuries. Pointing at the intern, she ordered, "You, chase after him."

"Yeah, see I can't run. Remember, I tore my ACL doing that Mud Run with the Barbie Twins back in September?" He gestured to the brace on his knee. He wasn't on crutches anymore, but that didn't mean he was cleared to go chasing a dog all over town.

"Shoot, shack, shipwreck!" she cursed, kicking off her ridiculous heels. What she wouldn't give for a pair of sneakers and some jeans right now. "Jacob, help Beau get cleaned up. There's a sewing kit in my desk, get it out and we'll repair his shirt. See if you can fix his glasses. Make sure the rest of the dogs are locked up tight. Do *not* answer the phone for anyone. Let it go to voice mail. And for the love of that St. Bernard, if Dr. Kessler returns before I come back, do not tell him you let his dog escape."

"What do I say?"

"I don't know. Tell him I took Herc for a walk or something."

"Right, like he'll believe that one," Jacob scoffed. "Dogs hate you, remember? So maybe you aren't like Dr. Dolittle after all, huh?"

"Jacob! Focus." Shelley headed for the door, calling over her shoulder, "Let's hope Dr. Kessler doesn't beat me back here."

Shelley shoved open the door. Sunlight poured in, along with a blast of unseasonably warm November air, belying the sodden state of the area after last night's downpour of sleet and rain. At least she wasn't running in her stockings in the rain or snow. This time. Yeah, like that single bit of good news made up for the fact that it was a Wednesday, and she was about to run outside shoeless on the still wet and most likely muddy ground.

Hercules, come back before anyone in town sees you doing your Born Free *impression.*

That would just put the stale dog treat on top of her already rancid dog-food bowl of a day.

TIDEWATER POLICE DETECTIVE Devon Jones pulled his black Lexus into the parking lot of Elkridge Veterinary Clinic. He cut the engine, imagining what he'd say when he saw Shelley again.

Her e-mail to him last week had been like a gift from God. He'd been searching for her for weeks. Even going so far as to track down her fiancé—his former roommate—and that was all kinds of a suckfest because Camden Figurelle, that rat bastard, was in Africa. In the *Peace Corps*. There was no way to get in touch with him, if it wasn't an absolute emergency.

What the hell was Cam doing in the Peace Corps anyway? They were supposed to be married by now.

Shells. Shelley Amanda Morgan.

He'd spent the past few weeks searching for Figurelle because the wedding should have happened last summer. Cam's family had listed the engagement in the society section of the *Baltimore Sun*. Dev read it, marked the date, and noted with some disappointment, he hadn't received an invitation. Not that he'd have gone. As much as he wanted Shells to be happy, he hadn't wanted to watch her marry the wrong man.

But she hadn't married Cam. Maybe Shelley had come to her senses and seen the prick for what he was and given him the old heave-ho. The thought brought a smile to Dev's face.

Still, wrong man or not, at least Cam had been a link to Shells. Without the connection, Dev had been stumped in the search for her. But then two days ago, she contacted him through an old e-mail address he'd kept from his college days. And damn if that wasn't some good luck.

Dev pulled his phone from his inside jacket pocket and clicked to her saved e-mail. He read it again, although he had it memorized.

Hey Dev,

It's me, Shelley Morgan. I know it's been a long time but I could use your help. I heard you're a police officer now but what I need is to use your puzzle-solving skills. Speaking of the police, I remember you wanted to be a detective. Did that ever happen?

Anyway, I was wondering if I could convince you to leave Tidewater for a few days and come to Elkridge. It's a little town on the border of Suffolk and Tidewater. Great place. Friendly people. Quiet community. Low crime. Sounds like heaven, right?

Well, something strange is going on. I think. See, there's this private zoo. Since I moved here last June there have been a number of unexplained disappearances of animals. I've tried contacting the USDA, but they're no help. It's hard to explain in an email but I just know something is wrong. I've tried investigating this on my own, but I can't piece it together. Plus, I have to be careful how much noise I make. People in small towns talk, you know.

If you could come and take a look around, I've got some papers, animal records, and old newspaper clippings. Maybe I'm paranoid and there's nothing really wrong here. But if I'm not, then your time could save the life of an animal. Or ten.

Email me back and I'll give you directions to the veterinary clinic where I work.

Hope to hear from you soon,
Shells

He darkened the screen and returned the phone to his pocket. Maybe he should have replied to her e-mail or called first instead of just driving over. But what could he say?

"Hi, Shells, long time no see. Can you believe it's been three years since graduation? Time sure flies and all that. While I want to know about this mystery you've unearthed, I'm more interested in the fact that you and Cam aren't together anymore.

I've been crazy about you since the first time you smiled at me. Had you not been Camden's girl in school, I would have moved heaven and earth to get you into my bed. I also have a big surprise for you. I've found something of yours. If you'll just come back to Tidewater with me, I'll show you."

Yeah, that would go over really well. He sounded like a stalker or like he was just hoping for a quick-and-dirty one-night stand. And a one-night stand was absolutely not what he wanted. Although, he'd settle for it if that's all he could have.

Dev gave himself a mental shake. He'd come to give her news she'd once told him she never thought she'd hear. Her older sister, Jules, was alive, well, happy, living in Tidewater, still seeing ghosts, and searching for Shelley.

The news of her long-lost sibling should be enough for Shelley to forgive his disappearance after graduation. But really, he hadn't known what to say. And Camden had made it pretty damned clear that Dev was not welcome in their lives. Plus, it wasn't like Shelley had called him, even once, in all that time.

Okay, so she'd been busy getting her veterinary license and building a happy life with Cam-the-sack. At least Dev had thought she'd been happy, until a few days ago. Although he couldn't quite ignore the pinch to his ego that she hadn't called him sooner. After all, they had been friends.

Christ, he was starting to sound like a freaking girl. First brooding over *feelings* and worrying about why she hadn't contacted him sooner. Next he'd want to start a knitting circle.

Okay, so his motives for coming here weren't completely altruistic. He was man enough to admit to himself that if a hint of the spark he'd felt for her back in college still ignited when he saw her again, he'd do it. He'd ask her out . . . This time, no one would stop him.

He'd use the next few days to let her really get to know him. Help her with her little zoo problem and take her to see her sister Jules. Maybe then, he'd have finally earned the right to spend time with the sexiest, most caring woman he'd ever met.

Dev shoved open the car door and stepped onto the damp cobblestone. His Ferragamos crunched over the wet, gritty street. He glanced around the nearly deserted road of the picturesque little town. Despite Elkridge's location on the scenic

James River—with no elks or ridges in sight—the place lacked one key element Tidewater was known for.

Salt air.

This afternoon, the scent on the warm November wind was rife with apples and cinnamon from the local shops. Refreshing and sweet.

Just like Shelley. Assuming she was as perfect as he remembered. Right. Like she could be anything other than the sweet, shy girl he'd crushed on so long ago. She'd probably be so grateful he had come to help her solve her mystery and had found Jules on top of it that she'd ask him out.

Dream on, man!

While he and his partner had wrapped up the biggest case Tidewater had seen all year, there were others that still needed his attention. A few days were all he could afford to spend away from the office. He'd really only taken the five days because he'd foolishly hoped he'd what . . . see Shelley and she'd finally fall in love with him? They'd run off to Vegas and get married?

Right and we'll have a unicorn and Elvis stand up for us at the ceremony.

Exhaling hard, he started to make his way toward a whitewashed brick building with the Elkridge Animal Clinic sign hanging over the front door.

A huge, blurry mass appeared so quickly in front of him, it seemed to pop into existence from nowhere.

Blam!

It flew at his chest, knocking him to the ground. Dev's head smacked the pavement. Tiny stars burst to vibrant multicolored life in front of his eyes.

The something was large and furry and pinning him. Still he managed to get a hand free. He reached for his sidearm, which . . . shit! . . . he'd left locked in the trunk of his car.

The damned beast burrowed its muzzle against his cheek and rumbled a deep, throaty growl.

A bear?

Cold fear slid down his neck. Or that might have been the animal's bloodthirsty drool. He might be a city boy, but he'd heard all about bear attacks in small towns like this one. He held perfectly still, eyes closed, playing dead as he tried to get a sense of the animal's size. If it were a bear, it wasn't fully grown. A cub, maybe? But a big one.

Relief at the thought evaporated at the next.

Where there's a cub, there's a mama bear somewhere. Dev couldn't just lie there; he needed to protect his vital organs before the animal figured out he was still warm enough to chew on. He rolled onto his side and into a ball, protecting his head, face, arms, and torso.

The bear seemed to tighten its hold on him. Its breath coming hot and nose hair curling against Dev's ear.

He was going to be eaten by a bear in the middle of this damned street while everyone in Elkridge was out to lunch. Trying to curl more tightly, he elbowed the beast in a front leg. It yelped.

Wait. Bears don't yelp. Plus, it wasn't trying to bite him. No, it was pawing at his arms, not painfully. *Playfully?*

A long, wet tongue slid across his hair, his ear, his *cheek*. And that growl he heard was followed by a deep woof. A dog, he was pinned by a dog. A great bear of a dog, but definitely the canine species as opposed to the Ursus americanus.

Dev slowly turned onto his back then drew his arms away from his face only to throw them up again when a slobbery tongue swiped from one cheek across his nose to the other. "Ugh. Serious dog breath. You need a breath mint, Fido."

Shifting onto his side, he attempted to scoot out from beneath the beast, but the dog took it as a game and began licking him in earnest down the neck of his suit. If he hadn't needed a shower before the dog knocked him down, between rolling on the cobblestone and the sloppy dog kisses, he certainly needed one now.

Hoping not to hurt the animal that was clearly looking for a playmate, Dev pushed at the beast's midsection in an effort to make a break for it. He'd barely touched the dog when someone yelled, "Stop it, you big bear! You'll hurt him."

Okay, that wasn't the first time in his life he'd been called a bear. Still, the words stung his pride. The average person might consider him to be bearlike, due to his large size, but he wasn't an animal. He was a police detective. A cop. A friggin' hero.

Although, at the moment he was in the least heroic position. Ever.

"Hercules, stop before you hurt him. You bad puppy," the voice said, closer now. "I'm really sorry about Hercules. Are you okay down there? Give me a minute. I've almost got his leash on him."

Ah, Hercules was the *dog's* name. She was calling the dog a big bear.

The relief coursing through him at that knowledge was quickly overshadowed by a sickening realization. He knew that voice.

There was a distinctive clink of metal on metal and the dog was off him.

"I'm so sorry," she said, then she laughed. The sound more exhalation of air than joy. "I'm really, *really* sorry. He doesn't normally do this. But I guess all creatures crave freedom, right? Are you . . . are you hurt?"

His gut shrank at her melodic voice. Now? She had to show up and see him covered in dog drool and muck, lying on the ground, pinned there by a playful bear-dog.

Maybe if I'm lucky, she won't recognize me beneath the slobber?

"Dev?" Her voice was closer now. He could feel her breath against his chin as she leaned down to look at him. "Is that you?"

"Uh . . . yeah." Dev lay there for a moment. His arm still firmly over his eyes and his head throbbing. His luck was good for buckets of suck.

"Why, bless your heart. Devon Jones, it *is* you." She sounded positively gleeful. "What are you doing down there?"

"Playing possum with Fido." He tugged his arm away and blinked open his eyes. The starbursts were gone, but he'd have a nice knot on the back of his skull later. It was already coming up.

And there she was. Leaning over him, her hair a cloud of red curls around her face. Concern and confusion crowded into her sapphire-blue eyes. Her pink lips twitched. "Thank God, it was you Hercules tackled. How do you do it? You always manage to show up just when I need saving."

If only that were true.

CHAPTER 2

"Hi, Shells, long time no see," Dev said, then inwardly winced.

Long time no see? He was an idiot. Couldn't he come up with something better than some lame-ass cliché?

Rubbing his doggie-licked face with his sleeve, he sat up but made no move to stand. Shelley Morgan was right here, in front of him. Even more beautiful than he'd remembered. Better. Unlike Jules, who was a little skinny for his taste, Shelley was full-figured. The kind of woman a man could take into his arms and not worry about snapping her like a twig. Her slim beige skirt hugged her hips like a groping lover. She bent closer to him, the buttons on her white shirt straining to contain her voluptuous breasts.

And suddenly, the cartoon wolves with their tongues rolling out at the sight of a beautiful woman made sense to him. He tightened his jaw to keep his own tongue in check. Three years of absence had done nothing to dim his attraction to his former college English tutor.

"Dev?" Shelley frowned, leaning closer to his face. "Are you hurt?"

"No." But the word came out as little more than a growl.

"Oh-kay." The dog tugged and she tightened her grip on the leash, then said in a rush, "Sorry about Hercules. He's really a good dog."

He glanced at her face, expecting to see the same nervous smile or blatant panic most people got when he growled at them. Instead, she beamed at him. Joy suffused her features, making her more beautiful.

"Thank you so much for catching him." The dog tugged for freedom again. She clicked her tongue at him and shortened the leash, looping it around her hand twice. "Your timing's impeccable, as usual."

"Happy to help." Rolling onto his hands and knees, he caught sight of the run in her stocking starting at her big toe and disappearing beneath her skirt. "Shelley, where are your shoes?"

She didn't respond to him, clearly too busy trying to convince the great bear-dog to stay.

Dev cleared his throat and straightened to his full height until he towered over her, but he couldn't stop staring at her toes. Her toenails were Christmas green and decorated with little white snowmen. He couldn't quite hide his grin.

Somewhere nearby a bell jangled and someone with a remarkably young voice shouted, "Doc, did you catch him?"

She glanced around the street, clearly nervous. She held up a finger as if asking Dev to wait, then called back over her shoulder, "I've got him, Beau. Everything's okay now. We'll be in in a minute. Go back inside and wait for me, please."

"Yes'm," the voice called again, followed by the bang of a door closing.

Then she stood there, staring at him. His mind completely blanked at the look of delight in her blue-blue eyes. Suddenly, his years on the force meant nothing, and he felt as awkward as he had in his first tutoring session. So he said the first thing that popped into his head, "I came to town to find you."

"I hope so. I sent you that e-mail asking you to come." She laughed, her shoulders relaxed, and her eyes sparkled. A wide grin spread across her lips. When serious, she was beautiful, but when she smiled like that . . . full-on blind-side knockout.

"Oh my gosh, I can't believe you're here." She squealed and

threw her arms around his waist. His arms went around her lush body as if they'd been designed for that express purpose.

Oh, sweet God.

She fit against him perfectly. He buried his nose in her hair. She smelled so good. Vanilla and sugar.

As spectacular as it felt holding Shelley close, the moment was definitely waning. Especially when the leash she still had looped around her wrist inadvertently tugged the massive dog tight against Dev's leg.

Yes, that was drool soaking into his slacks and plastering the material to his thigh.

If it was on his clothes and he was hugging her, then . . . "Oh damn, Shelley. I'm getting you filthy."

Shelley, still grinning, released him and bit her lip as she watched him fruitlessly try to de-slobber. He stepped back and tried to pull the Armani pant leg away from his body. What had he been thinking wearing them here? He should have worn his jeans, not just packed them. He knew this was a small town that had more farmers than bankers. Suits were fine for Tidewater, but here they just made him look pretentious . . . or stupid, since he *was* covered in muck.

"You're really here?" she asked, joy still making her voice lilt. "How long are you in town? Do we have enough time to visit before you help me, or do you need to get back right away? Why didn't you tell me when you were coming? Not that I'm sorry you're here, but I would have been more prepared, you know? Look at me getting ahead of myself. I should have asked if you did it. Did you make detective before your twenty-fifth birthday? Although . . ." She frowned. "I wanted to ask you in person, but Cam said your girlfriend didn't like us. So it would be best to give you two some space. I hope I didn't cause you any problems by breaking the silence."

Cam, you rotten sonofa . . .

Tension coiled in Dev's shoulders and he rotated them to relax it away. That bastard had lied to her. Again. But standing in the middle of the street was not the place to have *that* discussion. Dev needed to move them to some place with a little more privacy.

"It's great to see you too Shells. I'm in town for a few days. Why don't we go someplace we can talk?"

She smiled and nodded, then repeated one of her questions. "Did you make detective?"

Dev couldn't suppress the grin. "Yeah, I did. Last summer."

She squealed and threw her arms around his waist again. Shorter this time, and she'd already withdrawn when she said, "I knew it! I knew you'd do it. Where are you working?"

"I'm on the Tidewater Police Force in the burglary/robbery division. My partner and I just wrapped up a pretty important case. A real career-maker."

"I have no doubt you're going to be the best." The look in her eyes was pure hero worship. And a little unnerving. He'd seen that look from the police groupies he'd met over the past few years but had never expected to see it in Shelley's eyes. As if sensing his discomfort, she added, "I bet your partner considers himself lucky to have you. You were always so smart and careful and—"

The big dog decided he wasn't quite ready to give up his bid for freedom and gave a mighty yank. Shelley stumbled on the slick cobblestone. She might have hit the ground if Dev hadn't caught her and held her close.

Her back pressed against his chest, her elbows in his hands. Crap. He had really covered her front to back in muck now. But she didn't seem to notice. Or maybe she didn't mind.

"There you go rescuing me again." She tilted her head up and to the side to look at him over her shoulder. A mischievous glint in her eyes. "Should I swoon now too? You know, go for the complete damsel-being-rescued-by-the-knight act?"

A surprised laugh burst from him. "Thanks, no."

"That's good. I suck at playing the helpless female anyway," she said, chuckling. She pulled away, then turned to face him.

"Oh dear, you are covered. I'm really sorry."

Dev glanced at his mud-encrusted suit and forced a grin. "It could be worse. I just need a shower." Dev checked his watch. "Except, damn, I can't check into my hotel until three."

"Don't worry about it. You can shower with me."

Ah, yeah. Now there's a welcome any man could appreciate. His thoughts must have shown on his face because Shelley turned apple red.

"No! Oh God. I didn't mean *with* me. I meant at my place." Shelley blushed from her forehead to the collar of her tight top. "Oh my God. I can't believe I said that. Ha! Freudian slip, much? No really, I uh, meant you can come over to my place and use my shower after I'm done. Or before. You can use it before me. Either way is fine."

And that was one Freudian slip he could seriously get into.

Given the way she was blushing and rambling, Dev accepted with no small amount of regret that it probably was just a slip of the tongue.

"That would be great, Shells. I wouldn't mind an opportunity to de-funk."

Her lips curled into a grin. "You know, no one has called me that in years. *Shells.*"

"Really? You signed your e-mail that way."

"I did?"

"Yeah. I suppose I could call you Dr. Shells, but that just sounds too formal." He winked at her, relieved that some of his earlier awkwardness had disappeared. "I could call you Shelley, if you—"

"Shells is great," she said quickly. "Really great. You're uh, great. To . . . to come to Elkridge and help me with my problem. Mystery! The missing animals."

Despite the smudge of dirt on her cheek and the sludge on their clothes, a sexual awareness zinged through the air. Riveting and echoing. Time suspended until a strong wind whipped through the street, chilling Dev's legs.

"Like Hercules here?"

"What?" She blinked twice, then shook her head. "No, he's not missing. He's just trying to go on a walkabout." And the dog gave a mighty pull on his leash that damn near toppled Shelley again.

"Mind if I take the dog?" He slid his hand down her arm to take the leash from her. The touch sent another sizzle of awareness, this time straight to his groin.

"Sure." She stared at him another moment, her eyes hazy as if she too couldn't deny that pulse of heat beating between them. She blinked and her expression shifted to something distant but still friendly. Shelley gestured toward the beast. "Hercules is a great dog for most people. Loving and gentle. But puppies like Herc crave a bit of freedom from time to time."

"I'm glad to see your *issue* with man's best friend has been resolved." Dev slipped the leash off her arm. Immediately the animal sat down, his big tail thumping the cobblestone street. "Your gift of communicating with animals now extends to dogs? Or do you still call your gift a 'crift'?"

"My cursed gift." Her cheeks pinkened. "No, I don't call it a crift anymore. God, I can't believe you remember all that."

"Kind of hard to forget your Dolittle gift, especially after I watched you talk your roommate's cat out of that tree." Dev rubbed the top of the dog's head. "But then you couldn't go into Cam's house if his dog was there. I seem to recall Troian chasing you back into the car after a party our junior year."

"Yeah, not my fondest memory." She shook her head but grinned. "Nothing's really changed in the animal kingdom. Except for Herc here, every canine I've met since I turned seventeen freaks out on me." She glanced at the big puppy and shrugged. "I'm not sure why Hercules is different. Maybe because I helped deliver him by cesarean when he was born? I was the first human to touch him. Whatever the reason, I'm grateful he's mostly immune to my weirdness."

"Mostly?"

"We have an understanding. I rescue him from vicious attacking ferrets," she turned and spoke directly to Hercules, "and he *doesn't* run away and cost me my job."

"Your job?"

"Hercules belongs to my boss, Dr. Kessler." She glanced around anxiously, as if suddenly realizing where they were. "I really shouldn't be standing out here. I need to get him back inside the clinic before someone sees that his pet escaped. The number one commerce in this town is gossip."

At the other end of the street, the door to the diner opened again. Two women stepped out onto the street. They could have been twins, given their matching lace-collar tops, tan pants, and navy coats. Except the woman on the right was short, skinny, had blond hair and pale-white skin, and the one on the left was statuesque, had ebony skin and a short gray bob.

"Oh dear, the Elizabeths," Shelley muttered, stepping backward, as if to avoid being seen. "They see me out here shoeless, covered in mud, and talking to a stranger, and it'll be all over town in fifteen minutes."

"Gossip, right. Understood. Why don't you lead the way?" He gestured with his free hand, while he held firmly to the leash with the other. Shelley half-hopped, half-ran across the uneven stone street toward the clinic door.

Clicking his tongue at the dog the way he'd seen Shelley do a few minutes earlier, Dev signaled for Hercules to move. The dog responded immediately, trotting happily behind Shelley, but not too close.

The bells jangled as Dev, Shelley, and Hercules crossed the threshold. The door shut with a snap, and Shelley leaned against it. A wide, relieved smile on her face, she exhaled an exaggerated sigh. "Now that you're here, I'll show you around."

Shelley scrubbed her hand down her face, smudging the streak of dirt on her cheek. It made her look adorable.

"Great," Dev said, finding his voice.

But they didn't move. They stood there. Shelley shoeless, propped against the front door. Dev covered in muck and filth, and that spark he'd felt all those years ago turned into a brilliant shining flame of molten attraction.

Hercules woofed, breaking the moment. Shelley laughed and shifted slightly to rub her left foot. "I've got so much to tell you, Dev."

"Yeah, me too. But maybe you can start by explaining what happened to your shoes."

HER SHOES. FIGURES that he'd notice she wasn't wearing them. Not that it wasn't a hundred-and-eighty-percent obvious since she was rubbing her aching arch. But yikes. Could she look any more like a dork? Not that Dev had ever treated her like one.

"Just a sec," Shelley said, putting the Out to Lunch sign in the window. "To make sure we're not disturbed."

Dev bent down to stroke Hercules behind the ears. She used the opportunity to let herself really look at her old friend.

He was still huge. At six foot four, he was all powerful muscle and still heart-stoppingly sexy. His expensively tailored—and thanks to Hercules, now ruined—suit draped over his form in the most delicious way.

Most men as muscular as Dev would look beefy in a suit, but he didn't. No, where most guys worked out in a gym to get that pumped, Dev said a lot of his build came from genetics. She wasn't sure how true that was, because he also used to say he was the runt of the litter. The man definitely exercised regularly to stay fit. And if that hug he gave her earlier was any indication, he still kept himself in tip-top shape.

His sand-colored hair was slightly long in the front but cut short on the sides and in the back. And those eyes. God, she'd always loved his eyes. So pale blue-gray they were more like the color of storm clouds over the ocean. But from her vantage point, with him bent over, it wasn't his eyes she ogled. No, it was his model-worthy butt. Those slacks, grimy though they may be, hugged his backside and advertised that God really did dole out perfect bodies to a lucky few.

Dev straightened, then cleared his throat. When she met his gaze, the lazy half grin on his face said he knew what she'd been doing.

Busted! Heat scorched her cheeks.

"My-my shoes, right . . ." she stammered, desperate to discuss anything other than his yummy-looking butt. Because really, *I've had this fantasy of banging the headboard with you since freshman year* just didn't seem appropriate since he'd come to town as a favor for her. Plus, he'd been best friends with both Cam and Shelley. All through college he'd had an insanely jealous girlfriend. And really, what were the odds of him being single today? Given her luck, somewhere in the vicinity of nada.

Although, no ring.

"It's actually quite logical why I'm not wearing them," she said, forcing her mind back on topic. She reached beside the door and picked up her discarded shoes. Sliding her foot into one, she held up the other as evidence. "I kicked them off when I realized I needed to run after Hercules. They're four inches high. There's no way I could run in those crazy things. Not outside on the cobblestones anyway. And I certainly didn't think I'd catch him as quickly as I did. Thank you for that."

Before Dev could respond, both Beau and Jacob burst through the swinging door. Jacob was laughing about something, but the little boy appeared worried. Tiny lines appeared between his narrowed brows, the scrape on his arm, now nearly hidden by the repaired shirt. "I really am sorry, Doc."

"It's really fine, Beau. Are you all right?" Shelley jammed her foot into the other shoe, then hurried down the length of the counter to give the boy a hug, but stopped when Beau's eyes widened.

He pointed to her shirt. "What happened to you, Doc?"

"It's nothing." Not wanting to get the child dirty, she ruffled his hair. "Don't worry about me. Just a little dirt. And don't worry about Hercules either. My friend here caught him for us. I'd still be chasing Herc down the street, if not for his willingness to throw himself into the line of fire."

Dev shook his head, smiling. "I don't know that I intentionally did anything other than act as the human version of a bearskin rug for the big dog. But I'm glad I could help."

Shelley didn't miss the way Dev rubbed the back of his neck and didn't quite meet her gaze when he spoke.

She bit down hard to keep from smiling. At least that hadn't changed. Dev was as noble and shy as he'd been in college. Amazing, considering he came from money, wore a suit that would have cost her a month's salary, and was a police detective. If ever there was someone who might be expected to live like the entitled rich, it was he. Yet here he stood, embarrassed from a simple compliment.

Her pulse raced because . . . wow. There was nothing more scintillating than a shy man who looked like a sex god. Even when dirty.

Beau moved closer to her. His big brown eyes luminous behind his now-repaired glasses. "You got railroad tracks in your hose. Mama Margaret says that means pantyhose are ruined when that happens and money's been lost. Did you mess them up because *I* let Hercules escape?"

His bottom lip quivered and Shelley wondered, not for the first time, why someone like *Mama Margaret* would be allowed to remain a foster parent.

Shelley had already reported Mama Margaret on suspicions of abuse once. CPS was alerted to her. Not that it helped little Beau right now. Schooling her features to show only support and confidence, she squatted in front of him.

"No, it's fine. I have a spare pair in my desk. But how about you? How's your arm, little man?" Shelley asked, examining Beau's injury. Satisfied the boy would be okay, she suggested,

"Why don't you leave Mr. . . . uh, your *friend* here and I'll drop you at school. You can come by to get him *after* school gets out."

"Doc, it's a teacher workday. No school." Beau's eyebrows drew together to form one long, wavy brown line.

"I forgot about that. Well, then why don't I go get your friend for you, and you can take him home?"

"He's okay?"

"Definitely. He's completely healthy. Let him finish what's in his bowl before you refill it and you'll see he's eating." When he didn't do more than nod, she asked, "Don't you want to take him home right now?"

And there it was, that light in his eyes that made Beau look ages older than ten. "Nah, he likes it here. I'll work off the time. Besides, isn't it the same price if he's here for a few minutes or all day? I'm not finished bringing in the donations. And Jacob said I could help him in the doggie spa."

"Beau, that's very generous of you, but I've got to be out of the clinic this afternoon. Plus, you know how crazy Wednesdays are—" she said, but he cut her off.

"You know, Wednesdays aren't all bad, Doc. I met you on a Wednesday. That was definitely a good day."

"You're absolutely right." A lump formed in Shelley's throat at the sincerity in Beau's voice. It would be so easy for her to love this little boy, if he were hers. But that could never happen. She wasn't ever going to be anyone's mother.

"Dude!" Jacob called out and Shelley welcomed the interruption. She glanced at her intern who said with badly suppressed laughter, "You're a total mess. Did Herc do that to you?"

Shelley turned to see Dev futilely brushing at the grit on his suit with his fingers. He only succeeded in coating his hands in the fine black silt.

Wow. Would that come out with dry cleaning? And how would she pay for it? Between paying for health insurance, car insurance, and student loans, she was barely making rent.

"It's fine," Dev said to Jacob. "Doctor . . . ?"

"Sorry. Where are my manners? Dev, meet Jacob Durand and Beau Connors. Beau is our youngest volunteer, and Jacob is our very capable intern who's going to be a vet before long."

"Wow, thanks, Dr. Morgan." Jacob stood a little straighter, his chest puffed with pride.

"You're welcome, Jacob." She returned his grin. "Now, I think we've made use of the detective as a dogsitter for far too long. Can you please take Hercules to the back?"

Jacob gave an exaggerated sigh and slumped his shoulders. "And it's back to being the dog groomer. Ah, well." Jacob winked at her, then eyed the dog warily, patting his head. "Come on, Herc. *Eww*! Gross! You're filthy." Sparing a glance at Dev, he added, "What'd you do, roll in the street with him? I'm gonna have to give him another bath."

The white of the dog's fur had been tinged gray with dirt and grime. Dev hadn't faired much better. One of Dev's pant legs was plastered to him. And come to think of it, Shelley's blouse was sticking to her belly.

She glanced down. Fabulous! Her top showed off just how much exercise she *didn't* get. Talk about displaying all the wrong curves. Tugging the wet material away from her now-cold tummy, she added, "Just hurry and do it before Dr. Kessler gets back. We don't need him to learn his prized baby has been loose. I'd hate to upset him. He's having such a rough time these days. Although, he still might learn of the escape. I'm not sure if Mrs. Hoffstedder or Mrs. Blaney saw us."

"The Elizabeths?" Dev asked. When Shelley nodded, he added, "They didn't. Your secret's safe."

"Besides, it's not like Dr. Kessler'll remember ten minutes after he's told anyway. If he doesn't write it down, it's forgotten," Jacob said with a grin, but his smile quickly morphed into open-mouthed, bug-eyed horror. "I'm so sorry, Dr. Morgan. You-you won't tell him I said that, will you?"

Tempting.

"No, I won't say anything, if you don't. Just go and clean up Hercules." Shelley shooed Jacob toward the back door with her free hand. "I'm leaving the Out to Lunch sign up. Make sure you take it down at one. I'm headed home to clean up, then I'll be at the zoo this afternoon. Dr. Kessler should be back in the office by two. Think you can get all the guests in the doggie spa handled by then?"

"No prob." Jacob nodded until his bangs flew into his eyes

again. Then he jerked his head sharply to the left to clear the hair from his vision.

"Don't forget we've got a cat scheduled for a grooming this afternoon. Mrs. Blaney's old orange tabby. Make sure to place Morris in the cat sanctuary and lock that door tight when she drops him off. We don't need him strolling into the spa again."

"Gotcha." Jacob took Hercules's leash and hurried through the swinging door.

"Doggie spa? Cat sanctuary?" Dev asked at the same time Beau said, "I'll just finish bringing in the dog food."

Shelley glanced at the little boy so often forgotten by the town; she didn't miss the way his stomach rumbled. "Have you had lunch yet? You can go get something. Or I can drop you and your guinea pig at home. You can always come back after."

"Nah, no good." Beau grimaced. "Mama Margaret will be mad for sure if she sees you at her house, Doc. You know how upset she got the last time you tried to help me."

Shelley frowned at the memory. She took an instant dislike · to Mama Margaret on their first meeting. Probably because the old bat insisted that Beau call her Mama, all the time reminding Beau how no one wanted him and he was lucky she kept him.

Then Mama Margaret had turned her beady, greedy eyes on Shelley, as if daring Shelley to argue. Oh, she had wanted to, but refrained. Shelley remembered all too well how much uglier life in the foster care system could be when *outsiders* interfered.

That nasty meeting had been on a Wednesday. Another hard truth Shelley had to learn. The whole town had known Beau had been abandoned by his biological mother. That he was probably being neglected at best, emotionally abused at worst, by his foster mother—but no one could do anything about it without proof.

Shelley doubted it was love that kept Beau silent. And he was more than silent. Beau did everything he could to keep his failure of a foster mother from getting into trouble. Even denying allegations of abuse when questioned by the social workers.

But Shelley understood his motive. Having lost her sisters, Hannah and Jules, in that callous machine called the foster care system, Shelley knew how badly the program could fail. Even though she was eventually adopted by a loving couple, she still had nightmares.

So she couldn't blame Beau for wanting to protect his life, such as it was. After all, a known hell was better than an unknown one.

"Beau, surely Mama Margaret must be okay with you coming to see me here. I mean you're here all the time . . ." She let her words trail off at Beau's sideways glance. He chewed on his thumbnail and stared at the portrait of Dr. Kessler hanging over the couch. In the white suit, with that white hair and goatee, the vet looked more like Colonel Sanders than an animal doctor.

Beau's fascination with the picture was his tell whenever he tried to lie or hide something. A small headache formed behind her right eye. "Oh, dear. She doesn't *let* you come here, does she?"

"She *does*." Beau met Shelley's gaze briefly before shifting his eyes away. "She thinks Dr. Kessler lets me help *him*. That I don't see you at all. She told me if she found out I was lying, she'd get rid of Mr. Fuzzbutt so I won't have no reason to come back here. If I tell her it's you I've been helping—"

"I got it." She raised her hands in submission. And she *did* get it. The poor kid was being forced to choose between lying about spending time with someone who'd shown him an ounce of kindness or facing the harsh truth—and the inevitable cruelty that went with it. The child had chosen lies.

It made her stomach twist into knots. "How about I drop you off down the block? She won't see my car."

"I don't know . . ."

So many people in this town pretended not to see Beau. He probably *could* walk four blocks in tattered clothes and no one would know. Or care.

That sparked a rage inside of her so hot it frightened her. She wasn't this kid's mother. She had no claim to him whatsoever. She couldn't let herself get any more involved than she already was. Taking a mental step back, she pushed down her anger at the town's dismissal of one of its youngest residents and focused on getting him food.

"Wait one second." Shelley hurried to her office and returned within seconds, wallet in hand. She pulled out twenty dollars and handed it to the boy. "Go to the diner, buy lunch for you and Jacob. I'm sure he'd appreciate a break. And food. Then you can finish bringing in the donations. Deal?"

Beau's face lit up, then immediately dimmed. "I can't take your money, Doc. Ain't right."

"Excuse me," Dev's deep voice broke in. "But if you're helping out the clinic, it seems like a fair deal to me. I think that's called payment for services rendered."

"That's right. Thank you, Dev." She turned to Dev, who gave her a friendly smile. A strange green color pulsed around him. She blinked in confusion. *Are my eyes playing tricks on me?*

"Okay." A slow smile slid across the boy's face. "In that case, see ya!" He was out the door, the bells jangling as it closed behind him.

He bolted up the street as Shelley, fighting back tears, watched him through the window. Although she wasn't sure why her eyes stung. It's not like the boy was hurt, this time. Just hungry.

She couldn't let herself get so involved. She couldn't get attached. Not to a needy child. Not to anyone.

"You okay?" Dev whispered in a deep baritone.

"Yeah. Sorry. It's . . . it's . . ." What? Certainly not fine.

"Small-town life." Dev nodded. "I can imagine. It's why I prefer the city."

The silence that followed was awkward. Because, really, there was nothing to say to that. Nothing that would have made a difference anyway.

"So how about that lunch? And then we can talk about why you wanted me to come to town."

"Sure, but we need to go to the zoo first." She glanced at their clothes. "After our shower. *Showers.*" *God, I've got to stop saying that.* Because, yes, the image of a shared shower was hot and wet in her head. Hoping to hide the heat crawling up her cheeks, she hurried down the short corridor to her office calling over her shoulder, "Okay, just let me get my ferret."

Dev followed behind her, his steps nearly silent on the linoleum floor. "You have a ferret?" The wonder in his voice made her grin.

"Yes, and her name is Lucy. Wait till you see her. She's beautiful."

Shelley glanced at her reflection in the mirror hanging on the wall behind her desk. It was supposed to make the room look bigger. It didn't work. Instead, it afforded Shelley a frontal view of herself walking into the office.

Yeah, Lucy might be beautiful, her owner, however . . .

Shelley cringed at her reflection. She had dirt smeared down one cheek, the center of her shirt, and up both sleeves—no doubt from where she'd hugged Dev. Her blouse was once again hermetically sealed to her muffin-top tummy, accentuating every single curve.

Jeez! She looked like the before picture in a laundry-soap advertisement. Dev's reflection appeared slightly behind hers. Despite the mud caked on his suit and—*oh my Lord*—in his hair, he exuded a devastatingly sexy charisma. The kind that would have beauty queens lining up to offer him their showers along with a chance to run a loofah over his body.

The man might be quiet, but *day-um* he rocked the word *sexy*. And wow, it suddenly got very, very warm in her little office.

Resisting the temptation to fan herself, Shelley bent over and unlocked Lucy's cage. Gently, she tugged the sleepy pet from her paisley-green hammock and cuddled her close. Lucy nuzzled Shelley's neck then sniffed the air.

"Hello, Lucy," Dev said, bending over to peer at the ferret more closely.

Lucy twitched her pink nose.

Then leapt into the air, claws extended, aiming for Dev's head.

CHAPTER 3

S HELLEY WAITED UNTIL Dev started his shower before she spoke to Lucy. The ferret, locked in her cage in the bedroom, had finally settled down. But from the moment she had seen Dev at the clinic, she hated him.

"What is the matter with you?" Shelley asked, kneeling in front of Lucy's cage and feeding her special ferret treats in very small pieces. Lucy accepted a treat, nibbled it, then gazed at Shelley. Her beady black eyes sparkled in the afternoon sunshine pouring in through the bedroom window. "He's a great guy. Why did you attack him at the clinic?"

It had only been Shelley's quick reflexes and Dev's backward jump that kept the ferret from landing on his head. The moment Shelley caught her, she'd shoved Lucy back in her travel cage and hadn't let her out again until Dev was locked safely in her bathroom.

"Come on, Lucy. Talk to me."

This time, Lucy answered. Sort of. An image of the ferret gnawing on Dev's ear sprang into Shelley's mind.

"Okay," Shelley said, struggling for patience. "I understand you wanted to bite him, but why? He's a nice guy, and he came to town to help me."

Lucy gobbled the last bit of her treat then went into a weasel war dance. She hopped around, all fours paws leaving the ground. Her back arched and her tailed frizzed. All the time, she maintained eye contact with Shelley. That essential bond that allowed Shelley to read the animal's thoughts.

The anxious ferret sent a myriad of images flooding into Shelley's mind. Some were nonsensical and appeared centered around the steak-bone–shaped food pellets. Others were of Shelley crying after Cam had walked out, six months before their wedding. And then there was a distorted image of Dev's face. Overblown, like seen through a fishbowl, the black, red, and white image of the man's face appeared much too close to the ferret, in the most menacing way. As quickly as it appeared, it zapped out and was replaced by food again.

"You thought he was going to eat you?" Shelley frowned. "Gross. Just because you're obsessed with sleeping and eating doesn't mean humans are. I can guarantee you, Dev is a strictly non-ferret-eating kind of guy. Trust me. But what does that have to do with—?" Shelley cut her question short at the sound of the water being shut off. She leaned closer and whispered, "What is wrong with you?"

Again the image of Shelley crying flashed through her mind. "Do you think Dev is going to hurt me like Cam? Not a chance. No one will ever hurt me like that again. Besides, we're just friends. Now chill out."

Lucy leaped again. A new weasel war dance in motion.

The bathroom door opened and steam wafted into the bedroom. Lucy ran and dove into the small cardboard box tucked into the right corner of the cage against the wall.

"How's she doing?" Dev asked, stepping into the room. Dressed in snug, faded blue jeans and a heather gray sweatshirt that hugged his upper body, the man looked even more delectable than he had in a suit. He shook his head, then brushed the damp strands out of his face. His hair appeared almost brown when wet. And with his feet bare, he looked like a calendar model come to life in her bedroom.

"Um . . ." *Don't drool, remember what he asked.* "Lucy?"

The right side of his mouth kicked up in a half grin. "Yeah."

"She's fine. She's, uh, napping right now." Shelley pushed to her feet, facing him. He was clean and smelled wonderful, like

Irish soap. She, on the other hand, still reeked of dog and mud. She pointed to the bathroom door. "If you're done, I'd like to get cleaned up."

"Sure." He stepped out of her way. She started past him, but he caught her hand. His large, warm hand engulfed hers. "Thanks for the shower. And I'm glad to see you."

She couldn't hold back the smile. He was glad to see her.

Not half as glad as she was to see him. Maybe, just maybe, he could help her solve the case of the missing animals *and* indulge her in a long-time fantasy, the one of them naked, which she'd had all through college, despite being devoted to Cam. It was the kind of fantasy one might have about a superstar. Only her superstar stood deliciously real in her bedroom.

Oh, she couldn't do this to herself. When she'd brought up his girlfriend, he hadn't said a word about her being gone. Or even his being single. Frack! So her little fantasy was completely out of the realm of possibility.

She needed to focus. He was here because she needed his help to solve a mystery.

Extracting her hand from his, she stepped around him.

"Give me fifteen minutes to shower, and we can drive over to the zoo. I can tell you all about what's been happening on the way over."

"WAIT, IT'LL BE close to check-in time. Why don't I drive separately and we can talk at lunch after. There's someplace to eat over there, right?" Dev said, then wished he hadn't. Shelley looked slightly crestfallen.

"Sure, that makes sense. There's a little café across the street from the zoo. We can grab a bite to eat there. Then you can check into the hotel, it's just a few blocks up."

"How do you know where I'm staying?"

"It's Elkridge." She gave him a look that said she thought he was a complete idiot. "There's only one hotel in town."

"Oh, right." Way to go, Dev.

"I'm going to get cleaned up." Although her voice had lost some of the excitement, she pasted a smile on her face that was nearly believable. "Give me fifteen minutes and I'll be ready to go. Do you need anything? There's tea and coffee in the kitchen. Help yourself."

"Thanks, but I'm good. I've got a few calls to make." Dev pulled his cell phone out of the pocket of his ruined jacket, shoving the jacket and suit pants into his duffle bag. He zipped it up at the same time the shower turned on.

Dev stepped into the living room and exhaled a hard sigh. This was pretty damned weird. He hadn't seen or spoken to her in three years, and within thirty minutes of their reunion, he'd learned Cam had lied *again*, he'd been attacked by a dog *and* a ferret, and he'd gotten the impression his unrequited attraction to Shells wasn't so unrequited.

If the afternoon hadn't been *Twilight Zone* enough, Dev had gotten naked in Shelley's apartment. Too bad the naked part had been solo and relegated to washing up after said animal attacks.

Scrubbing a hand down his face, he dialed Seth's number. He slipped his wristwatch on while the phone rang.

"English here." Seth, his partner, formal as always, must not have checked his caller ID.

"It's me," Dev said. "I've found her."

Seth audibly exhaled. "That's great. When are you two coming back to Tidewater?"

"She doesn't know yet."

"Damn it, kid. What are you waiting for?" Seth's voice carried a mixture of relief and anxiety. "Tell her and come on home. I want to surprise Jules with the good news."

Dev rolled his shoulders to release the tension coiling in them again. "Look, it's been a crazy day. I'll tell her soon."

Silence.

And more silence.

Dev let it go on a bit too long because Seth said, "That's it? 'It's been a crazy day, I'll tell her soon.' Jones, help me out. Why are you taking so long? Just tell her and get your ass back here. We have a new case. They just found McGivern's partner, Colbert Rush. In pieces."

Pieces. Christ, that's gruesome. "Sounds like a case for O'Dell and Reynolds," Jones gritted out. As much as he wanted to work homicide, he and Seth were stuck squarely in robbery/burglary.

"You're right, but the captain wants us on it. Seems good old Colbert was stealing from his partner. He couldn't be smart about the embezzlement. No, the fool actually logged in the sales of more than $20,000 in semiprecious jewels, then walked out of the store with the cash over a period of ten years. Seems last month's murder had McGivern going over the records, and he stumbled across this little hiccup in the books. He claims he's been trying to find his partner to confront him. Instead, Rush has been dead for some time. I was going to fill you in on the case when you got back. Captain Peterson was so impressed by what we did with the Diamond Gang case, he wants us to solve this one. And did I mention Phil McGivern asked for us specifically? Reynolds and O'Dell are looking at him as the killer. McGivern wants us to prove he's innocent."

"Since when do we do anything but chase the evidence?"

"Hey, just sharing what he said." Seth laughed lightly. "McGivern is friends with the mayor. His Honor called the captain and asked for us to, quote, 'look into it' for him."

"Holy shit." Phil McGivern owned McGivern's Jewelers. It had been the last jewelry store the Diamond Gang had hit before Dev and Seth solved the string of burglaries turned murder.

"No shit. Seems McGivern's got pull in City Hall. So now the case is ours. Once you get your ass back here, that is."

They had begged the captain for a chance to work on the murder of one of the Diamond Gang members last month, and now they were being offered another murder case.

And Dev was here. In bumfuck Elkridge. Yep, his luck sucked.

Fine. He'd look into Shelley's case, then tell her about her sister. No doubt, the moment Shelley heard about Jules, she'd race him back to Tidewater. He hoped. A lingering memory of Shelley refusing to search for her sisters tickled at the back of his neck. Shelley *would* be happy to be reunited with her sister. Wouldn't she? Dev wasn't so sure, not that he'd tell Seth that.

Dev glanced toward the bedroom. "I'll be back ASAP."

"With Shelley?" Seth's voice was tinged with irritation and . . . desperation?

"Yes. Tell Jules I found her." The shower shut off and Dev stepped farther down the hall, lowering his voice. "Give me twenty-four hours and I'll be back with Shelley. I just need to check into Shelley's mystery of missing zoo animals, then we'll be on our way."

"Explain to me again how a town the size of a postage stamp can have a zoo and missing animals? And what in the hell Jules's little sister has to do with it?"

Dev ran a hand through his hair and down the back of his neck. "I don't know, but I damn sure intend to find out and get us both back to Tidewater before sunset tomorrow."

"WELCOME TO THE Elkridge Zoo," Shelley said, with a tentative smile twenty minutes later, as Dev stepped from his car and glanced around at the less-than-inviting environment.

"This is a zoo?"

She nodded, her eyes wide. "Believe it or not. Just give me a minute to pay for our tickets and we can go in."

We have to pay *for entrance* here?

Dev didn't shake his head. He didn't grab Shelley in a fireman's hold, toss her over his shoulder and haul ass out of this weird little town, but he sure as hell wanted to.

No, he waited.

The zoo was hardly a zoo. It looked more like someone decided to put up a wooden For Sale sign in the woods but instead of the words *For Sale*, they had painted the words *Elkridge Zoo*. The land itself appeared to be a nice piece of real estate, located on a small one-square-mile peninsula that jutted out into the James River.

Afternoon sunlight dappled the foliage. The red, yellow-green, and emerald leaves of the maple and oak trees were mixed with the dark greens of scrub pines and the lush, if somewhat overgrown, grass. Somewhere, just beyond the trees, the river lapped at the zoo's shores. Gulls cried overhead. Squirrels chattered. And a tiger roared.

Dev turned toward the sound but couldn't see anything past where the paths twisted through the trees. From the front gate there were three small dilapidated wooden signs sticking in the ground, marking the trails, and branching out into different directions. Each sign was freshly painted, despite the obvious deterioration of the placard. Broken and misaligned red-brick pavers made the rugged trails treacherous. The signs appeared to be a guide for the muddy footpaths that ran alongside them.

Dev squinted to read the signs and stepped closer. They bore clever names: Beaver Trail, Reptile Trail, and Tiger Monkey Trail.

What the hell is a tiger monkey?

"I can't thank you enough for doing this," Shelley said, breathlessly.

"Shells, what are we doing here? What do you have to do with the zoo?"

"It's complicated. Look, I'll explain it all after I show you. Just trust me, okay?" Her cheeks were pink with excitement, but her eyes were somber.

He should make her tell him everything, right now. But this was Shells. Sweet, honest, naïve Shells. "Sure. Of course, I trust you."

She grinned wide, then leaned closer and whispered, "Thanks. We need to hurry. Just play it cool walking through here."

"Play it cool?" That didn't sound good.

Shelley nodded and hurried up the muddy Tiger Monkey Trail. "Yeah, I'm not very popular around here these days."

"Wait. What? Shells," he called after her in a stage whisper, but she didn't respond.

Dev double-timed it to catch up with her. How could she jog in that hip-hugging skirt? Not that he didn't like it. He most certainly did, but it was distracting. It groped the curves of her ass and showed off her long shapely legs. Next to her, he looked decidedly underdressed in jeans.

Shelley, unaware he'd been thinking about her ass, said, "As long as we're quiet, no one should bother us."

Famous last words.

A man bearing a striking resemblance to Colonel Sanders—white hair and goatee, white suit, black bow tie, black-frame glasses, even a walking stick—stepped into the path. He blinked twice at Shells, who muttered a small oath under her breath.

"Dr. Morgan, what are you doing here?" he asked in a thick southern drawl. He glanced around, as if confused. "I didn't ask you to come here today, did I?"

"Um . . . hi, Dr. Kessler." Shelley nibbled on her bottom

lip. A small red flush crawled up her cheeks. She glanced over her shoulder at Dev, a plea in her eyes that he couldn't decipher. She glanced back at the older man, who was busy patting his pockets. With a smile that made Dev's insides quiver, she said, "No need to check your notes, sir. You asked me to check on Miah. I was just heading over there. How'd it go with Reverend Morrison's horse? Has Margo foaled yet?"

Dr. Kessler's brows drew together briefly before his expression cleared and he stopped patting his jacket pockets. "Why, yes, she did. The foal is healthy. Up and nursing. I was just headed up to give Mr. Jameson the good news. Seems he'd been a right bit worried since he sold her to the good reverend. Don't understand why he's worried, myself. Why that zoo owner sold his wife's mare, didn't he? But he seems especially concerned about the horse's well-being. But who am I to judge? Ah well, would you care to join me on my rounds this afternoon?"

As if seeing Dev for the first time, the old doctor smiled wide and extended his hand. "Good afternoon, young man. And you are?"

Dev opened his mouth to speak but was too slow.

"This is an old friend from college who's visiting me for a few days," Shelley said. "Dr. Kessler, meet Devon Jones. Dev, this is my boss, Dr. Kessler." Dev didn't miss her nervous grin or the fact that she'd left off his title. Odd. She'd asked him to Elkridge for his investigative skills.

Taking his cue from her, he shook the vet's hand. "Nice to meet you, Dr. Kessler."

"My, you are a big fella, aren't you?" the old man asked, a touch of awe in his voice. The gentleman said it kindly, but Dev recognized the wariness in the other man's gaze.

"Not as big as some of my cousins," Dev said with a smile and took two steps back. "Growing up, I was the runt in the family. Not anymore, though."

Colonel Sanders stared with knitted brows for a few seconds, then laughed. "I imagine not. Very nice to meet Dr. Morgan's gentleman. I've heard so much about you."

Dev turned to Shelley who gave an almost imperceptible head shake.

She sighed and said a little too brightly, "Well, I don't want to keep you, Dr. Kessler. I'll meet you back at the clinic after my lunch break."

"No, no. Enjoy your day with your young man."

"But the clinic."

The old man waved away her words. "Tosh, my girl. Take the afternoon off. As soon as I see Eddy Jameson about . . . about . . ." Again, confusion clouded the older man's features. He started to pat his pockets again. He withdrew a yellow sticky pad with writing on it. Giving it a quick glance, his expression cleared. He smiled. "Ah, here it is. As soon as I tell him the horse and foal are healthy, I'll be at the clinic."

Shelley opened her mouth to protest, but the older man simply held up a hand. She fell silent.

"I've run that place for four decades before you came along. I can handle one afternoon on my own while you and your gentleman spend a little time together." He turned to Dev and added in a stage whisper, "This girl works too hard."

He walked off without another word toward a building that sat atop a berm. Another low-tech sign that read Elkridge Zoo Visitor Center stood high between two mismatched posts in front of a two-story structure. Four windows on both floors of a long wall overlooked the zoo.

"Okay, I guess I'm off for the afternoon. That'll give us more time to discuss why I contacted you." But she didn't appear ready to discuss anything yet. Shelley turned and jogged up the trail in the opposite direction of her boss. "Come on, Dev, we need to hurry."

"Shells . . ." He started to ask about what just happened but stopped himself.

His neck tingled.

Someone was watching.

That sensation was unmistakable and all too familiar. Between being part of the wealthy McKinnon clan and being a cop, he experienced it enough to know when someone had eyes on him. Striding faster to catch up to Shells he surreptitiously searched the area like a fascinated tourist. Another zing beneath his collar had him searching harder. Then he saw it.

In the building on the hill, a curtain in one of the lower windows moved.

CHAPTER 4

SHELLEY CAUGHT SIGHT of the tiny monkey's hand a nano-second too late. The little guy latched onto her jacket sleeve. She nearly tripped, jerking to a halt to avoid injuring the primate.

"Hi, JoJo. How are we today? I don't have any snacks for you this time," she said, facing him. He chattered at her, but the blur of images he sent winging into her mind were jumbled and chaotic. "Slow down, I'm not getting what you mean."

"Everything okay, Shells?" Dev asked, a frown digging a line between his blond eyebrows. "Who's this little guy?"

"Hang on, JoJo." She turned her attention to Dev. "This, my friend, is JoJo. And you're looking at the Elkridge Zoo Monkey House."

When Dev frowned at the old cage, she shrugged.

"Don't judge." Then she looked at the house again. The cage had two trees in opposite corners connected by ropes. The trees, cut short to keep the monkeys from escaping, spread wide until their branches nearly touched each other. At one time, the trees probably offered a means of exercise for the monkeys as they leaped from branch to branch. Now the primates leaped only when the desire struck, not out of necessity.

"Okay, so it's little better than a heated barn with a green-colored chain-link cage attached to the front of it. But there are trees in there and a rope for them to play with . . . and why am I defending this place?"

"Is this what you brought me here to see?" Dev frowned at her, curiosity in his gray-blue eyes.

"I wish, but no." *If only it were that easy.* "I brought you here to see something much scarier."

"Scarier? He doesn't look scary to me." Dev placed his hands on the cage and tugged it, apparently verifying that it was more secure than it appeared. "So why are we here?"

"For something else." The tamarin grabbed Shelley's hair and tugged hard enough to bring tears to her eyes. "Ouch, stop that," Shelley said, untangling the primate's fingers then massaging her scalp. "Give me a minute, Dev. JoJo has something to talk to me about, and he doesn't seem willing to wait."

Dev didn't say anything, just arched an eyebrow and looked at the primate.

"You do know my gift goes beyond household pets, don't you? Or maybe you don't." She let out a nervous laugh despite the hollow pit opening in her stomach. "Um, seems I can talk to just about any living animal, including monkeys, guinea pigs, and, as I recently discovered, alligators. But that's a whole story in itself."

Dev grinned. His straight, white teeth gleamed in the afternoon sunshine. "Except dogs?"

"Right, dogs still don't talk to me. Hercules, notwithstanding."

"So JoJo here's got a story? I'm all ears." Dev stretched a finger toward the cage. JoJo wrapped his little fist around it. Dev smiled, then said softly, "You know, I'm kind of jealous that you get to talk to this little guy. I'd love to have your gift."

Shelley let out a pent-up breath. She should have remembered how accepting Dev had been of her Dolittle gift back in college. He'd never once questioned or doubted her abilities. Only her family had ever been so accepting. It was a bit unnerving . . . and wonderful.

JoJo rattled the chain link.

"Okay, JoJo, I'm all ears. What's on your mind?"

Without warning, JoJo released Dev's finger with a trilling call and then raced up one of the trees, disappearing behind the leaves.

"JoJo, where are you going?" Shelley shifted in front of the fence trying to see him in the tree. "Come back here or I'm . . . What am I doing? I can't understand him if he's not looking at me."

"Come again?"

She glanced at Dev over her shoulder. "The connection has to be eye-to-eye contact. I thought you knew that."

"Do now. So you can talk to them all day, but only if they're looking right at you."

She narrowed her eyes at him. "You sound skeptical."

Dev raised his hands and shook his head. "Nope. Just fascinated."

Shelley glanced at her watch and shifted again to try to see the animal.

"Do we wait?" Dev asked.

Shelley nodded. Although, yikes, did she feel silly. She'd asked him to come help her solve a mystery of disappearing animals that she hadn't even finished telling him about. And here they stood.

Waiting on a monkey.

"What kind of monkey is JoJo?" Dev pointed to the blurry laminated picture affixed to the front of the gate. The image showed two monkeys climbing the twin trees. With yellow manes, big black eyes, long fingers tipped with claws, and long prehensile tails, they looked like an odd cross between monkeys and lions.

"They're called golden lion tamarins. Their species is native to Brazil, Rio de Janeiro, actually. But these guys were born in captivity. Or so I've been told, though I have my doubts."

"Why's that?"

"Sometimes, when they talk to me, I see images of high canopied treetops and no humans around for miles. Something a tamarin born in captivity would never have seen.

"They're an endangered species. These little guys and the white tiger up the path are the big draw for this zoo. Everyone wants to feed a monkey. I've tried to persuade the owner away from that bad idea, but he's convinced that as long as he *sells* the food to people, nothing could go wrong." She blew a raspberry.

"You disagree?"

Before she could answer, JoJo was back with his mate. "Hang on, Dev. JoJo and BoBo need to talk to me."

"*JoJo* and *BoBo*?" The incredulity rang in his words.

"Hey, I didn't name them," she said turning away from him to give the primates her full attention. "Okay, what's up?"

The two raced up the cage and began to chatter at her. It was impossible to understand them both at the same time, especially in their heightened state of anxiety. "Whoa, slow down. One at a time." Shelley swung her attention left and right trying to lock eyes with one of them long enough to get an image. When she couldn't do it after thirty seconds, she put her hands up and stepped back. "Stop! BoBo, you talk to me."

Focusing her attention on the pregnant female, she found the connection she needed. Rapid-fire scenes whipped through her mind at a near dizzying speed.

An image of someone dressed in all black sneaking through the zoo in the dead of night. A tiger roared. Someone crashed through the woods and banged against the monkey cage. A distinct mewling cry went up followed by a second. A white-and-black striped cub's head popped through the center of the jacket where the zipper hadn't fastened the two sides together. It let out a mewling roar, small and weak and typical for a tiger so young. The thief pressed a gloved hand against its head and tucked it back, then zipped up the coat. In the distance, another frantic and somewhat odd-sounding roar rent the night.

A chill went down Shelley's spine. "Oh my God! The cubs?"

The tamarins chattered again. But she'd lost the telepathic connection. BoBo and JoJo were too upset to communicate effectively. They shook the chain-link fence and screeched.

Shelley couldn't breathe. She sucked in oxygen, but her chest constricted, squeezing her heart into her throat.

"Shells, what's wrong?" Dev put a hand on her shoulder, but she couldn't answer him.

"Just wait, Dev. Come on, BoBo, tell me more. When did this happen? Did you see anything else?" All of her attention was focused squarely on BoBo, the witness to the crime. The telepathic link sizzled between them, and the images leaped backward and forward in a jumbled maze for a moment before the little monkey zeroed in on the previous morning.

Eddy Jameson, the drunken owner, brought new toys for the tamarins. He might be a lush, but he made sure to deliver them every Tuesday morning like clockwork. Then the images skipped ahead so fast, Shelley's stomach gurgled. As quickly as they started, the racing mental pictures froze. In the pitch black, a small, cylindrical red fire glowed brightly then dulled. The same image repeated over and over before Shelley realized it wasn't repeating. Someone waited in the shadows, smoking a cigarette. The glowing red circle arced to the ground, then the shadowed figure raced up the path.

"Shells! Shelley, talk to me," Dev said. Both hands on her shoulders, he stepped between the fence and her. His handsome chiseled face wore a mask of concern. "What's going on? You've gone ghost-white."

"Someone . . ." Shelley cleared her throat, then pushed the words past her lips. "I reached you too late. BoBo saw someone steal a tiger cub last night. She'd been sleeping, but someone was smoking. Over there." Shelley hiked a thumb over her shoulder to the copse behind her on the other side of the footpath. "Then the person broke in and took the cubs."

"Cubs or cub?" Dev frowned. "Shelley, did she say if it was more than one?"

Shelley turned back to BoBo, but she and JoJo had already disappeared back into the treetop. Shelley searched her mind, fear and anger mingling inside her. Shaking free of Dev's touch, she clenched her fists and said, "I'm not sure, but I know how to find out. Come on."

WHEN DEV WAS small, his father had once told him to beware of a woman on a righteous warpath. As he chased Shelley through the zoo, his father's words echoed in his ears. If what those monkeys saw was right, Shelley was not going to be happy.

Thank God, he had good news for her.

Yeah and why haven't you told her already? Hoping to draw out this private reunion with her a little longer? His conscience pricked, but he shoved it aside and focused on getting Shelley through the next few minutes.

The tiger house was exactly that. A green-tinned roof, wooden cabin, and an open door with a ramp leading down to a lush green lawn. Centered inside a thousand-square-foot cage surrounded by an eight-foot-high perimeter fence and a three-foot-tall barrier fence, the tiger display was obviously the centerpiece of the zoo. Unlike the tamarin cage where the trees needed pruning, the tiger enclosure was pristine, and the grounds, immaculate.

Dev followed Shelley through the barrier fence.

"Wait here. I need to make sure Miah, the tigress, is secure in her cage, then I'll let you into the tiger house." Shelley bounced on the balls of her feet at the gate of the perimeter fence as she spoke.

"Okay."

Shelley disappeared around a corner.

The tiger house appeared to have two exits. One led down the ramp to the grass, the other led out of the back and into a six-by-six-foot cage. A roar went up from the back of the cage just before Shelley hurried around the perimeter fence near the tiger's house and raced across the rough path to unlock first the perimeter then the cage gates.

"Come on, Dev. We need to hurry," Shelley said, taking Dev by the hand and holding it until he passed through the gate. She dropped his hand, hiked up her pencil skirt, and broke into a run. Dev could have easily kept up with her, but given he was the outsider, he let her go first. Still, his training was too ingrained. He swept his gaze all around, searching for any threat as they went into the tiger house. No threat. No one else around. Whoever had been watching them before wasn't watching them now.

The house itself was little more than walls and floor with fresh-smelling straw for bedding. In a corner, partially hidden by the hay, three white tiger cubs slept on their sides, curled around one another in kitten-like fashion. Dev didn't get more than a glimpse of them before Shelley dropped down to her knees. Her body blocked the sleeping animals from his sight.

"One, two, three . . ." Shelley made a strangled sort of noise and counted them again before she started digging through the hay. "Dev, come here. Please help me dig. Look for the other two. They've got to be here. I couldn't be a day late. Not by a single, stupid, fracking day."

It didn't take a rocket scientist to wonder what she meant. Dev dropped to his knees and swept his hands through the hay. But in four short minutes they'd dug through the hay enough times; Dev was pretty sure they must have touched every straw. No matter how many times they counted, there were only three cubs.

Tears brightened Shelley's eyes as she sank into the hay near the snoozing cubs. The sight of her anguished, helpless expression made Dev's chest tight. "Is there any chance the mother tiger would have put them someplace else?"

"No, Dev." She let out an exasperated breath. "Miah wouldn't have separated her young. They were here when I examined them last week. All *five* of them. I weighed them, measured them. They were *here*. What am I going to do? How do I find them now? I don't even know who took them. I mean, I have my suspicions, but I—"

Shelley's words were cut off by the tigress's roar. She actually flinched. Although, truth be told, Dev wasn't exactly too confident sitting in a tiger's house with one pissed-off tiger nearby.

Just how reliable is that six-by-six-foot metal cell?

While he trusted Shelley's gift, he didn't know how useful it would be against an angry, grieving, man-eating carnivore.

"Shells, maybe we can take this conversation someplace a little less, uh . . . dangerous?"

Shelley blinked and her blue eyes cleared. Patting one of the waking cubs on the head, she said, "You're absolutely right. Miah is already upset. I don't want her trying to chew through her temporary cage."

"Can she do that?"

Shelley didn't answer. Instead she said, "Head back out. I'll meet you at the perimeter gate. Go now. I'll unlatch Miah's cage, once I know you're clear. Just make sure to wave when you get there. Oh, and remember to close and latch the gates behind you."

Dev didn't want to leave her, but Shelley seemed to know what she was doing.

Quick as he could, he crossed through the gates, latched them, then waved. Seconds later, the tiger roared and bounded toward the green-roofed house. Shelley came through a side door near the perimeter gate and padlocked it behind her.

Another tiger cry. This time from inside the wooden house. Then a white-faced tiger with black stripes and startling blue eyes appeared at the top of the ramp. She looked directly at them. At Shelley. The animal roared twice.

Both times, Shelley flinched as if struck. Her face pinched and her eyes became misty.

"I will," Shelley whispered. "Now go be with your other babies. I promise."

The tiger turned, flicked her tail, and disappeared back inside with her cubs. Shelley sagged beside Dev only to jump when a twig snapped behind them.

"What in the blue blazes of hell do you think you are doing here?"

"Hello, Reyna." Shelley smiled and appeared calm despite the dancing pulse in her neck.

While Dev was surprised, he didn't react. Truthfully, he'd been so focused on what was happening inside the cage, he hadn't noticed the approach of the exotic-looking woman in a tight yellow dress. But his training taught him to never lose the upper hand—especially when surprised.

"Don't 'hello' me. What are you doing here today?" Reyna propped her hands on her hips.

"I'm on a date," Shelley said lightly, then grabbed Dev's hand and squeezed.

"Ha! Good one. Figures only *you* would bring a date to this place," Reyna replied. Her gaze skated over Shells dismissively before she zeroed in on Dev. Artfully, Reyna extended her hand to him, like a princess greeting royalty. "I don't think we've been introduced. I'm Reyna Jameson. My family owns this land. And you are?"

"I'm Devon Jones. What a beautiful tiger y'all have here." Dev accepted her limp handshake with his free hand and realized too late the mistake he'd made. Shelley withdrew her hand from his and clasped her hands behind her back. He missed her warmth.

Reyna narrowed her eyes at Shelley and a distinctly

unfriendly smile curled her mouth. Although physically beautiful, with long, wavy dark-brown hair and curves that the
average woman paid money for, there was something ugly in
Reyna's eyes.

"Dr. Morgan, you weren't trying to examine the tiger, were
you? You do remember that you're barred from working with
the animals behind that fence," Reyna said gleefully, pointing
at the tiger cage. "And if you've violated that rule, why I think
my daddy will have to officially ban you from the whole park
before you cause another scene." She pointed one finger in the
air and pulled a cell from a pocket of her dress. Impressive.

"Don't bother calling anyone. We're leaving." Shelley
waved and started toward the path back the way they'd come.

Dev started to follow Shelley, growing more confused by
the second. If Shelley thought tiger cubs were missing, why
didn't she tell the owner's daughter? He didn't have time to
wonder long because Shelley hadn't taken five steps when
Reyna called out, "Don't go stirring up trouble again, because
I will get the sheriff involved this time. No matter what my
daddy says. I won't have you raising a stink here anymore."

"Me? You're accusing me of stirring up trouble?" Shelley
spun around. The blue blazes Reyna mentioned earlier seemed
to shoot from Shelley's eyes.

In the distance, three men made their way up the trail, led
by an older man in a blue jumpsuit. Dr. Kessler's white suit
shone like a beacon in the afternoon light. The man really did
dress like his office picture. His silver-topped walking stick
glinted as he struggled to keep pace with a lanky man in a tan
deputy's uniform and hat.

Not good. "Let's go, Shells," Dev said, placing a gentle
hand on her shoulder.

She shrugged away his touch and squared off with Reyna.
"No. I don't stir up trouble. I'm the one who you've had to call
multiple times in the past six months to clean up the messes
you and your family have made. Or did you forget?" Shelley
plunked her hands on her hips. "Wasn't it last month your
daddy burned the body of a five-year-old green iguana instead
of properly disposing of the poor animal? I didn't even get a
chance to examine it first. Or are you now claiming that I

raised a stink when I asked to do that before you got rid of the creature? So there would be documented proof about what killed it? Green iguanas can live twenty years in captivity."

"My daddy was perfectly within his rights to burn that disgusting lizard. It was dead." Reyna stepped forward, mirroring Shelley's stance. "There's no requirement that says he has to perform a lizardtopsy—"

"It's called a necropsy," Shelley hissed. "And it should have been performed."

"Necro? *Ewww* . . . Whatever it's called, why should he bother? The thing was dead." Reyna narrowed her eyes further. "You think we should let you cut it up just to satisfy your suspicious little brain? Not that it would have mattered. In your mind, we're already convicted of animal cruelty. You even called the USDA on us!" Reyna stepped closer and raised her voice. "Lucky for you, they have better things to do than to worry about smelly old reptiles."

"Lucky for you, you mean," Shelley shot back. Her face nearly as red as her curly hair. "Had that been a mammal that died under your tender care, the USDA wouldn't have been the only one involved. It wouldn't have looked good for this town if word got out that its landmark zoo has animals dying and disappearing mysteriously."

"Oh my God! You're going to tell me there's some sort of conspiracy going on here? You are one crazy bitch if you believe that."

The man in the blue jumpsuit sprinted the last few feet up the path, leaving the other two behind. He put a hand on Reyna's shoulder.

"Reyna, please," he slurred slightly. Up close, his uniform was crisp and freshly pressed with ELKRIDGE ZOO emblazoned on the front left pocket. In his early sixties with thinning gray hair, a florid complexion indicative of excessive alcohol use, and bloodshot, watery eyes, he swayed slightly. "Dr. Morgan was only trying to help."

"Really, Daddy?" Reyna spun on the man. "Stop defending her. How can you say she was only trying to help? She threatened you last week."

"I did no such thing." Shelley crossed her arms over her

chest, her blue eyes still shooting sapphire sparks. "I just told him no other animals better disappear under mysterious circumstances."

"I believe your actual words were much worse." Reyna laughed like a hyena. "Isn't that right, Deputy Munro? You were contacted that day, I believe."

The deputy double-timed it up the last few feet of the trail at the woman's call. He stepped up beside her and withdrew a small black notebook from his pocket. Beneath his wide-brimmed hat, it was difficult to read his expression until he glanced up. He flipped open the notebook, glanced at Eddy, Reyna, then finally Shelley and said in his nasally voice, "I believe it was reported that your exact words to Mr. Jameson on October the twenty-eighth were 'No other animal had better die or mysteriously disappear or I'll make sure you pay for it.'"

"I think we've heard enough, Payne . . . um, Deputy Munro." Reyna turned to Dr. Kessler, who'd finally caught up to the group. She shook her head. "I'm sorry, Dr. Kessler. While we respect you and your work, I think this time we really must ban Dr. Shelley Morgan from these grounds. Permanently."

"Now wait just a minute—" Shelley started at the same time the deputy gave both women a wary glance, then sighed in obvious frustration. Dev could relate. He was none too happy with the day's events either.

"Shells," he whispered into her ear. "Why don't—" His words were cut off by the deputy.

"I've told you before, Reyna, it's your father's place. He decides who stays or goes."

"Ask him then." Reyna crossed her arms beneath her ample chest and glared. "Daddy, are you finally going to stop her now?"

"Stop me from what? Do you even know what's going on here?" Shelley demanded as another person stepped out from the line of trees.

This individual, like Eddy Jameson, wore a blue zoo uniform but looked distinctly different from everyone else. Perhaps it was the shovel he carried over both shoulders, or it might have been the quick flashes of surprise and fear on his face before he regained his composure. He glanced over at the small cage where Shelley had locked the tiger while they'd checked on the cubs, then sighed as if in relief.

No one else noticed his behavior, because the deputy, Shelley, her boss, and now a growing crowd of zoo visitors were avidly watching Reyna plead with her father to have a no-trespassing order filed against Shelley.

"Just look what a scene she's made this afternoon." Reyna gestured to the half dozen onlookers, who weren't even pretending to ignore the drama unfolding a few feet from the tiger display. "We can't have her coming back here."

"I didn't do anything wrong. I just walked up to the cage when you started freaking out," Shelley lied. The red on her cheeks could have been because she was in high temper, but Dev knew better. Shelley blushed like that back in college whenever she told a lie. Which wasn't often. Why was she lying now?

Reyna spun and leveled a glare at the newest staff member to join their party. "Is that true, Tomás? Don't lie for her."

There was something threatening in her tone. Dev glanced at the young man in the dirty blue jumpsuit as he shot a nervous glance at Shelley.

Reyna didn't give him an opportunity to answer. "You didn't just walk up to the cage, Dr. Morgan. I saw you several minutes earlier from the window of the visitor center. She didn't just stand outside the cage the whole time, did she, Tomás? She went inside the tiger's house, didn't she?"

Tomás pressed his already thin lips together and exhaled through his nose before he answered in a thick Spanish accent, "*Sí*, I saw you lock Miah in the cell, then go into the tiger house."

"And she's done it before, hasn't she, Tomás?" Reyna asked, not missing a beat. "Didn't you tell me that last week she went in without Dr. Kessler present? That she had insisted on evaluating the cubs, *alone*?"

"Tomás?" Shelley said, her eyes wide, the color draining from her face.

There was so much disappointment in that one word, it made Dev's chest ache for Shelley. He wasn't surprised when Tomás winced before nodding.

The sudden burst of questions from the group wasn't a surprise. Clearly, only Tomás and Shelley knew about her visits. Dr. Kessler kept patting his pockets, searching for something he couldn't seem to find. The deputy frowned, watching Reyna continue to demand her father have a no-trespassing order sworn out.

Eddy licked his lips and swiped an arm over his sweaty brow as he alternately listened, then responded to his daughter's angry words.

Shelley waved her hands high above her head like she was signaling for a plane to land. "Excuse me, but there's something everyone needs to know," she said, when she had their attention.

"Not everyone," Eddy said, swaying slightly as he approached the onlookers and then ushered them back down the path. Once the zoo-goers were out of earshot, he rejoined the group.

"Now," Reyna said, a sneer in her voice. "What more could you possibly have to say?"

"I did check on Miah this morning. You were right. But there's something you need to know. Two of the cubs are missing. I think they were stolen last night."

"Yes, we already knew that," Eddy said, his voice slurring again. "It's why Deputy Munro's here."

"You *knew*?" Shelley goggled at the owner. "Why didn't you say something?"

"He did. To the *real* vet in this town," Reyna said and pointed to Dr. Kessler.

The old vet patted his pockets again, this time pulling out a crumpled yellow sticky note from his left pants' pocket. He held it up and read it aloud. "Ah, I have it here. 'Discuss missing cubs with Dr. Morgan.'"

"I find it convenient that *you* would show up today to tell us about the missing cubs. And why didn't you tell me when you first saw me?" Reyna didn't give Shelley time to respond. "For that matter, why didn't you want Tomás or Dr. Kessler in the tiger house with you last week? And how did you know the cubs were taken *last night*, if you haven't been here for a week? It could have happened at any time. I'll tell you why. Because *you're* the tiger thief."

CHAPTER 5

"SHE'S OUT OF her mind!" Shelley said for the fifth time since she and Dev had sat down at the Wight Café.

The restaurant with Italian spices in the air was her favorite place to eat. Today she could barely stomach the sight of her antipasto. Probably because their bistro table had a clear view of the zoo entrance, where Reyna and Payne were speaking with Eddy.

"I can't believe Payne actually escorted us off the premises like I was a criminal or something. He knows me. They all know me. I went there to help and that . . . that *woman* accused me of stealing the cubs."

She tore her gaze away and glanced at Dev across the table. He silently munched on a fry, his expression impassive. He appeared interested in what she was saying, so she continued to vent her frustration.

"And Tomás? What was he thinking? How could he just stand there and not say a single word to defend me?" Shelley stabbed her fork into the provolone hard enough to shred it. Giving up, she pushed the fork and plate away and massaged the ache in her right temple. "Tomás knows I'd do anything to protect those animals. He's even helped me with them. How could he throw me under the bus by telling that . . . that *harpy* that I'd insisted on being alone with the cubs? After all the time we've worked together, I thought he was my friend. But no, he let her make it sound like the time I spent alone with the cubs was something sinister. And he knew exactly why I did it. Frack! He'd agreed it was a good idea at the time."

Dev cleared his throat, slid his own empty plate away, then folded his hands together on the table. "Why *did* you insist on being alone?"

"Because I needed Tomás to help Dr. Kessler check on Miah. He's a sweet old man and was once a very good vet, but lately his mind is going. When I got here last summer, the memory slips were minor. I'm afraid to leave him alone with an animal anymore. Two weeks ago, he tried to spay the same dog he'd spayed the day before. Then there are his massive mood swings. He's normally sweet, but without warning, he's angry. Not violent or anything, just furious. Then twenty minutes later, it's like he's forgotten the whole episode. So leaving him alone with an animal isn't exactly wise right now. I couldn't even have taken the afternoon off if Jacob wasn't at the clinic."

"So you asked Tomás to keep an eye on the doctor while you worked with the cubs." When she nodded, Dev straightened and pulled a small black notebook and pen from his pants pocket. "You wanted to make sure nothing happened to the tiger—"

"Or to Dr. Kessler," she interjected.

"Or to Dr. Kessler," Dev agreed, jotting down notes. "These cubs just went missing, so if you didn't contact me about them, what made you contact me?"

"Oh, I was worried about the cubs, but only because of—" She cut herself off and glanced around to make sure no one was near enough to overhear her. She whispered, "What the lizards told me."

Dev paused in his notes and glanced around the café. It was mostly empty, since the lunch rush was over. "Come again?"

She leaned closer to the table and whispered, "The lizards."

"Yeah, I got that part. Why are you whispering?" he asked, his voice soft and low. He answered his own question. "Right, crift. Got it. Continue. You were in the reptile house and . . . ?"

"Not the lizards in the reptile house. The five-lined skinks that run wild in the zoo." When Dev simply stared at her, confusion clouding his gray eyes, she gave a quick explanation. "Five-lined skinks are commonly called blue-tailed lizards. They're native to Virginia and they hang out in the deciduous part of the zoo, mostly under logs."

"What did the lizards—"

"Shhh." She glanced around again at his voice.

Dev shook his head. "What did *they* tell you?"

"That they'd seen someone carrying away snakes in the middle of the night in September. Funny thing, there was no record of some of these animals. Had I not examined the eastern hognosed snake the week before, even I wouldn't have known it was missing. But since I did, I went to see Eddy about it."

"And what happened?" Dev asked, continuing to scribble in his pad.

"He said he had no idea it was gone. He called Tomás and Cristos in, but they didn't know either."

"Who's Cristos?" Dev flipped to another page and scribbled, then flipped back and continued writing.

"Eddy's son. He is technically the zoo manager, but he's about as interested in the zoo as Reyna is."

"She seemed pretty interested to me."

Shelley snorted. "All that woman is interested in is Payne Munro and causing trouble. She hates the zoo. The animals—" She paused when the waitress passed their table to deliver drinks to a couple three tables away. After the waitress left, Shelley said, "They all tell me that Reyna refuses to feed them or clean their cages. She puts on a smile for the tourists, but the moment people aren't around, she's mean. JoJo told me Reyna once took his new toy away from him and threw it in the trash can just out of his reach. You know, if anyone stole the cubs, I bet it was her."

"Let's back up. You say the lizards saw animals being carried off. Aren't there cameras at the zoo? If so, theft should be easy to prove."

"Oh my God! There *are* three cameras; one at the visitor center door, one inside the monkey house, and one inside the tiger house." Shelley raised her hand high into the air to signal for their check. Pushing to her feet, she pulled her wallet from her jacket pocket and tossed her last twenty on the table. "Dev, you're a genius. No one could have taken the cubs without being caught on video. We've got to get back to the zoo and tell Eddy to check the tapes."

Dev pushed the cash back at her and grabbed her wrist lightly, halting her movements. "Wait, Shells. If the sheriff's office is involved, they've probably already considered that. I bet they've already reviewed the tapes. I would have, if it were my case. And since you weren't on the tapes, my guess is that's why you were escorted off the premises and not to jail."

Shelley tugged and Dev released her, but he didn't stand. "Oh, you're right."

Deflated, she sank back into her chair and glanced out the window. Eddy, Reyna, and Payne were gone. The parking lot was nearly empty.

"Shells, did the—" Dev cut himself off when the waitress returned. He handed her the check and his credit card.

The twenty dangled between Shelley's fingers. "Dev, you didn't have to do that. I can pay for my own lunch."

"From what I can tell, you've already paid for two lunches today. Beau's and your intern's." He gave a roguish grin. "I've got this."

Shelley hadn't asked him to come to town to pay for things, just to help her with the zoo problem. Her immediate reaction was to refuse him, to pay her own way. But this was Dev. She consented . . . sort of. "Thanks, but I'll get the tip."

A muscle ticked in Dev's jaw, then he gave her a quick nod.

"Great. Now you were about to ask something?"

Dev glanced at his notebook then said, "Did the an-uh . . . your friends describe anyone to you? Is that the right term? Describe?"

"More like pictures in a silent movie." Grimacing, she shook her head. "What they gave me wasn't very clear, because it was night and their view was at ground level. The thief dropped a cardboard box and several snakes fell out. The thief with shiny black gloves scooped up at least five—but one, the hog-nosed, got away."

"That's it? Shiny black gloves and a cardboard box?"

"You gotta remember, they're skinks. They think in terms of food, prey, and mating. Some crickets hopped by and the snake wasn't hunting, so they lost interest in it. But not before getting a good look at it. It's how I knew which snake it was."

"Doesn't matter anyway." Dev scratched his head and whispered, "It's not like we can log into evidence the witness statements of a lizard spotting a snake thief or a monkey reporting stolen tiger cubs. Let's stick with what we can report and what we know. Two cubs and a hog-nosed snake were stolen from the zoo. Any other animals go missing?"

"Yes, a bilateral gynandromorph eastern bluebird." When he stopped writing and simply stared at her, she explained. "It's a bluebird with a rare genetic disorder. Basically, it's male on one side and female on the other. Even the coloring is split down the middle."

"And it was on display in the zoo?"

"Yes, but at the end of August when I asked Eddy what happened to it, he said he came in one morning and the cage was open. It must have flown away."

"You don't believe that?"

"I did at the time. It was the first animal to disappear since I moved here. After today, you've got to believe that I'm onto something here."

"Snakes and birds aside, I'm inclined to agree." Dev nodded.

Relief had Shelley exhaling a deep breath. "I'm so glad, Dev, because I think another animal went missing too. Earlier than the bird. But I'd rather show you my notes. Since I've got the afternoon free, we can drop off your car at the hotel and I can drive you back to my place."

He nodded as the waitress returned with his credit card. He signed it and rose to his feet. Shelley followed, leaving the tip on the table. She had been relieved that he agreed with her that there was something wrong at the zoo, so why was she suddenly nervous?

They gathered their things and stepped outside. They walked across the street and were approaching their cars when Dev said, almost casually, "Did you really tell the owner you'd make him pay?"

The incredulity and disappointment in his tone made Shelley cringe.

"Yes, but Reyna made it sound a lot worse than it was. Of course, I didn't mean I'd kill him or anything. I meant I'd call the USDA, the *Post*, even PETA, if I had to. And you heard Eddy. He said himself that he didn't feel threatened."

"I'm not worried about you killing someone. I know you wouldn't do something like that, Shells." Dev frowned and crossed his arms over his brawny, distracting chest. "But you can't go around telling people that you'll make them pay. It can be construed as a threat. Which *is* illegal. It's a good thing for you he didn't press charges. His daughter might change his mind if you aren't careful."

Shelley blinked in surprise at Dev's harsh tone. "Would you have really arrested me?"

"Not my jurisdiction," he said.

Was that a joke?

"Hey, Shelley. Good to see you back." Cristos, Eddy's derelict son sauntered over to her. With a strong jawline, long black hair pulled into a ponytail, and startling green eyes, he was hot and knew it. He often used his looks to skirt the rules he didn't like. Like wearing uniforms. Today he sported a black leather jacket with a burning skull on the back, jeans, and biker boots. The metallic chains draped across the boots caught the sunlight and shone right in Shelley's eyes. She blinked and averted her gaze.

Dev seemed to get taller as Cristos pulled Shelley into a quick semipersonal embrace. The kind he delivered to most of the women in town. The very hug she tried to avoid. "Ain'tcha gonna introduce me?"

"Hi, Cristos." Shelley stepped back, out of his reach. "Cristos Jameson, meet Devon Jones. Cristos is Eddy's son. Dev is an old friend visiting from out of town."

They did that greeting that men sometimes do where they nod their heads and part their lips like they're going to speak, only they remain silent.

"Shelley, I'm glad you're here," Cristos said. "If you've got some time, we could use something to calm down ole Miah. She's been freaking out since last night."

"Probably because two of her cubs are gone," Shelley said, then bit her bottom lip to stem the sudden urge to scream in frustration.

"You heard?" He rubbed his neck as if it pained him. "We're trying to keep it quiet. Don't want the town panicking. I can see the headlines now, man-eating tiger cubs on the loose, news at eleven. Missing cats really aren't good for business. But you already know that. Leonardo's escape almost shut down the whole town."

At the questioning look on Dev's face, Shelley said, "The week before I moved here, the male white Bengal tiger, Leonardo, went missing."

"You've had more than one tiger escape here?"

Cristos waved his hands in the air in a gesture that clearly meant keep your voice down. "Leonardo escaped his cage but not the zoo. Tomás had to put him down because the tiger went to attack him when he tried to catch him."

Shelley frowned in confusion. "I thought you and your father put him down."

Cristos gave her a narrow-eyed glance and shook his head sharply. "Not me. Dad said Tomás did it."

And Tomás had told Shelley he hadn't been there when the tiger was caught.

She glanced at Dev, who watched them with an impassive expression.

"See, this is what I mean about cats on the loose being bad for business. A year after and no one, outside of those who really were there, knows what happened. But everyone *thinks* they do," Cristos said, his tone light, but the expression on his face was dark.

"I can't figure out how the cubs could've escaped. Tomás said the fence was locked when he opened the zoo this morning," Shelley said, determined to make Cristos see there was something else at work here.

"And I thought last month's tortoise fiasco was bad," Cristos said in an obvious attempt to change the subject.

"Tortoise fiasco?" Dev echoed.

"Yeah, I left the gate open and a couple kids got too close. But no one was seriously hurt." Cristos laughed, but quickly lost his sense of humor. He got a calculating look in his eyes, then said, "Shelley, maybe the cubs aren't missing at all. Miah could have eaten another litter."

"Another litter?" Dev intoned at the same time Shelley

said, "Miah didn't do anything. Someone had to have stolen the cubs."

"That's bullshit. No one could get near Miah's cubs without her attacking them. Well, except you. And you wouldn't have taken them, right?" Cristos frowned and shook his head. Shelley started to reply, but he went on. "She could have eaten them. I saw this report on television that talked about big cats eating sick young. And all of them are ill according to Dr. Kessler's report."

"What report? I haven't seen any report like that." That didn't make any sense. She wrote the reports. "Wait, Cristos you sound like you haven't seen the cubs at all."

"I haven't," Cristos said with an air of *Are you nuts?* in his tone. "The camera feed in the tiger house has been down since Leonardo escaped. Only you and Dr. Kessler have been in with them."

Frack! There went her one hope of quickly getting proof of last night's abduction.

"What other litter?" Dev said sharply.

Shelley and Cristos both glanced at him. Dev's face was impassive but his hands curled in loose fists at his sides and his wide stance showed his irritation.

Cristos shrugged. "A year ago, Miah had another litter. Only one cub. One day both mama and baby were there. The next, just Miah. If we hadn't seen the cub on the feed the day before, we wouldn't have known it had been there at all. She must have swallowed it whole. Not even a bone left over. It's the reason why my father and I wanted Drs. Kessler and Morgan to keep an eye on her. To make sure she didn't do it again."

"No way, nuh-huh." Shelley ground her teeth at the matching dubious expressions on the men's faces. "It's not that it couldn't have happened, theoretically. But there's no way Miah would have done that. All she ever wanted was to be a mother. She loves all her cubs."

"*Hmmm.*" Dev's sound could have been one of agreement or doubt. Shelley couldn't tell because his dubious look faded away, replaced by a blank expression. Her heart sank.

"Are you coming in or heading out?" Cristos asked. "Because if you've got time, I'd like you to check on the monkeys. They were making a lot of noise last night too."

"Heading out," she said quickly. "And I really can't go back in. Um . . . Reyna wouldn't like it."

Cristos rolled his eyes. "Threw you out again? She finally bend Dad to her will and make it official?"

"Not yet, but the day's still young."

"Well, don't worry about it. I'll go smooth things over. But you'll owe me."

Shelley forced her lips to curl into a smile and hoped it didn't look phony. "Right."

Cristos grinned wide and clapped his hands together once. "I should go see what Pop wants me to do this afternoon. I'm sure it will be something sexy, like clean the reptile house. I know you're jealous. I get all the cool jobs." Cristos shuddered in mock excitement, then strode toward the gate. He turned back with another laugh. "Catch you later, Shelley."

She turned to Dev, not surprised to see the questions lighting his gray eyes.

His phone rang out with the song *Bad Boys* from the old TV show *COPS*. He pulled the phone from his belt clip. He silenced the music and returned the phone to his hip. He scrubbed a hand over his mouth.

"Bad news?" she asked, guessing from the look on his face.

"No. It's not bad. It's just something I need to take care of."

"Well, can it wait until after I show you my notes? I should have thought to bring them with me."

"No, it can't wait. Shelley, I want to help you. And I will. But first, I need you to listen to me for a minute." Dev closed his eyes and shook his head. "I was really glad to get your e-mail. I've been looking for you. I tried to contact Cam. I didn't know he had joined the Peace Corps. When did that happen? I thought you two were getting married." Before she could answer, he waved his hand in the air. "I'm talking too much. I need to stop stalling."

There's something you don't hear a stoic man say often.

"Dev, whatever it is, just tell me."

"Shelley," Dev paused, exhaled, and said, "I need you to come to Tidewater with me. I found your sister Jules."

CHAPTER 6

S HE COULDN'T BREATHE. All the oxygen had been sucked out of her lungs.

"Are you all right?" Dev placed a hand on her shoulder. Shelley could only imagine what she must have looked like.

All right? Was she? Instead of answering his question, she slid away from his touch and asked one of her own, "Is . . . is she dead? She must be. Why else would you have been stalling?"

"No! Oh, damn it, Shelley. I'm sorry. Jules is fine. She's very much *alive*."

Alive. She's alive. Shelley was still processing that thought when Dev moved. Suddenly his arms were around her waist, and he was holding her close. She wrapped her arms around him and pressed her nose against the soft combed-cotton of his shirt. She inhaled the warm delicious scent of Dev and Irish soap, a combination that both soothed her spiraling emotions and fired her hòrmones. Yet all she could say was, "She's really alive?"

"She's really alive," Dev whispered into Shelley's hair. "I didn't mean to scare you, Shells. Jules is fine. Better than fine, fantastic even. She's engaged to my partner on the force. She's been looking for you for years."

Shelley tightened her embrace slightly. Dev answered by

swaying slightly; they were almost dancing beside her car, pressed chest to chest and thigh to thigh. She'd dreamed of him holding her like this for years, and at this moment, sex should have been the furthest thing from her mind. But, wow. All she could think about was sex. Except he wasn't offering sex. No, he wanted to comfort her because he'd found Jules. Dev being Dev just seemed to know that would devastate her emotions. That knowledge unleashed the memories she normally kept locked away. She shuddered.

Dev tightened his hold, rocking her. "It's okay, Shells. This is good news. I swear to you, it is."

"You're right." She didn't argue. She couldn't. While she'd told Dev about losing her sisters in the foster care system, she hadn't told him all of it. Childhood screams echoed in her ears, and tears she thought she'd never shed again threatened.

"You look just like her," Dev whispered quietly into Shelley's ear.

She sniffed back her tears. No more tears. She was finished crying over Jules. Right, like she hadn't promised herself that more than a decade ago.

"I'm glad Jules is happy and has a good life. She does have a good life, doesn't she?"

Dev pulled back and she reluctantly broke contact with him. Without his arms around her, the November wind felt brisk. Cold.

"Yes, she's happy. Well, as happy as she can be considering her . . . crift." He whispered the last word.

"Does she still see—?"

"Yes." Dev cut her off and glanced around as if making sure they were alone. "Come see her for yourself. Let me drop off my car at the hotel and . . ." He checked his watch. "Still too early to check in, but I can leave the car there. We'll head back to your place, talk about Jules and Tidewater, then see what we can do to find these missing cubs. Sound good?"

She'd almost forgotten where she was. The zoo parking lot. She was lucky no one had walked up and found her getting misty-eyed. That would be mortifying.

It was bad enough Dev saw her weak. But the look on his face wasn't pity. It was so full of compassion and hope, it made her stomach knot.

"Let's do that. I can even drive you to the hotel after, if you want."

A horn beeped, then a powder-blue Cadillac rolled to a stop at the curb on the street. Dr. Kessler called out, "Dr. Morgan? Shelley, my girl. What are you still doing here?"

He shifted into park and stepped out. Silver-topped cane in hand. "I've been looking for you."

"Hello, Dr. Kessler. We were eating lunch at the café." Shelley's back straightened, but she greeted her boss politely. "You gave me the afternoon off, remember? Shouldn't you be at the clinic?"

"Quite right. I'm headed there." He rapped his cane on the ground in two staccato taps. "You have put me in a pickle, my girl."

"Yes, Dr. Kessler, and I am sorry for that. But I promise you, I've done nothing wrong."

"Be that as it may, it doesn't change the fact that several people are very unhappy with you. And when they're unhappy with my staff, they take business away from me. What am I supposed to do about . . . about? Dagnabit, where did I put that note?" The elderly vet patted his vest pocket with his free hand and pulled a yellow sticky from it. He glanced at it, then wrinkled his brow. "About Reyna Jameson demanding that I fire you?"

"Fire me?" Her words slipped out on a squeak of alarm. "Oh, sir, you cannot believe—"

"It's not what I believe or don't believe. It's what's best for the clinic." Dr. Kessler slipped his paper back into his pocket and rested both hands on the round silver handle of his stick. "I brought you on to help me run the clinic. You were supposed to become my partner and take it over. Now I cannot even get you into the zoo to help me with the animals."

"But that's not necessarily true. Cristos and Eddy both—"

Dr. Kessler held up one hand to silence her, and she obeyed. "Now see here, if you cannot help me at the zoo, then you cannot remain a staff member."

"You're *firing* me?" A ball of ice formed in her chest and dropped razor-sharp icicles into her belly. "But this job is all I have. It's everything."

Dr. Kessler stroked his white mustache and gave his head a small shake. "I don't like this any better than you. But you brought this down on yourself. I warned you last month not to mess with any of the founding families of this town. Even *I* cannot go up against the Jamesons.

"Now, don't take it too hard, my dear. I'll give you a good recommendation and allow you to turn in a resignation letter. Take the weekend to draft it. Be at the clinic before opening on Monday to collect your things. Don't look so sad, my dear. I'll make sure you'll be able to secure employment with another veterinarian. I have a friend who's looking for someone to . . . to . . ." He sliced his hand through the air in annoyance. "Bah, I'll make sure you're taken care of. But you cannot remain at the clinic. I am sorry, my girl."

Dr. Kessler continued to talk, but she didn't hear him. It wasn't until Dev reached across her to shake the old vet's hand that any words registered. "Yes, sir, I'll see her home."

Dr. Kessler patted her shoulder gently. "Such a shame. I like you, girl. You're one helluva vet, even if dogs do go barking mad at the sight of you." He shook his head again, then climbed into his ancient Cadillac and drove away.

Shelley blinked her tearless eyes and listened to a single thought echo through her mind. *I'm fired.*

DEV DIDN'T KNOW what to do. Shelley crumbled right in front of him. She didn't move, barely even breathed, but all the color in her face drained, and her beautiful blue eyes unfocused.

And damn it, he'd seen her upset enough back in college that he didn't want to watch her suffer another second. "Shelley?" No response. "Shells, are you all right?" He stroked a finger down her silken cheek.

"He-he *fired* me. But I didn't do anything. You saw. You were with me. I didn't threaten anyone. I was only trying to help the . . . the . . ." Her words trailed off.

"Why don't we head back to your apartment and talk about this?"

She nodded, then slid behind the wheel of her old Buick. Dev closed her door but tapped on her window. After she rolled it down by the hand crank, he said, "Are you sure you're all right to drive?"

"Yeah, it's only a couple of blocks." She answered as if he

hadn't followed her over from her apartment, but Dev didn't correct her.

"Okay." He turned and had barely hit the unlock button on his key fob when Shelley called out to him.

"Dev, wait. Something's wrong with my car. Again." She turned the key in the ignition, but nothing happened. The engine didn't even try to turn over. "God, I hate Wednesdays. First the cubs go missing. Then I get fired. Now my fracking car won't start."

"Pop the hood. Let me take a look at the engine." Dev moved to the front, staring at Shelley through her windshield.

She shook her head. "Don't bother. I know what's wrong. The mechanic told me last week that my alternator was dying. I was hoping it would make it until my next payday before it died. I'll call the mechanic when I get home."

"Yep," Dev agreed, hoping to lighten the mood. "Could this day suck any more buckets of doggy-drool?"

Despite the frustration in her tone, the corners of her mouth curled up slightly.

Dev chuckled. "At least you've still got your sense of humor."

The would-be grin vanished, but she said in a light tone, "If your world's going to hell in a handbasket, might as well enjoy the ride down."

"Come on. I can drive you home," Dev said, opening her door and offering his hand. She accepted it, her tiny palm cool against his skin.

"I can't believe he really fired me. What am I going to do?"

Again the glow that lit her from within was snuffed out. Her smiles were a show, a front. She was trying to be brave, but there was no need to fake it with him.

Surely she knew that.

"Ready to go?"

She glanced at him and another too-bright smile appeared on her lips. This time he noticed how much of it didn't reach her eyes. "I'm all set. No wait, I've got to tie the trunk closed."

"What?"

"It's nothing. The latch is broken. Some kids broke into my car when I was still living in Baltimore, and I never got the trunk fixed." In short economical moves, she tugged on the bungee cords holding the trunk lid down.

"That's not very secure."

"It's more to keep it from flying up in case it rains tonight." She shrugged. "There's nothing in there to steal."

Without another word, she moved to his car. Dev opened the passenger door of his Lexus and waited until she'd buckled herself in before closing the door.

It was so quiet at the zoo, it took Dev a minute to recognize that even the normal sounds of squirrels chattering and birds chirping had ceased. He glanced up to the trees surrounding the lot. The few animals there stared down at his car and presumably Shelley in stony silence.

Their stillness was made more ominous by Dev's complete lack of knowledge on how to handle the situation. So he did what he did best, kept quiet.

A breeze carried the scent of the river, warm and brackish, along with the rich aroma of fall in the woods. Long golden shafts of midafternoon sun shining through the surrounding trees cast half of Shelley's face in shadow.

The Shelley he knew from college would have argued for her job. Fought to keep it. But the woman before him hadn't. She rallied enough to smile when he addressed her, yet she slid into the passenger seat like a ghost. Barely aware of where she was and what she was doing.

It was jacked up. He'd always remembered Shelley as the brave one. The girl at school who not only ran for SGA president, but won. She tutored football players in biology and English for fun. And made him and his teammates enjoy every moment of it too. Shells was never down. Never cried. Not even when she told him about her parents' death. The only time he'd ever seen her shed a tear was the night she'd had a bit too much to drink and admitted that she'd had another family as a child. That she had two sisters lost in the foster care system. Sisters she was both desperate and afraid to find.

That had been the same night she'd announced to Cam and him that she was getting a tattoo. Cam had thrown a fit and stormed out. Shells hadn't caved. She knew what she wanted and wasn't afraid to go get it.

Dev, worried for her safety because she was headed to a seedy part of town, had gone with her.

After it was over, Dev had asked about the three

roses—one yellow, one red, and one purple—wrapped in a green banner with the name *Scott* on it. Each rose was artfully designed with the name of the sister it represented. Until recently, he'd thought that tattoo on her shoulder had been a one-of-a-kind piece. That is, until he learned from his partner that Jules had an identical one on her back. What were the odds they would pick the same design?

Coming out of the tattoo parlor four years ago, he had asked about the artwork. She had mentioned the mingled feelings of desperation and fear when it came to searching for and possibly finding her sisters. The desperation he understood. People needed connection, a sense of belonging. And he had that in spades with his dozen cousins.

But the anxiety, he didn't get. She refused to elaborate on it. Still, he'd remembered how she trembled and changed the subject after her tears started to fall.

It was why he had wanted to be the one to tell her that Jules had been found. Ease Shelley into the idea of reuniting with her first family. Give her an ally and maybe a chance to discuss her concerns before she saw Jules again.

Shelley sniffed, and Dev glanced over at her. Her eyes were dry, but her hands were twisted together in her lap, her knuckles white.

"Shells, Jules is go—"

"I'm sorry, can you just give me a few more minutes?" She glanced at him and smiled again. This one was considerably less potent and more heartbreaking.

"Sure."

Silence he could do. Very well. So he'd wait until she was in control of her emotions again. He focused on driving the four blocks to Shelley's building. The tires spun and dipped along the cobblestone street, but the Lexus absorbed the shock.

He was tempted to just drive past her apartment and take her straight to Tidewater. Perhaps delaying the trip wasn't the best idea.

As if she could read his mind, she said, "It's a good thing we're headed home now. I need to feed Lucy."

Her ferret. Right.

Pulling into the parking lot behind her building, Dev struggled to find something to say. Cutting the engine, he racked his brain. He'd always been much better at listening than talking. "Shelley, it's going to be okay."

And yes, ladies and gentleman, that is perhaps the stupidest statement of all time.

She'd just been fired, she was conflicted about seeing her sister again, and she was worried sick about two missing tiger cubs.

She snorted, not quite smiling but definitely not doing the catatonic stare anymore. "Thanks, Dev."

She shoved open the passenger door and hurried across the gravelly lot for the building's front door. She barely paused long enough for him to catch up before she took the steps, two at a time, to her second-floor apartment. She didn't bother to close the door after unlocking it but left it open for Dev.

He entered, locked the door behind him, and waited for her to return from her bedroom.

Shelley left the bedroom door propped open when she came out less than a minute later. The ferret appeared to be sleeping in her cage, but the gate was ajar.

"Is that a good idea?" Dev gestured to the unlatched kennel.

Shelley shrugged. "Lucy's fine. She tends to wander around the apartment when I'm home. I lock her up at night for safekeeping or when I'm not here." She sank down on the couch beside Dev only to jump up again when her cell rang. She searched for it.

Dev spied it on the coffee table and handed it to her.

Frowning, she listened to the caller who apparently didn't wait for a salutation. Whatever was being said, Shelley's mood brightened then dimmed before she frowned. Within thirty seconds, she was shaking her head. "Oh, that's not necessary." Pause. "I'm not really comfortable—" Pause again. "Really, I'd rather talk to him myself. Please don't do anything to confuse him more." This time the pause went on longer and her frown faded. Her head bobbed twice and she smiled. "The clinic guests would be fine. Now *that* I can get onboard with. Thanks." She paused to listen again. "Oh, and Jacob, thank you."

She chuckled at whatever Jacob said, then clicked off.

"Give me a second." Shelley dashed off to the bedroom, shutting the door behind her.

Dev wanted to ask about the conversation, but given Shelley's state, he didn't want to push. She'd tell him when she was ready. He hoped. If not, he might not want to push, but that didn't mean he wouldn't. He was a cop, after all.

"Sorry about that. I needed to change into more comfortable clothes. I feel better now," she said, a few minutes later when she returned. In a blue cashmere top and jeans, she sat down on the other end of the couch from him and grinned. With her hair down and her blue eyes sparkling with life again, she looked good enough to taste. And taste. And taste.

Stop it. You're supposed to be helping her.

Dev clasped his hands together in his lap to resist the temptation to touch her. When she was sad, it was okay to hold her. He did it to comfort her. Sure, he did. Like he didn't have to resist the temptation to kiss her tears away.

But she was back to her usual joyous self. Going after Cam's ex was just wrong. Or maybe not. Cam had clearly lied to her about Dev's fictitious girlfriend at some point. And the rule about not dating a pal's ex surely had an expiration date when said former pal was a douche. At least, that's what his cousin Ryan always said.

Dev's phone beeped again, signaling another text. He tugged the phone from his pocket and checked it. The one he'd received earlier had been from Seth. So was this one.

It read, File sent to your email. Call me. Need you back here ASAP.

Crap, if Seth was pushing for Dev to work on the case, it had to be important. Until this morning, Seth's primary reason for contacting Dev off the clock had been to ask about finding Shelley.

"Shells, I know I told you I could stay in town for a few days, but something's come up at work. How about we alter our plans a bit?"

Her smile dimmed. "Oh. Okay."

"Great. How much time do you need to pack?"

Shelley raised her brows in obvious confusion. "What?"

He tried again. "Pack a bag? We can head back to Tidewater now. If we hurry, we can be at Jules's place by dinner. I know—"

She was already shaking her head. "I don't think so." Shelley ran one hand through her hair, then rubbed her temples. "I can't leave right now. My job—"

"Which you were just fired from—"

"I know, but I still have responsibilities here," she continued, narrowing her eyes at him. "The tiger cubs are missing and—"

"The sheriff's office is investigating it. You can't really believe you can do more than the sheriff, can you?"

"Well, I can interview witnesses they can't. Like members of the animal kingdom."

"Not gonna help, inadmissible evidence. Besides, your monkey didn't tell you much more than a smoker stole a cub or two. JoJo—"

"BoBo."

"*BoBo* wasn't even certain how many had disappeared last night." He slid closer to her, taking her hands in his. "Shells, you can't do any more here than in Tidewater. Bring your notes, we'll go over everything, and you can meet with Jules."

She withdrew from his touch and moved to sit on the arm of the couch as far from him as possible. Dropping her head in her hands, she muttered, "It's not that simple."

"Yes, it is." He paused at the panic in her eyes. "Shells, I'd planned to be here for a couple of days. Ease you into the idea of seeing Jules again. But the text I just received and the one earlier were from my partner. We have a case that just landed in our laps. I need to be in Tidewater. Someone's been murdered, and we've been specifically requested by the mayor to help."

"The mayor. Wow, that probably doesn't happen every day." She straightened, but the look on her face read defeated, not excited.

"It doesn't. This is huge, and I'd be crazy to pass it up." He ground his teeth at the resigned way she nodded.

"I get it, I do. But I have responsibilities here myself. That was Jacob on my cell. He's got this lame idea to help me get my job back. You saw Dr. Kessler with his notes?" Dev nodded.

"Okay, Dr. Kessler hired me a year ago because he's going senile. He knows it. On some level he does, anyway. But suffice it to say, he forgets it. A lot. I mean he forgets everything.

"My office is neat, but if you walk into his, there are sticky notes all over his walls and computer. And you saw him. He carries notes and notepads in every pocket. Plus, he keeps a calendar on his computer that's linked to his phone. It beeps to remind him to do everything, including to take his high blood pressure medication.

"Anyway, Jacob wanted to steal the notes about my being fired and replace them with notes about how much I'm needed."

Dev started to protest, but Shelley waved away his concern and said, "I think I talked him out of it. But I'm not positive. He said he wanted to do something to help me, so I suggested he keep an eye on the clinic animals for me. When he worried he wouldn't make the right call for the emergency cases, I offered to be available for consultation. Not that I expect too many emergencies, but you never know. Plus, something in his tone makes me think he might still try to trick Dr. Kessler. So I can't leave now."

"What can you do here that you can't do from Tidewater? Talking to Jacob over the phone is easy to do whether you're in your apartment or an hour and a half away."

Shelley drew her legs beneath her crisscross style and folded her arms over her chest but didn't say anything. Still, multiple emotions flitted across her face. "I don't know."

"Are you going to tell Dr. Kessler what Jacob said?" Dev asked, turning his body to face hers.

"It wouldn't matter. If it's not written down, he might not remember. Wow, that sounds callous. I didn't mean it like that. My primary job at the clinic is to keep the office running smoothly. I ensure the pets—guests—are properly vaccinated and groomed, the animals at the zoo receive their checkups, and the accounts and billing are handled in a timely fashion. It's why I should be here to stop Jacob."

"So you're going back to the clinic before Monday against Dr. Kessler's orders?" When she shook her head, he asked, "Are you going to the zoo?"

"No, but . . . the animals need me."

"They need you to not get arrested." Dev leaned toward her. "Staying here won't stop Jacob, and it won't keep another animal from going missing. But coming back to Tidewater with me will reunite you with your sister and give me time to go over the files you said you have on your computer."

"I don't know, maybe you're right." She shook her head. "If I stay here, I'm bound to run into Reyna this weekend. Jacob said she'd already called the clinic asking to speak to Dr. Kessler. And she claims I stir up trouble."

"What's with you and Reyna? Seems a little more personal than zoo-management ethics."

Shelley grimaced. "Yeah, in my defense, I didn't know she and Payne had been an item before I moved to town."

"The deputy?"

Shelley nodded. "He asked me out. It was one date to a restaurant outside of town. Honestly, the food was more exciting than the date. He spent the whole time talking about his recent breakup."

"With Reyna?"

"You guessed it." Shelley rubbed her right temple as if it pained her. "Anyway, a week later they were back together. And it seems he told her about our dinner. Ever since, she's been out for blood."

"All this over a meal?" Dev asked. "Seems a little melodramatic."

Shelley shrugged. "I've never done anything else to her."

"All right, what does this have to do with Dr. Kessler?"

"Oh, well, since that date, he's received one complaint after another from Reyna about me. His short-term memory might be shot, but he's received enough complaints that while he cannot remember the details, he knows there are problems with me. Today, she finally won. I'm fired." Shelley groaned and dropped her hands to her lap. "What am I going to do? I can't even afford my rent, let alone my student loans, without that job. Dev, I'm an animal empath. I should be using my gifts to help animals."

Dev understood her frustration. He knew what it felt like when the thing you wanted most stared you in the face, but you couldn't touch it.

"Dr. Kessler sounded like he had a line on another job for you already," Dev said. When she made a noncommittal noise, he said, "I know it sucks right now, but maybe this is for the best. You can go to Tidewater. See your sister. Hang with me for a few days. Maybe even check out the zoo there. They've got lions and tigers. This could be your chance to do what you always wanted. Be a big-cat vet."

She glanced up, her eyes wide with surprise. "Whoa, you remember that? I mentioned that goal five *years* ago."

"Of course, I do. It's all you talked about when you started veterinary school. I thought that was why you chose the school

you did. Didn't the vet program offer some special training
with big cats?"

The smile she gave him made his heart clang against his
rib cage. Damn, she was beautiful.

"You're right, it did." She laughed softly. "But it's a lot harder
to start making money right away as a big-cat vet. All the best
zoos in the places I wanted to live didn't need me, because I
didn't have experience. Oh, they offered jobs with the opportunity for growth. I really wanted to take a couple of the offers,
but I couldn't afford to start at the bottom. Even if I had put my
student loans on temporary deferral, a year wouldn't have been
long enough to move into a better-paying position.

"See, that's why I took this job as Dr. Kessler's associate.
He offered me an incredible salary and a chance to work with
big cats. We're talking guaranteed access to the local zoo and
great pay. It sounded like a dream come true. Too bad I had no
idea what a farce of a zoo that place would be before I accepted
the position. You saw it, it's barely a zoo . . . especially with
the number of animals that have gone missing lately."

"Then it's settled, we'll head back to Tidewater tonight."

"I thought you were checking into a hotel room. Why are
you pushing me to leave right away?"

"Well, I figured with you being fired, there's no reason to
wait."

"Gee, thanks so much for your support." She sighed and
stretched out her legs until her foot brushed his knee. A zing
of awareness rocketed up his leg. A moment later, she shifted
and tucked her feet beneath her again, a blush on her cheeks.

Did she feel it too?

"Okay, I get it. I do. You need time to get used to the idea
of Tidewater. So, how about we go in the morning? Treat it
like a vacation. I've got this cottage, right on the ocean. It's
beautiful. You'll have a private room, your own bath, plus,
there's a hot tub with a Jacuzzi on your balcony." She tilted her
head as if considering and Dev pushed on. "You'll love it. Plan
to leave tomorrow and stay for the weekend."

"But my car is dead."

"Call the mechanic. I'll even pay to replace your alternator." Dev hoped his offer wasn't too over-the-top, but she

needed to agree. And he sure as hell needed to get back home to find out about the murder case.

"Dev, the last time Jules and I saw each other—"

"You were both children." Dev scooted closer to her on the couch and took her hands in his. "I don't know everything about what went on with you two, but I remember enough to know the last time you saw her was hard. On both of you. Shells, give her a chance. I've gotten to know her. She's a great person. A lot like you. And I know she misses you."

"She does?" There was no missing the doubt and confusion in her eyes.

"She does." He nodded. "Give yourself a chance. You deserve to know your family. Take it from someone who will never get an opportunity like this. What you have here is a gift. Grab it with both hands, Shells."

The touch of her cool, delicate hands between his much larger ones sent a jolt of awareness through his body. From the way her eyes widened, she must have felt it too.

Shelley sucked in the right corner of her bottom lip. The sight of it thundered straight to his tightening groin. "All right. I'll go with you to Tidewater, tomorrow. But that ocean view had better be spectacular," she joked.

"Satisfaction guaranteed."

"Thanks, Dev." She beamed at him, then cleared her throat and pulled free from his touch. "Your girlfriend is one lucky woman."

Cam, I'm going to pound you, if I ever see you again.

"Shelley, that relationship ended a long time ago. I . . . uh, don't have a girlfriend."

"You broke up? I'm sorry to hear that." But the smile on her face and the dilation of her pupils belied that statement. She licked her lips and leaned closer to him. Her soft fingers entwined with his rougher ones again. "Really sorry."

Awareness rocketed through him.

"Don't be. I'm not." And, oh God, her lips were right there. The scent of Shells, vanilla and sugar, teased his senses. His mouth watered for just a taste. Just a sample. Slowly, giving her time to pull back, he lowered his head.

And screamed like a little girl.

He launched off the couch. Lucy, the demon ferret, held onto his crotch with all four paws and her evil little teeth.

"Lucy! Stop that right now," Shelley called out, reaching for her ferret. Her fingers brushed against the undeniable but rapidly deflating bulge in his pants. "Dev, hold still or you'll hurt my baby."

"Hold still?" Her *baby* was trying to gnaw through his jeans. Her daggerlike teeth were biting way too close to his testicles, which were currently burrowing into his body for safety. He held himself still. With his hands behind his head, he resisted the urge to grab the ferret and toss her across the room like a slingshot flying-monkey toy.

The knuckles of both of Shelley's hands rubbed against his crotch and his cock jumped even as his testicles drew up higher. She twisted and tugged the ferret, searching for better purchase on the animal.

"Lucy, let go of Dev this instant," Shelley said in a voice that reminded him of his second-grade teacher, Mrs. Clark-McBride. "Look at me. He needs all his . . . parts."

Shelley's gaze collided with his for a moment, then she blushed. It would have been funny had his dick not been in danger of becoming a ferret chew toy.

Finally, Lucy let go and Shelley plucked the weasel off his package.

Shelley held her up, so she could stare eye to eye with her pet. Some silent communication appeared to pass between them because Shelley's already pink cheeks flamed to bright scarlet. "Yes," she said to the ferret as she headed to Lucy's cage in the bedroom. "Well, that's none of your business. Now take a nap."

The door to the ferret cage latched shut with a snap.

Dev cupped himself quickly to make sure no blood had been drawn. *Nothing sexier than blood drawn by a wild animal during the first kiss.*

"I'm really sorry about that. Are you hurt?" She gestured to his jeans.

Dev took a step back. Now that he was not on the ferret's menu, reality set in. He'd come here to help her with her missing-animals case and to bring her home to see Jules, not get in bed with her. Although he intended to pursue her, but only after he reunited her with her sister. Because he had a feeling, given the opportunity to get her into his bed, he might not want either of them out of it before Sunday night. Or ever.

"I'm not hurt," Dev reassured her. Hiking a thumb over his shoulder, he added, "But I should probably get to my hotel. I've got that case file to review for Seth. And you need time to adjust to the idea of seeing Jules again before tomorrow."

"Oh. You don't have to go now, do you? You only just got here." She glanced at her watch and her eyes bugged. "Three hours ago. It's past three thirty. If you want, we could do dinner later? I'm a great cook."

His cell beeped, indicating another incoming text before he could answer. He checked it quickly, then shook his head. "I'd love to, Shells, but that's my partner again. He wants to discuss our case. It could be hours before I have time to eat." Not to mention, he liked the idea of spending the evening with her and possibly picking up where they'd left off before the ferret attack. And he doubted they'd stop with a single kiss. Then they'd never make it back to Tidewater.

"I understand." Disappointment flashed across her face so fast, he doubted he'd seen it once it disappeared. "I need to work too. I've got to make notes from today on my own files. Frack. I left my thumb drive in my car."

"You keep your files on a thumb drive?" In the age of Internet clouds?

"I work on two different networks, home and the clinic. I tried e-mailing stuff to myself but ended up with too many different versions, and I couldn't keep it all straight. The thumb drive was easier." She sighed. "Maybe you're right. We both have work to do." She rose from the couch and wandered to her front door. She twisted her fingers together, a telltale nervous habit.

Stupid as it sounded, now he wished he hadn't said a damned word about work. What were the odds he'd have more than a few minutes alone with her after she saw Jules again? He should just go for it. Tell her he'd been crazy about her for years. He stepped closer, but she said, "And I could use some time to adjust—good word, by the way—to all of the day's revelations. I don't think I'm up to being good company after all. God, I *really* hate Wednesdays." She rolled her eyes.

His timing was good for shit. Following her to the door, he kept his tone casual. "Want a lift to your car?"

She shook her head. "No, thank you. I want to write my notes first. And I could use the walk to clear my head."

He stepped through the open door and paused, wanting to ask more about the case, the attack ferret, that near kiss. Instead, he said, "Sure. Take it easy. I'll be back in the morning to pick you up."

And there it was again. That zing of awareness between them. It practically sizzled in the air. Then time suspended.

She drifted closer to him until he inhaled her vanilla-and-sugar scent with each breath. With just his fingertips, he touched her silken cheek. She closed her eyes and tilted her head back.

Dev leaned down and brushed his lips over hers. A gentle touch that was innocent but definitely not enough. He kissed her again, softly, teasing his senses with the feel of his mouth on hers.

Shelley turned to human fire in his arms, ramping up the kiss. Rising on her toes, she threw her arms around his neck and drove her tongue into his mouth. She both owned the kiss and demanded more from him. And more he was happy to give. Grabbing a handful of her luscious ass, he pulled her tighter against him. She moaned into his mouth.

A door slammed downstairs followed by loud voices floating up the stairwell.

Shelley's eyes flew open. Ah, hell, she pulled back from the kiss and out of his arms. Her cheeks flushed and her eyes went from lust-filled and hazy to shocked, then to something else entirely. She took two steps backward and into her apartment. A phony smile slashed across her face but didn't quite disguise her shuttered expression. Why did she just shut down? She'd been the one to ramp up the passion.

"Okay. I'll see you in the morning." She smiled, but it didn't quite reach her eyes, then she crossed her arms over her chest. "It was—is—good to see you again, Dev."

It could be better if you'd invite me back inside. Given her protective posturing, that was less than zero on the possibility scale. Damn, once again he had missed his chance with her.

Dev cleared his throat and focused on tomorrow. "Are you still an early riser? I can pick you up at seven."

Shelley chuckled. "Yep, some things don't change. But aren't you a night owl? We don't have to rush back first thing

in the morning. Jules can wait a few hours. It's been years."
She shook her head before he could answer her question. "No,
I know you need to get back for your case. I'll be ready."

"Shells, I know this is probably strange for you. It's why I
wanted to tell you in person. I'm here if you want to talk before or after you see her. Just know, Jules *is* your family. She
loves you."

"Thanks." She cut her gaze away, shrugging. "I'm okay
with it."

"If you change your mind," he said, taking her hand in his.
When her eyes lifted, he said, "I promise you, Shells. I'll be
right there with you tomorrow. Or if you want to talk tonight,
you can call me."

A grin tilted her lips at the corners. "I don't have your
number."

Dev pulled out his cell, keyed in her number, then sent her
a text. "Now you do."

"Yeah. I guess I do." She glanced over her shoulder. "I
should have named her Houdini. I'm going to have to padlock
that cage."

Lucy, the ferret demon, was making her way through the
apartment. Dev took an automatic step back and fought the
urge to cup himself. If Shelley noticed his reaction, she didn't
let it show.

"Better close the door before she decides to make a break
for it. See you tomorrow. And, Dev, thanks for coming to
Elkridge."

"Couldn't have kept me away." Dev took another step back,
then two. "I'll see you at seven a.m."

The door closed with a snap. He headed down the stairs
when Shelley opened the door a crack and called out, "Dev, if
Jules is so happy to have found me, why didn't she come here
herself?"

"Because I volunteered."

CHAPTER 7

DEV HAD VOLUNTEERED.

The knowledge shouldn't have made Shelley's heart beat faster, but it did. That gorgeous, shy guy she'd known in college was a devastatingly handsome police detective today. And every bit as kind and caring as he'd always been. Maybe her superstar sex fantasy with Dev in the leading role wasn't so far out of the realm of possibility. Provided Lucy, the attack ferret, left them alone long enough. She might have invited Dev back in, had she not heard Lucy playing with her little jingly ball. Sneaky beast had escaped her cage again. There was no way Shelley would risk another ferret attack on Dev's impressive package. She might never get him into her bed if Lucy had her way.

Shelley locked the door behind Dev and spun around. Lucy sat up on hind legs, glaring, ball forgotten in the middle of the living-room floor.

Shelley glared back. "I cannot believe you tried to bite his . . . his . . . you know what. Jeez, Lucy! What was all that about?"

An image of Shelley and Cam kissing flew into her mind, courtesy of Lucy. The memory was a ferret's-eye view of the day Cam left her, just six months before the wedding. Shelley had been on the couch, Lucy at her side, addressing the last of the wedding invitations when Cam came into their posh living room in Baltimore.

Shelley didn't need Lucy to remind her of that horrid afternoon. Even now, almost a year later, her stomach still cramped at the memory. Cam had announced he couldn't marry her. He'd never loved her and had realized it the moment she'd told him she was pregnant. He hadn't been excited. He'd felt trapped. The miscarriage had been a relief for him. He'd actually said, "Now we can be free."

As if losing the baby hadn't been hard enough.

Shelley's tears had started then. She'd dropped the pen. It had rolled off the coffee table and onto the pristine white carpet where it had bled a black mum-shaped stain.

The flashes of Lucy's memories winged faster and faster through Shelley's mind, until she thought she might hurl from the spinning images. Shelley crying on her bed. On the couch. At the kitchen table, eating a bowl of cereal. Shelley crying, as she packed and moved out of the apartment she'd shared with Cam. Then without warning, the mental pictures shifted to Dev's face as he'd leaned in to kiss her on her couch. The expression on his face was intent, lustful, and dear God, hopeful.

The thoughts zapped out.

Lucy might not have even understood what she saw, but Shelley did. Dev *wanted* her. If his half-hooded, nearly obsidian gaze was anything to go by, he really wanted her. Something she'd been positive she would never see. Not on his face. She wasn't his type. And she knew all about his type. Cam had always compared her to those superskinny football groupies who'd followed Dev everywhere back in college. Shelley hadn't been skinny since puberty. Tonight though, Dev had been looking at her with hunger in his sexy gray eyes. And again, the superstar knocking-boots fantasy became a little more attainable. It wouldn't be more than that. No one stayed with her forever. It just didn't happen. Everyone left or died. She was meant to be alone. Still, even the lone wolf gets to experience a little companionship.

A slow grin curled the corners of her mouth. Maybe getting fired today was a good thing after all. It freed her up to spend

the next couple of days with Dev. Perhaps tomorrow might not
be so bad.

She liked the idea of staying at a place with an ocean view.
Tidewater was beautiful all year long. And she could see Jules.

The muscles in her shoulders knotted at the thought of facing her older sister. Shame filled her, remembering her
behavior all those years ago. Jules searching for Shelley
seemed illogical given their last *conversation*. She pushed
away the thought and focused on Dev.

She touched her fingers to her lips, recalling his amazing
kiss in the hallway. She could indulge herself in a few lusty
nights of fun with an old friend. Besides, after a night or two,
her fantasy would be fulfilled. And Dev probably had women
slipping him their phone numbers at the grocery store, so
there wouldn't be any risk of him wanting what she could
never give.

Tidewater was looking better and better. Then she could
come back to Elkridge and beg Dr. Kessler for her job back.
Or if that didn't work, see if his offer to help her find another
one would lead to a new adventure. In the meantime, she'd get
Dev to help her solve the mystery of the missing animals.

"Oh, Lucy," Shelley said, gently cradling the ferret and rubbing her belly. "You can't protect me from everything. I wanted
him to kiss me. Dev isn't Cam. He can't hurt me. I happened to
adore the look you saw in his eyes. So please, don't interfere
again. Otherwise, I won't be able to take you with me tomorrow.
And I need you with me if I'm going to see Jules."

Lucy went boneless at the tummy scratch, then yawned and
lifted her head to make eye contact again. An image of Shelley
saying, "I promise," winged into her mind. It was the closest
Lucy could come to actually saying the words and it touched
Shelley's heart.

While she booted up her laptop, Shelley let Lucy run free
in the apartment. The computer hummed to life. Opening a
new document, she spent the next hour documenting everything she'd seen, heard, smelled, and sensed today. She
reached for her flash drive but remembered it was back in the
zoo parking lot. As much as she hated duplicate files, she
didn't want to risk forgetting the details. Saving the file to her
hard drive, she shut down the computer.

Scooping Lucy from her latest hiding place, Shelley's computer bag, she said, "Want to go for a walk? I need to get something from my car. Come on, we can both use the exercise."

Shelley grabbed the leash and harness from the hook on the wall near the front door. Settling on the couch, she helped Lucy wriggle into the apparatus. Five minutes later, they were on the sidewalk headed toward the zoo parking lot. Corner streetlights buzzed to life as the setting sun's rays faded. At barely five o'clock, the tourist shops had started to close for the night. Main Street was busy with people heading home from work. Four cars waited for the light to turn green at the corner of Main and First. Ah, rush hour in a small town.

"He's gone? Missing?" The words carried on the wind.

Shelley glanced around to see two familiar shop owners, Mrs. Blaney and Mrs. Hoffstedder. The Elizabeths, as Shelley often thought of the pair, were gossiping outside of Elkridge Antiques. Both hard of hearing, the women stood close together, heads bent, but their voices were too loud to be considered whispering.

"Why, I saw Colbert last week. He stopped in my shop on the way to his cabin. Told me to put that lovely carnival-glass butter dish aside for Janice. She's been wanting it to complete her collection, you know," Mrs. Blaney said. Her blond curly hair bounced as she bobbed her head. "Told me he'd be back yesterday to pick it up."

"Oh, the blue dish? That was a nice piece," Mrs. Hoffstedder said. She frowned, pushing her black horn-rimmed glasses up on her nose. "And he didn't show? Curious. You know, Maureen said that Colbert Rush didn't come to the barbershop for his monthly trim either. First haircut he's missed in thirty years."

"I tell you, it's just like what happened last summer with John Wallace," Mrs. Blaney said. "He went missing too."

"Tosh. You read too many mysteries. Everybody knows John Wallace ran off with some woman he met on the Internet. And Colbert, that man has barely been a part of this town in twenty years. He's some uppity jeweler in Tidewater. He only comes here for the antiques and his haircuts. He probably just forgot about your carnival glass." Mrs. Hoffstedder waved away the other woman's concern. "You mark my words, he'll call next week wanting that dish. And when he does, you should charge him double."

At that moment, the pair caught sight of Shelley with Lucy.

Shelley's cheeks heated. She didn't mean to eavesdrop, but it was kind of hard to ignore them. Plus, they were discussing *two* missing men from Elkridge. "Good evening, Mrs. Blaney, Mrs. Hoffstedder." Shelley pretended not to have heard their conversation just like the shop owners pretended they hadn't been gossiping.

"'Evening, Dr. Morgan," Mrs. Blaney said with a grin. "Lovely night for a walk."

"Yes, it is," Shelley agreed, stepping up her pace to get past the two busiest bodies in twenty miles. "Have a nice night."

"Good night," the two owners called out in unison.

Turning left at the corner, Shelley made her way up Zoo Lane. One more block and she'd be at her car. Good thing. Lucy's pace had slowed considerably. "Hang on, girl." Shelley bent down and scooped up the exhausted ferret. Lucy might love her walks, but she'd worn herself out attacking Dev this afternoon. "I should make you walk for trying to eat Dev," Shelley groused teasingly, then tucked Lucy inside her coat.

The day had been unseasonably warm, but the moment the sun set, it definitely felt like November in Elkridge.

Once Lucy settled inside her jacket pocket, Shelley continued strolling. Her mind replayed the beginning of that interrupted seduction scene on her couch.

Oh my, just remembering the heat in his gaze as he'd stared at her. She'd licked her lips intentionally, just to see how he'd react. It had been the first time she'd been certain he was looking at her with that intensity. The few times she thought she'd seen it, he had looked away before she could be sure. And man alive, on the couch, he looked at her as way more than his old college buddy.

And that incredible, soul-melting kiss at the door.

Chances were, if Lucy, that little magician, hadn't escaped her cage, Shelley would have pulled him back into her apartment and would still be kissing him. Maybe more.

Definitely more.

And suddenly her coat was stifling. Unzipping her blue fleece-lined jacket, she started to fan it. Lucy popped her head out of the pocket and Shelley froze. "Sorry, girl. Forgot you were there." She zipped the jacket back up.

Dang, she needed a cold shower or Dev to come back and finish what he'd started. *Next time, I'm locking Lucy in her cage in another room. Possibly on another floor.*

Shelley crossed the street at the light, still lost in thought. She passed the squat evergreen bushes that framed the parking lot of the zoo and was nearly to the entrance when she stumbled over something.

She flew forward but managed to clutch Lucy to her with one hand. Tumbling down, her knees and right palm skidded along the cracked white sidewalk, but Lucy remained safely clasped against Shelley's chest.

"You okay, girl?" Shelley righted herself and unzipped her jacket enough for the ferret to poke out her head. Her round pink eyes were wide and searching before she sniffed the air. Lucy sneezed, then burrowed back into the warmth of the coat. "I'm fine. Thanks for asking."

Shelley turned her palm and blew cool air on the skinned heel of her right hand. She started to rise, still blowing on the stinging wound and searching for the source of her fall.

A pair of blue sneakers protruded from beneath a nearby bush. A very familiar pair of sneakers. Fear had her bolting to the shrub, her skinned hand all but forgotten.

"Beau?" She gently patted his leg through his threadbare jeans. "Beau, speak to me. Are you hurt?"

"Doc?" His voice sounded thick. Like he had a bad cold.

"Yes, it's me." Relief flooded through her at the sound of his voice. If he could talk, then he was conscious, breathing, and had a pulse. All good signs. "Can you come out from under there?"

"No, ma'am. I don't think that's a good idea." He paused, then added. "Sorry I tripped you."

"Beau, that's okay. I'm not angry." When he didn't respond, she said, "I really must insist that you come out. You could get hurt lying on the ground like that."

Beau made a derisive noise and muttered something that sounded like "Too late."

The fallen leaves crunched on the ground, and the shrubbery rustled as Beau drew his legs farther beneath the bushes.

More rustling leaves and branches. Then he slowly poked his head out. He lumbered to his feet with one arm wrapped around his midsection and awkwardly shuffled just beyond the reach of the halo of light cast by the streetlamp. In the fading strains of the sunset, he was mostly in shadow.

Even in the dimness, he kept his head down, his eyes not meeting hers. A chill sank into her bones. Then a Carolina chickadee hopped out from the bush he'd just been under. It made eye contact with Shelley and images washed through her mind like a rapidly rising river.

Beau, right eye swollen and lip bleeding, ran up the street. He raced past the shrub, past the zoo gate, to stare through the zoo's chain-link fence, only to run back again. He dropped to his belly and army-crawled under the bush. His hair and shirt snagged on branches as he burrowed farther inside until his whole body was camouflaged. His head dropped to his knees.

A hand jutted through the bushes. Beau's head snapped up, his eyes dark with fear. Red-tipped fingernails scraped across his face. He turned his head and bit the attacker on the wrist. A fist slammed through the bush, colliding with his left ear, knocking him sideways into the many branches.

The little bird flew out of the bush in a panic and into the face of Mama Margaret. Her eyes as wild as her wiry orange hair, she swatted at the chickadee. It jerked back and circled her head once before taking safety in one of the tall scrub pines dotting the zoo's entrance. The woman reached for the boy's legs, which were now sticking out from beneath the bush and yanked. When she couldn't pull him out, she kicked the soles of his feet twice and stumbled away.

The images blinked out and for an instant Shelley's mind was a white slate. The world and the chickadee came into focus once more. Caressing the bird on its tan breast, she whispered, "Thank you."

The bird chirped once and flew up to perch in the scrub pine. Shelley turned to the boy who still hadn't lifted his head. His shoulders were hunched forward and down, his chin and chest seemed to be one connected body part, and his hands were jammed into his pockets. It was as if he were trying to fold in on himself.

Fury and heartbreak warred inside her, but neither would

help Beau. Shelley needed to examine him, get him to a safe place, and make another call to CPS. First, she needed him to talk to her. Just because she knew the old bitch had crossed the line didn't mean she could make the call, because her only proof came from an avian witness.

"Why was Margaret so angry? Why did she hurt you?"

Beau's head snapped up and he stared at her with the eye that wasn't swollen shut. "How did you know?"

"A little birdie told me." *And wasn't that the truth.*

"Someone at the diner told her I came in with money. She wanted to know where I got it. She said I stole it from her purse and demanded I give it back. I told her I got it at the clinic. That you gave it to me. I had to tell her. She kept smacking me, saying I couldn't steal from her. She said she was going to take away my dumb rat so I won't have no reason to go back to the clinic. And . . . and I got so mad. I yelled at her. Told her Mr. Fuzzbutt was a guinea pig not a rat, and she was too stupid to know the difference.

"That just made her madder. Said she was going to drown Mr. Fuzzbutt and put him out with the trash. She went into my room and started tearing things up looking for him. When I wouldn't tell her where he was, she hit me again and again. Said that's what heathens get for being bad. I'd get a lot worse if I didn't give her Mr. Fuzzbutt. So I shoved her and ran away." Tears leaked from beneath the swollen eye and made his open brown one shine like polished stone behind the cracked lens of his glasses. "I know it's bad and I'm gonna go to juvie now. But I think she would have really killed him. I couldn't let her. If I get sent away, you've gotta keep him, Doc. Don't let her hurt him."

"*¡Ay Dios mío!*"

Shelley and Beau both jumped at the exclamation. Shelley turned to see Tomás running up the sidewalk.

"Beau! *Venga aquí.*" He shook his head and said in English, "Come here." Tomás dropped to his knees in front of the child and opened his arms. Beau moved in short, painful steps until he stood in front of Tomás. The man placed gentle hands on his shoulders, examining the boy's injuries.

Anguish gave way to fury in the man's dark eyes as he took in each bruise and abrasion. "*Mijo*, who did this to you?"

"Mama Margaret." Beau's words were husky sounds, barely intelligible, but Tomás nodded as if he understood.

"Come inside," Tomás said, taking Beau by the hand. Tomás glanced at Shelley, "Thank you, Dr. Shelley. I will take him."

Without another word, Tomás and Beau headed to the employee entrance.

Shelley stood stunned. Tomás's reaction seemed almost paternal. She knew he and the boy were close, but she'd had no idea how much of a bond they shared. Then the bird's-eye view of Beau's run for safety flashed through her mind. He hadn't been standing near the fence. He'd been near the employee entrance. Searching for Tomás.

"Wait!" Shelley called out, catching up to the pair. Not missing the way Tomás stiffened, she said quickly, "I might be a vet, but I'm still a doctor. I'd like to tend those cuts and make sure he doesn't have more serious injuries."

Tomás seemed to wage an internal battle, then gave a curt nod. "*Sí.*"

Together, they made silent passage up the Tiger Monkey Trail. Around them, the nocturnal creatures chattered, chirped, or sang. She walked a few feet in the expanding twilight before asking Beau softly, "You were trying to get to Tomás, weren't you?" He nodded. "Why?"

"He loves me," Beau said simply, allowing Tomás to lift him into his arms. Beau snuggled against Tomás's chest, while quiet tears tracked down his bruised cheeks.

Shelley followed. Her instincts were to take Beau into her arms. Hold him and comfort him. It was illogical, but deep inside her, the need burned. She didn't act on it. She doubted that neither man nor child would willingly let go of the other. They seemed to share a bond she could only dream of. Here she'd thought she'd known both so well. Clearly, she didn't know everything. And until she was certain Beau was safe, she wasn't letting him out of her sight.

"KEEP YOUR HEAD down until we get past the cameras," Tomás said, indicating one of the security cameras affixed above the employee entrance to the zoo's visitor center.

Shelley lowered her head then realized the stupidity. "My hair is bright red. Everyone in town knows me."

Tomás yanked a key from the retractable fob on his belt and unlocked the door. "You are right. I was not thinking."

He moved through the dark hallway with a snuffling Beau in his arms. Tomás didn't bother to turn on any lights. He clearly knew where he was headed, so Shelley followed them through the converted warehouse.

Tomás pulled out another key and opened a door on his right, this time flipping on the lights. The small office was neat and tidy. A sturdy wooden desk and chair were functional and solid if slightly chipped and showing age. The windowless space had probably once been a utility closet, but it appeared to serve Tomás's purposes. The walls of the office were covered with paintings of desert sunrises, giving the space a warm, welcoming feeling. A brightly colored braided rug covered the floor. On it lay dozens of Lego creations, crayons, coloring books, and a very familiar-looking backpack.

Shelley and Tomás worked together silently cleaning Beau's cuts and icing down his bruises. When the child yawned and blinked his good eye sleepily, Tomás pulled out a sleeping bag and tucked Beau in for bed. To a passerby, it looked as if Tomás had a room full of toys and stuffed animals shoved into one corner. The child was all but invisible.

Tomás whispered something to the boy in Spanish and kissed him gently on the top of his head before gesturing for Shelley to follow him back into the hallway. She couldn't go without making sure for herself that Beau was okay with being left alone.

"Beau, are you going to be all right for a few minutes? Tomás wants to speak with me in the hallway. If you'd rather I didn't leave you, I won't. I can stay right here with you, or you can come home with me." She reached out a hand and stroked his beautiful black hair.

"I'm safe here," Beau replied. He didn't smile, but his tone suggested confidence. He yawned again, then his eyes slipped closed. He mumbled, "As long as I'm with him, no one will hit me."

Shelley's heart broke. Her eyes stung as she replied, "And no one will hit you if you're with me."

"I know." Beau's bruised mouth curled slightly at the corners before relaxing into sleep.

Shelley stepped into the hall and Tomás closed the door behind her, unlocking another door across the hall. Again he flipped on the light. This time they stepped into a closet. A clipboard with a pen tied to it hung on one wall. Brooms, mops, buckets, and cleaners were jammed into every corner of the space. There was barely enough space for one person to stand, but Tomás squeezed in next to her. His brown eyes had the look of a haunted man.

"He's your son, isn't he?" She tried not to feel hurt when Tomás nodded slowly. Tried and most definitely didn't succeed. "All this time. We've been friends all this time. We worked together every week for hours and hours, sometimes pulling all-nighters here. I trusted you with my private notes on the animals when you said the zoo's files had begun disappearing. You trusted me with snakes and tigers but not enough to tell me Beau is your son. Why?" Then anger burned. "And how could you leave him with that bitch?"

"Do you think I want him with her?" Tomás snapped, his dark eyes full of fury. "He is not mine *legally*. I have petitioned to adopt him, but the courts are slow. Especially to a single man who only just became a U.S. citizen last year."

Tomás scrubbed a hand down his face; weariness replaced the anger. "Beau is the son of my love, Claire. He is all that I have left of her. She died when he was three. I went to see her when she lay dying, and she told me that he was mine. Made me promise to raise him. But her parents hated me and him. They blamed us both for her death. Claire's heart was always weak. Childbirth made her sicker.

"When I tried to take him after she died, her parents refused to give him to me. I don't know why Claire hadn't listed me as the father on his birth certificate. Without it, I could not claim my son. When they gave Beau away, I could do nothing. I was not a citizen. I could not foster him. But I did follow him to Elkridge. I became the zoo manager to be near him. I got my GED and I became a U.S. citizen for him."

Realization dawned, and tension drained from her shoulders. "You changed your life to be with him."

"*Sí*, yes." He smiled. Hope glimmered in his eyes. "I find out next week if my petition has been accepted."

"Does Beau know you're his father? That you want to adopt him?" When Tomás nodded, Shelley echoed the head movement. "That's why he ran to you when Margaret attacked him?"

"Margaret," he spat on the floor, "that *punta* will pay for what she did to my boy." Tomás's eyes widened. "*Lo siento*. I am sorry for my language."

"No, I think you've got her description about right." Shelley waved away his apology, then it struck her. "You're the reason why he won't allow Social Services to remove him from her house. He's waiting for you."

It wasn't a question, but Tomás answered anyway. "*Sí*, yes. He knows I'm trying to adopt him."

"But can't you prove paternity by taking a test? You shouldn't have to adopt your own child."

He stared at her as if dumbstruck. His mouth moved, but no sound came out for several seconds. Finally he said, "I could take a test?"

Her heart broke for this man. The same man who'd all but fed her to the proverbial lions earlier today. "It's not a quick turnaround like you see in the movies. It usually takes six to eight weeks to get the results."

Tomás shook his head. "The petition is being decided next week. I wish I had known about this test months ago."

"I wish you would have told me. I could have helped you."

Tomás straightened his shoulders, steel in his spine. "I thought you knew. He talks about you all the time. Why did you never ask him about his parents?"

Guilt pinched at her. She had kept Beau at arm's length, hoping to avoid getting too close to someone who would likely leave her too. And in the end, he'd wormed his way into her heart. "I should have asked. You're right. I'm sorry. But you could have trusted me too."

Tomás nodded. "*Lo siento*. I am sorry too."

From across the hall, Beau called out, "Papi?"

They paused their conversation to check on Beau, who'd awakened frightened. One glance at them and the child settled down quickly. There were times Beau seemed so much older than ten and times like these, when he seemed years younger.

Something in Shelley's chest tightened as she watched the child drift back to sleep. No one should harm any child. And if she were his mother, no one ever would. But she wasn't his mother. And he already had a father, a good, honest man. One who was ready and eager to claim him.

Tomás nodded toward the hallway. Shelley followed him out on tiptoe. Back in the broom closet, he narrowed his eyes and glared. "I will not let him go back to her. She will not beat my child again."

"What can I do to help? I was going to call Child Protective Services."

He shook his head and checked his watch. "No. I'll make the call. Thank you, my friend."

She clasped his arm. "You're welcome, Tomás. He's lucky to have you."

Tomás gave her a smile that faded quickly. "You must go now. If they catch you here with me, I will be fired. I cannot lose this job."

"That's why you didn't defend me this morning, isn't it? You were afraid if you sided with me in front of Reyna, she'd get you fired?"

Again, Tomás nodded in apology. "I need to be near my son."

"I understand." And she did, but that didn't mean she had to like it. Another thought occurred to her, and Shelley's heart began to pound. "But the security tape. I'm on there coming into the visitor center with you tonight."

"*¡Ay Dios mío!* I almost forgot the tape." Tomás opened the door and ushered her out of it. "I will erase it. Go now, quickly."

She started to go, but first she said, "Tomás, I'm going to be out of town for a couple days. Will you call me and let me know how Beau's doing?"

He paused long enough to grin at her. "Of course, my friend. I will call tomorrow."

CHAPTER 8

THE SECURITY OFFICE door stood ajar. Voices floated into the darkened hallway.

For a moment, Adam stood frozen. He'd seen the vet leave ten minutes ago. Watched the groundskeeper lock up and head out the front door shortly after.

The voices stopped with alacrity. A strange whirring sound erupted, followed by the voices speaking again. It was a video playing. And Adam was on it.

His spine stiffened in alarm. The act made a decade-old injury ache anew.

Adam had snuck into the visitor center tonight to take another cage. He'd been careful to only nick one every few nights, so as not to raise suspicions. This would be the final cage needed before he could collect the remaining cubs.

But someone was here. Someone had a tape of him. It wouldn't have alarmed him. Being on the security tapes was almost expected, given his position. But it was the second voice on the tape he heard that made his chest too tight to breathe and his fists clench.

Colbert Rush was blubbering and pleading for help. For forgiveness.

"Shut up. You fucking asshole. You deserve everything I'm going to do to you." He cringed at the sound of his own voice followed by the tiger roaring. *Fuck! All the cameras had been disabled that night hadn't they?*

Adam's heart pounded in his chest. Did the sheriff know? Had anyone else seen the footage?

"*¡Ay Dios mío!*" someone cursed.

Fuck! It was Tomás in there.

For a moment, Adam stood helpless. Hopeless. Just as he had been twenty-two years before. Lost. Alone. Panic clawed at his chest, stealing his breath. It was all falling apart. Every plan, every adjustment was for nothing. Not-one-fucking-thing!

Never let the impossible stop you. There's always a way. His momma's voice flowed through him. Washing away the fear and angst. She was right. There was always a way.

Adam hadn't spent all this time planning his revenge to fail now. He would succeed. He just needed to improvise. But killing Tomás *wasn't* righteous. It wasn't supposed to happen. He wasn't on the list. That poor bastard hadn't done anything except stick his nose where it didn't belong. Justice or not, it had to be done for the greater good.

Quietly, his boots barely scraping the floor, Adam slipped into the room and locked the door. Tomás, unaware, rewound then replayed the footage again.

Adam cleared his throat.

Tomás spun around; fear rounded his eyes. His lips trembling in a nervous smile, he said, "Good evening. I did not know you were here." As he spoke, he reached behind him and shut off the monitor where Adam's profile had been clearly visible and frozen in the act of murder.

Adam nodded slowly. "What are you doing, Tomás? I thought you left with the vet."

"No." His right eye twitched uncontrollably. "You-you saw Dr. Shelley leave? She is not supposed to be here, you know. I-I forgot to erase her from the tapes. I came back for that. Just for that."

The groundskeeper hiked a thumb over his shoulder to the darkened screen, then blanched. He side-stepped twice heading for the door, but Adam blocked the exit.

"I'm sorry for this. No one was supposed to see that video," he said clamping both hands tightly around Tomas's neck. The groundskeeper pawed uselessly as Adam tightened his grip. "It's not your fault. It's that vet's. But don't worry. I'll make her pay."

THE CHILL OF the night air nipped at Shelley's ears as she hurried up Main Street. She'd forgotten to call the mechanic earlier, but one glance at her dead car in the glow of the parking lot's streetlight reminded her. After finding her flash drive, she pulled her cell out of her other pocket and called the local garage. Someone answered after the fifth ring.

"Ken's Hunting and Towing," Kenny answered.

Only in a small town. Shelley grinned. "Hi, Kenny, this is Dr. Morgan. My car died again. It's at the zoo parking lot. Can you tow it to the garage?"

Kenny Parran, a fifty-year-old retired Marine, laughed in gravelly tones. "I surely can hep ya, darlin', but I can't do it 'til Terry comes back. He's over on the other side of town helping his brother. Bunch a college kids from Norfolk decided to go mudding, not giving no thought to the rains last night. Got six SUVs stuck up to their axles in the Great Dismal Swamp. They're damned lucky they ended up in the shallow section. Some parts of the swamp could swallow a car whole."

Shelley shuddered at the thought. "How long do you think it might be?"

"Oh, darlin', I don't know. Hours probably." Kenny paused, then asked, "You need a lift home? I can swing round in the wife's wagon."

"No, that's okay. I'm almost home. Can you give me a call on my cell after you've had a chance to check it out tomorrow?"

"Sure thing, darlin'," Kenny said.

"Thanks, I'll wait for your call." Shelley clicked off and shoved her phone in her pocket.

Yikes, for such a warm day, the evening had gotten cold quickly.

She was almost to her door when she had the oddest sensation, like a cold finger tracing down her spine. She shivered and looked around. No one was there. Just a stray dog nosing around the front step of her apartment building. It caught her eye and growled. It was a Jack Russell terrier, and its short white fur stood on end. It bared its teeth at her. *Of course, this fantastic day just wouldn't be complete without a dog attack.*

She didn't have time for this. She was cold, hungry, and just wanted to go home. In her most soothing vet voice, she said, "It's okay, fella. I'm not going to hurt you. I'm just going to go into my apartment. Let me in without biting me, and I'll bring you a nice juicy hot dog. Wouldn't you like that?"

The dog growled louder and snapped its teeth twice.

Okay, so hot dogs were bad for dogs anyway.

She was about to offer another bribe and pray that this dog would be like Hercules and just let her be, when it yelped and leaped into the air as if shocked by something. Then it ran down the street. She watched the dog for a moment, amazed at her luck. *Well, that's new.* Not wanting to tempt fate, she fished her key out of her pocket and hurried inside.

Two hours later, after eating dinner and watching a *Bones* rerun, Shelley poured herself a glass of merlot and headed to the bedroom to pack.

Lucy was curled up in her hammock asleep. Shelley latched the cage door. Lucy had had enough playtime today. The last thing Shelley needed was for her ferret to go digging into her overnight bag.

Taking another hearty sip of wine, Shelley wondered aloud, "What does one wear when seeing an estranged sister for the first time in more than a decade?"

Lucy continued to sleep. No help there. Fine, Shelley could figure this out on her own. She'd just pack what was comfortable. Shelley was definitely a sneakers-and-no-makeup kind of woman on the weekends.

Another flaw Cam never failed to point out.

Why was she thinking of him so much today? Maybe because Dev was in town. In college, Cam had said he and Dev were like twins. And they were, in everything except skin color. Where Dev was a beautiful light mocha, Cam had been pasty white. Otherwise, they had the same classes, earned the same grades, and even dated the same girls.

Not me.

That's true. Cam had once told her that Dev had asked out every girl Cam had ever shown an interest in, but never Shelley.

Maybe not, but Dev had certainly appeared to have changed his tune this afternoon. And she fully intended to keep his attention on that particular song.

She packed her duffle and carried it to the front door. Leaving it there, she headed to her little kitchen and rewarded herself by pouring a second glass of wine, a truly decadent night for her. Someone knocked on her front door. She hurried through the apartment, stopping only to tug the bedroom door closed. If this was Dev returning—God, she wished—she didn't want Lucy interrupting.

"Coming," she called out.

Unlocking the door, she opened it, and then blinked in surprise. "What are you doing here?"

Something sharp pierced her arm through her sleeve. She had only seconds to recognize the pain before the world faded away.

CHAPTER 9

❧

SHELLEY AWOKE TO her cell singing about Mick Jagger and his moves. She reached for her alarm clock on the bedside table and read the time: 6:45.

Whoa! Who hit her in the head with a hammer? Her head didn't just ache, it spiked pain right into her eyes.

Man, not another migraine.

Worse, her mouth felt like she'd spent the night sucking on cotton balls. Shelley sat up slowly, pleased that the room didn't spin, just tilted a little. The headache didn't worsen but definitely didn't improve.

She needed caffeine and a shower. Sometimes they could knock out a migraine without her needing to take pain meds.

Lucy, who'd been curled up in her hammock, stretched and yawned then headed to the water bottle affixed to the inside of her open cage. *Didn't I lock that last night?*

She tried to think, but that only made her head ache more. She'd think later, when the migraine spikes eased a bit.

Those moves of Jagger belted from her cell again.

"Hello? Hello?" She glanced at the phone's darkened screen. Two missed calls.

Whose number is that?

She stared for a moment, her mind still muzzy. Searing pain burned behind her eyes, but her brain started to function again. That was Dev's number.

All at once, yesterday came rushing back, along with today's plans. Dev was on his way to pick her up. To. See. Jules.

Her headache was buried beneath a surge of adrenaline, and she bolted out of bed.

Shelley should call him back, but she hated to admit she'd overslept. Better to shower, dress, and be ready when Dev arrived. Otherwise, he might just show and find her soaking wet and wearing only a towel. Hmmm . . . the thought had merit, but not with her head threatening to cleave in two.

Instead, she hurried to the bathroom, stripped, and stepped under the spray. Only then did she notice her right bicep ached. She glanced at it; saw nothing but a million freckles. No time to waste. With the speed of an Olympic sprinter, she cleaned up and was running a brush through her damp hair when Dev knocked on her front door.

A flash of opening the door last night sprang to mind along with the image of David Boreanaz standing there.

That is the last time I drink that wine.

The knock sounded again, louder. The noise made her migraine grow, and the memory faded.

DEV TRIED NOT to worry when Shelley didn't answer the phone. She could have been in the shower. But when she didn't answer the door right away, he couldn't ignore the feeling. She had been wary of seeing Jules. Would Shelley really avoid him to keep from going to Tidewater? God, he hoped not, but he had to admit, he didn't really know her anymore. People change.

He knocked again. His eyes starting to water a bit at the thick scent of cleaner in the air.

"Hang on!" Shelley called, then the door swung open. She grinned up at him. The mingled aromas of vanilla and sugar wafted off her. A much better fragrance than the oranges. "I'm almost ready."

Her wet hair hung in loose curls around her shoulders, as if she'd just hopped out of the shower. Droplets of water

glistened on her pert, lightly freckled nose. But she already
had on her short brown leather coat. She ran down the hallway
to her bedroom, zipping up the jacket as she moved. "I need
to get Lucy into her carrier."

"Do you need my—" He started to offer his help, but then
remembered Lucy's sharp teeth. "On second thought, how
about I get your suitcase?"

Shelley laughed with him as if she knew why he let his first
offer trail off. "It's by the door."

The purple paisley bag bulged. It looked like she had tried
to cram everything she owned into it.

"Light packer?" he joked.

"Not really," Shelley admitted, striding out of her bedroom
with Lucy's cage. The ferret, up on her hind legs, wrapped her
front paws around the bars and stared at him balefully. Shelley
didn't seem to notice. "I need a cup of coffee. Want one? Oh,
shoot! I forgot to buy coffee yesterday."

Dev glanced to the left where the half wall hid the entrance
to her kitchen. From this angle he saw the whiteboard on the
refrigerator with the words *Buy coffee, TODAY.* He picked up
her suitcase, grinning. "Come on, we'll stop at the Starbucks.
My treat. If you're nice to me, I'll even toss in a muffin."

Shelley gave him a grateful smile, then sucked air between
her teeth and grabbed her head with one hand.

"Wow, you are a caffeine addict if you're already getting a
withdrawal headache," Dev said sympathetically. He could relate. While he wasn't addicted to caffeine—no, his vice was
peanut butter cups—his partner was. Seth could be a real
beast when he didn't get his morning three cups. "Come on,
I'll get you fixed up."

CHAPTER 10

B Y THE TIME they'd pulled out of the Starbucks, Shelley had caught Dev up on her events from the night before. No wonder she had large bluish circles under her eyes. Between rescuing Beau and writing her report, she'd barely slept.

"And, of course, I pick today to have a migraine. I haven't had one in months. It's my own fault for drinking that second glass of wine. Cheap wine does not agree with me." She pushed a small pill out of a blister pack and popped it into her mouth. She swallowed it with a gulp of coffee and sighed.

"Better?"

"Give me twenty minutes, and I'll be right as rain in springtime." She smiled, but her eyelids drooped. "Anyway, what was I saying?"

"You were talking about Tomás and Beau. Do you want me to call my friend at social services?" Dev knew Abigail Harris, his contact in the department, would love to help. And considering she'd once been Shelley's caseworker, she'd probably help on that principle alone. "She might be able to help Tomás get an emergency allowance to foster Beau."

Shelley yawned wide, covering her mouth with her hand. "Tomás said he'd contact CPS. He promised to call me today.

If he still hasn't done it or it sounds like Beau is going back with that awful woman, I'll take you up on it."

She yawned again, then fell silent. A mile passed, then two. Dev glanced at her. Shelley had dozed off. He'd ask about the thumb drive when she woke. Not like he could do anything with it right now.

Switching on the radio, Dev tuned to the classical music station. Strains of Bach drifted through the car.

With Lucy in the back seat, still safely ensconced in her carrier—thank you, very much—Dev relaxed and enjoyed the drive. The only thing about small towns he did like was the lack of city traffic.

Shelley slept for most of the hour-and-a-half drive from Elkridge to Tidewater. While she rested, Dev used the time to mentally review his murder case.

He'd called Seth just after dawn this morning, but so far no new information on the murder case. Dev hated not being able to examine the case details himself, but Seth had promised to go over everything with him this afternoon. Once Dev dropped off Shelley with Jules, that is. *Please let the reunion go smoothly.*

"You don't have to play this music for my benefit." Shelley rubbed her eyes, yawning.

She arched her back. Her lush breasts pressed against her blue silky top. God, she had an amazing body. He really should be watching the road, not her. And definitely not at the way she shifted sideways in her seat to look at him.

"I don't mind." And he didn't. He'd actually grown fond of Bach back in college. "You got me hooked on it when you tutored me. It's very relaxing," he said on a yawn.

"Well, we can't have you too relaxed." She shut off the radio.

Only the tires rushing over the road cut through the sudden silence. He would have liked to have filled the space with something other than the gentle shushing of rubber on the road, but had no idea what to say.

"How's your mother doing?" Her question surprised him. The two women had only met once.

"She's good." He took the exit off the interstate and frowned at the sudden traffic at the end of the very short ramp. *This could tack on another thirty minutes to the drive.*

"She's a nurse, right?" She sipped her now cold coffee and grimaced. "Wasn't she working toward a degree?"

"Good memory. Yeah, she's a nurse at Tidewater General," he said, sliding onto the highway between two tractor trailers. Once in the flow of traffic, he added, "She earned her master's last year and is a nurse-practitioner now. She's talking about leaving the hospital to run the community clinic my great-grandmother started. Hours aren't great, but it's a chance to help folks who really need it."

Shelley reached up and pulled the band out of her hair. She'd put it up into a messy knot just before they stopped for coffee. It fell down around her shoulders in curly waves. The scent of vanilla and sugar hit his senses and arrowed straight to his groin. He'd found that fragrance erotic only on her.

"HEY, DEV?" SHE paused as if unsure, running a hand across his dashboard. "What happened to your dad's car? Don't get me wrong; the Lexus is amazing. But in college you said you'd drive it forever. And since you worked on it yourself, I figure it should have outlasted my Blue Bomber."

"Your car is sitting in the parking lot at the zoo," Dev reminded her with a grin.

She glanced at her phone and held up the text for him to see. "Yep, it's still there. Kenny, the mechanic, left a message two hours ago that his sons were still out of town. He hopes to get to the car by tonight. And don't think I didn't miss that you changed the subject. Don't tell me if you don't want to. I'm just trying to find something to talk about to keep my mind off yesterday and . . . what's coming today."

Shelley shifted in her seat so she could look out the passenger window.

He was an ass. *Smooth. Way to put her at ease.* "No, it's fine. I'd still be driving my dad's old Charger except some drunk plowed into it the night I made detective."

She straightened in her seat. "Oh, my gosh! You were hit by a drunk driver?"

"Nah. The car was sitting empty in a restaurant parking lot while my family and I celebrated my promotion. Seems some repeat offender from the bar across the street piled into her car, shifted into reverse instead of drive, and slammed into the Charger. She was damned lucky she didn't kill herself or anyone else that night."

"Repeat offender?"

"Yeah, drunk driving. Her third strike." Dev shook his head to dispel the images of his entire extended family pouring into the parking lot to examine what was left of his father's prize possession. "Anyway, because of the damage, I needed a new car. I have a cousin who owns a Lexus dealership. She convinced me to buy this while I rebuild my dad's car."

"Whoa, I knew you had a huge family, but exactly how many cousins do you have?" She smiled and placed a gentle hand on his arm. The sensation of her touch burned him through his sleeve.

"Oh, uh, eleven on my mom's side, but that doesn't count their kids, who are my first cousins once removed. Or are they my second cousins?"

"Beats me. I never had any cousins." She withdrew her touch and straightened in her seat.

"Right, sorry." Dev could kick himself for not considering Shelley might be a bit uneasy talking about all of his family relations.

"What about your dad's side?" Shelley asked, surprising him. A quick glance at her inquisitive face and he relaxed.

"My dad was an only child. He might have cousins back in Haiti, but I have no way of knowing. His parents changed his name fifty years ago when they adopted him."

Her eyes sparked with interest. "I didn't know your father was adopted."

Now it was Dev's turn to tense. Why had he brought up his dad? He never talked about him to anyone except his family. It wasn't that he was ashamed of his father. Quite the opposite. After losing his father at fifteen, he'd never managed to get over the death.

Shelley shifted in her seat, facing forward, hands folded in her lap. "It's okay, you don't have to talk about it. I know not everyone is comfortable with adoption."

"No, it's fine. My dad's parents were missionaries. Story goes they helped at an orphanage where they found my dad when he was two years old. My grandparents were in their sixties when they adopted him. Pops died before I was born, but I remember when Memaw died. I was eleven. My dad pulled out the baseball Pops had given him for his eighteenth birthday. It was from the first home run my dad hit in Little League. Dad also showed me the baptism gown Memaw had crocheted for him. He told me he'd pass both to me when I turned eighteen." Dev's chest grew uncomfortably tight. "Damn, Shells, I haven't thought of that day in years."

"Painful memory?" Apology was written all over her beautiful face.

"No, a nice one. Thank you for that." Dev cast a quick smile that she mirrored.

The traffic thinned and they turned off the highway onto the main strip of Tidewater. Twenty minutes to his place or thirty to Jules and Seth's apartment. Maybe he should drive to Seth's apartment, but one glance at the time and he changed his mind. Seth and Jules should be leaving for work in a few minutes.

The plan was for Dev to reunite the women at the flower shop, but Jules wouldn't be there yet.

"Shells, we made much better time than I thought we would. We've got time to drop off your stuff at the cottage. Sound good? We'll grab a bite to eat and head over to see Jules after." He left off the part about running into the station for a few hours while she and Jules got reacquainted. Better to gauge the reunion as a good time for him to leave. Not that he had much time to spare. His captain's dentist appointment that morning was the only reason the morning meeting was delayed until eleven. Dev had to be at the station by then at the latest. "Sounds great," she said, a note of relief in her voice. "It'll give me a chance to freshen up before I see her. We can even go tonight or tomorrow, if it's easier. You know, work on the zoo case today."

"Now that the sheriff's office is involved, we may not have much to do." A quick glance at the narrowing of her eyes and he amended, "I'm willing to go over the files with you and see what I can find. Just know, now that the sheriff is involved, my help may not be wanted."

"I want it," she replied, quickly.

"And I'll give it. How about we talk over breakfast?" he

said, unsurprised by her quick acceptance of delay. "After, I'll take you to Jules. I know she is more than ready to see you again. Sound good?"

Shelley nodded silently.

Dev wanted to give her time to talk about her feelings and hoped she'd take the opening. She didn't. He drummed his fingers on the steering wheel, hoping for inspiration to help her open up when she asked, "So one of your many cousins convinced you to buy a Lexus. Where's your dad's car?"

"The Charger's in my garage." Okay, he'd let her change the subject. "Another cousin, Ryan, is helping me restore it."

He slowed to a stop at a light on Seventeenth Street. They were now in the heart of the business district. Several storefront owners, dressed in shorts and polo shirts, were on ladders hanging Christmas lights, taking advantage of the unseasonably warm weather. The blue sky reflected in the glass fronts gave an odd mural look to the shops that offered everything from puka-shell necklaces to boogie boards.

"You know, my dad's folks gave him that car the day he graduated high school? Even after he married my mom during their freshman year of college, he hung on to it. Mom likes to say that when I came along, Dad had to choose between the car and the groceries. He joined the army instead."

"So he got both." She gave a light laugh. "Smart man."

"Yeah." Dev nodded and slowed for another light. "Mom says she doesn't know who cried harder the day Dad announced he was going to help with Operation Enduring Freedom, her or my pa."

Damn, for a man who never talked about his dad, he couldn't seem to shut himself up.

"Sounds like your mom's parents really loved your dad too." Shelley's lips curled into a smile.

"Yeah, Gram and Pa did love him. When Dad got called back up to Iraq after September 11, he sat me down and told me I would be the man of the house while he was away. Made me promise . . ." He paused. "He made me promise lots of things, including that I'd earn my college degree. He said if anything happened to him, I had to promise to take care of my mom. He said she'd need me."

Dev ignored the sting of tears behind his eyes. In a weird way, he needed to finish telling her what he'd never told anyone, not even his beloved Pa. Shelley might be the only person who could understand.

"He died three months later when his helicopter crashed just outside of Baghdad. I was fourteen. I . . . I always wondered if he knew he wouldn't come back. I mean, my pa told me Dad made out a will, set up a bank account for me, even set up a fund for my mom. Not much in there to start with. He came from poor missionaries, and she was a McKinnon at birth. But it was hers alone, and something truly from him." He paused, then asked what he'd always wondered, "Do you think people sometimes just know they're not coming back?"

She didn't respond for two traffic lights. And coward that he was, he couldn't bring himself to look at her.

Finally, she exhaled a long, slow breath. "I think . . . I think sometimes people do. Animals do. Wait, that didn't come out right." She waved her hand in the air. "I don't know from people, but I know humans are more animal than mineral, so hear me out. At the clinic, there was this cat, Walter. His owner kept bringing him in because he was sick. Walter would bolt every time anyone opened his cage. He'd always head for the same spot, underneath his owner's porch steps. Finally, she stopped bringing him in. She told me later that that was where she had found him after he passed. Underneath those porch steps. He looked like he'd just gone to sleep."

Dev did glance at her then. Because what did a cat have to do with anything?

As if she'd read his mind, she said, "I think some of us, human, canine, feline or other, know when our time is coming. My first mother did, but she fought it every step of the way. My second mom and dad had no idea. Just one wrong skid on the ice, and they were gone. No chance to wonder or worry."

A car horn blared. Dev glanced up to see the light switch from yellow to red. He'd been so caught up in Shelley's words that he'd sat right through a green light.

Shelley used the opportunity to make a joke. "So tell me, Officer, would you issue a ticket for something like this?"

The light turned green again and Dev joked, "My jurisdiction, but not my department."

SHELLEY WAS GAWKING. There was simply no other way to describe her behavior. Her jaw was slack and her eyes were so wide they watered. Still, she couldn't help herself.

She sat in the car staring up at the palatial house Dev had dubbed *the cottage*. The house had to be four thousand square feet. It sat right on the beach in the highly prized section of Tidewater named Ocean Front.

The house's white siding seemed to glow against the cerulean sky behind it. The grass was vivid green and perfectly trimmed. Not even a dandelion dared to impugn the front lawn. Purple, red, pink, white, and yellow pansies lined the cement walkway like hundreds of little guardians with their faces pointed to the sky. The neat rows of flowers led all the way to the sedate gray front door. It stood solid, flanked by matching arched picture windows. There were no curtains on them, yet she couldn't see inside.

"This is a cottage?" Shelley asked when Dev opened her car door.

Dev rubbed a thumb along the corner of his lip, then shrugged. "It's the name the house came with when I bought it from old man Mansbach last year."

He'd started to open the door to the back seat but paused. "I did say I had a cottage. I assumed you'd use one of my guest rooms. If you'd rather stay at a hotel, I can rent you a room at the Cavalier—"

"No, I don't mind staying with you," she cut him off, then flushed at her own words. "I-I mean, the guest room would be great. But you said rooms, how many guest rooms do you have?"

"Three." He rubbed the back of his neck. "My cousins Ryan and Ian stayed here for a while to save money when they first opened their business. But now they've got a place across town. Be grateful, Ian's a slob."

Dev grinned, reaching to grab her suitcase from the floor, at which point Lucy's cage shook. He hopped back as if the cage might launch at him, or she might chew through the bars or do something equally terrifying, like bursting into song with a top hat and cane like the frog from the old cartoons.

"Sorry, let me get Lucy." Shelley sidled past him and caught a whiff of his Irish Spring soap scent. Her skin tingled at the near contact. She tried to cover her hormonal reaction by saying, "She's really very loving."

"Loving? Her?" His eyebrows rose and he glanced nervously into the back seat. "Tell you what, Shells, I'll carry your suitcase inside. You carry the man-eater."

"She's not a man-eater." Shelley laughed, collecting Lucy's cage.

"My crotchless jeans beg to differ. She tried to bite off a part of my anatomy I'm rather fond of."

She couldn't help it. She knew she shouldn't have done it, but . . .

Shelley's gaze zeroed in on Dev's groin, which definitely wasn't crotchless. Dang it.

"You know if I did that to your breasts, you'd slap me."

Don't be so sure.

Clutching Lucy's cage tighter to her body, Shelley hoped her flaming cheeks were sexy rather than silly and said in her best femme fatale voice, "It's not like you can see anything through this cage, anyway. So look at the girls all you want."

Dev's eyes widened and sure enough, his gaze dropped below her chin then zipped back up again. His cheeks darkened.

Score one for me.

Emboldened, Shelley headed to the front door, calling out, "Come on, Dev. I want the grand tour."

DEV'S HEART AND cock were going to explode before the day ended. Sweet Shelley Morgan was openly flirting with him. And, oh holy God, he hoped she was serious. Because it was too cruel to consider the alternative.

He unlocked the door and led her inside. She sucked in a breath and swept her gaze through his house. The slate foyer opened to a long hallway that ended in sliding glass doors overlooking the Atlantic. He hadn't changed it much since he bought the place. The house was still decorated in East Coast shoreline decor with chair-rail-high beadboard walls painted

Nantucket white butting up to the blue walls. He couldn't even claim the Stickley furnishings. They'd been left by the former owner.

The one thing Dev had changed was the kitchen. All the appliances were high-end, matching brushed steel. The linoleum countertops had been replaced with dark blue granite. The cottage fit him. It was a man's house. While there was no leather furniture, everything was sturdy but classy. Definitely not filled with the lacy curtains and shabby-chic stuff his mother used in her home.

"Oh my," Shelley said, taking two tentative steps down the hall. She stopped next to the cherrywood staircase leading up to the second floor. Her eyes sparkled. The morning sunlight filtering down the hallway caught the red in her hair, giving her an ethereal glow. Like a goddess come to earth. "This place is absolutely incredible."

No, she was the incredible one. It was a house. But he couldn't quite stifle the pride filling his chest at her approval. "Come on, I'll show you around upstairs. Wait till you see the view from your room." The next to his with the adjoining balcony.

Shelley's eyes lit up and she nodded. "Lead the way."

At the top of the stairs was another picture window. Shelley *ooh*ed when she glanced through it. "I see a pod of porpoises swimming offshore."

The sunlight glinting on the water was occasionally dulled by small, blunt dorsal fins cutting through the surface. Then the heads of the porpoises would pop up for air before diving down again, continuing their morning swim. "Yeah, I usually see them playing early in the morning when I go for my run on the beach. This place is so private, we can see them all year long, even during high tourist season."

Shelley hefted Lucy's cage higher, either to show the animal the view or because the plastic traveler was getting too heavy to hold. Figuring it was the latter, Dev opened the door to his right and set her suitcase just inside.

"This is your room. Why don't you bring Lucy in here?" Dev frowned into the darkened room. "Sorry, the maid closed the curtains for some reason." Dev hurried to draw back the heavy black-out curtains.

"You have a maid?" Shelley asked, then gasped as sunlight poured into the room, highlighting the peach-painted and white beadboard walls. Her mouth gaping, she glanced around. The guest room was laid out similar to his, all Mission-style furniture like downstairs. A queen-size bed faced the wall opposite the door; a dresser and mirror were placed on the opposite wall from the window. And there was a door leading to a walk-in closet between the bed and that wall. But this room had his mother's feminine touch. She'd told him when she came to visit, she wanted a room that didn't feel like an antique version of a bachelor pad. Dried roses, lattice, and baby's breath filled a carnival-glass vase on the dresser. The duvet on the bed had been tatted by his great-great-grandmother.

Shelly ran a hand lightly over the bedspread. "Whoa, this is amazing."

Choosing to avoid the maid topic as long as possible, Dev slipped Lucy's cage from Shelley's hands and set it on the ground. "Your bathroom can be accessed through your walk-in closet. Step inside and there's a door to your right. The previous owners added it decades ago. The bath is shared with Ryan's room on the other side. But, like I said, he doesn't stay here often."

"Is it okay if I let Lucy out? She's not used to being pent up for this long."

"So long as she keeps her teeth off my body, sure."

Shelley, her eyebrows lifted, slipped past him to squat before Lucy's cage. The scent of vanilla and sugar lingered, making his heart race. She whispered to her pet, but Dev heard her anyway. "Don't chew anything, please. Or I'll have to keep you in here until we go home." Shelley straightened, then wrapped Lucy around the back of her neck like a live fur stole. "How often does the maid come? I don't want to freak her out with Lucy."

"The maid won't be here again till next week. So don't worry."

Shelley grinned, a glint of mischief in her eyes. "Too busy solving cases, or still as lazy as you were in college?"

"Ha. Very ha." Dev tried not to smile, but one glimpse of the twinkle in her eyes, and he couldn't help himself. "This is why I didn't want to mention the maid. I knew you'd start in on me. I hired her when Ian still lived here. Back then, she was here every week. Now she comes once a month. Some weeks on the force, I work seven days straight. The last thing I have the energy to do when I get home is wash windows."

There, he managed not to sound like some hapless bachelor incapable of cleaning his own house.

"Oh, so you're still lazy." She laughed at the scowl on his face, then raised her hands in mock surrender. "Just kidding. If I lived in a place this big, I'd definitely hire a maid. And she'd come way more often than once a month. Although, if I had a house like this one with a view like yours, I might never leave it. So I probably wouldn't need a maid. I'd find excuses to spend all day here. I can't get over the view."

He watched, silent, unsure what to say. The thought of her living here didn't set off internal panic bells that normally sounded when a woman eyed his home. He rather liked the idea.

Too soon. Don't rush.

Shelley pulled her laptop out of her suitcase, set it on the dresser, and fired it up.

"I know you said with the sheriff involved you can't do much, but I feel much better knowing you're looking into the mystery personally." When he didn't answer her, she laughed and patted him on the arm. "Come on, Monk. I was only kidding about the maid. I thought we were on a schedule. I've got a lot to show you, so let's get started."

Dev didn't know why he grinned. "Did you just call me Monk?"

"Yeah. I haven't thought of your nickname in years." She laughed. "Don't people call you that anymore?"

"God, no." If Seth heard her call him Monk, it would be hours, possibly even minutes, before every cop in the station jumped on the Monk wagon. He had a hard enough time with everyone at the station calling him *kid.*

Dev really needed a cup of coffee before he started on these files. "Hey, Shells? I'm hungry. Why don't we move this downstairs to the kitchen. Bedrooms are meant for more intimate entertainment." He'd spouted his cousin Ian's favorite phrase, then felt his cheeks go hot.

Her reaction was instantaneous. She glanced at the bed and

blushed. Right, he was in the bedroom with her. Mentioning intimate entertainment that, okay, yes . . . he'd *really* like to have with her. The room went stifling.

"Oh. No, no. When I said intimate entertainment, I didn't mean to imply that you and I should . . . God! Let's just go to the kitchen."

Shelley, who'd been smiling, albeit nervously, began to frown. Her cheeks reddened, and she whistled. "Wow, when I get my signals wrong, I really get them wrong. Why don't you go downstairs? I need a minute to, you know, salvage my pride."

She handed him her laptop. It buzzed softly in his hands.

The very hands that itched to toss it to the floor and bury themselves in Shelley's hair as he kissed her like he had last night. He'd have done it too, except at that moment Lucy lifted her head and bared her teeth in silent warning.

So he took the laptop and headed toward the door. Just before pulling it closed, he glanced back. Shelley rubbed her cheeks with her hands as if trying to scrub away the splotches of red there. She looked so damned adorable. And vulnerable. Before he could think better of it, he said, "When I said I didn't mean to imply that we should, it didn't mean I don't want you. I do. Willing and eager. So you didn't entirely misinterpret the signals."

And shut the door behind him.

THE DOOR CLOSED with a snick and Shelley blinked. Her heart raced like a cat overdosing on catnip.

You didn't entirely misinterpret the signals. She shivered, recalling his words.

Lucy, who'd been on her shoulder, shifted. Her tiny claws dug through Shelley's long-sleeve blouse. Unlooping the ferret from around her neck, Shelley said, "You, my friend, need to stay up here. I'll give you food and water. But I need a little time to think."

Settling Lucy back into her crate, Shelley filled the food dish and refilled the water bottle. All the while, thinking. Dev had come to Elkridge to help her out. And to tell her about Jules. In a day or two, Shelley would be back in Elkridge and Dev wouldn't. Every bit of help he'd give her on the case would happen here. And if she wanted to explore their apparent mutual attraction, it would happen here too.

Shelley caught her reflection in the mirror. The headache was mostly gone, but there were still the telltale smudges beneath her eyes. She couldn't do anything about those, but she could fix her hair. She fluffed her curls with her fingers, and put any thoughts of Dev's signals out of her mind.

She had a mystery to solve and tigers to find. She ignored the niggling doubt that was whispering she might never be able to locate the missing ones. She had to find them. She had to. She needed Dev to help her piece together the seemingly incongruent clues of what was happening to the missing animals.

The rest she'd worry about later.

Shelley grabbed the thumb drive out of her overnight bag, squared her shoulders, and opened the door. She found Dev on the first floor deck, speaking quietly into a cell phone. Not wanting to disturb him, she headed to the kitchen. He'd left her computer on the counter that doubled as a bar. She plugged the flash drive into the laptop and searched for the zoo files. And blinked in confusion.

The thumb drive was empty. She ejected it and plugged it in again. No change.

Her stomach squeezed north into her throat, clogging her airway. She searched the hard drive for the notes she'd written last night. But no matter where she looked, the answer remained the same.

No results.

Every last file was gone.

CHAPTER 11

*H*OW CAN EVERYTHING *be gone?* Shelley's headache, which had settled to a dull throb, roared to full-on agony. Her blood pressure shot up and, frack it all, tears stung her eyes.

She glanced across the open living room to see Dev still speaking into his cell on the porch. He paced back and forth, grim-faced, seemingly unaware of Shelley watching him.

Panic rose in her throat. She wanted to call out to him but held back. Her vision blurred as thoughts of the last six months of work, the animals that had disappeared, and Miah's mournful roar clamored in her mind.

If she didn't find those files, she'd be letting down all the creatures that had come to rely on her. And Miah. That poor tigress was lost without her babies. Shelley couldn't break her promise to the Bengal.

There had to be something on her computer. Files didn't just vanish. Not without crashing. And everything had been there last night when she'd hit save and shut down.

The sliding glass door shushed open. Crashing waves, the cry of seagulls, and the comforting scent of salt air filtered down the hall before the door slid closed again.

Dev made his way slowly through the living room. The

phone still pressed to his ear. He spared her a quick glance, then did a double take.

Shelley quickly schooled her features. She needed to be strong. Smart. She needed to find a solution, not weep like a child. Forcing her lips to turn up at the corners, she gave him what she hoped was a reassuring smile.

Dev cocked his head sideways and slowly arched a single blond brow.

Rising from her barstool, Shelley gave him her full attention and blocked her laptop at the same time. It was foolish. He was going to find out in a few minutes anyway. But he looked so intense on the phone, the last thing she wanted to do was distract him. She wanted his undivided attention, so she'd wait to tell him about the missing files. She ratcheted her smile up another two notches.

That did the trick. Dev's brow lowered and he gave her his back, saying into the phone, "I hear you, partner. We'll discuss it at the station. I thought the meeting was at eleven. No, I can't break away yet."

He paused, long enough for Shelley to wonder what he intended to break away from. Was he planning to leave her sitting here while he went to work? What about her case? Well, now that the files were gone, there wasn't much to go on. But Dev didn't know that, yet.

"Got it," Dev added, turning to shrug apologetically in her direction. "I'll be there in two hours, provided I can get off the phone." Another pause, this one ended with Dev exhaling a burst of laughter. "Not a problem."

Dev clicked off the phone and pocketed it. "Sorry about that."

"Is everything okay? Do you need to be someplace?"

Dev snapped the fingers on both hands, then clapped his hand over his fist several times in a row. "Yes, everything is fine. What I need is some breakfast. I checked the fridge while you were upstairs. I forgot I hadn't gone to the grocery store this week, so it's pretty bare. How about we grab a bite to eat and discuss the case downtown? There's a great place down on Twenty-third Street open for breakfast called Doc Taylor's."

Shelley automatically checked her watch. The pink breast-cancer-awareness ribbon pointed at quarter to ten. The simple act of glancing down sent the pain in her head thundering past her ears.

Two hands gripped her elbows and she found herself nose to neck with Dev. His fresh clean scent both fired her hormones and seemed to ebb the tide of pain lacerating her skull from the inside out.

"Whoa, Shells. You're not going to faint on me, are you?" His gray eyes, filled with worry, traced the contours of her face as if searching for something. As if caressing her skin with his gaze.

"N-no." Shelley swallowed, her throat inexplicably dry. Slowly, she shook her head. "No, I'm better now."

With him holding her this close, it would be so easy to press her nose against his soft cotton shirt and breathe him in and see where this attraction might take them. If, that is, her files weren't missing. If the animals didn't need her. If her life weren't in absolute turmoil.

She stepped away and bumped into the barstool.

Catching it before it crashed sideways to the floor, Dev righted it, then frowned at the *No Records Found* blinking on Shelley's laptop.

"I'm sorry. I woke with a massive migraine. Normally, one dose of my migraine meds knocks it out. I thought my nap in the car was a sign it was going away, but that didn't fix it. I should have put something more in my stomach than coffee. I guess my blood sugar's low, and the headache's coming back."

"I've got some ibuprofen, if that'll help. But we do need to go out for food. Or I can go out and you can lie down until I return."

"Thank you, but I'm sure I'll feel better once I've had a meal." She rolled her shoulders and admitted, "I could really go for a burger."

"Let's go to Doc Taylor's then. They serve the best in Tidewater."

"Except I'm vegetarian. I don't know why I'm craving it. Maybe I need the protein?"

Dev frowned. "When did you go vegetarian? In college, weren't you the one who argued with the professor that animals eating one another was part of the cycle of life? That if tigers and lions were given a choice between grass or gazelles, they'd pick fresh meat."

She snorted, which only made her head ache more. "I can't believe you remember that. You really have an incredible mind, Monk. I became a vegetarian about two years ago after Cam went on a mission to help families in Puerto Rico affected by a hurricane. The stories he told me about what some of the poorest islanders ate after the disaster convinced us both to drop all meat from our diets.

"It's been a long time since I've had actual beef. I've been living off tofu or garbanzo beans for so long, I'm not sure my body would react well at first. It's safer to stay meatless this morning."

"You know, Shells," Dev said, scratching his cheek with one finger. "We seriously need to talk about what went down with you and Cam."

Oh, frack no!

The panic must have shown on her face because Dev quickly added, "Later. This morning we'll get food. Bring your laptop."

She glanced over her shoulder to see the vile words still blinking on her screen. "That might be pointless. I'm not sure what happened, but every file on my computer is gone."

Dev bristled. Shelley would have stepped back, but had nowhere to go. Literally, the man seemed to both widen at the shoulders and grow taller. But it was the way his steely gaze bore into hers, then around her body to frown at the useless computer that was disconcerting.

"*Every* file is gone? Are you certain?" Dev's frown melted away and was replaced by an inscrutable expression that probably served him well on the force. When he interviewed criminals. "How long have you known the files were gone? Did you accidentally wipe them?"

"Yes, Dev. That's exactly what I did." She let the sarcasm drip from her voice. Crossing her arms over her chest, she reined in her temper and explained, "I just discovered they were missing when I came downstairs. I looked at the files last night. I walked to my car and got the thumb drive and added yesterday's notes before I ate dinner. There should be two sets of notes from yesterday. The notes I wrote when I didn't have the thumb drive, I saved to my hard drive, but they're gone too. I don't know how I could have erased them."

"Do you have them saved anywhere else? In a cloud?"

Shelley shook her head then remembered. "Wait. Tomás has a copy of the files too. I e-mail them to him for safekeeping after I update each file. I've been doing it for months, ever since he told me that the zoo files disappeared along with the animals. Frack! I can't remember if I e-mailed last night's notes to him. But he'll have something. There's enough in there to help you get started."

"So he keeps your notes on the zoo's computer network?"

She shrugged. "I don't think so. They're probably on his home unit."

Without waiting for Dev to respond, Shelley dug her cell out of her pocket and dialed Tomás. After the fourth ring, it went to voice mail. Frustrated, but not completely surprised— it was feeding time at the zoo after all—she left a message. "Hey, Tomás, it's Dr. Morgan. Do you still have the files I e-mailed you last week? I really need to see yours. I lost my copies. I'll explain when you call. Thanks, I'll talk to you soon. Please let Beau know I'm thinking of him."

She clicked off and stuffed her phone back in her jeans pocket only to dig it out again and set the ringer to loud. Glancing at Dev as she pocketed it again, she explained, "I usually have the ringer turned off. I hate to be interrupted when I'm working."

Dev smiled, his gray eyes sparkling. "I know the feeling."

"I'll bet you do." She couldn't help returning his smile. There was something peaceful and yet undeniably exciting about being around him again. It made her want to believe in all those things she had believed in as a child. Before her first mother died. But she wasn't a child anymore. And if she didn't find those files, those animals could be lost forever.

Her smile faded.

His expression also sobered. "Look, let's get some breakfast. Forgive me for saying so, but you look worn out."

"Thanks so much."

He backpedaled. "That came out wrong. You look like you feel much better than when I picked you up this morning, but you still look rundown."

Shelley closed her laptop and thought about it. "I am still pretty wiped. I guess yesterday took its toll on me. You know, I don't actually remember going to sleep last night?"

"Is that unusual?" Dev's tone was light, but his gaze had sharpened.

"Yeah, very. I remember taking Lucy for a walk, calling Kenny about the car, working on my notes for the zoo, but not going to bed. Heck, I don't even remember putting my laptop away. Guess yesterday was a bigger strain than I'd realized. Then again, I can do all sorts of things when I have a migraine and not remember. It comes from pushing too hard. But when there's only me to do the job, I have to work, headache or not. So, I guess it isn't all *that* strange. I did have the start of this migraine yesterday. Plus, I had some wine on top of it."

"Hmmm . . ." he said vaguely. An odd expression crossed his face. He slipped her pink laptop covered in Save Ferrets stickers from her hands and headed down the hall toward the front door. His loafers hardly made a sound on the slate floor. "Got your purse?"

"I don't carry one as a rule. Just my keys, wallet, and cell. They all fit in my pockets." Shelley narrowed her eyes at him, teasingly. "So Mr. Monk doesn't notice all? You're losing your touch, Dev. Back in college, you'd never have had to ask me that question after spending more than fifteen minutes with me."

He froze midstep and gaped at her. There was no other way to describe it. His jaw went slack and his sexy gray eyes, normally set at half-mast bedroom-style, were wide.

"What?" She tried to move past him, but he kept her still, placing one hand on her shoulder.

"You didn't call me Monk. You said Mr. Monk? As in that old television show with the crazy private detective who got kicked off the police force?" His voice cracked as the words kicked off.

"Y-yes." Shelley scratched the back of her neck. "I started calling you that, ever since you helped Professor Gose solve the mystery of his disappearing laser pointer from our Economics class. The way you walked into the room, glanced around, picked up and touched almost every object on his desk, then turned and told him, 'I know what happened' reminded me of the character Adrian."

Dev's wide-eyed stare faded. He started to chuckle. The chuckle transformed into a laugh. A laugh that shook him so hard, he leaned his head on his arm against the doorjamb.

Afraid he might drop her computer, Shelley tried to reclaim it, but Dev straightened, still chuckling and shaking his head. "Oh, damn. That's the best laugh I've had in a while. For years, whenever I heard you call me Monk, I thought you were referring to . . . But you really meant the TV show . . ." His words trailed off as he laughed again.

He thought *what*? "Want to send up a clue or a signal or a semaphore flag or something?"

Dev shook his head, still chuckling. "Nah, I'll tell you later. Let's go eat."

He opened the door and waited for her to exit through it. As she moved past him she could have sworn he muttered, "Thank you, sweet baby Jesus."

DOC TAYLOR'S WAS just Dev's style. A quiet little restaurant on a side street that had the best food in the city. A fresh-faced waitress in a white shirt and black pants approached.

"What's good?" Shelley asked Dev, setting aside her menu and spreading a linen napkin in her lap. Her laptop and cell phone sat closed on the table.

"My favorite is Eggs Benedict a la Graz. They make the best Hollandaise sauce here that you'll ever taste."

"Sounds delicious." She beamed at him, then turned to the server. "I'll have that, but no meat, please. And a glass of sweet tea."

"Make that two."

When they were alone, Shelley said, "I'm so thirsty this morning. You'd think I have a hangover between the headache and the thirst."

"Do you?" He couldn't resist asking. The Shelley Morgan he'd known in college wouldn't have touched alcohol. But this new Shelley, the one who chased windmills in the shape of lizards and tiger cubs, was a mystery to him.

"Sometimes. I probably drink once every six months or so. I'm not a teetotaler or anything, I just don't like to be out of control. I think I've had four glasses of alcohol in the past year. Two glasses of champagne my best friends bought me the night I announced Cam and I were finished, and the wine last night."

Interesting.

"Your friends bought you champagne?"

Shelley's ivory cheeks went scarlet. It only made her more beautiful.

"Yes, well. My maids of honor, Kim and Donna, hated Cam. They said for all his posturing, he was nothing but a self-centered little boy. So when er . . . *we* broke off the engagement, they took me out to celebrate. And I woke up with a fracking hangover that made me swear off champagne forever."

Who left who? He wanted to ask, was about to when Shelley tapped her fingers on the table, then her eyes went wide.

"Jacob has a copy of the files on my flash drive. He needed to borrow one for a paper he was writing when his died. I lent him my spare. There were files on there."

She snatched up the phone again and punched in a number. A few heartbeats later, she started to speak, her voice rife with excitement. "Hi, Jacob, it's Shelley, um . . . Dr. Morgan. Do you remember that thumb drive I let you borrow on Monday? Do you still have it? Terrific. Is it with you at the clinic?"

As she listened to whatever Jacob was saying, her sapphire eyes lost their luster. Her grin faded until it was as forced as the cheeriness in her voice when she added, "No, no I understand. You don't have to keep apologizing. These sorts of things happen. But you wouldn't, by any chance, have saved it to your computer? No, no, of course not." She paused, then added, "I'll figure something else out. It's okay. No, I'm not home right now. Thank you, but no, I haven't changed my mind about your offer."

The waitress returned with their drinks and their breakfast. The aroma of eggs, Canadian bacon, and Hollandaise hit Dev's senses, making his stomach rumble. Loudly.

Shelley shot him a surprised look that quickly morphed into a grin. While the excitement was gone from her face, her usual positive attitude had returned. She ended the call, saying, "Jacob, I've really got to go. It's no problem at all. I'll see you on Monday."

She set the phone down on her closed laptop and sighed. "So Jacob had a little accident with my flash drive. Seems he was really tired after printing off his paper and somehow dropped the drive into his thermos of coffee."

"Into the thermos? How on earth did he accomplish that?"

"It's Jacob. If there's a way to make it happen, good, bad,

or utterly weird, he can do it. Seems he hadn't returned the drive because he was hoping once it dried, it could still work. He's got it in a jar of rice trying to dry it out."

He'd heard of putting cell phones dropped in water into containers of rice to dry out the circuits. Perhaps it could work for a flash drive drenched in hot coffee.

Shelley picked up her fork and knife and started to eat. Dev followed suit. They ate in companionable silence for several minutes.

After finishing his breakfast, he said, "So, you told me about the missing snakes, the tiger cubs, and the bilateral gigando—"

"Bilateral gynandromorph eastern bluebird," she corrected then popped a forkful of egg into her mouth.

"Right. Have any other animals gone missing?"

Shelley glanced at him, chewing her breakfast thoughtfully. Swallowing the food, she said, "Not exactly missing. At least, not officially. There was a green iguana that poofed one day."

"The same one you and Reyna argued about?"

Shelley jutted out her chin. "Yes. The story is that The Machine, that was his name, died one night when I was helping the sheriff's cat during a difficult labor and delivery. By the time I got to the zoo the next day, they'd already destroyed the iguana."

Dev didn't miss the tone in her voice. "You don't believe that?"

"No. I don't. There was something off there." She rolled her eyes. "Frack! I wish I had my files."

"Look, Shells, I know this is frustrating, but the sheriff's office is on the case now. You called me in when there was no one else, but give your local police a chance to do their jobs. It's really all you can do for now."

She sighed then gave her head a short shake. "No, I'll work on my notes. I'll try to rewrite everything from memory. You said you'd help me; I need to solve this. I promised Miah."

And there it was. The real reason Shelley wouldn't relinquish control to the police. She'd made a promise. To a tiger, yes, but still a promise. Dev had made one as well, to Shelley.

"All right, work on your notes. I've got to go into the station for a few hours while you and Jules get reacquainted. Later, we'll go over everything you can remember."

The waitress returned to refill his coffee and her tea and to clear their empty plates. She asked, "How'd y'all enjoy your breakfast?"

"The food was fabulous, thank you." Shelley grinned.

"I'll be back with your bill." The waitress left to greet new customers.

"I can see why you like it here, Dev. The food is amazing. "

"Yeah, I have to double my run times after eating here. But it's worth it. Great food and an extra-long run on the beach."

"I don't think I could do it. Great view or not, I hate running. Murder on the knees."

He laughed. "I hear that, but I love the ocean. So many people live in Tidewater but only see the water on Memorial Day or Labor Day. You know?"

"Yeah. The view from your house was breathtaking," Shelley agreed. But something in her demeanor changed. Dev couldn't put his finger on it. Her smile didn't fade. She didn't slouch. She didn't even blink. But *some*thing had changed from the moment he'd mentioned her sister.

"Shells?"

"Want a to-go cup of coffee this morning, Detective Jones?" the waitress, who seemed to pop up from nowhere, asked.

"No, thank you, Angela." Dev pulled out his American Express Blue Card and handed it to her. With a smile and promise to return, she disappeared almost as quickly as she had appeared.

"You ready to go?" Dev asked, then immediately regretted it. This time, the change was clear. Shelley straightened to ramrod stiff in her seat and began twisting her linen napkin on the table.

"Dev, are you sure Jules wants to see me? I mean, bad timing and missing files aside—both of which I need to talk to you about—are you certain this is what she wants? It's been over thirteen years."

"I'm not sure what you mean by bad timing, Shells," Dev said, reaching across the table and covering her hands with his. She stopped torturing the fabric. But it didn't ease the worry in her eyes, so he went on, "And we have been talking about the case. So you can't show me the files. We'll work around that.

Make your notes like you'd planned. I promise you, this evening I will sit down with you. You can tell me everything you remember. You're smart, Shells. You always have been. Now that the sheriff's involved, I don't think you need me, but I'm happy to help you. Before I can do that, you need to meet with Jules. "

Shelley pulled her hand back.

He instantly missed the connection that seemed to transcend flesh and jolt straight to his soul. *Where the hell did that thought come from?*

"Dev, I never told you what happened at the end. I know you think you know me, but I'm a very different person than I was in foster care."

"Of course you are. You were just a child the last time you saw your sister."

Shelley glanced nervously around the dining room, then pressed her lips together until they formed a thin line.

If the sisters were going to reunite, it had to be in the best setting possible. Which started with easing Shelley's anxiety. Dev glanced at his watch. Half past ten. Seth would be pissed if Dev didn't make it into the station before eleven. Then again Seth would be furious if Shelley didn't go to see Jules.

Let this be the right decision.

Dev rose to his feet and extended his hand. "Come on, Shells. Let's go for a walk on the beach."

She accepted his hand. A sizzle of awareness raced up his arm, and he had to work to keep from pulling her closer to him to see if that sizzle would travel all the way to their lips.

"Maybe this is a bad idea. It's chilly. I was so distracted at your place by the missing files, I forgot my jacket. I swear, every day has been a Wednesday."

"Still think those are cursed?" He grinned at her nod. "I've got something you can wear."

Stopping by the Lexus on the way to the boardwalk, they dropped off her computer and grabbed one of his old sweatshirts from the trunk.

"Thank you," she said, pulling on the royal blue sweatshirt emblazoned with white lettering that read Tidewater Police Department,Virginia's Finest.

Shelley rolled up the sleeves three times, then held her arms wide. "What do you think? Is it me?"

Oh yeah.

She looked so damned adorable in his clothes. Seeing her like that filled him with an illogical pride. Like she'd claimed him or something. Ridiculous. She was just wearing his sweat-shirt because it was windy.

Still, the idea of her claiming him as hers warmed him in a way that he didn't want to examine too closely.

"Come on." They crossed Atlantic and headed straight for the boardwalk, where they removed their shoes and socks. Together, they stepped onto the cool sand.

Sandpipers chased waves, searching for meals. Seagulls squawked and soared overhead. The water lapped and shushed as waves rolled in and out. Shelley seemed not to notice. In-stead, she waited for him to pick a direction, worry wrinkling her brow.

"Let's go this way." He pointed south, in the direction of April's Flowers, the shop where Jules worked as the manager.

Shelley fell into step beside him, occasionally bending over to examine a seashell, only to leave it behind.

"So what happened between you two?" Dev asked, hoping Shelley was ready to talk about her childhood.

"With Cam or Jules?"

Both? "I was talking about Jules."

"Oh." She examined another shell, picked it up, tossed it into the ocean. "You know part of it. My mom had breast cancer when I was young. She was diagnosed after my baby sister, Han-nah, turned two. Around that time, our father took off. Anyway, Momma fought for several years before the cancer got her.

"I remember when I started first grade, I was determined to get the best grades. Momma told me that she needed me to always do my best. That it wasn't enough to go halfway. So in my seven-year-old brain, I thought if I was the best little girl I could be, then my mother would get better. She didn't."

Shelley slowed to a stroll, the shoes in her right hand seem-ingly forgotten as she picked up another shell and threw it into the water.

"I don't know why I'm telling you this. It's not like you haven't heard it before." Shelley waved her hand in the air dismissively.

"I want to hear about it." Dev touched her shoulder. When

she turned to look at him, he stroked his thumb down her cheek. "It's on your mind, Shells. For a reason. So get it out of your head. Talk to me."

Shelley turned her cheek into his touch. He cupped her face in his hand, loving the softness of it. All too soon, she pulled away and resumed her stroll up the beach.

"When we ended up in foster care, we had a run of bad luck. Our first social worker, whose name completely escapes me, was a nasty old woman. Looking back, I think she suffered from short-timer's syndrome."

"Short-timer's syndrome?"

"You know, close to retirement and doesn't really give a frack about her job." She shrugged. "Anyway, we weren't in the system four months when she arranged for Hannah to be adopted. Jules and I didn't even know. We came home from school one day, and our foster mother was crying because they'd taken Hannah that afternoon right out of preschool."

Assholes. Dev didn't say it. What good would it do? But who does that to children? Especially children who'd already lost so much. "You didn't get to say good-bye?"

"No." There was no missing the bitterness in her voice. "I thought maybe there would be a drawing—Hannah was always drawing pictures—or something in our bedroom. There wasn't. They'd even taken her Little Mermaid sheets. There was nothing left in the bedroom I shared with my baby sister but a mattress and box spring."

Dev wanted to reach out and touch her again. Hold her. Promise her everything would be all right, but he didn't dare make a promise he couldn't keep.

"They moved Jules into the room with me. She'd been sleeping on the couch until then. Jules was moody and having trouble with ghosts. We lost our first foster home because our foster parents thought Jules was crazy. They tried to keep me, though. After they sent Jules away, I went into the garden and talked to the woman's dog. He told me she loved her flowers more than anything. So I took a pair of scissors and cut the heads off every single one."

"Very clever." Dev grinned at the pride in her eyes. "How long did it take for you to reunite with Jules?"

"Two days." Shelley made a sound that could have been a

laugh or disgust. "That social worker was ticked. She told me if I didn't get my act together, she'd spank me herself."

Dev ground his teeth against the caustic remark he wanted to let fly.

"But it was always the same. Every foster family kept us long enough to collect the month's allotment, then didn't want us anymore. While I could hide my crift, Jules had a harder time. Animals seemed to get when people are evil and must be avoided. Ghosts, not so much. I remember this one time, we were sitting at the dinner table with foster family three . . . or was it four? It doesn't matter. Jules got really quiet, then started to talk out of one side of her mouth, like you do when you don't want to get caught talking. But the foster monster mother heard her say the name Charles. Good ole FMM apparently had a son who had died of a drug overdose in the house. He was warning Jules to be careful, that his mother liked to taint snack food with sleeping pills so she could get a break from the kids.

"Jules called our social worker, but the old bat wouldn't listen. That night one of our foster siblings was rushed to the hospital for a drug overdose. That ended that. The kid survived, but we all went our separate ways, except for Jules and me. We were assigned a new social worker, Mrs. Harris. Great lady. But by then I was so full of anger and preteen rage that I'd started acting out."

Shelley grew quiet and stayed that way for several minutes, giving Dev time to digest some of what she'd been through. It was amazing the woman had any compassion at all. She'd been abandoned by her father, lost two mothers to early deaths, had her sisters taken from her. Thank God for her gift of talking to animals, or she would have been all alone in the world for years.

The sign for Seventeenth Street came into view. Count on Tidewater to have the beach-access roads well labeled. Only a few more blocks and they'd be at the shop. *Time to hurry this along.*

"How did you and Jules get separated if your new social worker was better?"

Shelley glanced up as if startled by the question. "Well . . ." She rolled her shoulders. "My last foster family didn't like Jules. I think they were afraid of her. They kept making overtures about keeping me—adopting me—but sending Jules away. So I did to them what they threatened to do to Jules. I left. I ran away five times. Never made it far. Only as far as the bus station, but I didn't have any money. Plus, I didn't want to leave without Jules.

"Then I met my adoptive parents, Jill and Nate. They were amazing. Even after hearing that I'd been running away, my grades had gone from perfect report cards to barely passing, and I was angry all the time, they still saw the good in me. Believed in me.

"They kept coming back to see me. Trying to prove that they wanted me. That I was safe with them. They even bought a puppy that I'd seen in the pet store. Let me name him. They promised I could play with him whenever they came to visit. It didn't take long for me to love them enough to want to go with them.

"I thought, given enough time, I could talk them into adopting Jules. But when I presented my plan to her, Jules refused. We had this horrible fight. I don't remember most of what we said. You know, it was one of those 'scream whatev-er's on your mind, even if it isn't true' moments."

It wasn't a question, but Dev answered like it was. "Yeah. I know what you mean."

Her blue eyes misted. "I do remember the last thing I said to her. I told her I hated her and that she wasn't my sister any-more. I'd found a better family. One that wasn't filled with freaks. God, I was so awful. After all she'd done to care for Hannah and me. And I threw it back in her face."

Shelley covered her mouth with her free hand and blinked fast, clearly trying to stave off the tears. Something about that move was familiar. He'd seen her do that in college after fights with Cam. She always calmed down. Never shed a single tear. And he wondered if she ever let herself truly grieve for anything.

He reached for her, but she shook her head. "I'm-I'm fine." *Right, and I'm Joan of Arc.* "You sure?"

She dropped her hand and inhaled a long, slow breath. "Yeah. I'm okay. I just haven't talked about that."

"In a long time?"

"Ever."

"You need another minute?" *How had she gone thirteen years and not talked about it?*

"No, I'm good." She smiled at him briefly, then studied the sand beneath their feet. She bent over and picked up a fully formed but tiny—smaller than her fingernail—seashell. Cupping the pure white Common American auger in her palm, she held it up to him. "Look at this, it's beautiful. Perfect. I think I'll add it to my collection."

She pocketed the keepsake and continued walking.

"You collect shells, Shells?" He grinned when she groaned.

"Usually I collect rocks. They're sturdier. I try to save one from every new place I visit. Just seems wrong somehow to collect a rock from the ocean when there are so many shells to choose from."

Now that confused him. "Weren't you born in Tidewater? How have you never been to the beach?"

"No time to play." She shrugged. "Plus, Tidewater's a big city. And we grew up in the middle, geographically speaking. So unless we took a bus or someone drove us, we didn't go anywhere that was more than five blocks from the house. Momma was an only child, we didn't know Daddy's family, and our grandparents died long before Jules was born, so there was no one to take us anywhere."

"Sounds lonely."

She shrugged again, this time less convincingly. "Nah. When Momma was alive, we were happy."

Dev again wondered at her upbringing. It was so different from his, where family seemed to sprout up like weeds in his mother's flowerbed. It made him want to wrap Shelley in his arms and hold her close. Or take her to his Gram's for Christmas so she could see what a big family gathering was like.

Somewhere in the distance, a car horn blared. Dev glanced to his right. Whoa. They'd covered the distance faster than he thought they would. He turned them up the access road. On the opposite side of Atlantic Avenue lay the strip mall with April's Flowers and . . . Jules.

CHAPTER 12

"WE'RE HERE." DEV muttered so softly, Shelley wasn't certain he'd said it at all. Then she glanced across the street to see a pretty redhead hanging garland in the front window of a florist shop.

Shelley's heart thudded in excitement. In trepidation. In confusion. She took an automatic step back.

"I promise, it's going to be fine," Dev said, catching her by the elbow and halting her retreat. "Better than fine, Shells. Your sister is going to be thrilled when she sees you. Trust me. What happened that last time you spoke won't matter in the least."

Maybe not to you.

She should just leave. Go back home. She was needed there anyway. Animals were disappearing. Miah was suffering and only Shelley could talk to the tigress. Provided Reyna didn't have her legally banned from the zoo.

As if reading her mind, Dev tightened his hold on her arm. Not painfully, but just enough to let her know he wasn't going to let her run. She glanced up at him when another horn blared. Dev's eyes widened, then he dropped her arm.

Raising his hands high in the air, he attempted to stop traffic. It took a split second for Shelley to figure out why. In the
center of the road was a small calico kitten. Its little wet body
shivered as cars whipped past.

"Oh my God!" Shelley dropped her shoes and hurried into
the street.

"Wait, Shells." Dev raised both hands in a clear demand for
the oncoming gold Toyota to stop. Brakes screeched as Shelley raced past.

Dev called out, "Can you get it?"

Shelley scooped the frightened animal into her hands and
continued across the street, seconds before a red Porsche blew
past, horn honking. Once on the other side of the road, she
cradled the wet animal to her chest.

She tucked the kitten, which couldn't have been more than
three weeks old, beneath the sweatshirt Dev had loaned her.
Tiny sharp claws dug into her thin blouse, as the little animal
sought purchase in the dark.

"Did you get it?" Dev asked, when he met her on the sidewalk. He handed Shelley her shoes. He must have gone back
for them after she crossed. "Is it alive? Does it need a vet?"

"I am a vet." Shelley arched an eyebrow at him.

"Right. But I meant do we need to go to a local clinic?"

"Let's get away from the street so I can talk to her."

Shelley glanced back at the shop, hoping for a place to go
that was convenient. A teen in black pants, combat boots, and
a black T-shirt with hundreds of white skulls on the front stood
frozen in the storefront window. A string of evergreen garland
in her hands, she stared at them. The open-mouthed, narrow-
eyed expression all the more disturbing because her radically
black hair framed a face covered in Goth makeup. White
powder, black eyeliner, mascara, and matching lipstick.

How on earth did I mistake her for a redhead?

Dev waved to the teen, then tugged Shelley's sleeve.
"Come on."

He didn't wait for a response but led her to the front door.

Chimes tinkled as they walked into the shop. The scent of
roses and freshly cut evergreens made the little store both
homey and welcoming.

"Hey, Diana," Dev said to the Goth teen. "Is Jules around?"

* * *

SHELLEY JERKED AS if in surprise. Clearly, during Operation Kitty Rescue outside, where they were must have slipped her mind.

"Yeah," Diana said, hiking a thumb over her shoulder. "She's recycling boxes, but she'll BRB."

Shelley made a hissing sound between her teeth. Dev turned to see her awkwardly trying to remove the sweatshirt with one hand, while reaching beneath it with the other, presumably to hold the kitten in place.

"Who's your *friend*, Dev?" Diana asked, her southern Tidewater twang more pronounced than usual.

"Diana, this is Shelley." Dev didn't bother to continue, instead he said, "You hold the kitten, Shells, and I'll tug off the sweatshirt." That idea didn't work, because every time she let go of the kitten with one hand to pull her arm free, it sank claws through the sweatshirt, halting the upward movement.

"Do you want me to hold the kitten while you try to pull off the sweatshirt?"

Shelley blushed. "Um . . . no. Kitty's partially wedged under my bra. She managed to get her head beneath the underwire. I think she's stuck and panicking. Ouch! She's scratching my stomach. I'm holding her still so she doesn't strangle or claw me to death."

"You've got to be kidding." Diana's laugh cut across the room. "You've got a live animal stuffed down your shirt? Where'd you find this chick, Dev?"

Shelley turned to glare at the girl. "You could offer something useful, like the direction to the ladies' room."

It was Diana's turn to glare. She narrowed her brown eyes to slits and folded her arms.

"Back there," Dev said, pointing to the doorway behind the counter. He didn't wait for Diana to lift the hinged counter. He did it himself, guiding Shelley through.

"Do you want me to come in with you?" he asked, his face heating. Thank God, he didn't blush like she did. Because damn, he would be Dev the Red-Faced Detective right now. The idea of helping Shells out of her bra did things to his dick it just shouldn't have, given the circumstances.

"I—ow!" She danced backward into the small white-tiled bathroom. "Yes, jeez, I think she's out for blood."

"How do you know the cat's a girl?" Dev asked, searching the tiny bathroom for a first-aid kit.

"She's a calico kitten. Except for a rare few, none are male—" She sucked air between her teeth and shifted the bulge under her shirt. "Calicos are female. It's a genetic thing." She glanced over at him. "What are you doing?"

"Kicking myself for leaving my car at Doc Taylor's. I have my first-aid kit in there. I can't find one in here."

"You're such a Boy Scout." She laughed, then hissed in pain.

"CPR instructor," he said.

Jules appeared in the doorway. "Dev, Diana said you have a crazy woman back here with a live animal stuffed down her bra?"

He gestured to Shells, who was still doing the dance of pain beneath the slowly brightening lights of the bathroom. "Surprise, Jules. Shelley's here."

CHAPTER 13

A WKWARD. SHELLEY COULDN'T speak. She couldn't stand still. She had a kitten clawing its way out of her bra and shirt like some twisted feline version of *Alien*. And Jules was just staring at her, like *she* was an alien.

The kitten shifted and slid, dragging its razor-sharp nails down her rib cage. It let out a strangled mewling noise and really started struggling. "Frack this! She's going to strangle to death or tear me to ribbons or both. I need someone to help me get my clothes off, fast."

"I'll help her," Jules said, taking charge. "Dev, go get the first-aid kit from under the desk in my office." Then she shut the door in Dev's face and began the process of peeling the layers of clothing off Shelley's body.

"Well, this is not the reunion I pictured us having," Jules said, dropping the sweatshirt to the floor. "I thought we'd have dinner and maybe some wine or meet for breakfast somewhere. But stripping my little sister naked in my flower shop was definitely not on my list of top one hundred ways to reunite."

"Me neither," Shelley replied with a surprised chuckle, then winced as the kitten used her body as a scratching post. "But hey, we can always go for the wine thing tonight after

I've had the three thousand stitches I'm going to need once this kitten is free."

Jules grinned, her emerald eyes sparkling. And just like that, it was as if no time had passed. They were sisters dealing with another crazy animal Shelley had brought in out of the rain. Just like when they were kids.

Why was I worried about this?

The blue gauzy top Shelley had chosen for the day was a pullover with strings that tied at the neck. Jules took one look at it and her smile faded. "Oh, dear."

Shelley glanced down but couldn't see anything past the kitten head moving steadily upward between her breasts.

"Let's do this one step at a time." Slowly, Jules peeled the gauzy top from Shelley's body, then it too joined Dev's sweatshirt on the floor. "Turn around and I'll unhook your bra, then the kitten will be free."

Shelley turned, staring at the bizarre painting. "Jules? Why is there a painting of a field of penises in your bathroom?"

"That's a cornfield, gutterbrain," Jules said with a snort.

The bra unhooked, and the kitten's head popped free. The kitten fell into her hands and curled up, mewling.

Jules glanced over her shoulder. "All better?" When Shelley nodded, Jules added, "Hold still and I'll fasten you back up."

Another snap and the bra was securely back in place.

Dev knocked on the door and called, "I have the first-aid kit here. Do you want me to leave it by the door or—?"

"Come on in, Dev. The important parts are covered," Jules replied, cutting him off.

"What?" Shelley whipped around to stare at Jules.

"He teaches people first aid. This is right up his alley." Jules's eyes shifted to Shelley's clawed belly and her face took on a greenish tinge. "And, oh, I think I'm going to be sick."

A memory from their childhood surged. When Shelley was six, Jules had come into the backyard where Shelley was bandaging the bleeding leg of a stray she'd found. Jules turned green and started yakking in the bushes.

"Oh, God, you still can't handle the sight of blood?" she asked Jules, who made a gurgling noise. "Ah, come on, it's not *that* bad."

"It's the smell."

Dev opened the door and his jaw dropped. Shelley spun to face the penis-like–cornstalk painting again, then spun back around, mortified. She held the kitten pressed against her chest, much higher than where it had climbed to earlier. It purred against her flesh.

"I-I . . ." Dev's words trailed away. His gaze drifted down her body and froze on her midsection. "Damn, Shells. She got you good."

Shelley arched her back to discover the little beast had drawn blood. A lot of it. As if to remind her, the kitten clawed at her palms. She yelped in surprise, but didn't do more than shift her position so she could communicate with the animal eye to eye.

"Dev can help you get cleaned up." Jules, greener still, plucked the kitten from her hands. "I'll, uh . . ." She made another gurgling noise. "I'll take the kitten to my office."

Jules rushed out of the bathroom, yanking the door closed behind her.

And there they stood. Shelley half-naked and bleeding from the world's youngest attack kitty and Dev. Dev, who stood all tall and sexy and indescribably adorable as he bounced his gaze up and down her body, as if unsure where to keep it trained.

Something wet and sticky seeped beneath the waistband of her jeans. Shelley swiped a hand at it and it came back covered in blood. Turning to the mirror over the sink, she stood on tiptoe trying to assess the damage. Which was beginning to seriously sting.

"Here, let me help." Dev set the first-aid kit on the sink, placed his hands on her hips, then slowly turned her to face him. Kneeling in front of her, he unzipped the red bag and pulled out gloves, antiseptic cream, and bandages.

Not one to stand by and allow another person to coddle her, Shelley yanked a few paper towels from the roll on the wall, dampened them in the sink, and began to blot away the blood.

"I can do that," Dev said, his voice oddly huskier than usual.

"No, it's really fine," she lied. Truth was, having Devon Cary Jones on his knees in front of her half-naked body was something straight out of one of her fantasies. She needed to feel the sting of pain to keep her grounded in reality.

* * *

A TRICKLE OF sweat slid down Dev's back. *Ah, God.* This shouldn't turn him on. Okay, it didn't really. Seeing the blood on her torso was a complete soft-on. But the moment she wiped it away, only minor scratches were revealed on her voluptuous body. Hidden only by a lacy, nearly transparent, turquoise bra with little sparkling rhinestones on the cups. Now that did rev him up. And up. And up so much, he was glad he was on his knees so she couldn't see just how aroused he was.

"Thank you," Shelley said, as he dabbed the triple-antibiotic ointment on the deepest of her cuts.

"No problem, the scratches aren't bad." He applied several bandages.

She hissed as he smeared more ointment on a two-inch-long shallow gash. "Ooh, I meant, thank you for this too. But I was thanking you for seeing the kitten in the street. Helping me rescue her."

"I'm just glad you were able to get to her in time. Did she tell you how she got there?" He put another bandage on.

"No, I didn't get much from her. I think the poor thing is in shock. I'll try again in a few minutes."

Dev applied one more bandage, then ran a hand over her midsection, searching for any wounds he might have missed.

She shivered.

"Sorry," he said, pulling back.

"No, it's fine. I'm just . . . uh, cold." Goose bumps covered her arms.

Snatching the sweatshirt from the floor, he handed it to her. "Here. There's a little blood on it. Your blouse is ruined I think." He held up the gauzy top with several claw marks running down the front.

"Thanks for the loaner. I'd be naked now if I hadn't borrowed your sweatshirt for our walk," she said, chuckling. Her cheeks pinkened. "So how often do you go around bandaging half-naked women in bathrooms?"

"Not very." He snorted. "I only teach CPR. I'm not out there riding an ambulance and saving lives."

"No, you just catch criminals *and* train others to save

lives." She stroked a hand down his cheek. Her touch singed him to his toes. "I think you're pretty amazing."

"Said the woman who speaks to animals."

The warmth in her gaze and her touch lingered even after she'd tugged on her shirt. "Speaking of animals, I should probably check on our kitten."

"I'll clean up and meet you," Dev said, repacking the first-aid kit.

"Thank you for coming to my rescue again, Dev." Shelley kissed him on the cheek, then was out the door before he could respond.

Dev repacked the kit, tossed out the trash, and washed up. He found Jules, Shelley, and the kitten in Jules's office. Shelley had the feline on the desk, examining it.

"I don't have my stethoscope, but Callie the kitten seems healthy. Young, though. I think she can't be more than three weeks old." Shelley glanced at her sister. "Y'all seen a pregnant cat around here? Where there's one kitten, there are usually more."

Jules shook her head; her short, straight, red ponytail swung back and forth. "I haven't seen any. You found her in the street?"

"Right in the middle. She was on the double yellow lines, shivering and frightened."

"Shelley, has the kitten told you anything yet?"

"No, I wanted to check her out first. Make sure she didn't have any broken limbs before I tried talking to her. She's just a baby. There's no telling how much she'll be able to communicate."

"Are animals like people? Do they need to learn language?" Dev asked, handing the first-aid kit back to Jules, who returned it to the box beneath her desk.

"Not language exactly. She needs to learn to communicate. It's not completely instinctive," Shelley said, scooping the kitten into one hand, while running two fingers down the cat's spine. The kitten arched her back at the touch and purred. "It's why most mammals raise their young with such care and don't abandon them at birth. They need someone to teach them how to survive in the world, how to hunt, avoid predators, what specific noises or calls mean."

She returned the tiny animal to the desk, took its little face between her two palms and stared.

"So how did you come to be in the middle of the road?" Shelley sat motionless for about thirty seconds, then blinked several times. She frowned and kissed the kitten on the top of its head between its mismatched ears. Snuggling the kitten close, she said, "It seems our little friend here has had a rough day. Her mother was living in a trash can when she gave birth. This little girl and her four brothers were in it this morning when the trash man came. He saw the kitties and dumped the can onto the grass. Callie ran for cover but chose the dump truck's side rim. She fell off after the truck hit a pothole filled with water."

"Oh, you poor thing," Jules said, scratching the kitten's black, white, and orange back. "I've got milk in the refrigerator and a blanket in my desk drawer. We'll get you all warmed up and feeling better soon."

Shelley bumped shoulders with her older sister. "I see you're still taking care of everyone in need."

"Ha!" Jules retorted, tossing an arm lazily around Shelley's shoulders. "You're the one who saved the kitten. I'm just giving her a little food and comfort. I'd say you're the one still saving the world."

Dev's cell rang. Seth's name appeared on the display. He stepped out of the office to answer it and quickly updated his partner on the morning's events ending with, "They're fixing the kitten."

"Now that Jules and Shelley are together, think you can break away long enough to go over this case with me? Or are you too busy rescuing house pets?" Seth asked, humor in his tone.

"I am on vacation, you know. I could technically skip the meeting at the station."

"Kid, we're on a homicide case. That trumps vacation time. Aren't you wondering exactly what kind of animal munched on the hand of our deceased victim?"

Actually, he wasn't. "I am now."

"Haul your lazy ass to the station. I'll meet you there and we can go over the case." Seth barked a laugh.

"First, I have to haul my lazy ass back to Doc Taylor's to get my car."

"Come again?"

"We had breakfast there before walking to the shop."

"Why'd you walk?" But before Dev could answer, Seth added, "I don't care. Just stay put. I'm almost to the shop. I'll pick you up."

Seth hung up without giving Dev an opportunity to disagree. Pocketing his cell, he spun on his heel and nearly knocked over Diana. In her platform combat boots, she was almost six feet tall.

"Oops," she said, glancing to his right where Jules and Shells were speaking quietly. "So, uh, who's your friend? I swear she could be Jules's twin if you KWIM."

"I know what you mean. And they look alike because they're sisters. That's Shelley."

The Goth teen goggled, her mouth agape. "OMG, seriously?"

"Yeah."

Dev was saved from further explanation when the bells on the front door chimed. Diana hurried to the front to help the arriving customer. She returned moments later with Seth on her heels.

Seth was in his typical navy suit and sedate tie, and the intense expression on his face said he was completely in cop mode. But his expression softened when Jules came out of her office. He held up a brown paper sack.

She rushed over, took it, and then threw her arms around his neck with a squeal of delight. "I have someone I want you to meet. Seth, this is my little sister, Shelley."

She tugged him by the hand, closer to her sister. Holding Seth by one hand and Shelley by the other, Jules finished the introductions. "Shelley, this is my dashing fiancé, Detective Seth English."

Shelley and Seth exchanged nods in greeting, then Jules launched herself at Dev. He caught her with one arm as she hugged him fiercely. Pulling back, she said in a thick voice that threatened tears, "Thank you! Thank you."

Dev glanced toward Shelley. Unsure whether Jules's emotional reaction would make her feel good or send her running for Elkridge. "Told you she'd be happy to see you, Shells."

"You were right." She turned to her sister. "You know, you weren't this emotional when I arrived."

"You had a kitten lodged in your underwire and blood on your shirt. I was a little focused on saving your skin and the cat's neck. Forgive me." Tears sprang to Jules's eyes. "I can't believe he really found you."

She let go of Dev and threw both arms around Shelley.

Shelley blinked once, then again. To Dev's surprise, she let her tears fall too.

Dev glanced to Seth for support. His partner shrugged and hiked a thumb over his shoulder, saying, "Precious, Jones and I are headed to the station. You two going to be okay for a while until we get back?"

Jules mumbled something incomprehensible and waved them off.

"See you in a little while, Shelley."

"Dev, wait." Shelley let go of her sister and pulled him aside. "I know I promised you I'd stay for a few days, but I really think I should get back to Elkridge, today. I'm really worried about the tiger cubs."

Maybe she's not as happy with this reunion as she appears. "I thought we were going to go over what you remembered when I get back?"

She shrugged. "Without my notes, I really feel like I should head back to Elkridge."

Her cheeks reddened, and he knew she was lying. He tried not to be pissed. Tried to understand this was probably all a bit overwhelming for her, but couldn't quite kill the feeling. But he *could* hide it until they had time to talk later. "Okay, Shells. I get it. But I'm needed at the station right now. Can you wait a bit to go back?"

"I don't know." She ran a hand through her hair. "I suppose. I mean, it's not like I've been able to reach Tomás yet. But he's probably working or taking care of Beau or both."

She shifted from foot to foot as if too anxious to stand still. With every passing second, Dev grew more certain she was afraid and wanted to run. He had no idea what had set her off, but he was positive her sudden need to return to Elkridge was less about the animals and more about her own fears.

Well, he wasn't about to let her run from him.

"Tell you what," he said, nodding toward Jules. "You enjoy the day with Jules. I'll work and then tonight I'll take you home after dinner. I'll even get another room in Elkridge and stay there until we solve your mystery. Sound fair?"

She blinked and narrowed her eyes at him. "Considering I thought that was why you had come to town in the first place, yeah. I think that'll work. And don't worry about a hotel. You can stay at my place."

But her place only had one bed and a very uncomfortable couch.

Does she mean . . . ? Maybe he wasn't one of the things she was running from.

Jules pulled Shelley back into the office, and Seth ushered Dev out into the sunshine.

Stay with her in her apartment. Oh yeah. Things were looking up.

CHAPTER 14

"**W**HAT MAKES YOU certain the animal bite occurred after death?" Detective O'Dell asked Dev.

Dev, who'd only been in the station two minutes prior to the meeting and hadn't yet read the coroner's report, glanced at Seth for help.

"According to the coroner's report, the lividity showed the bite on the left hand happened after the victim was killed," Seth answered.

As usual, when Peterson called Dev, Seth, O'Dell, and Reynolds into his office, O'Dell and Reynolds, the actual homicide detectives, took the only available chairs. Dev leaned against the captain's credenza while Seth leaned against the opposite wall near the window.

Captain Peterson, a balding man in his early fifties, sat behind his large cherry desk, his fingers steepled. To Dev's surprise, the man addressed him, "What do you think of this case, Jones?"

"Honestly, sir. I'm not sure what to think." Dev ignored the impulse to whack Reynolds in the back of the head when he snickered. "I've been out of town and was only handed the latest update as I walked into your office."

"Reynolds," the captain said, turning his eagle glare to the man. "Catch him up."

Reynolds, who looked like he'd rather play with cat puke, cleared his throat. "Okay, kid, here's what we know. The vic, Colbert Rush, was embezzling money from McGivern's Jewelers for about ten years before his partner found out. Vic disappeared one night last week. Wife says she didn't report it right away, because she thought he was on a business trip. She called McGivern and found out there was no trip. She reported her husband missing. A search of her place turned up a key she doesn't recognize, and close to fifty grand in cash.

"Yesterday, pieces of the vic start showing up on beaches from Chicks Beach down to Tidewater Bridge. Not in the water. Dump sites. Someone broke his neck then cut him into pieces. The hand on his left arm had a single animal-bite mark. Too big to be dog or coyote. We have no idea what decided to take a nibble out of this guy."

If a scavenger had bitten him, it would have continued to gnaw until it had eaten its full. But what kind of big animal would bite and let go without eating? And why?

"Ideas, Jones?" The captain put him on the spot. Dev should be flattered. He knew that part of the reason they'd solved their last case was because he found a connection to the killer no one else had. But he'd also done a buttload of research while Reynolds and O'Dell slept.

"I think, sir," Dev began and prayed he was right, "what we should do is talk to someone who might be able to help us identify the bite wound. If it was a clean bite, perhaps we can work backward. If we figure out what bit him, then maybe we can identify the actual crime scene."

Captain Peterson's brows drew together to form one long salt-and-pepper one. "Good idea. Anyone have other suggestions?"

"The key," Seth and O'Dell said at the same time. The men glared at each other, then Seth added, "We'll go back and talk to the wife again. If we can get her to let us search the house, maybe we can find what the key went to."

"Didn't you say she thought the key went to a house of some kind?" the captain asked Reynolds. When the man nodded, Peterson said, "Good. You two search public records. See if this guy had any other property in his name. Give whatever you find to English and Jones, then get back to working the construction-site homicide. I have the builder's association breathing down my neck wanting that case solved."

Reynolds and O'Dell nodded. The captain dismissed them but asked Dev and Seth to wait. Once the door had closed, he said, "Jones, I need this case solved. I know you asked for time off, but dismembered bodies take priority. Keep it quiet. I don't want the press hearing about this story until we have a killer in cuffs."

"Understood, sir." Dev nodded.

The captain picked up his office phone and began to dial. Recognizing the action for the dismissal it was, Dev and Seth walked out.

Once at their desks, Seth said, "I thought you told Shelley you'd go back to Elkridge tonight and help her solve her mystery."

"I did."

"How are you going to do that and solve this case with me too?"

Damn good question.

"So, WHICH ONE are you? The middle one or the baby?"

Shelley, who'd been settling the kitten in an old box, glanced up at Diana's question. The girl held out a white plastic bag containing two cans of kitten milk, a two-ounce bottle, four nipples, cotton balls, and a heating pad.

"Ah, thank you, Diana. You're a lifesaver." Shelley smiled at the girl, who beamed with pride. "And I'm the middle sister. I take it you've heard about me?"

"A little." Diana's smile faded. "Enough to know that Jules has been looking for you. Does this mean you're going to come to work here too? I'm never going to get promoted."

Shelley chuckled. "Don't worry. I'm a vet in Elkridge. I'm just back here for the weekend."

"So you're *not* staying?" Then Diana muttered, "TGFT."

"Diana, I'm glad you're back." Jules hurried into the office, making the small space feel even more cramped. "We still need nine dozen roses wrapped before four, and there are two women out front wanting to review some of your floral arrangements for their dog's gravesite. Can you go help them and keep the front covered while I wrap?"

"Sure thing, Jules." Diana started toward the archway between the back and the storefront, then paused to ask, "Are we closing early tonight?"

"If Mrs. Marcos picks up the roses on time, we are. Do you need to call your mother to tell her?"

"Nah, I'll just ask Dev to drive me home again."

Something ugly and sharp erupted in Shelley's chest. Jealousy? No way. She couldn't be jealous. She'd seen Dev for what twenty-four hours? Who was she to care if he was . . . ? But jeez, that girl was *young*.

"Ignore her," Jules said, laughter in her whispered voice. "Diana's been chasing after Dev since the first time she saw him."

"I don't care. It's none of my business," Shelley replied, although that ugly spark died a quick death. But that didn't make her jealous. Did it?

Opening the bag and pulling out the bottle and one of the nipples, Shelley glanced around. "Got a coffeepot or hot teapot in here somewhere?"

Jules blinked and pointed to the coffeemaker sitting on a gray filing cabinet behind her desk. "I only use it for hot water for tea, though. I might have some instant coffee somewhere in my desk."

Shelley held up the supplies. "No worries. I need to sterilize the bottle and nipple before I feed Callie."

As if recognizing her new name, the kitten began to meow. She crawled around the inside of the box, sucking on the blanket.

"Is that normal?" Jules asked with a frown, pulling down the coffeemaker.

"She's just hungry. Actually, moving around is a good sign. I should have thought to ask for a rectal thermometer to check her temperature, but she's not shivering anymore."

Jules grabbed the glass pot off the heating element and headed for the door. "I doubt Diana would have bought it. Don't let her fool you. She's pretty squeamish about bugs, boys, and butts."

Shelley stripped the wrappers off the bottle and nipples. The nipples had been pre-pierced with two tiny holes. Go Diana! She'd found and bought what were likely the best nipples at the store. Shelley set them aside and picked up Callie.

Jules returned, poured the water into the coffeemaker, set the pot on the element, and turned it on. "Should be ready in three minutes. Do you think the water will be hot enough?"

"It'll do in a pinch." Shelley would have preferred a rolling boil, but that wasn't an option.

Jules was staring at the kitten with longing in her eyes.

"Want to hold her?" Shelley asked, then grinned when Jules practically danced over. Shelley carefully set the kitten in Jules's hands. "Okay, be careful, her little claws are pretty sharp."

"I deal with thorns all day. This is no big—ouch." Jules shifted the kitten so she could snuggle Callie against her chest. "Wow, they are sharp. No wonder you were such a mess in the bathroom. Lucky you had such a large sweatshirt on. That's Dev's isn't it?"

Shelley glanced down at the white letters on the shirt. Virginia's Finest, indeed. "Yeah, we were at breakfast when we decided to take a walk on the beach. I didn't have my jacket with me."

Jules didn't reply. She just stroked the kitten and grinned.

Heat burned up Shelley's neck. "Anyway, I figured my own shirt was destroyed, so I put it in Callie's box. At least I lost it to a good cause."

"And you had Dev's shirt to wear now. TGFT."

"Diana said that too. TGFT. What's it mean?"

Jules's smile flashed to surprise, then a grimace. "Great, now Diana's got me talking in text speech. TGFT is 'Thank God for That.'"

"Diana seems nice. I need to thank her again for the bottles and food." Shelley heard the tightness in her voice and wanted to cringe.

"She lives for this stuff. She might dress tough, but she's got a big heart."

"Is . . . uh, she in college?" Shelley asked, *not* fishing for information about Dev's potential suitor. Because, yeah, she'd seen the way Diana had lit up when Dev came through the door.

"No, she's only eighteen but will start at Tidewater U next fall. Like I said before, Diana's been chasing after Dev for weeks, but he's definitely not interested."

"Oh." Shelley tried to ignore the little thrill of relief that drained the tension from her shoulders. "Well, that's . . . um, fine."

"Yeah, you're so hot for him, you're practically melting."

Stunned by her sister's rather accurate description, Shelley blurted, "How is it that I haven't seen you in thirteen years and yet you still seem to know what I'm thinking?"

"Ha, you weren't thinking. You were feeling and it was written all over your face." Jules laughed, then glanced at Callie and frowned. "Uh, do kittens have bladder control at three weeks?"

"Sort of. They can go on their own without help. Why?"

"I think Callie just christened my apron." Jules handed the kitten back and sure enough, there was a little wet spot right in the center of the white apron. Jules laughed. "I guess this means she likes me."

Shelley put Callie back in her box. "No, I think it just means she had to pee. But I'm glad she did. It's a good sign. Means she wasn't exposed to the elements too long."

"Jules," Diana called from the archway. "Mrs. Marcos just called. She's going to be here at three to pick up the flowers. Something about the caterer got the time wrong when he placed the order."

"Oh, dear." Jules tugged on her left ear. Something she did when she was worried back when they were children. "I'd love to help you with Callie, but I need to wrap about a hundred roses in silver and blue ribbon. Individually."

The coffeepot hissed, then clicked off, indicating the water was ready. "Tell you what, let me finish feeding Callie, then I'll come help you."

"You know how to wrap roses?" Jules arched both brows.

"No, but my sister's a good teacher. She taught me to read. I figure she can teach me the fine art of rose-wrapping."

Jules's eyes misted. And shoot if Shelley's own eyes didn't too.

"Go work." Shelley shooed Jules out of the office. "I'll be in to help you soon."

Jules hugged her and left. Shelley could still feel that hug and smell Jules's strawberry scent lingering in the office. For a moment, she let herself imagine what it would be like to live in Tidewater. See Jules every day. See Dev every day. Have a real home. A real family again.

Then she thought of Nate and Jill, Momma and Daddy, even old Barty the Bay retriever, and the ache of losing them stole her breath. Just as it stole her sleep more nights than she wanted to count. Of course, Jules, Hannah, and her ex, Cam, hadn't died, but they had all left. Sure, Jules was here now, but what about in a week or a month or a year? Everyone Shelley had ever loved had died or left her.

She couldn't stay here. Not with these people. She had Lucy and Miah and all the animals at the zoo who needed her. They needed her to care for them, protect them, and solve the mystery of the disappearances. She couldn't abandon them . . . not after the way they'd been there for her after all the times *she* had been abandoned.

She needed to get out of Tidewater and back where she belonged in Elkridge.

CHAPTER 15

ADAM PUT HIS car in drive and slowly backed out of the swamp. He drove the mile back to the public parking lot. His tires crunched over the gravel as the sun beat down on the hood of the black SUV. Pulling into a spot between two mini-vans, both black, he put the car in park with the engine running, and waited.

He'd heard from Kenny, the mechanic, about the teens getting their cars stuck in the swamp last night. He nearly choked on his lunch when Kenny's older son, Marcus, described the spectacle of the four cars buried up to the door handles in the mud. Kenny and his kids were heading back after lunch to dig out car three of the four.

When Adam had offered to come help, the hick actually appeared grateful. So here he sat, waiting for the men to appear in their beat-up red tow truck.

His pulse thumped steadily. While Adam had been terrified the mechanic might have figured out what he had done, it quickly became clear that Kenny had no idea. He honestly thought Adam only wanted to help.

What Adam wanted was for this part to be over already. But until all three of the bodies were discovered, he didn't dare risk leaving town. Someone might, quite rightly, start looking at him for the crimes.

He would call the sheriff's office but couldn't risk doing that without incriminating himself. How could he know where the body was, unless he had put it there? But it had been four months, and the fucking department hadn't found the body. Fuck, for his plan to succeed, every body needed to be found before he exacted punishment on the last man.

Then there was Tomás. His body needed to be found, too, but that required that nosy little bitch to go to her fucking car. Where was she? Any other time the vet would be hounding him.

A horn blared musically, reminding Adam of that old television show his mother had liked when he was a small child. Except instead of an orange Dodge Charger with a Confederate flag painted on it, a beat-up red tow truck pulled into the lot.

Adam cut the engine, pretending to have just arrived, and exited the vehicle.

"Thanks for the help. Hop on in, son," Kenny said, using the moniker he gave to all men under forty.

Adam ground his teeth to bite back the angry retort. He wasn't this small-town hick's son. And the only reason Adam did not kill him for the insult was because Kenny wasn't on his list or in his way.

He forced himself to smile as he climbed into the passenger seat of the cab. "Where are your boys?"

"Ah, they'll be along right soon enough," Kenny managed between snaps of gum. The man chewed gum like a cow gnawing on fetid grass. "We'll just head over to the site. Boys thought they saw somethin' in the dark last night. Somethin' other than them four kids' cars. Figured we could have a look before they get here. Sound good?"

Adam smiled a genuine, relieved smile. Finally, something was going right today. "Works for me."

And it did because if the old coot couldn't find it, Kenny would make sure to stumble across the body of that asshole of a retired D.A., John Wallace.

DEV WASTED TOO much time at the station. Rush's widow was out of town and couldn't be reached. His inbox was overflowing with bureaucratic forms that basically repeated one another on the station's new computer software system. Why the hell had they switched systems? It only made his job harder. Instead of logging in and glancing over records, Dev played hide-and-seek with the needed files.

"Kid, you're supposed to be on vacation," Seth teased, tugging on his jacket.

Dev glared at his partner, who, two months ago, would have glared back.

Today, Seth just laughed. "Come on, Jones. Jules closed the shop early. She's making dinner at our place. Let's go eat."

Dinner? Dev glanced at his watch. "Christ, it's nearly five. I can't believe I've been sitting here for four hours." He scrubbed a hand down his face.

"I can. Jules has called me twice in the past half hour. Seems Shelley is worried about a *ferret*? I thought you two found a kitten this morning."

"Crap." Dev closed down his program and hopped out of his seat. "I forgot Lucy, the attack ferret, is locked in my house. Shelley doesn't have a key to my place. Damn thing is probably hungry. Or she's eaten her way through the cage and is now munching on everything of value I own."

"Attack ferret?" Seth grinned.

"I'll explain later. I've got to get my car and pick up Shelley. Can you drop me off at Doc's?"

"Jules can take Shelley over to our place, while you get your car and the ferret."

Dev shook his head. "No. *No.* Shelley has to get her ferret. Lucy doesn't exactly like me as anything other than a chew toy. Besides, I don't know if you want that beast in your place."

Seth laughed. "Look at you. Big, bad cop afraid of a little weasel."

"Yeah, we'll see how much you laugh when Lucy goes for your balls."

"ARE YOU SURE you want to take Callie with you?" Shelley asked, holding the kitten in her little makeshift box-bed, while Jules locked the front door to April's Flowers. "Have you ever owned a cat this young? She's going to take some work."

The door clicked and Jules set the alarm. She turned, arms outstretched. The sun had set forty minutes earlier, and the early evening sky blazed with colors from pale pink to deep indigo. The streetlamp on the corner buzzed to life, shining on Jules's smiling, eager face.

"Shelley, you told me yourself you have a ferret. Seth and I have been talking about getting a dog. I think Callie will fit perfectly in our life," Jules said, hugging the box close to her chest.

"A dog and a three-week-old kitten aren't the same." Shelley wasn't sure why she was arguing. Jules was right. Lucy would never stand for a kitten invading her home. While most ferrets were good with other animals, Lucy was different. She tolerated the guests at the clinic because she knew that at home she reigned supreme.

"Don't worry. If Seth doesn't want her—and I know he will—I have other people who will. My parents, April and Big Jim, are definitely cat people."

"Big Jim?" Shelley asked.

Two sets of headlights flashed across their faces, as two cars pulled into the parking lot. Jules waved with one hand, while holding tight to Callie's box with the other. She glanced back at Shelley. "Remember all the Jims who fostered us? Well, Big Jim—whose real name is Ernie—was my last foster dad. Great guy. You'll love him and April when you meet them. They're out of town this week, attending some writers' convention in Baltimore. Big Jim announced about a month ago that he's secretly been a romance novelist for years. April's read his stuff and thinks he should make a go of it. Anyway, they'll be back next week. And you'll see them at Christmas."

A twinge of something cold and painful settled in Shelley's chest. Jules sounded like she expected Shelley to stick around. "Jules—"

"Ready to go, Precious?" Seth's voice cut across hers.

Shelley stepped back. The couple shared a kiss that was at once passionate and pure. As if they were doing more than greeting one another. They were reaffirming their commitment to each other.

Not wanting to be a voyeur, Shelley swung her gaze to the parking lot. Dev was crossing toward her. The sight of him made her stupid heart skip. The expression of heat in his eyes made her idiotic pulse race. Thank God she maintained enough self-control not to do anything foolish.

Then it happened. He was bathed in a warm red glow. Sexy and alluring. It made her mouth go dry and her core wet. Until it hit her that she was once again seeing things that couldn't be. She blinked her eyes and the color disappeared.

"Hey, Shells," he said. His incredibly sexy voice rumbled low and deep.

She strove for casual. "Hey, yourself, Monk."

The heat vanished. He laughed for some reason. "Ready to get Lucy? Jules and Seth invited us to dinner at their place."

"Okay, but I need to check my messages. My cell phone died, and I left my charger at your house."

In truth, she needed a little time away from Jules. Not because the reunion had been difficult. It hadn't. Whatever Shelley had been expecting, an insurmountable chasm maybe, hadn't happened. It had been wonderful. The few hours she'd spent with Jules had resurrected memories and feelings she'd buried long ago. Not put away out of pain but out of necessity for survival. Everyone she'd ever loved had left her. Everyone. And now she was being given an opportunity to rekindle her relationship with her sister, but how long could that really last?

It had been shockingly easy for Shelley and Jules to fall right back into their old roles, like no time had passed. Yes, they were both adults now, but that bond they'd shared as children was still there. And Shelley didn't know what to do. Besides run, before it all went to hell again. Run and rebuild the walls around her before Jules could leave her first.

Dev moved closer, draped an arm around her waist and whispered, "Did everything go okay? You seem upset."

At the moment, her body burned where he was casually touching her. Other than that, she was definitely not okay. Yet she couldn't seem to convince her body to break the contact that felt so fracking good.

"Meet you back at my place?" Seth called out, startling her.

Shelley did move then. Out of Dev's arms and several more feet away.

Jules and Seth were halfway to his car, the kitten box now

in Seth's arms. A loving smile on his face as he glanced at his fiancée.

"See you in thirty." Dev waved at them, then turned and extended his elbow to Shelley. "Come on, let's get Lucy. I can drive you back to Elkridge after dinner."

CHAPTER 16

A S SOON AS she arrived at Dev's place, Shelley let Lucy out of her cage and set her on the bed. The ferret yawned and stretched before slinking across the covers. Shelley watched her from the corner of her eye, while she pulled out her cell charger and plugged it into the wall.

The phone beeped, indicating it was taking a charge. She turned it on and waited impatiently for it to come up. No messages.

She tried to stem her frustration, but frack, why hadn't Tomás called? With effort, she kept the annoyance out of her voice. "Hey Tomás, it's Dr. Morgan again. Please call me when you get this message."

Shelley paused, phone in hand. Where was Kenny? He was supposed to have called when he picked up her car. She dialed him. He answered on the first ring. "Hi, Kenny, it's Dr. Morgan."

"'Evening, Doc. Sorry, but I can't talk right now." Kenny, normally slow talking and friendly, sounded cold and nervous. His speech fast and clipped. "I ain't got to your car yet. I'll call you tomorra when I getta look at it."

Something in his tone made her empty stomach knot. Kenny was never ruffled. He was definitely upset now.

"Kenny, are you all right? Are your boys okay?"

"Yeah, sorry, Doc." Kenny lowered his voice and said, "Marcus and Terry are fine. We, uh, found a body out here in the swamp, and the police want to talk to me. Seems old John Wallace didn't run off. Somebody killed him."

"John Wallace?" The name rang a bell, but she couldn't remember where she'd heard it.

"The retired D.A. that went missing last summer," he said, then paused. A muffled sound of someone putting a hand over the receiver crackled in Shelley's ear. A thunking sound and then Kenny spoke again, "I gotta go. I'll call you in the morning when I get a chance to tow your car. I'm sorry I didn't get to it today."

"Don't worry about it." Shelley's mind reeled. Someone in her little town had been murdered? "Take care of yourself. Have your sons call me if you need anything."

"I do appreciate it," he said, then hung up.

Dev knocked on her bedroom door. "Shelley, are you ready to head over to Jules's and Seth's?"

Lucy's head popped up at the sound of Dev's voice. She wriggled down on all fours as if ready to spring into the air. Shelley grabbed her about the middle and held her close before opening the door.

"Yeah, I guess. I just hate leaving Lucy locked up again. She's not used to being in such a small cage for so long."

Dev eyed Lucy with distrust. He brushed a hand through his sandy-blond hair, sighing. "If you want to bring her along, it's fine. I'd already mentioned the possibility to Seth. But you might want to bring her cage just in case she decides to attack anyone else."

Shelley laughed. "Lucy's a very loving animal. She doesn't usually attack." Lucy pushed all four paws against Shelley's chest, as if preparing to launch herself at Dev again. "On second thought, maybe she should stay here. They've got the kitten over there now."

Bringing Lucy up to eye level, Shelley said, "I'll give you some extra treats and let you run around when I get back." *I also don't want you attacking Dev anymore.* She sent the thought winging into the ferret's mind.

Images of Lucy's hammock, munching on treats, and

snuggling with Shelley came flying back in response. She'd started to smile until another image hit her—of Lucy latching onto Dev's jeans in Shelley's apartment.

That's not funny. She mentally scolded Lucy, who sent back an image of her doing the weasel war dance . . . Lucy's way of laughing.

"Yep, she'll be fine here," Shelley said, glancing at Dev as he opened the door. A soft blue-white light surrounded him. At first she thought it was coming from the lamp in the hallway, until the colors shifted around him, appearing to cling to him as he moved into the room.

Lucy squeaked and her little body tensed, threateningly. Shelley quickly tucked her back in the cage and latched the door.

"Everything okay, Shells?" Dev asked after she straightened. He stroked a finger down her cheek. "You're flushed."

Little did he know his touch was making her blood race. It took every ounce of restraint she possessed, and the knowledge that Lucy was watching them, for Shelley not to give into her seemingly never-ending urge to kiss him again. And again. And again.

His full lips quirked up into a sexy half smile that mesmerized her. His gentle caress of her cheek slid down to her neck. He cupped her chin in his hand, tilting her head back until she stared into his sensual gray eyes. The light around him, which had been a pure blue-white light pulsed to a clear, vibrant red that seemed magnetic. Drawing her closer to him.

Deciding restraint was the losing part of valor, Shelley brushed her lips against his.

The light touch, barely a kiss, exploded through her. Every one of her senses was on fire. His taste, salty and clean, made her hungry for more. Driving her fingers into his silky hair, she tugged him down and kissed him again.

Dev groaned, then his arms went around her, lifting her off the ground. He tugged her tight against him, surrounding her completely. Yesterday's kiss had been hot. Tonight's was scorching.

He kissed her like he'd done it a thousand times before, but would never get bored. He kissed her as if it were their first time touching, pure and raw. And still he kissed her until she was drowning in the sensation of pleasure. And she prayed he'd never stop.

But he did. Slowly. Carefully. First setting her on the floor again, then unwrapping his arms and cupping her face between his huge, warm hands. Finally, he pulled back from her lips, taking care to kiss each of her cheeks, her forehead, the tip of her nose.

Shelley, awash in sensation, couldn't open her eyes. The pleasure was too much.

Dev chuckled. "Wow."

She peeked an eye open then both flew wide at the sight that greeted her. Dev was bathed in a deep red light that encompassed his body. It seemed to emanate from the center of his chest and pulse like a heartbeat.

Shelley stepped back from him, tripped over her duffle bag, and nearly fell on Lucy's cage. Lucy chattered at her angrily.

Dev extended a hand to her. A distinctly non-glowy hand. Whatever color she thought she saw was gone.

I'm losing my fracking mind.

"Sorry," Dev said, when she didn't move fast enough. "I'd always wanted to sweep you off your feet, but that's not quite how I pictured it."

"Oh, that was bad." She laughed and accepted his proffered hand. Once standing on her own, she said, "If not for being named Shelley Grace, I'd have no grace at all."

"I don't think that's true." Dev's watch beeped. He pressed a button on it and said, "We'd better hurry. Jules is making her mother-in-law's lasagna, meatless-style in your honor. If we're late, Seth might just eat the whole thing."

He grabbed her by the hand as if he'd done it a hundred times before, and escorted her down the stairs, out the door, and to his car. He opened the door for her like she'd seen men do in old black-and-white movies.

Sliding into the car, Shelley's body hummed with pleasure. Pleasure from his touch. Pleasure from his attention. Pleasure from the sense of belonging she hadn't experienced in a very long time.

She decided not to examine that last too closely. Everything ended.

*   *   *

TEN MINUTES LATER, Dev parallel parked his car outside of
Seth and Jules's brownstone apartment building. Shelley
hadn't said a word since he climbed into the car. The ride over
had been quiet but companionable.

He cut the engine and Shelley reached for her door handle.
He stretched across her body, covering her hand with his.
"Let me."

She glanced at him, one eyebrow arched. A slow, seductive
smile curved her lips. "I appreciate the offer. Lord knows, I
don't want to risk chipping this fine manicure on your Lexus."

She waved her short, unpolished nails in the air. Damn, she
was beautiful. Without makeup or polish, she was the sexiest
woman on the planet. And her sense of humor jacked up her
beauty to a full-on eleven.

"Can't have that, now can we?" Dev laughed and hurried
out of the car.

He'd just opened her door, when he heard the noise behind
him. Somewhere down the sidewalk, just beyond the lamp
post a dog growled. The guttural sound was menacing.

Shelley had already slammed the door closed before Dev
had a chance to warn her. The dog growled again, lower.
Louder.

"Where is it?" she asked, becoming a human statue beside him.

As if in answer, a large German shepherd stepped out of
the shadows. The fur on its body stood up in a line down the
center of its back. Its tan and black coat appeared more sinister
beneath the twilight sky.

"Can you talk to it?" Dev whispered from the corner of his
mouth. He inched slowly to his left, hoping Shelley would do
the same.

"I'm trying, but I don't think it's working. All I'm getting
are random images of him leaping into the air and devouring
a steak. I can't be sure, but I think *I'm* the steak in that scen-
ario," Shelley replied back. "Where are we going?"

"Into the building. If this dog is going to attack, let's make
him work for his meal."

Shelley exhaled a breath that puffed white in the chilly night air. The temperature was so cold, the hair on the back of Dev's neck stood up.

The dog whimpered then pawed the ground. Oddly, it backed into the shadows as if it had changed its mind.

Dev took Shelley by the elbow and urged her sideways up the short flight of steps to the building's front door, keeping his gaze on the shadow where the dog had gone. Dev twisted the knob and pulled open the door when the dog launched itself at the steps.

Sharp, white teeth dripping with spittle aimed for his face. Dev threw up an arm to shield himself, only to tumble backward through the open doorway. Just like that, the door slammed closed and the dog barked ferociously, throwing itself against the glass.

"Did it bite you?" Shelley, who he'd fallen on top of, squirmed out from under him. She scooted around, then bent over him, her hands sliding up his arms and chest, searching for wounds. "Are you bleeding?"

"No. How did you *pull* me inside?" Dev glanced to the door where the dog was still barking and scratching on the glass pane. Then he recognized it. "Holy shit! That's Theresa's dog."

"The door just sort of popped open, and I grabbed you." Shelley sat back on her heels, trembling. "Who's Theresa?"

"Seth's daughter." Dev sat up, dug his cell phone out of his pocket, and dialed. The moment Seth answered, Dev cut to the chase. "Seth, T's dog is down here. I think it's gone crazy or something. It tried to attack Shells and me."

"Crap! I'll send her down."

"I don't think that's a good idea." Dev argued, but was talking to static.

Above them, a door opened and slammed closed. The sound of feet pounding down the steps preceded three people—Seth, Jules, and Theresa appeared on the landing. Theresa, Seth's curly haired, brunette daughter, let a leash dangle from one hand as she stared open-mouthed out the window at her dog attempting to claw its way inside.

"Wait," Shelley said, rising to her feet. "I think it's me. Give him two minutes after I leave, and I'm sure he'll be fine."

"What's going on?" Theresa asked, confusion all over her

face. "I'm so sorry. He got out. He's never attacked anyone before. Are y'all hurt?"

"No, T. Everyone's okay."

Shelley turned to the girl, apology written all over her face. "Look, Theresa, I didn't do anything to your dog. I think I scare him for some reason. I'm positive once I'm out of sight, he'll be back to normal. Is there a back door out of this place?"

"You're not going outside until the dog is on a leash," Dev said, afraid Shelley might just sneak out through a window if she couldn't find a door.

"Dev—" Shelley began to protest but Jules cut her off.

"Dev's right, Shelley. Come with me. We'll let Theresa and the guys sort this out."

Shelley nibbled on her lip as if uncertain, but allowed her sister to lead her up the stairs.

"What the hell happened?" Seth asked.

"I'm not sure. Shells got out of my car and the dog was there. It just sort of, uh, lost it." Dev tried to explain without getting into too many details. He wasn't sure how much Theresa knew about her father's fiancée or their inherited family crifts.

Outside, the dog stopped barking and sat down on the stoop.

Theresa glanced at Dev, then at her father, then up the stairs, then back at the animal. "Do you think it's safe?"

"She said wait two minutes. Let's do that." Dev scrubbed a hand through his hair. It was going to be an interesting dinner.

"DOES THAT HAPPEN to you often?" Jules asked as she led Shelley into an apartment on the second floor. It was sparsely furnished but clean and neat. On the wall over the fireplace hung a picture of a blond Jules and two other people.

"It's not usually that bad," Shelley admitted, stepping nearer to examine the painting more closely. Upon inspection, she realized it wasn't a painting at all, but a photograph on canvas.

They looked like the perfect family. Happy.

"That's Big Jim and April," Jules said, moving to stand beside her. "I was big into my assimilation phase back then. You know, I wanted to look like them. I even wore colored contacts. Danged things got caught in my eye one night, and I had to go to the ER to get one of them removed."

"Ouch." Shelley glanced at her sister, whose hair was so like her own. "Decided to go back to your natural color?"

"Yeah. That phase didn't last long." Jules turned and cocked her head. "Did you go through that too?"

"What?"

"The assimilation phase? Where you wanted to look like your adoptive parents?"

Shelley didn't miss the odd note in Jules's voice. What was she digging for?

"Not really. Jill and Nate, my adoptive parents, already had red hair. People just assumed I was theirs. Plus, we moved to Baltimore not long after the adoption, so no one ever knew I wasn't theirs unless we told them."

Jules nodded her head slowly, then led the way into her kitchen. With a wrought-iron, glass-topped table pushed to one side of the room, there was space to move around, despite the small size. "Want a drink?"

The apartment smelled vaguely of strawberries, but no spices. Where was the dinner Dev had mentioned? "Sure. Got any apple juice? Jules, are we eating out?"

Jules pulled a bottle of juice from the fridge and poured it into two glasses before returning it to the refrigerator. Handing Shelley the wineglass full of apple juice, Jules said, "No, we're eating across the hall. I'm not sure where they're going to put the dog yet, and Theresa left her purse in Seth's apartment."

Shelley scratched her head in confusion. "You two don't live together? The way Dev talked, I thought you did."

"Oh, we do. But I'm still the legal tenant of this place for another year. I'd just signed the lease when I met Seth."

"How long have you been together?" Shelley asked, sipping her drink.

"We met in October."

Shelley nearly choked on her juice, coughing at the ridiculously short time before they decided to move in together, let alone get engaged. Jules pounded on Shelley's back until she stopped coughing.

"Isn't . . . isn't that a little fast?" Shelley wheezed.

Jules laughed. "You'd think so, wouldn't you? But if you'd been here, you'd understand. Some people are together their whole lives and never know each other. Others meet and boom . . . instant connection. Seth and I are the latter. Plus, he knows all about my crift and other weirdness and is okay with it."

"I assume you mean the ghosts. You still see ghosts, right?"

"I do. It's not like when we were kids, though. I've started to learn how to better deal with the crift. I'm even assisting lost spirits now. Not long after Seth and I met, I helped him with a case. So it's good, a lot less of a curse than it used to be." Jules smiled. *Maybe.*

"What other weirdness?" Shelley had to know. "What could be stranger than seeing ghosts . . . besides talking to animals?"

"You'd be surprised." Jules laughed, leading the way back to her living room. She settled on one side of an overstuffed beige couch and patted the seat next to her. "Let's just say, Seth can't hide his moods from me."

Sitting down on the comfy sofa, Shelley frowned in confusion. "I don't think I understand. You mean, you make him talk? Or did you develop telepathy over the years?"

"Gosh, no!" Jules shivered. "The last thing I want is to hear anyone else's thoughts. Hearing the dead is bad enough to keep me awake some nights. No, what I mean is I can see his aura, so I know his mood."

Shelley frowned. "Come again?"

Now it was Jules's turn to frown. "Do you know what an aura is?"

"Charisma?" Shelley said, fairly certain that was the wrong answer.

"Think of auras like they're lines of color. Each color represents a different emotion. For example, the color red respresents passion. Passion in the most positive sense is love. But the negative is hate. A green aura can mean someone is at peace or is incredibly jealous. Blue is intuitive or despairing. Yellow is hopeful or afraid. Instead of seeing colored lines, I see them around Seth. Although, I've never seen yellow around him. Mostly, he's red or green. Loving and protective. Darn, I'm not sure I'm explaining this well."

Oh, Jules explained it well enough.

"I think I got the idea. This aura, does it pulse like a heartbeat around his body?"

Jules's eyes widened, and she set her juice glass down on the table. "Can you see his aura too? Seth's the only living person I can do that with. Can you do it with other people?"

"Yes . . . well, no. Not exactly." Shelley rubbed her forehead. "It just started yesterday. Or maybe it's nothing. I might just be imagining things."

Jules blew a raspberry at her. "You don't believe that. *I* don't believe that. You asked a specific question because I think you can see auras." She frowned and said more to herself than to Shelley, "Dang, I thought that was special."

"You thought what was special?"

"Seeing Seth's aura. But if you can do it too." She shook her head. "I guess it doesn't mean what I thought it did."

"I can't." When Jules didn't look relieved, Shelley added, "I can't see *Seth's* aura. I see Dev's."

Jules's eyes sparkled and her lips twitched. "You see Dev's? And this just started? You never saw it when you were in college?"

"How did you know we went to school together?" Shelley asked, then answered her own question. "Dev told you." She exhaled slowly and ran a hand through her hair, only to snag it in her ponytail. She searched her memory. "I don't remember seeing any weird lights around him back then. Except . . ."

"Except what?" Jules urged when Shelley didn't immediately continue.

Shelley took another swallow of juice, stalling for time and trying to sort out her memories. "I thought I saw something the first time I met Dev."

"Really?"

"Don't look at me like that. It's not what you think. I was Dev's tutor. He was late for his first session with me. I waited for him for close to half an hour. It was cold and the sun had gone down. I got this creepy feeling I was being watched. I tried to call Dev from my cell, but the school was notorious for dead cell zones.

"Next thing I know, I'm knocked to the ground. Some guy is ripping my backpack off my shoulder. I tried to scream, but the guy slammed my face into the cement. I saw stars and thought I was dead. Suddenly he was off me and running away. With my backpack. When I looked up, I saw—"

"Dev?" Jules asked, a wide grin on her face.

"No. Cam, my ex-fiancé. Although he was a stranger at the time."

Jules's smile dissolved. "What does this have to do with Dev?"

"Dev's roommate, Cam, saw the attack and scared away the mugger. Turns out, Dev called him to tell me he was running late. They had a big football game coming up, so Dev had stayed late for extra practice. Anyway, Cam was escorting me back to my dorm room, when Dev caught up with us. At first, I didn't see anything, but then Dev caught sight of the bruise over my right eye, and I don't know. He seemed to . . . this is going to sound nuts but . . . *radiate a green glow*. It pulsed like it was coming from the center of his chest. Until you mentioned seeing Seth's, whatchamacallit, aura, I thought it was just stress. My eyes playing tricks on me."

"No, it's definitely real. You described what I've seen with Seth." Jules patted her arm. "Just another Scott family crift."

Shelley smiled at the use of the surname they'd been born with . . . Scott.

Muffled voices floated in from the hallway. Seth popped his head in. He glanced around until his gaze landed on Jules. A slow, contented smile slid across his face.

"Hi, Precious. T's taken the dog home. She said not to wait dinner on her. Would you two like a little more time, or do you want to eat now?" He gestured across the hall with a nod.

Jules glanced back at Shelley, question in her eyes. She didn't need telepathy to know her sister was asking if she wanted to eat. Shelley nodded.

"We're starved," Jules said, then hopped up from the couch.

Shelley followed them into the hall and found Dev waiting for her. No green glow. No glow at all, but still as sexy as ever. He draped an arm around her waist and whispered into her ear, "Want to fluster Seth? Ask him how he met Jules. It makes for great dinner conversation."

CHAPTER 17

"A HOOKER?" SHELLEY didn't mean to laugh, she really
didn't. But she couldn't help herself. The idea of her
prim and proper big sister in a leather skirt and bustier sneaking into a cop's bedroom in the middle of the night was hilarious. Catching her breath, Shelley said, "Come on! You
climbed into his bedroom dressed as a prostitute?"

Across the little round table, Dev snickered then shoved a
forkful of lasagna into his mouth while Seth glared at him and
muttered, "Thanks, Jones. I guess I should be grateful you
didn't tell everyone at the station too."

Seth's eyes rounded and his mouth gaped. "Ah, crap. You
didn't. Right?"

"Holy Toledo, Seth, it was a costume," Jules said, her face
pink, and her green eyes sparkling with humor.

"Yes, but if Gareth had seen you that night, you probably
wouldn't be sitting here today." Seth touched Jules's cheek as
if to reassure himself.

Tension replaced the humor in the room.

"Who's Gareth?" Shelley asked at the silence that had
redefined deafening.

"He was a police officer—" Jules began.

"No, he was a bastard dirty cop who murdered a woman dressed exactly like you, then went after you too," Seth corrected.

Jules laid a hand on his and said quietly, "But he didn't. I'm fine."

Seth exhaled a hard breath, then cast Jules a weary grin. He kissed her on the temple. "I know, Precious. I know."

Dev leaned close to Shelley and said in a low, rushed voice, "Gareth had been a police officer until October. We didn't know he was behind a string of jewelry thefts until he started killing people. One of his victims was a woman. Before she died, she'd accidentally switched purses with your sister. Stolen diamonds were sewn into the lining. Gareth realized it and went after Jules."

Shelley glanced at Jules who nibbled on what was left of her dinner. Her sister had been in the sights of a murderer? A shiver went down Shelley's back so fast, she shuddered.

"If it hadn't been for the ghosts, he might have killed me," Jules said. "But they kept sending warnings . . . messages. Finally, the dead woman, Aimee-Lynn, told me where to find the diamonds and what to do with them. Dev here played a big part in helping to catch that psycho."

"Dev did?" Shelley expected Jules to name Seth, not Dev.

"Yeah." Seth nodded grimly. "If he hadn't convinced me to stop wearing my ass for a hat, and believe in Jules's abilities, I might have lost her forever."

Seth's watch beeped. Jules hopped up and shuffled into the bedroom. She returned moments later with Callie the kitten and handed her to Seth.

"Your turn to feed her," Jules said with a grin.

The kitten meowed loudly. "Ooh, that's a good sign," Shelley said. "Despite the way we found her, she's strong. Her lungs are definitely working."

"I noticed that when I got home from work." Seth rubbed the kitten on her patchwork head. She closed her eyes and purred.

"Is T coming back?" Dev asked, glancing around.

"No. She decided to stay at her place when Jiovanni called," Jules said, returning to the table with the filled bottle. She handed it to Seth. "Theresa's still trying to convince Seth that she's ready to get married."

Propping the kitten on the table and cupping his hand over her little body to keep her from falling, Seth gently inserted the nipple into the kitten's mouth. Once the kitten started to drink, Seth said, "She's only nineteen, Juliana. I don't care if she's mad at me. She's too young to get married."

Jules held her hands up. "I'm not arguing with you. I just think you two need to talk about it. Calmly."

Dev caught Shelley's eye and winked. That one little gesture did crazy things to her heart. And when he reached out and took her hand in his, the organ previously known to pump blood through her body did somersaults in her chest.

Oh, she shouldn't let herself get close to these people, especially Dev. She didn't belong here. Not really. And yet . . .

"Don't you agree, Shelley?"

Shelley tore her gaze from Dev's handsome smile and stared blankly at her sister. *Her* sister. The idea that they were really together again was still hard to process.

Jules frowned at her. "Shel? You all right?"

She was about to say yes, when the temperature dropped. She shivered and glanced around. Dev rubbed his arms through the sleeves of his navy crew neck. Seth stared at Jules, who'd gone pale.

Her eyes were open and staring blankly at Shelley, or maybe through her.

Shelley had the distinct impression that Jules didn't really see her.

"Juliana?" How could Seth load so much love and concern into a single word? He turned to Dev, handing him the bottle. "Jones, take Callie."

Seth slid out of his seat and squatted next to Jules. Dev shifted and took the vacated spot, so as not to disturb the kitten.

Shelley, unable to sit idly by, knelt next to her sister. There was something familiar about touching Jules's hand during a vision. She didn't have time to think about it long before Jules snapped out of it. Or rather, slumped against Seth's shoulder.

A ripple of fear went through Shelley. "Is she unconscious?"

Seth and Dev wore matching frowns.

"Yes, don't worry," Seth said. "She does this sometimes after a vision. Haven't you seen her do this before?"

That was what was familiar. Shelley *had* seen Jules go into a trance before. Not long before Shelley was adopted. "Once."

"Oh, this is typical. She'll be all right in a few minutes. She'll probably be tired," Seth said, picking Jules up from the chair and carrying her into the bedroom.

Uncertain what to do, Shelley cleared the dishes from the table and washed them in the sink while Dev continued to feed Callie.

The urge to run back to Elkridge hit her squarely in the midsection. In Elkridge, the animals needed her, and she had a purpose. There in that little town, she was safe. She was needed, but *she* didn't need anyone. One afternoon with Jules and Shelley's need for her older sister sprang to life again. It was too easy to fit in, here in Tidewater. Too easy to fall prey to the false sense of actually belonging to a family.

Shelley scrubbed the plates with more force than necessary and reminded herself to keep her expression neutral. God, she was being irrational. But she couldn't shake the feeling that the joy she felt—and frack it all, she *did* feel it so much her eyes misted—could all end without warning. Then what would she be but an empty husk of who she'd been before? She couldn't do that. She couldn't wait for fate or Jules or even God to decide she should be alone again. Shelley, and only Shelley, had to be the one to make that decision.

Seth appeared in the open bedroom door without Jules. His face showed concern but not fear.

"How's she doing?" Dev asked.

"She's out." Seth quietly closed the door behind him then reached for the kitten. Well-fed and sleepy, Callie snuggled against his chest. "It's been a crazy week. One of our neighbors fell and broke her wrist. Jules has been running meals over there every morning and every night. The shop's had extended hours because of the holiday rush. Everyone in Tidewater wants one of Jules's handmade wreaths. She hasn't had much sleep. Until tonight, she hadn't had a vision in a while. I guess with everything, it just wore her out."

Seth absently ran a finger down Callie's spine, then glanced around his kitchen. "Shelley, you didn't have to clean up."

"I didn't mind." Shelley stepped closer to Seth and rubbed

Callie between the ears. "Did she say what the vision was about?"

"No." Seth sighed. "This one hit her hard. Sometimes they make her physically ill. Others knock her out. This was the latter. My guess is she'll sleep until morning." He gave Shelley a wan smile. "I'm sorry. I know she was really excited to spend time with you. But how about we try this again tomorrow night?"

Shelley smiled, unsure how to answer. She didn't want to still be in Tidewater tomorrow. "Maybe we can reschedule? I really need to get back to Elkridge. The animals are counting on me."

"You're not staying for the weekend?" Seth cast a curious glance to Dev, then back at her.

"No, I don't think I can. Like I said, the animals need me." Shelley glanced at her watch. Frack! It was after eleven. She couldn't ask Dev to drive the hour and a half back to Elkridge tonight. And he *had* asked her to stay. "On second thought, why don't you bring Jules by in the morning? We can do breakfast. Right, Dev?"

"Absolutely." There was no missing the relief on his face or in his stormy eyes.

Oh yeah, she could definitely delay her trip home by a night, especially if Dev kept looking at her like that. Maybe they could try out his Jacuzzi . . . naked?

Seth cleared his throat.

Heat whooshed up her cheeks. Dev winked.

"Shelley, you talk to animals, right?" Seth asked.

"Well, not as much as they communicate with me," she replied, trying to pretend she hadn't just been imagining Seth's partner naked.

"So what happened with T's dog earlier? Couldn't you talk to it?"

"Well, dogs are special. They um . . . don't always want to communicate with me." She smiled, but Seth didn't return the grin.

"So you talk to all animals *except* dogs?"

"Sounds crazy, right?"

"No crazier than my fiancée talking to ghosts. Sounds like your crift comes with limitations, like Juliana's." Seth shrugged. "So maybe your crift isn't as much of a curse?"

"No, talking to animals has been the one thing that's kept me from being lonely all these years."

Frack! Why did I say that? Looking for an excuse to end the conversation, Shelley spotted a dirty glass she'd missed earlier, swept it up from the counter, and headed to the sink to wash it.

Dev, as if sensing her discomfort, said, "Seth, you were going to lend me the files to review tonight. Can I get them?"

"Sure, hang on." Seth disappeared back into his bedroom with Callie. He returned moments later without the kitten, but with two thick manila folders in his arms. He handed them to Dev. "I'll pick them up when Jules and I swing by for breakfast."

"Sounds good." Dev tossed an arm around Shelley's waist and guided her toward the door.

Seth cast her a big grin. "Great. Well, get some rest, you two. And for God's sake stay away from big dogs."

SHELLEY DIDN'T SAY a word all the way back to Dev's place. And damn, it was starting to make him nervous. He'd escorted her to her room, where she'd promptly said good-night and closed the door. An hour had gone by, and she still had her light on.

Not that he was stalking her room or anything. He'd just noticed the light shining underneath the door when he'd gone downstairs to check the security system. And when he'd gone to make sure the coffeepot was set for the morning. And when he'd slipped down to get a glass of wine because he couldn't sleep.

So now he stood in his bedroom, a half bottle of wine and a full glass, both untouched. Thinking. About Shells.

Her little speech about being needed back in Elkridge didn't sit well with him. Okay, yes, she'd asked him to come to the little town to help her with some mystery of disappearing animals. But the sheriff's office was investigating now. She didn't *need* to be there.

He would've thought it was all out of her hands, except for the files she said she'd had only yesterday. Proof that tracked at least six months' worth of strange happenings at the zoo. Proof that had suddenly vanished. Crap, she probably was needed back in the Elk-less Ridge. Which meant Dev was being a prick by not helping her solve her mystery. Well, he'd fix that right now.

He yanked open his door, only to find Shelley there, fist in the air as if about to knock. She wore a pair of plaid sleep pants and a faded black T-shirt with the words Vets Do It Doggie-Style. She held a yellow legal pad in her hands.

"Hi," he said, then could have kicked himself for not just kissing her, because she backed up two paces and lowered her hand to her side.

"Sorry to bother you, Dev, but I noticed your light was still on." She licked her lips then pressed them together. "I need you to promise that you'll take me back to Elkridge tomorrow. I can't sleep, because I know something's really wrong at the zoo. I think it goes beyond the missing cubs. Plus, I still can't reach Tomás. I want to check on Beau too."

"You're right," he said when she paused.

"I know my proof vanished . . ." She continued as if she hadn't heard him at first, then frowned. "What did you say?"

"I said you're right. The animals need you. And I promised to help. I was just coming over to talk to you about it." He opened the door wider and gestured for her to come in. "But since you're here, why don't we talk in my room?"

The smile on her face was dazzling, and it warmed him. More than warmed him. Made him damn hot. But she wasn't sidling into his bedroom so she could fulfill his fantasies. Or even part of his fantasies.

Closing the door behind her, Dev waited to see where she'd sit. His bedroom was twice the size of hers. It had a small round table with two leather-padded desk chairs near the sliding glass door. There was of course, his king-size bed, which she promptly walked straight past to get to the chairs.

Damn shame.

While she sat down, he opened the slider a crack to let some fresh air flow. The sound of ocean waves rolling against the shore and the scent of the cool, salty night air washed through the room.

Dev clicked on the small lantern-style lamp on the table and turned off the overhead lighting, reducing the glare in the room. He hadn't done it for the romantic effect, but Shells, bathed in the combination of moonlight and the soft light of the lamp, was definitely erotic.

He claimed the chair across the table from her and waited.

Shelley bent her head sideways, revealing her long swan-like neck.

Swanlike neck? Since when do necks turn me on?

She smiled at him.

Oh, now.

The combination of her innocently seductive smile and her silky throat did a number of things to his cock, not the least of which was making it go rock hard.

"So." He cleared his throat. "Did you work on your notes this afternoon? Think of anything new?"

"I was kind of distracted helping Jules. But I did think of something just now." She set the pad she'd brought into the room on the table and pushed it toward him. "While writing down what I'd seen at the zoo, it hit me. Yesterday, Cristos told you that Miah ate one of her cubs. That was completely untrue. Miah never harmed a single one of her cubs."

"You sound pretty certain." He searched the table for his own notepad before realizing he had left it and the pen on his nightstand. He crossed the room, collected them and the wine bottle and glasses, then sat back down. "How can you be so sure?"

"Do you normally keep wineglasses in your bedroom?" Shelley stared pointedly at the stemware, red brows arched.

"Not really. I brought up a glass and the bottle tonight before remembering I'd left one in here from a few nights ago. I fell asleep before I had a drink." When she continued to stare at him with a dubious expression, he tapped on her yellow college-ruled paper with his pen. "You were telling me you were certain Miah didn't eat her young."

Shelley's brow relaxed. "Right. Well, Miah's a tiger, isn't she?"

"Yes, she's a tiger, but I don't see how that explains anything."

"Lying is a human condition," Shelley said, eyeing the wine bottle. He couldn't tell if she wanted some or wanted it to go away. Curious, he pushed it closer to her. Shelley paused for three heartbeats, lifted the bottle, and poured herself a glass. Taking a hearty sip, she grinned. "Heaven."

"I thought you didn't drink?"

"Not as a rule. But my migraine's gone and after today . . .

Well, a good wine is worth a slight dulling of animal-empath senses from time to time." She grinned and sipped again.

Dev picked up his own glass and drank. "You were saying about tigers?"

"Huh?" Shelley blinked then nodded. "Lying is a human condition. People lie to each other all the time. They lie to themselves more. Animals do not. When a dog steals food off the kitchen table, it might cower and hide from its owner, but it doesn't deny the theft. And the monkeys on St. Kitts in the Caribbean might take your beer and drink it, but they don't pretend they're not drunk. It's only humans who lie."

She stared at him earnestly; her wide guileless blue eyes looked at him imploringly. And he wanted to follow her train of thought but hadn't made the connection yet. "So some people lie."

"Not some. *All* people lie. Animals do not." Shelley took another mouthful of wine and said, "Animals are incapable of telling a lie. They see the world for what it is, be it dangerous, beautiful, or deadly. And when they communicate with me, they wing images into my mind. Sometimes I have to figure out what they mean because an animal cannot reference what it has never seen. Still, what they tell me or show me through their mental pictures can only be the truth."

"Okay, some humans lie. Not *all*, but we'll save that discussion for later." Dev held up his hand when Shelley opened her mouth, presumably to argue. "You mentioned that Cristos was wrong about Miah killing her first litter. Why do you believe that?"

"Because I asked Miah about it when I first heard the rumors," Shelley said, as if that alone would satisfy his curiosity.

"And?"

Shelley took a swig of wine, downing half the glass. She set the stemware back on the table. "When I asked her about the first cub, her memories were fuzzy, which was really odd. Tigers have better memories than humans. She should have remembered everything clearly, but she didn't. The images she sent were scattered and blurry, like looking at an old photograph through a dirty pane of glass.

"I think she was drugged. I can't prove it, unfortunately.

But it makes the most sense. If she were drugged, even for sedation purposes, her memory could be impaired. Hazy. Plus, this happened at night. Dr. Kessler wouldn't have done anything with her in the middle of the night. Not without documenting it somewhere. His memory has holes, but he wasn't nearly as confused then as he is today. I told you he hired me in part to help at the zoo? Well, I think he suspected something was wrong but didn't trust his memory."

Interesting. Dev jotted down notes about the vet and the tiger. "Have you noticed any change in the animals since you've been in Elkridge?"

"Yeah." Shelley gave him a small smile. "It's been better. I've been keeping a closer eye, not just on Miah but on all the animals in the zoo. And then there's Reyna."

"The zoo owner's daughter?"

"According to the town gossip, before her mother died last year, Reyna hadn't set foot in the zoo in two years. Now she's there all the time, but makes no effort to hide her hatred of the zoo or the town."

"Really?" Dev jotted that down on his notepad.

"Yep. Rumor mill claims she ran off to New York right out of high school. Left Payne Munro behind so she could be an actress or something. Anyway, she returned for her mother's funeral last year. Eddy talked her into staying in town. Reyna took back up with Payne—except for those few days when he'd asked me out.

"Folks say that Eddy built the zoo for his wife. Those animals meant more to her than her own children."

"Nice." Dev penned that note too. "So what—Eddy just stopped caring for his wife's animals after she died?"

Shelley frowned, setting the glass down. "No, the way I heard it, he fell apart. They say he *was* a recovering alcoholic. When a drunk driver killed his wife, Eddy fell off the wagon into a fifth of whiskey. He hasn't come out of the bottle yet."

So would that drive the man to slowly get rid of his wife's animals one by one? Could be motive. Or it could potentially clear him if he were simply too drunk to commit the crimes.

Dev sipped his wine and noted his questions on his pad. He glanced up to find Shelley trying to read his paper upside down.

"Honestly, I don't think Eddy could do anything to the

animals, not intentionally," she said. "When Cristos left the tortoise cage partially open and one got its head wedged in the chain-link fence, Eddy cried in relief when—after I put eight stitches in the reptile's neck—I told him the tortoise would be okay."

"I won't take him off my list yet, but I will move him to the bottom of the list of probable suspects." Dev put a star next to Eddy's name. "Do you think Cristos left the gate open intentionally?"

She shrugged. "I don't think he cares enough about the zoo to want to harm the animals. But I could see him trying to sell them. He's always looking for an easy paycheck. Since I've known him, he's had six jobs, lost every one, opened a failed e-Bay store to sell zoo merchandise, and even tried to start a zoo-friend hotline."

Dev paused in his note-taking and glanced up. "Zoo-friend hotline?"

"For the incredibly cheap price of $29.95, you too can have Miah the tiger call your son or daughter and wish them a happy birthday in tiger-ese." She rolled her eyes. "He spent God knows how much money on advertising and didn't make ten dollars."

"How would you know what the tiger was saying in tiger-ese?" Dev asked, then amended. "Okay, you would know, but how would the rest of us know?"

"Ding, ding, ding. People in town asked the same question. And he didn't even bother to use a real tiger voice. The one person who called said it was obviously Cristos on the other end."

Dev shook his head and reviewed his notes. "Back to Reyna. What else can you tell me about her?"

"Not much. She's into shoes, Deputy Munro, and hates the zoo, the town, and me in equal measure."

"Would you say she hates the zoo enough to make the animals disappear?"

Shells tapped her chin with her finger. She had the most adorable little dimple there. The kind that begged to be licked.

"No, that would require Reyna to get her hands dirty," Shelley said, unaware he'd been fantasizing about using his tongue to trace the indent in her chin. Dev shifted slightly in his seat to hide his growing erection.

"Or getting someone else to do it. Since she's finally wrangled an engagement ring out of Deputy Munro, I don't see her risking her relationship on a few tigers."

Dev glanced at his notes again. So far they'd discussed the owner, his children, and the deputy. "What about the other staff members at the zoo? Tomás, for instance."

Shelley went very still. Slowly, she said, "Tomás would never hurt Miah or her cubs. I know it looked like he was on Reyna's side, but he's got his hands full with Beau. Nope, he couldn't have had anything to do with what's wrong in zooville."

"Are you sure? Selling tigers on the black market could definitely help him financially. Having kids is expensive."

Shells shook her head vehemently. "Nope. You're wrong. It's not Tomás. He was the one who alerted me to the situation at the zoo in the first place. My first day there, he showed me into the reptile house so I could see how overcrowded it was. He also told me about his suspicions that Miah had been drugged around the time her first cub died."

"Tomás told *you*? Why didn't he go to Dr. Kessler or the USDA himself? Why did he wait for you to do something?" Dev set his pen on the pad and folded his hands.

Shelley's pink tongue peeked out between her teeth and moistened her lower lip. "He couldn't. He told the first person he trusted what he thought was happening. Me. Tomás didn't go to the authorities, because he didn't want to risk losing his job. He's trying to gain legal custody of Beau."

"You told me that." And wasn't that a fucked story. Man's trying to adopt his own kid. "Why should that stop him from getting custody?"

"Tomás is afraid if he doesn't do what Reyna says, she'll have him fired. She's already had the former zoo manager and two other caretakers booted in the past five months. If he loses his job, he could lose his petition to gain custody of Beau. So you can see why he wouldn't want to risk it."

Dev picked his pen back up. "Understood. As long as he has nothing to do with the missing animals, I see no reason to make trouble for him or Beau. The kid seemed sweet."

"He is." She nodded. "Thank you, Dev. Now about the zoo. Most of the people in the town barely go there anymore. So I can't think of anyone else who would come into contact with the animals on a regular basis. If you want to know about the animals, though, I can tell you lots."

Sure, why not. "Okay, start with the tigress. What did Miah tell you about her cubs?"

"I thought I was never going to get to tell you." Shelley's entire face lit. "She showed me pictures of her looking at the cubs. I think she heard a noise because she stared at the front door of the tiger house before getting up to investigate. She stepped outside and she jolted. Like something struck her in the neck or the side. She went back to sit with her cubs, all *five* of them. The smallest, Shanti, was hungry and wanted to nurse again. She cleaned him as he fed while his brothers and sisters slept. When he'd finished, she tried to stand but nearly fell on her cubs. The room spun and went dark. She kept trying to lift her lids, but all I saw were hazy shadows. Ooh, right before she fell, she pawed at her nose like she smelled something."

"Can't you identify the scent?"

"No, only sights translate to my head. Think Charlie Chaplin and silent movies." She pretended to stab an invisible dinner roll with her pen and make it dance.

Dev grinned at her impression of the classic Chaplin move. "Go on. So you can't hear or smell what the animals do. Only see what they see." He paused then asked, "Does that mean you only see the images in black and white?"

She nodded. "If those are the only colors the animals see, then yes. Lucy sees three colors—black, white, and red. But tigers can also see green, blue, and sometimes red—when Miah sends me a mental picture, it's pretty vivid."

"What happened next?" Dev glanced to see what he'd last jotted down. "You said the room started to spin and get dark."

"Right," she said, tapping that dimple on her chin again. "The next thing Miah saw was sunlight. Shanti was gone and so was Anna, one of the girls. Miah searched all over the house, then the yard. She saw Cristos and Eddy coming up the trail and Tomás down by the monkey house. And . . . that's it."

"You're sure. She didn't see who came into the tiger house and stole her cubs?" Dev asked, penning the last of the notes. When Shelley didn't answer him, he glanced up.

"Please tell me you believe me. I can't exactly go to Deputy Munro with this. Everyone in town agrees I'm gifted with animals, but I don't think they'd be quite so keen on me if they knew the animals could actually communicate with me." Her eyes were warm and her cheeks flushed. A brilliant smile seemed to light her from within. "I mean, people do lots of things in front of their pets, like hide money and jewelry, meet with illicit lovers, surf porn."

"Whoa, the animals tell you all that at the clinic?"

"You have no idea. Like I said, animals don't lie. I once asked a cat how his leg got hurt, and he told me his mistress's lover tripped over him as he snuck out the back door when her husband came home."

"Yeah, I can see why you wouldn't want folks in your town to know their secrets aren't safe. Could be bad for business."

"True." She nodded. "Did I give you enough information? I can't think of anything else."

"It's not a lot to go on. Certainly nothing I could take to the sheriff's office. And I feel the need to remind you here, that Deputy Munro was working on the case when we left town. So there is an investigation in progress. I have to be careful not to step on any toes. Elkridge isn't my jurisdiction. But, I think when we go back there tomorrow, we have a couple of places to start looking for information. Strictly off the record. Anything we uncover that can be proven beyond what a tiger, monkey, or lizard saw, we'll share with the sheriff's office, deal?"

"You do *believe* me?" she repeated, rising slowly from her chair.

Dev stood too. "Of course, Shells. I believe you."

"Yes!" She launched herself at him.

Dev was glad he was standing and could catch her. Her arms went around his neck and she rained kisses over his cheeks interspersed with the words, *thank you, thank you, thank you.*

Dev's body shook with laughter as he hugged her. Damn, she was the perfect shape. Her body molded to his like God had designed her especially for this moment. For him to hold her in his arms while she covered his face in butterfly-soft kisses.

"I knew I was right to contact you," she said, breathless, still hugging him. She'd stopped kissing him and was currently squeezing him against her. "I knew I could count on you."

"We might not be able to prove anything," he warned.

She tilted her head back to look at him. The fierce determination in her eyes told him she wasn't about to give up until she found those cubs. "We'll find them. Between my Dolittle qualities and your incredibly Monk-like ability to solve any mystery, we *will* find them."

"Shells," he said, wanting to prepare her for the fact that even when people go missing, they aren't always found. And with tiger cubs, it could be next to impossible to locate them. But when he opened his mouth, she kissed him. A full-bodied, tonsil-dueling, soul-sucking kiss. And if he'd thought the kisses they'd shared earlier had been incredible, this one melted his socks off.

Or would have, if he'd been wearing any.

Her slender fingers buried in his hair and tugged him down closer to her. She moaned in his mouth and he captured the sound. Her voluptuous breasts were unrestrained beneath her T-shirt. Her pebble-tight nipples rubbed against his chest. And God in heaven, he wanted to taste them. To bury his face between them and spend hours just licking her, pleasing her, tempting her.

And okay, he wasn't a saint . . . or a monk, he wanted to dissolve in the pleasure too. The bed was just a few feet away. But what if this amazing kiss was only her getting swept away by the moment?

As if in answer to his inner musing and in answer to one of his oldest prayers, Shelley reached between them and cupped him in one hand.

He groaned as she stroked him through his pajama bottoms. Not wanting her to stop, he ratcheted up the kiss.

Normally, he held back with his lovers. He was so big, he worried he would scare them if he let loose his passion. Shells wasn't scared by the intensity. She kissed him as if to say, "I'll see that fire and raise you to a solar blast."

God, she was everything he'd ever imagined. Sexy, soft, and hungry for him. He wanted to do this right. Take it slow. Show her how much she meant to him. How much she'd *always* meant to him.

She slid her cool, slender fingers inside his pajama bottoms and he hissed in pleasure. Fuck slow. At this rate, he'd be lucky if they made it to the bed.

"Shells," he said, breaking the kiss and wrapping a hand around her delicate wrist. "Slow down."

She nipped his chin. "Not a chance."

She reached for him again. His cock jumped, eager for her caress. Luckily, Dev's brain was still engaged. He twisted his hips away from her.

"You're not going to tell me you're shy, are you?" Shelley laughed, trailing her fingers up his chest beneath his shirt.

He laughed too, chills covering his body at her touch. "God, no. I've just been imagining you in my bed for the past two days. I don't want to rush it."

Shelley froze, her intense blue eyes wide. "Really?"

"Hell, yes!"

With his hands on her hips, Dev walked her backward until her knees hit the edge of his bed. She fell back and Dev leaned over her, supporting his weight on his hands beside her shoulders.

Damn, the woman epitomized sexy. Not cover-model-starve-yourself-waif perfection. No, Shelley was a real woman, incredible curves, soft skin, and the most beautiful blue eyes he'd ever seen.

"I've wanted you in this bed from the moment you bent over me in the street." He loved the way her eyes softened at his words. Like she was melting for him. Only fair. He'd melted for her long ago. "I've wanted you in *my* bed since the first time you tutored me in college."

She frowned at him now. "But you set me up with Cam?"

Fucking brilliant! He'd made her think of her ex.

Dev rolled to her right side and propped his head up on his fist. "I didn't set you up with Cam. I was running late and asked him to tell you."

Realization dawned on her face. "Oh, and he arrived as I was getting mugged."

Dev didn't flinch at her statement. He should have been there to protect her. Instead, Cam the asshole had been her hero. Her lover.

"So why didn't you ever ask me out?" Shelley rolled onto her side and mirrored his pose.

"You were with Cam after that," he answered honestly.

Shelley bent her knee and rubbed her calf against his. "I'm not with him anymore."

"I see that." Dev scooted a little closer to her, so that with just the right angle, their lower bodies would touch.

She propped up on one hand and leaned over him, forcing Dev to lie back. He stared into her blue eyes, now dark with arousal. Her cloud of red hair formed a curtain around their faces. "So . . ." she whispered, sliding her right leg over his body until she straddled him. "What are you going to do about it?"

DEV DIDN'T HESITATE. One large, warm hand wrapped around the back of her neck, the other around her waist and he kissed her with so much ferocity, Shelley wondered if he wasn't trying to suck out her soul. Oh, fracking God, the man could kiss.

He tugged her tightly against his body, threw his leg around her hips and in one deft move, he flipped them over until Shelley was between the black Egyptian cotton bedspread and Dev's rock-hard body.

And still he kissed her. Dev wasn't a run-the-show kind of lover either. He moaned in pleasure as she met him stroke for stroke.

Dev plucked her right nipple through her thin sleepshirt until the pleasure of it bordered on pain. Then he switched to the other. All the time never breaking that soul-searing kiss.

Too many clothes.

Shelley tugged the hem of Dev's tee up his back and ran her hands over his smooth light-mocha skin. God, the man was so cut, he even had well-defined back muscles. She delighted in gliding her fingers over his narrow hips and up his back, but she kept running into his bunched-up shirt.

She headed south, feeling his tight butt through the cotton pants; she gave it a gentle squeeze. Dev moaned into her mouth and ground himself against her.

More. She needed more. Her knees fell apart until Dev was grinding himself, through their clothes, at her core. Oh. Dear. God. He was huge all over. The pleasure was too much to bear. Too much to stop.

And still, they had on too many clothes. "Dev," she panted, turning her head and tugging at his T-shirt again. "Off. Take it off."

He leaned back long enough to rip it over his head and kissed her again. The man could have won an Olympic gold medal for kissing.

She shoved at his pajama bottoms until her hands came into contact with his perfect round backside. It flexed and bunched beneath her fingers. Dev arched his back and pulled his lips away from hers.

"Stop, or I'll finish before we get started," he warned. Then he bent down and lightly bit one of her nipples through her top.

It was her turn to arch her back.

He suckled her through the cotton until her aching tip pressed against the damp material, threatening to pop through it. And just like when he'd used his fingers earlier, he switched to the other breast until she had two painfully erect nipples pressing against the wet cotton of her shirt.

Dev sat back on his heels, straddling her hips, and looked down at her. The heat in his gaze made her shy. She reached to cover her damp breasts with her hands, but Dev stopped her by manacling her wrists with his own. "Don't hide. You're beautiful, Shells."

"I'm in a wet T-shirt, Dev," she pointed out.

"Best damn one I've ever judged."

She arched an eyebrow. "And how many have you judged?"

"Just one. No one on earth could be sexier than you."

"Nice line," she said, making a joke because the intensity in his stormy eyes and the sincerity in his words were too much. So beautiful that she needed to do something or risk getting all weepy with him.

"Not a line," he said, frowning slightly. Then a glimmer of something teasing lit his eyes and he gave her a cocky half grin. "But it might have been the 'Vets Do It Doggie-Style' that convinced me."

Shelley glanced down at her shirt, mortified. "Oh, frack. It was a gag gift from a lab partner for graduation."

"If it's embarrassing," he said, fingering the hem, "how about we just take it off?"

In one fluid motion, he sat her up, stripped off the top, and tossed it over his shoulder. He had her on her back again before she could blink.

And yes, God! This was even better. Skin to skin. His chest

muscles rippled against her flesh. Again, she slid her hands beneath his pajama bottoms and squeezed his perfect ass.

"More," he said, loosening the pull-string of her bottoms. "Damn, Shells, I don't know how much longer I can wait. I wanted our first time to be slow, but you've got me aching for you. I need to be inside you now."

Shelley shoved at his hips, trying to force his pants down, but only succeeded in almost knocking him off the bed. Laughing, he let go of her to step out of his clothes. She took the moment to shake her bottoms and panties down her legs.

Then Dev was gloriously naked. His cock stood proud, jutting toward her. Moisture glistened on its tip. And she wanted to taste him. She crawled across the California king-size bed and Dev climbed on it, meeting her halfway.

Lowering her head, she licked him from tip to base. Dev shuddered, clasping her shoulders. When he didn't try to stop her, she did it again. This time, swirling her tongue over the tip, licking every drop of the salty moisture, while she gently cupped his sack.

"Shells." His voice was guttural, strained. "Please."

She licked him again, trailing her tongue along the vein running down his shaft. He groaned.

"Do you like that?" she asked, already knowing the answer. She lazily tasted him. He shuddered, his fingers tightening on her shoulders. "Do you want me to do this?"

She took him completely in her mouth. She had only slid halfway down his cock when he wrenched away.

"I want to be buried deep inside you when I come."

"Do you have any condoms?" she asked, stroking a hand down his length.

"Yeah. Hang on, just let me . . ."

He opened the drawer in his end table and pulled out an accordion of individually wrapped condoms. Dev's elbow knocked into the lamp on his nightstand, knocking it to the floor.

The room darkened, but the moonlight still made it possible to see his gorgeous smile. His two front teeth were slightly crooked, but he was still the most handsome man she'd ever seen.

"Now, where were we?" he asked, covering himself, protecting them both.

"I think we were about to start a game of chess."

Dev laughed. "God, I love your sense of humor, Shells."

Then in one long, deep stroke, he pushed himself inside her, all the way to the base.

Her every nerve ending sizzled with the pleasure exploding through her. Was it possible to come that fast?

Dev withdrew slowly and . . .

Oh, hell, fracking YES.

She was unraveling from her center outward. Pleasure pinged every nerve ending from her toes to her eyelashes. Sensations crashed through her entire body. Wave after wave of passion washed through her until she didn't want it to end.

And Dev was still moving, like a man on a mission. He grinned at her, closed his eyes and continued to push harder, push her higher until she was flying.

Somehow, she reached down from the heavens and grabbed two handfuls of his perfect, naked butt. He groaned her name, was flying with her. His orgasm set off another one in her. This one so intense, when it faded to the lovely afterglow, all she could do was lie boneless beneath him. Dev, amazing man that he was, found the strength to shift his weight to one side so that he still covered her body but didn't crush her.

For several long minutes they lay together unmoving. Shelley, sated and more content than she'd been in years, didn't want to move. Ever. Again.

Dev gestured to his flagging condom-covered erection and said, "I need to take care of this."

He kissed her head and slid off the bed. Seconds later, he was back, tucking her beneath the covers.

He spooned behind her, wrapping one muscled arm over her chest.

Shells peeked an eye open and saw the tattoo encircling his bicep. "When did you get that?"

Dev mumbled something into her hair she couldn't understand.

"What?"

"Long story," he said, yawning. "Tell you tomorrow at breakfast."

"Want to go to sleep?" she asked, wide awake and seriously hoping for another round.

Dev nudged his hips against her backside and nibbled her neck. "Nah, I was thinking about taking some of that wine we have left and licking it off your body. Then making you come three or four more times before we fall asleep at dawn." He slipped a hand between her thighs and began to stroke her. He whispered into her ear, "I want you to come with me. All. Night. Long."

THE SKY WAS lightening. Shelley lay motionless in Dev's bed listening to the sounds of dawn. Seabirds sang to the sunrise. Waves crashed. Dev snored softly; each breath puffed warm air against her bare shoulder.

She'd been lying there for twenty minutes, basking in the afterglow of the night's lovemaking.

Last night with Dev had been fun. Okay, she was lying to herself. It hadn't just been fun. It was better than any fantasy she'd ever had. Would ever have.

But it couldn't last. She had a life in Elkridge, and Dev had one in Tidewater.

A sliver of unease pricked at her. She shouldn't stay here. It would be too easy for her to take this one night of amazing sex and want to make it something more.

She couldn't do that.

She wouldn't allow herself to want it. If she did, it would only end in disaster.

CHAPTER 18

ADAM COULDN'T HAVE planned this better if he had tried. Sipping his coffee at the café, he pretended to be engrossed in whatever the stupid bitch was saying. She always found her own company more enjoyable than he did. But he needed her with him this morning. He didn't trust her not to fuck up his plans again, especially since she'd just told him that she'd been the one to reset the video in the tiger cage.

Ignoring her, he watched through the large picture window at the three men arguing across the street. Dr. Morgan had parked the piece-of-shit car she owned at the very edge of the zoo parking lot two days ago. Around him, people chattered like geese. Loud, obnoxious noises that meant they had little more to do with their lives than follow whatever pattern the current leader dictated. And today, he was their leader. Too bad only he knew it.

Any second now they'd pop that trunk. It wouldn't take much. He'd barely closed it. Not bothering to latch the bungee cords, but letting them dangle. He'd hoped that nosy bitch would find the body. This was so much better. The winch creaked and whined as it lowered the hook. The old man in the Marines ball cap attached the winch to the front of her car while the two younger men piled into the front of the truck. The creaking started again.

The trunk lid flew open.

So did the old Marine's eyes. Arms flailed over his head as he gestured for the tow-truck driver to cut the engine. The two younger ones hopped out and ran to the back to see what happened.

"What's going on over there?" she asked, craning her neck for a better view. Whatever topic she'd been rambling on about was instantly forgotten. Her gaze focused entirely on the events unfolding in the parking lot. "Hey, isn't that Dr. Morgan's car?"

"Looks like." He mimicked her gawking stare. Sure enough, the geese-like patrons of the diner followed suit, watching through the window.

His pulse raced through him, sizzling in his veins like the coffee had sizzled in his throat. The rush was extraordinary. He hadn't felt that before. When he'd killed the others, there had been relief, joy, even a sense of pride.

But this man *hadn't* been on his list. The fool had gotten in the way.

Adam's entire body thrummed with excitement as he watched. His heart tripped in his chest like a jackhammer.

He might just have to change his plans and be there when the final body was discovered. Until now, he'd never expected to surpass the high he felt when executing those sadistic bastards who'd let his mother die. And he still had the main one to punish.

Hal, the restaurant owner, clearly tired of waiting, pushed open the door and yelled, "Whatcha got there, Kenny?"

The old man cupped his hands around his mouth and yelled back, "Better call the sheriff. Someone's killed Tomás."

SHELLEY AWOKE TO the incessant ringing of her cell phone. Bleary-eyed because she'd hardly slept after sneaking out of Dev's room at almost five in the morning, she tried to focus. Slapping her hand on the nightstand, her fingers collided with the noisemaker. She dragged it to her ear.

"Hello?"

"Dr. M? Did I wake you?" Jacob's too-cheerful voice

called into the phone. "It's like eight thirty. Aren't you normally on your morning run by now?"

"Jacob, you're the one who likes morning runs, not me. I don't run. Is-Is there something you need, besides checking my daily schedule?" She tried not to grouse into the phone, but it was hard. Man, she needed about five more hours of sleep.

Jacob laughed as if he'd just heard the funniest joke. Ever. "Yes. Say, 'Thank you, Jacob. You're my hero.'"

"Why would I thank you for waking me up?"

"You wouldn't." He snorted. "But you would thank me for making sure you still have a job."

Shelley sat straight up in bed, suddenly wide awake. "What have you done?"

"I got you your job back. Dr. Kessler just called to remind me that I was handling your workload today because—and I quote—she's on vacation." He paused then added, "Now what do we say?"

"Jacob! I told you not to do that." Shelley stifled the urge to scream. "I can't come back to the clinic like this. Dr. Kessler might be suffering from dementia, but I won't take advantage."

"I did it for you." Jacob's tone was terse and angry.

"I know," Shelley said and sighed. "I appreciate your help. I do. Look, when I get back to the clinic, we'll sit down and talk. Figure out something."

Jacob was so silent on the other end of the line, Shelley might have thought he'd hung up, except for the noises in the background. A lone dog barked two quick yips—Mr. Montgomery's Pomeranian, most likely. Another dog howled in reply, then a series of *whoop, whoop, whoop*s.

She frowned. "Is that Beau's guinea pig in the background?"

"Seriously? I tell you I just pulled off the most amazing feat ever of getting you your job back and you ask me about a rodent?"

"Jacob, I do appreciate your help. It was very thoughtful of you." *And unethical.* But she didn't say that part. She needed his help, the kind she could actually accept. "It's just . . . I need you to tell me if that's Beau's pet I hear."

"Yes, Dr. Dolittle, it's Mr. Fuzzbutt. I'm in your office refilling his water bottle. You said to leave him here until the kid comes back, right? I assumed you wanted me to keep it fed and watered."

"Yes, I did. Didn't Beau come in yesterday? Or maybe Tomás?"

"No," he replied drawing out the word. "You want me to give the rodent to the zoo?"

"Oh, no. Beau is uh . . ." She didn't know if Tomás wanted her to talk about his family situation. Deciding to keep it to herself, she said, "Tomás was going to sit for the guinea pig for a few days. I just thought he or Beau would have been in to pick him up by now."

The background noises changed and Jacob groaned. "Ah, man! One of the cats escaped and is freaking out the dogs. I gotta go."

He hung up.

Shelley dropped her phone onto the bedside table again and glanced at the sunlight peering between the curtains. Below the window, Lucy stretched, then sat staring expectantly.

"Good morning, girl," Shelley said, unlatching the cage. She lifted Lucy into the air until they made eye contact. "Stay in here. No sneaking out of the room. I'll get you some breakfast and fresh water."

The image of Lucy doing the weasel war dance flew into Shelley's mind. *Agreed.* Lucy, clearly happy to be out of her carrier, was content to stay put.

In no time she'd fed and watered Lucy, cleaned her carrier, taken a shower, and dressed. Throwing the curtains wide, sunlight poured into the bedroom. Waves crashed on the beach below. The blue, cloudless sky seemed to beckon her outside.

Lucy, who'd already returned to her hammock, was snoozing. Locking the cage, Shelley ventured out of the room and down the stairs.

Dev sat, his sock-covered feet propped up on a coffee table in the living room. A partially empty Kiss the Cop coffee mug on the end table. The television, tuned to a news station with a red ticker scrolling across the bottom of the screen, was on mute in the middle of a large entertainment center.

Dev's head was back, his eyes were closed, and two manila case files were facedown on his T-shirt-clad chest. Sunlight streaming through the sliding glass doors threw a spotlight on him, making even his hideous camo cargo pants charming.

His golden hair was almost white; his beautiful light mocha skin glowed with health. Even his long, dark lashes shone in the sunshine. In quiet near repose, Dev could have been an angel.

Everything about the man was breathtaking. His biceps bulged against his white T-shirt making her hot. She pictured herself pushing those files aside, straddling his lap, and waking him with kisses. Well, kisses for a start. She'd love to rip that shirt off him and explore all of his delicious muscles with her tongue and teeth.

Whew, when did it get hot in here?

Since when did arms turn her on?

Space. She needed to go for a walk. Clear her head. Or she might just cave in to her desire. Although, why shouldn't she enjoy another healthy round of sex with this man? Except he was asleep, but that could be remedied.

Had she played her cards right, she could have awakened this morning to intimate caresses and perhaps another love-making session instead of Jacob's phone call.

But all through dinner and the ride home, Shelley had kept thinking about Jules's explanation of auras. Something about auras. That Jules only saw Seth's. Then she'd asked Shelley if she'd seen anyone else's. A shiver went down her spine, even as something bloomed in her chest.

It wasn't the fear that had made her pull back and retreat to the guest room alone last night. No, it had been the warmth. That sensation of belonging. Even seeing Dev in the bright light of morning still haunted her.

Dev yawned and blinked open his eyes. "Good morning," he said, his voice rough with sleep. He plucked the files from his chest, closed them, and stacked them on his coffee table. "What time is it?"

"About nine." She stepped back from the couch because she could see he was really awake.

All. Of. Him.

Dev shifted to hide his "oh my there is a sex god" erection, but Shelley would have to have been blind to miss it. And it made her hotter than she'd been before.

"Going somewhere?" he asked, his stormy gaze smoldering.

Not if you keep looking at me like that.

"Yeah. I, uh . . . I wanted to take a walk on the beach." There, she'd gotten the words out and managed not to sound like a complete imbecile.

Dev stretched his arms wide and rolled his shoulders. "Give me five and I'll join you. I wasn't sure how light of a sleeper you were, so I didn't want to go out and risk waking you."

Her heart melted just a little at his thoughtfulness. "Oh."

Brilliant conversationalist, Shelley.

Dev pushed to his feet, and she couldn't help herself. Her gaze swung to his waist, where his tent had been. And to her surprise, the flagging erection grew.

"Or we can skip the walk," Dev suggested.

"Yeah?" she said, when what she really wanted to do was scream, "You got it. Now get naked so I can see how many ways I can make you come."

Dev sauntered toward her. Shelley backed up from where she'd been standing beside the couch to give him room to move. And possibly throw her onto it. But this was Dev. He didn't do anything in a hurry.

He lowered his mouth, passing her lips and went straight for the pulse point on her neck. Gently, lazily, he suckled it. Goose bumps erupted all over her whole body. Liquid heat pooled low in her core.

She reached for him only to have Dev encircle her wrists with his hands. "Shhh . . . slow down, darlin'. Let me taste you."

He trailed feather-light kisses up her chin. Brushed the corners of her mouth. Teased her lips with his tongue, but still held himself back, whispering, "I've wanted you forever. I don't want to rush through. I want it to last."

A shiver went down her spine. But instead of him continuing to kiss her, he pointed to the television.

"Holy shit, is that *your* car?"

Shelley turned. Dev gaped at the television. A pretty blond reporter in a royal blue suit stood in front of the Elkridge Zoo. The camera panned to Kenny's tow truck hitched to her Blue Bomber. But the car wasn't being towed. In fact, it looked like a small crowd had gathered.

Shelley reached for the remote at the same time as Dev.

They knocked heads. She hissed in pain as lights burst before her watery eyes.

"I got it," Dev said, unmuting the television.

"For those just joining us, I'm Christie Michaels live at the Elkridge Zoo where a body has just been discovered in the trunk of a car. The body was found by this man, Kenny Parran, owner of Ken's Hunting and Towing. Kenny, can you tell me what you saw?"

The camera panned to Kenny. Deep purple bruises beneath both eyes indicated he hadn't had much sleep. In his customary jean overalls, faded red T-shirt, and Marines ball cap, he gulped at the camera much like a fish out of water. When it became clear to the reporter that he wasn't going to talk, she spoke again. "Right now, the local sheriff's office is keeping quiet about the list of possible suspects. No names of either the victim or suspects have been released. But when they are, we'll update you. This is Christie Michaels with Channel Nine News, live in Elkridge, Virginia."

The image changed to a commercial about diapers. Dev muted the television.

Shelley was too stunned to do more than glance down. There, on Dev's couch was a file labeled Colbert Rush. A picture of a severed hand with a bite mark had fallen out. There was something familiar about the name and the bite mark, but she couldn't put her finger on it.

Dev pulled out his cell phone, began to tap the keys, and opened the balcony door.

"What are you doing?" she asked, too numb to feel anything except slight curiosity.

"Calling for backup," he said, stepping outside. He'd barely finished one text when he tapped out another. Just before closing the door he added, "My cousins, Ryan and Ian, own Tidewater Security Specialists. They specialize in difficult cases. If it comes down to it, I might be limited by the law, but they aren't."

CHAPTER 19

THIS WASN'T REAL. It just wasn't. Things like this didn't happen. People don't just end up stuffed in a trunk. Certainly not in *her* trunk.

The pretty reporter was back on the screen. Shelley unmuted the television.

"This just in. My sources tell me that the owner of the car, one Shelley Grace Morgan, a local vet here in Elkridge, is missing. Could she be another victim of foul play or perhaps the murderer? Deputies are searching her apartment on—"

The television clicked off. Shelley jumped. She hadn't heard Dev return. His lips were pressed into a thin line, and his square jaw was so tight a muscle ticked. He glanced from the blank screen to his phone to her. "That sucks."

Shelley snorted a laugh. "I'm sorry, it's not funny. I just . . . Maybe I should turn myself in."

"And say what? That you've been staying in my house for the past twenty-four hours? We don't know how long that guy's been dead. What if twenty-four hours isn't a long enough alibi?"

Her stomach shrank. "Oh, God. If the cops find me here, what'll happen to you? To your career?" She answered her question. "This could destroy your career. Unless . . ."

"Unless what?" Dev narrowed his eyes.

Shelley swallowed past a sudden painful lump in her throat. She hated to even say it. She hadn't done anything wrong. But if it could keep from implicating Dev, she could do it. "Unless you arrest me first."

"No. That's crazy. Right now, they don't even know if you're another victim or not." Dev scrubbed a hand through his hair, making the blond strands stick up in all directions. He frowned, sank down onto the couch, and sighed. Shelley joined him, placing a hand on his knee.

"I don't want you in trouble, Dev."

"Okay." Dev blinked his gorgeous gray eyes and asked in an almost casual tone, "Did you kill anyone?"

She tried not to be hurt by the question. Tried and failed. Withdrawing from him, she clasped both hands in her lap and said in a controlled voice, "No, I didn't."

"Do you have any reason to think someone would want to frame you for murder?"

It was her turn to blink. "Those missing animals could definitely cost someone prison time and a whole lot of money if they got caught."

"It's a big leap from tiger-napping to murder." Dev grabbed his ever-present notebook and jotted something down but covered it before she had a chance to read it.

"Do you have any idea who might be in the trunk?"

Shelley went cold at the thought of someone lying dead in her car. Then a sick, oily feeling slithered into her belly. It curled around itself until she was certain she'd vomit from it.

"I haven't been able to reach Tomás since Wednesday night. He's rarely out of touch. He promised to keep me updated on Beau's condition. But he's not answering the phone . . . Oh God, it's got to be him. Dev, if it *is* Tomás in my trunk, where's Beau? The last time I saw them, they were together."

Unable to sit still, she shoved to her feet, pacing. This couldn't be real. It couldn't be happening. Who would kill Tomás? Why? A balloon of panic swelled inside her until her chest ached.

Dev's arms went around her. Her face pressed against the soft cotton of his T-shirt. "Shhh . . ." he whispered into her hair. "We don't know anything yet. Let's take it one step at a time."

He rested his forehead against hers. The gesture was so sweet, so supportive—tears stung the back of her eyes. She didn't know how to handle it, so she slid away from his touch.

Striding across the living room, she stepped out onto the porch. She leaned both hands on the white wooden railing and stared at the beauty in front of her. The ocean waves crashed against the shore, indicating a storm front moving in, but the sky was still a deep cerulean. Laughing gulls danced in the wind, flapping their wings only occasionally to stay in the sky. Sandpipers raced between the larger black-tailed godwits as they all sought a midday meal.

Even surrounded as she was by majestic sights and sounds, all Shelley could think of was her friend, possibly dead, and what awaited her in Elkridge.

The porch floor groaned. The sliding glass door closed with a thunk. Then Dev's profile appeared to her left. He mimicked her pose, resting his hands on the railing. She'd expected him to speak. He didn't. He simply stared at the ocean too.

"Ever notice, disasters always seem to strike on the prettiest days?" Shelley asked, unsurprised at the tremor in her voice. "Like Mother Nature is laughing at you?"

DEV GLANCED AT Shelley's profile. Her red hair shone like curly copper flames in the sunlight. This morning she looked younger. Vulnerable.

To think he'd been frustrated when he awoke to an empty bed. What he wouldn't give for that to be the biggest issue of the day. The man in him wanted to comfort her. Tell her everything would be all right. But the cop in him needed answers.

"Shells." He waited for her to look at him. "My cousins will be here soon. Along with Seth and Jules. We need to work out a POA."

She frowned and turned to face him, resting her back against the railing. Arms folded over her chest, she asked, "POA?"

"Sorry. Plan of action." When she didn't do more than stare

at him, he added, "We need to discuss your alibi for the murder."

"Murder," she repeated. Tears glistened on her lashes but didn't fall.

"I'm sorry, Shells, but we need to talk about this."

She smiled weakly. He didn't miss the fear in her eyes, but he didn't know how to remove it without solving the mystery first.

"Let's go inside," he said. "The guys will be here soon."

Shelley gripped her elbows until her knuckles turned white. "I don't want Jules here. She's got a good life. The last thing I want to do is mess it up again."

"I don't know if I can keep her away. Seth already knows about the murder. I texted him as soon as I saw the news report. He's looking into getting more information for us as we speak." When Shelley opened her mouth to say something, no doubt to argue, Dev held up a hand. "Seth already told Jules. She texted me as I was coming out to the porch to say they'll be here soon."

"Then I won't be." Shelley stormed into the house.

She made it to the bottom of the stairs before he caught up to her. Grabbing her hand, he held on, forcing her to stop. Eyes flashing with anger and fear, she spun on him. "Let. Me. Go."

"No." Was she nuts? Dev strove to keep his voice calm. "Why are you running? Everyone is coming here to help you."

She jerked her hand free. He could have kept her in his grasp, but he didn't fight. He could chase her if he had to, but for now he wanted her to feel safe. Maybe then she would stay put.

Shelley glared at him, unshed tears making her blue eyes swim. "I don't want anyone else's help. I asked *you* for help with the missing animals, but instead of staying in Elkridge and going through the files, you had me come here. Now the files are gone. The animals are gone. And Jesus, if the worst is true, Tomás is gone too. So no! I don't want any more help. I just want to go back to Elkridge and talk to the sheriff. Maybe he'll believe me when I tell him I think the murder is related to the missing tigers."

"I *do* believe you," he yelled, frustrated that she was right. He hadn't taken her concerns seriously. Christ, if her friend was killed because Dev was too focused on getting her to

Tidewater, she'd never forgive him. "What are you going to do if the sheriff doesn't believe you? You do realize you could be arrested for capital murder?"

"You think I don't know that?" she shouted, her fists on her hips, her face practically nose to nose with his. "But I didn't do anything wrong! It doesn't matter anyway. I still have to go back."

"Why?" He couldn't believe he was arguing with her against turning herself in. But something just wasn't right in this whole situation. Before she went back, he wanted to make damned certain she wasn't going to be charged for a crime she couldn't have committed.

"Because the animals are counting on me. If whoever is taking these creatures killed Tomás, then there's no one there to protect them." Conviction radiated from her.

There was no way to win this part of the argument. He'd seen that look before in the faces of mothers searching for their missing children. The look of utter determination that vowed no rest until the mission was accomplished.

He sighed. Raising his hands in surrender, he said, "Okay, I'll take you back."

"Thank you," she said, relief in her voice.

He held up a finger. "After we sit down and talk this out. I *am* going to help you. With the murder investigation and the missing animals. I made a promise. I keep my word. To do that I need Seth and my cousins."

Lips pressed together, she slowly shook her head. "Not Jules. She's got a life and doesn't need me messing it up. It's not like she can do anything to help. She's useless. I don't want her here."

"Now that's the stupidest thing I've ever heard you say," Jules said, announcing her presence in the hallway.

Dev glanced past her to see Seth, Ian, and Ryan filing in through the sliding glass door. Relief went through him at the sight of the cavalry. It was short-lived.

Police sirens blared outside the house.

CHAPTER 20

"ALL CLEAR. JUST cops in pursuit of a speeder," said the man, who bore a striking resemblance to a young Brad Pitt from *Troy*. Tan, buff, with long golden hair and piercing blue eyes, he wore tight blue jeans, black T-shirt, and black cowboy boots.

Shelley blinked in a mix of shock and confusion at the uncanny resemblance, as the movie-star double walked through the front door and locked it behind him. His gaze bounced to everyone standing in the foyer until they landed on Shelley. He winked at her and said, "Guess you're safe from the law for now."

Dev growled low in his throat, belying the smile on his face. "Thanks, Ian. Give us a minute. Shelley and I'll join everyone in the dining room."

"Yup," Ian said, but it came out in two syllables, *ye-up*. "Got any green tea, Dev?"

Shelley had to be dreaming. A body had been found in her car, the police were looking for her, and Dev was discussing beverages with Brad Pitt. Things like this did not happen to her.

"How do you drink that crap?" Dev gave a mock shudder. "I have whatever you left when you moved out. Hey, Ian, put on another pot of coffee for the real men while you're at it."

Ian offered a middle-fingered salute and led Dev's other cousin with Seth and Jules down the hall to the kitchen. Their muffled conversations lent an air of privacy to the house's large entryway.

Shelley kept glancing at the front door. Afraid that any minute now, the police *would* arrive to arrest her.

"I know you didn't want Jules here," Dev said, running a consoling hand up and down her arm. "But she's here now. No one is going to judge or accuse you. I know you and Jules have some shit . . . pardon, *stuff*, to work out. Save it for another time. Right now, we're up against the clock. It won't take long for the police to put out an arrest warrant for you if the circumstantial evidence doesn't point to anyone else, so we need to get your story. All of it."

A shiver went down her back, but she refused to cower. "Okay. I'll tell you everything I know."

Dev gave her a weary, relieved smile.

"But after, you have to take me back to Elkridge. Or I'll catch a bus."

His smile vanished, in its place the tight-lipped expression of a cop she hardly knew. "Fine. Let's go."

She followed Dev down the hall. Voices of the men and Jules floated in the air. Their conversations were quiet and the words unclear, but the tension was thick enough that it clogged Shelley's throat.

It took several minutes of closing the curtains in the dining room and clearing off the table before everyone gathered around it. Shelley made herself useful by helping Ian and Jules make coffee, tea, and toast in the kitchen.

Jules worked with her, side by side, occasionally giving her odd glances, but never speaking. Shelley could practically feel the weight of her sister's displeasure, like a Great Dane sitting on her chest.

Ian carried a tray laden with mugs out of the kitchen.

"Jules, I'm sorry," Shelley said, the moment they were alone. "What you heard me say earlier about you being useless . . . it's not how I meant it. I meant you can't help with the case is all."

Jules's green gaze, loaded with hurt, collided with hers. "Well, that's a relief. But, Shelley, that's not what's bothering me. There's—"

But Dev's other cousin, Ryan, a giant of a man at six foot six, swathed in black from neck to toe, poked his shaved head into the kitchen. "Dev's ready for you," he said in a voice that made Dev's deep voice sound positively falsetto.

"We're coming right now." Jules picked up the sugar jar, creamer, and spoons, and nodded to the toast and jelly. "Grab those. We'll talk about this later."

"Fine."

"We will." Jules paused to meet Shelley's gaze.

Something earnest burned in Jules's eyes making Shelley's chest tighten. God, that look was so like their mother's. And for a moment, she took comfort in the sense of family. Shelley wished that the sense of belonging she had found wouldn't disappear again.

"Let's get this meeting over with," Jules said. "Then we can talk. Privately."

Shelley followed her sister into the dining room. The four men were seated around the large rectangular table. Four of the six chairs were occupied. The only two seats left were next to Seth and Dev. Jules, not unexpectedly, filled the empty space next to her fiancé, leaving Shelley to claim the chair beside Dev.

Dev reached beneath the table and gently took her hand in his. The move was so pure, so comforting to Shelley's frayed nerves, it nearly had her weeping.

Gah, I'm becoming a major wimp.

"Okay, let's get introductions over with." Dev released her hand and pointed to the giant on his left. "This is Ryan McKinnon. He owns half of TSS, Tidewater Security Specialists."

Across the table, Jules sat up a little straighter. Her eyes wide. She glanced to the man on Shelley's right and asked, "Does that make you, Ian McKinnon?"

Ian flashed that Hollywood smile and nodded. "Sure does. Have we met?"

"This is my fiancée, Juliana Scott," Seth said, placing an arm around Jules's shoulders.

Ian didn't seem at all bothered by Seth's macho leaning. If anything, the guy smiled wider. "Why, Ms. Scott, how nice to meet you in person."

Jules glanced to Shelley, explaining, "Ian and I spoke last

month when I started the official search for you and Hannah. He was out of town and asked Dev to handle the case for him."

"Oh." Shelley wasn't sure what to say or even feel. So she did what she did best. Pasting her best smile on her face, she extended her hand to Ian and said, "Congratulations. TSS solved that case. Dev found me. Do I get part of the commission because I really found him first?"

Ian laughed and shook her hand. "Nah, I think we'll call it a draw, considering why we're here now."

Right, and thanks so much for the reminder.

As if sensing her discomfort, or maybe he was just tired of the delay, Dev said, "Let's start with what we know. According to the news, a body was found in the trunk of a car at the Elkridge Zoo. We know that car belongs to Shells."

Seth's cell phone buzzed. He glanced at it and tossed it onto the table. "And now we know the name of the victim. He has been identified as Tomás Rodriguez, age twenty-eight."

Shelley couldn't help it, she started to cry and hated herself for it. "I mean, I suspected it was Tomás, but he was my friend." Then it hit her. "What about Beau? He wasn't hurt was he?"

"Who's Beau?" Ryan asked at the same time that Ian said, "Why would you think that?"

Ian handed Shelley a white handkerchief. The act was so anachronistic with everything about the man, it momentarily stunned her.

Who carried around a handkerchief these days?

"Thanks," she told him, then wiped her face. Turning to Ryan, she explained, "Beau is Tomás's son. At least he would have been legally next week." Shelley explained the legal entanglements Tomás and Beau had been facing. "The last time I saw Tomás, he and Beau were together. Beau was asleep in Tomás's office at the zoo's visitor center when I left them Wednesday night. Don't you see? If Tomás was killed at the zoo, Beau was there. So where is he now? I need to call Jacob."

"Why?" Dev asked.

Shelley explained about the morning's phone call from Jacob. She left out the part about Jacob trying to trick her boss into hiring her back and focused on the pertinent details of the situation. "Wednesday night, Tomás told Beau he could leave the pet at his place. But Beau never picked him up."

Without warning, the temperature in the room dropped twenty degrees. A cold wind blew from the vents on the wall. Ian frowned, rubbing at the goose bumps on his arms. "Dev, what's with the heat in this old house? I thought you had the HVAC replaced last spring?"

"I did," Dev said, calmly.

"Is she okay?" Ian asked, nodding at Jules.

Jules's face went blank, as if she'd gone into a trance. Seth had his arm around her. Dev gave Shelley's hand a quick squeeze, then he released her. All attention was on her sister.

Shelley recognized the look. She'd seen it more than once when they were children and again last night after dinner. Still, it unnerved her every time.

Shelley shivered. Dev moved to drape an arm around her shoulders. She wasn't sure whether he was comforting her or himself, until he said, "Don't worry. Seth warned me that she's done this twice since dinner last night. He said she's been snapping out of it quicker. Give her a second."

Just as Dev predicted, Jules blinked and her expression cleared. But she didn't look happy. No, Jules glanced at Shelley and Dev, past them to the curtained windows, and finally to the ground.

"Is she all right?" Ryan asked, looking at Jules with concern.

"Just a little light-headed. I need a minute—I feel a bit queasy," Jules answered, pushing to her feet. She wobbled and to Shelley's surprise, Jules reached for her. "Can you give me a hand? Excuse us, gentlemen."

"Sure. We'll be right back." Shelley looped Jules's arm around her waist and led her across the hall to the small half bath. Once inside, she grabbed a cloth from the shelf, ran it under cold water and dabbed it on her sister's forehead and neck. "Better?"

Jules took the cloth with a weak smile and nodded. Several moments passed in silence. Just when Shelley would have suggested returning to the dining room, Jules spoke.

"He's here."

"Who?"

"Tomás."

"Wait, what?" Shelley blinked at her sister's solemn expression.

Jules swiped the cloth over the back of her neck again, tossed it into the sink and said, "Tomás is here. He's been dead for a couple of days. The last thing he remembers is seeing you at the visitor center Wednesday night, then going to the security office."

"Why is he here?" Shelley wasn't sure she wanted to know, but she needed to at the same time.

Jules shrugged. "Same reason most spirits hang around. He has unfinished business. He said he's been looking for you and Beau but hadn't been able to find either of you. Not until he heard you calling his name."

"Oh, my God, he doesn't know where Beau is? Don't the dead always know everything after they die?"

Jules shook her head. "From what I can tell, being a ghost is nothing like in the movies. Sometimes they can't even remember their own names. So I'd say your friend Tomás is doing pretty good for a recently deceased spirit."

Shelley couldn't quite see that. Tomás was dead after all. "Jules, do the dead always hear their names? Can they see other ghosts?"

"Not always." Jules picked up the cloth and dabbed her cheeks. "It's selective. They see those spirits they seek out. Kind of like how we can walk down the same street every day and never notice the guy with long hair who checks his mail at the same time each afternoon. He's there, you know it, but you don't really pay attention. Then one day, he calls to you and you see him. Really see him. Ghosts are the same way."

"Does that mean that if I call for someone who died a long time ago, she'll hear me?" Shelley asked, temporarily distracted by the idea of talking to her dead parents.

Jules pursed her lips with an apologetic look. "I've only been really trying to learn more about my crift for a short time, but no, I don't think so. Spirits can only hear their names if they're on this side of the light. I've never heard of anyone crossing back from the other side."

For an instant, just a brief moment, the room's temperature dropped. Shelley could almost swear she felt someone touch her cheek with an icy finger. She shivered.

"Shelley, we need to go back out there." Jules pointed to the door, her eyes wide and her tone urgent. "You need to tell them everything that happened Wednesday night. Tomás says it's important. That there's something he's trying to remember, and it has to do with you. And his murder."

DEV HATED KEEPING secrets from his cousins, especially when they were here to help him. But it wasn't his place to tell them about Jules's ghost-seeing abilities. Granted, Ian and Ryan probably wouldn't even flinch at the mention of ghosts or animal whisperers. Lord knew they had their own share of relatives with shiny talents that science couldn't explain.

But without Jules's consent, Dev was forced to sit and wait for the women to come back, while dodging his cousins' probing questions.

"You sure she's all right?" Ian asked. "She kind of looked like Aunt Marlene at the punch bowl."

Aunt Marlene owned a crystal punch bowl that she swore, when filled with vodka, gave her glimpses into people's past lives. Dev suspected it was more because of the vodka she would siphon off when she thought no one was watching than any real shiny talent.

"Juliana's fine," Seth said gruffly to Ian, but then rose. "Excuse me." He disappeared into the bathroom.

Seconds later, Shelley emerged and joined Dev at the table. She sat with her hands folded, arms resting on the cherrywood tabletop. "Where do we start?"

Dev glanced at his cousins, then back to her. "Start at the beginning. If you're right and you stumbled onto something that someone thinks is worth killing for, then we need to know everything you do."

She nodded. "You know part of it. I moved to Elkridge last year from Baltimore."

"Why did you move?" Ryan asked.

Dev wanted to silence his cousin, but understood. Ryan and Ian needed to hear it all too. Before she could answer, the bathroom door opened. Seth and Jules silently rejoined the group.

"I needed a fresh start after my fiancé . . . uh, left me,"

Shelley said, staring fixedly at her hands. She quickly high-lighted her trek from Baltimore to Elkridge. "When I first moved to town, everything seemed relatively normal. I mean the zoo was a little strange. But it was private, and the smaller zoos get away with more unusual stuff than the larger ones."

"What sort of stuff?" Seth asked.

Shelley wrinkled her nose, clearly thinking. "Private zoos aren't monitored as closely as the larger ones. So little things, like overcrowding in the reptile house, or having smaller-than-acceptable cages for the birds or improper feeding of the animals can happen."

"Did you see all these things?" Ian asked.

She nodded. "And more, but what really bothered me was when the animals in the zoo would change from week to week. One week there'd be four green iguanas, the next none. Rare birds mysteriously flew away. Tortoises escaped and wandered the grounds. Sometimes their cages would not only be cleaned but filled with an animal from another part of the zoo."

"Shells," Dev said, placing a hand on her cool ones. "I'm not sure how much time we have, so let's stay on track. You e-mailed me about missing animals."

"Right." Shelley exhaled audibly and explained about the missing snakes, birds, and escaped tortoises. "After I'd started documenting everything, Tomás took me into his confidence. As the groundskeeper and animal caretaker, he'd noticed the strange happenings too. He told me to watch out for the tigers. He explained that before I came to Elkridge, Miah, that's the female white Bengal tiger I mentioned earlier, allegedly ate her cub. She didn't. I'm sure of it. *He* was sure of it too. Now he's dead, and I have a feeling what's happening now is related to what happened then."

When Ian and Ryan just frowned, Shelley glanced at Dev, confusion on her face.

"Shelley, I think maybe you need to tell the tiger part of the story chronologically. Go back to when you first arrived in town."

She nodded and backtracked. "Okay, by the time I started working in Elkridge, Miah's mate, Leonardo, had somehow escaped his cage one night. Rumor has it he was put down and the body disposed of. But no one can say for sure who put him down and who disposed of the body."

"Did you try to find out what happened?" Ryan asked, his impassive face giving nothing away.

"Not really. I was new, and Miah was already pregnant with another litter. She had them at the end of the summer. Tomás called me the night she went into labor. He and I waited and watched her deliver five cubs."

"How did you watch?" Ian asked.

"At the time, we had a camera working in the tiger house." She swept her glance around the table. "There's a security room in the old converted warehouse that serves as the visitor center on the zoo's grounds. We watched from there. It was pretty amazing."

"Tigers giving birth." Ian grimaced. "Yeah, that's prime-time television, all right."

"Shut it," Ryan said out of the corner of his mouth, before Dev could.

Ian winked at Shelley. "Sorry, darlin'. Go on."

Shells stared at him as if he were some new species of monkey she'd never seen before, then smiled, tentatively. "Um . . . okay. Where was I?" She paused then snapped her fingers. "Right. When Dev and I went to the zoo on Wednesday, there were only three cubs. And Cristos told us the camera feed to the house had stopped functioning, so they don't know when the cubs disappeared. But I think it happened Tuesday night."

"What do you think happened to them?" Ian asked at the same time Ryan said, "What makes you think they vanished on Tuesday?"

She glanced from one man to the other then sighed. "I think the cubs were stolen. Like I told Dev, there's a black market for exotic pets. People pay a lot of money for tiger cubs, especially white Bengals. And to answer your question, Ryan, I'm certain they disappeared on Tuesday, or I'd have heard from Tomás. He checked on them daily and was in charge of Miah's care and feeding."

"Any idea who would take them?" Seth asked.

Shelley seemed to deflate. "That's just it. I have no idea. Everyone in town loves the tigers, well, except for Reyna. She's the zoo owner's daughter. And she accused *me* of stealing them. I just can't imagine her wanting to risk her manicure by taking the tigers. I can't figure out who's sabotaging the zoo and taking the animals. It's the reason I contacted Dev in the first place.

"If I'd had proof of wrongdoing, I'd have taken it to the authorities right away. Reptiles and birds might not be in a protected class, but tigers are. The USDA would have come in and investigated if I'd had one shred of evidence that anything was wrong."

Shelley slapped her hands to the table. "Why are we just sitting here? Tomás is dead, two cubs have been stolen, and Beau is missing."

"Shells, I know this is stressful, but you need to trust us. Ian and Ryan will believe whatever you tell them. Let us work out a plan of action. Together." Dev covered her hand with his. Although he wasn't surprised when she withdrew from his touch. He'd sensed her putting up her guard last night, but it didn't make it suck any less.

"Shelley, you need to remember everything that happened Wednesday night," Jules said suddenly. Still pale, Jules grabbed Shelley's hand as if to steady herself. Unlike with Dev, Shelley didn't withdraw from her sister's touch. Jules licked her lips nervously and said, "Tomás came to me and said he needs Shelley to remember what happened on that night. It's tied to his murder."

"I'm trying to tell them everything." Color flooded Shelley's cheeks. "Dev was with me until after three. I typed up my notes. Remembered I needed my flash drive, which was in my car. Walked to the zoo parking lot, where the car had died earlier. Called the mechanic on my way home. Ate dinner, packed, and. . . ." Her voice trailed off. Her red brows knitted together in concentration. "I don't know. I think someone knocked at the door, maybe? Then nothing. Just a migraine the next morning." She shoved to her feet. "This is a waste of time. There's nothing else to remember."

"This is not a waste of time, we're gathering information," Dev said. He wanted to be the one to soothe her, but she refused to listen to him.

"I've got to get back to Elkridge. I need to find Beau." She pushed to her feet.

"Shelley, you cannot just take off. You heard the television report yourself. The sheriff is already looking for you. Going back to town will just land you at the station at best. Or worse, they'll arrest you on the spot."

"Seriously?! Aren't you supposed to be telling me to turn myself in?" she asked, nonplussed. "Couldn't just talking to me hurt your career?" She glanced at Seth. "And yours?"

"She's right," Seth said. Jules gasped her fiancé's name and glowered at him. "Precious, if they have already issued an arrest warrant, then Jones and I are jeopardizing our futures, hell, our freedom, by not bringing her in. We should be trying to convince her to go to the station." Seth included Dev in his argument. "You know I'm right, Jones. We need to take her in."

"That's not going to happen." Dev fought the rise of fury burning in his chest. "Seth, you didn't question Jules for twenty-four hours after she found that body in October. Don't lecture me about doing the right thing for my career now."

"I'm not going to allow anyone to risk their futures for me." Shelley crossed her arms, defiant in her eyes. "I can handle this on my own."

"How do you propose to do that?" Damn it, why was she being so stubborn?

"I'll go talk to Deputy Munro. He knows me. He can't honestly believe I'd hurt anyone."

Jealousy, ugly and green, pricked Dev in the center of his chest. "Your old boyfriend?"

"It was one date! And who are *you* to judge me? One night in bed with you doesn't give you the right to dictate my life. You want to arrest me? Go ahead. Otherwise, get out of my way."

Christ, she was going to make him crazy. In his head, he had known this was coming, had sensed it from the moment she'd snuck out of his room this morning. She was pushing him away. But he hadn't expected it to hurt this much.

Perfect! His cousins and partner get to witness his humiliation. Seth, Ian, and Ryan were all staring at the ceiling as if it were the Sistine Chapel.

"I've got to go. I rescind my request for help, Dev. I don't need you. I don't need anyone." She must have seen Jules's pained expression because she added, "I mean I don't need anyone else to get hurt. Not because of me. I can handle this.

I was wrong to contact Dev. Wrong to come here." Her face crimson and her eyes swimming blue sapphires, Shelley turned to leave.

"Please wait, Dr. Morgan," Ryan said, softly. His deep, calm tones reverberated through the room. "I respect your situation and the difficulty we all face, but don't leave yet. I think you've given us more information than you realize. Let me consult with my cousin."

Dev could only assume Ryan meant Ian because the two men put their heads together and whispered.

Shelley, seemingly placated by Ryan's quiet demeanor, slowly sank back to her chair. Her face still red, she clasped her hands together until her knuckles were white. She refused to glance at Dev. Instead, she stared at the table. Dev's gut twisted at the chasm building between them. He had no intention of allowing anyone to arrest Shelley for a crime she couldn't have committed. But she seemed determined to throw herself under a bus in order to find a missing boy and a pair of tiger cubs she might never be able to locate.

Ryan nodded at something Ian said and cast a meaningful glance at Dev. He knew that look. It made him both hopeful and nervous at the same time.

"Do you think you might have opened the door that night?" She nodded.

"But," Ian interjected, "you don't remember clearly."

Shelley looked askance at Dev, but he'd already figured out their line of thinking. Apparently so had Seth because he said, "And you woke up with a headache."

"Yes, but what does that have to do with anything?"

"Your missing files," Dev said on a sigh. "Damn it! I should have thought of that. You said your migraine medicine didn't work and your files disappeared. Shelley, I think you were drugged. I think the killer was in your apartment."

She blanched.

"Your theory about the murder being tied to the missing animals is probably on target. And the murderer wants you quiet."

"So why not kill me?" she asked, color returning. "If he or she was in my apartment, why just wipe the files? Why not kill me too?"

Ian and Ryan shared a look that made Dev tense. One that said they didn't know. If they didn't know, then Shelley could be in danger from more than a possible false arrest.

Several silent moments passed. Finally, Ian said, "Tell me about the boy, Beau. Where's his mother? Is there any chance Beau could be with her?"

Shelley shook her head. "His mother died a few years ago. He's in foster care right now with a woman who wouldn't blink if the kid didn't come home. She's only in it for the money."

"Do you have a name and address for the foster mother?" Ryan asked her before glancing at Dev. "I think, since Shelley's determined to go find the little boy, maybe we should go and make contact with him. Make sure the kid's okay."

Ian nodded, adding, "While we're in Elkridge, we can check out the Jamesons. See if we can't get them talking."

"I appreciate you going to find Beau, but he doesn't do well with strange men. He wouldn't come to you because he doesn't know you. But if you could talk to Eddy and the gang at the zoo, maybe you can figure out who's behind those thefts."

"Shells—" Dev began, frustrated with her obstinacy.

"Why don't you let us try," Ian said with a slow, lazy grin. "I've got a way with children. Give us a list of hiding places, his current address, and a few hours. Ryan and I can do this."

"Please, Shelley," Jules spoke up. "I think you need to trust them."

Shelley stared at her sister, her expression completely unreadable. "Fine. But what am I going to do? I can't just sit here."

"You're not going to," Dev said. "You're going to write down everything you can remember from the past few days. Every conversation you've had. Everything you've seen. Let's see if we can't piece together a list of who might have motive to kill Tomás. "

"But I've just told you everything. Wouldn't I be more help if I went to Elkridge with Ian and Ryan?"

"Not until we know what's waiting for you there," Ian answered before Dev could.

"I have to go to the station to check in with our captain about our own murder investigation. While we're there, I'll see what I can find out about the murder in Elkridge," Seth said.

"Oh, frack! Wait a second, Seth," Shelley said, eyes wide. She jumped out of her chair and hurried down the hall. She returned moments later with the files he'd brought home last night. "Dev, I just remembered where I heard that name Colbert Rush. He's from Elkridge."

CHAPTER 21

AFTER SHARING WHAT she knew of Colbert Rush with Seth and Dev—which wasn't much more than the Elizabeths' gossip—everyone left, except Dev. He radiated concern. Part of her wanted to curl up in his arms. She retreated to the privacy of the guest room instead.

An hour later, Jules knocked on the door. "Shelley, can I come in?"

"It's okay, Jules," Shelley said, relieved it was her sister and not Dev. "Come in. I was just giving Lucy some free time."

Closing the door behind her, Jules crossed the room and sat down on the edge of the bed next to Shelley. She glanced at Lucy, who was curled up and sleeping on Shelley's lap. "Free time, huh?"

"Lucy ran around, ate a few treats, then tuckered herself out." Shelley shrugged. "I thought you and Seth left at the same time as Ryan and Ian."

Jules nodded. "We did. Diana's running the shop for me today. So I went home and picked up Callie. I thought you could use some company."

"Where is she?"

Jules grinned. "I handed her off to Dev. I figured all he's

doing is checking the news and reading some reports. He could watch her sleep for a while."

Shelley tried to return her sister's smile, but failed. "Dev shouldn't be here. He should be at work. Frack, at the very least, he should be getting me as far away from him and his home as possible."

"It's not in his nature to abandon anyone in a time of need," Jules said with a frown. "Surely, you know that. I mean, the way Dev talked about you, I assumed you two were close once."

Not as close as we were last night. Satisfaction shimmered through Shelley at the thought before she could completely shove it away. "We were friends in college, if that's what you mean. And you're right. I do know him. He's loyal to a fault."

Dev knocked on her door, then called through it, "Shells, we need to talk."

Dreading the conversation, but surprised it hadn't happened earlier, she turned to her sister, who was rising from the bed. "Please stay."

Maybe with Jules there, Dev wouldn't ask the dreaded, "Why did you bail like some fracking weirdo coward last night?"

"Just a second, Dev. Let me put Lucy away." The ferret woke with a squeak. "Shhh, girl," Shelley reassured her. "I'll bring you back out in a few."

Once the ferret was securely locked away, Shelley opened the door.

"She's been fed and is sleeping again," Dev said to Jules, handing her the box that held a sleeping Callie. Jules set it on the dresser next to Lucy's cage.

"Shells, I've got to go." Dev's handsome face was clouded; a frown drew his eyebrows so close together, they seemed to be one long one. "Seth just called me. The medical examiner is headed over to Elkridge. The sheriff requested him when he discovered something. The deputies found the murder weapon in your apartment."

"What?" She shivered. She couldn't help it. A killer *had* been in her apartment.

"Don't worry," Dev said, pulling her close. "The sheriff also said he found something odd with the victim and wants the M.E.'s opinion. Take it as a good sign. It means the sheriff's office is making sure they have a solid case before they arrest anyone."

Anyone, right. She pulled away from him and hugged herself. "You mean, me. They're making sure they have an airtight case before they arrest *me.*"

"Shells, I won't let you go to jail for something I know you couldn't have done," Dev said, his voice adamant. A soft, green light glowed in the center of his chest, then expanded and shifted until it encompassed his entire body. The color changed from a soothing green to a strong, clear red. The light seemed to pulse around him like a heartbeat.

Shelley blinked and glanced over her shoulder at her sister. If Jules saw it, she gave no indication.

"I need you to trust me, Shells," Dev said, drawing her gaze back to him. The light faded somewhat, but still pulsed rhythmically around him. "I'll do whatever it takes to make sure you don't spend even a single night in jail."

She believed him. And it scared the holy hell out of her. This beautiful, amazing man was willing to risk his career for her. But she'd never let him.

"Thank you, Dev. Your faith in me means more than I can say," she said. "I know you wouldn't let me go to prison."

Dev reached for her but dropped his hands when his cell phone sang out "Bad boys, bad boys, whatcha gonna do?"

He snatched it from his pocket and answered. "Detective Jones."

Shelley pressed her lips together to keep from laughing at his choice of ringtones. She glanced at Jules who mouthed, *"Cops?"*

Shelley shrugged, grinning.

"I'll be there in ten." Dev cut the connection and glanced at Shelley, an apology forming on his lips before he said, "I have to go to the station. Your tip about Colbert Rush helped. He has a cabin in Elkridge that he uses for hunting. According to Mason Hart, Rush was eager to dump the land and Hart Construction was set to buy it."

"Mason Hart?" Jules's asked, her eyes wide. "Are you sure?"

"Yeah, that's why I'm headed into the station." Dev's phone

vibrated. He glanced at it and shoved it into his camo shorts. "After I change."

"How did Mason get involved in another crime?" Jules sounded weary.

"Who's Mason Hart?" Shelley asked.

Jules and Dev both opened their mouths, but Jules answered first. "He's an old friend of mine. Back in October, his fiancée was killed. He helped save me from her killer."

"He's nobody's hero." Dev snorted. "But he did come into the station this morning when he read about Rush's murder. Seems he didn't know Rush was a silent partner in McGivern's Jewelers—the site of his fiancée's murder. Your tip about Rush's ties back to Elkridge helped jog the widow's memories. Seems she never went there, it was where Rush went for boys' time with old friends."

Dev exhaled a slow breath and said, "I shouldn't be gone long. And before you start to worry, no arrest warrant has been issued for you. But that doesn't mean you should go wandering. Let me find out what the M.E. learned and then we'll talk. No one outside of our group knows you're here. Let's keep you hidden as long as possible."

"I'm really not comfortable with this. I should be actively helping. Not sitting on my hands like someone too weak to take care of herself."

"No one who's ever met you could call you weak. Shells, it's called plausible deniability. If no one sees you wandering around Tidewater, no one will have any reason to ask me about you. If no one asks, then *I'm* not doing anything wrong by not bringing you in on a case I'm not even working." Dev rubbed the back of his neck with one hand. "I don't like it any better than you do, but please wait for me to get back. For all our sakes."

Every instinct in her body screamed that she needed to do *some*thing. Before she could answer, Jules spoke up. "Go to the station, Dev. I'll stay with Shelley."

"I don't need a babysitter."

"Yes, you do," Dev and Jules said in unison.

Fisting her hands on her hips, Shelley pasted the most plastic smile on her face and gritted, "Fine."

Dev exhaled a relieved breath. "Thank you, Shells. Back

soon." He swooped down, planting a quick kiss on her lips and was out the door before she could react.

That kiss, innocent though it may have been, both warmed her and made her uneasy. It was too familiar. Too comfortable.

"Seth owes me a massage," Jules said with a snicker.

Shelley turned to find her sister squatting in front of Lucy's cage, running a finger down the ferret's back.

"What are you talking about, Juliana?"

She straightened and said with a grin, "I bet Seth a massage that Dev was in love with you back in October. Seth thought I was imagining things. Ha. I win. I think I'm going to make him do it naked while feeding me caviar."

"Eww!" Shelley recoiled. "Thinking about my sister getting it on is TMI."

Jules laughed. "I said nothing about sex. Although that will definitely happen too."

Shelley pressed her hands to her eyes. "Stop! Where's the mind bleach when I need it?"

"Okay, so we'll talk about *your* love life then," Jules said, plopping down on the bed.

"There's nothing to tell." Shelley claimed the seat next to her.

"I saw what just happened. Dev was working hard to keep it casual, but he totally wanted to play tonsil hockey with you."

"You've really got to stop that," Shelley said, failing to keep her lips from twitching. "Dev and I are just friends."

Who had amazing sex last night.

"Why are you fighting it?" Jules draped an arm around Shelley's shoulders. "You already admitted you two had sex last night. You clearly want each other again. And you do the aura thing."

"The aura thing?" Shelley asked. Anxiety and hope made her chest tight.

"You see his aura. Just like I see Seth's." Jules leaned back on her elbows. "That can't be coincidence. I'd never seen one around a living person before Seth. You said yourself, you'd only ever seen Dev's. It's a sign you belong together."

Shelley liked that idea. Really liked it. Too much. She shook her head. "I'm also locked in his house with you as my babysitter because some nut stuffed the body of my friend in the trunk of my car."

And just like that, the mood in the room shifted again. "It's not your fault, you know," Jules said after a few minutes.

"You don't know that."

"I know that a murderer was in your apartment, and you're lucky you're not dead too," Jules said, the color leaching from her face. "I'm glad you weren't killed too, Shelley."

"But Beau . . . what if he's hurt or dead?" Shelley blinked back tears. God, when had that little boy come to mean so much to her? She wasn't supposed to get attached to people. She knew better.

"I don't think Tomás would still be on this side of the light if something had happened to Beau. I've seen families in the afterlife. If they're close, they find each other. Travel together." Jules shook her head. "No, I think Beau is alive. Ian and Ryan will find him. You'll see."

Shelley hoped, no she wished, with everything inside her that Jules was right. "You know, without Tomás, Beau is on his own. That sweet little boy is stuck in the system all alone, just like we were."

"He's got you."

Shelley started to disagree when Jules suddenly said, "Besides, we're getting off topic. You and Dev have a connection. Like Seth and me. Like Momma and Daddy . . . well, if I hadn't messed that up."

Jules dropped her arm and sighed with a faraway look in her green eyes.

"Momma and Daddy weren't happy, Jules. That's not to say you and Seth won't be, but I don't know why you think they were."

Jules stood up and paced the floor twice before facing Shelley again. Tension had her sister coiled so tight, Shelley wondered if the woman wouldn't turn into a human spring and bounce off the walls.

"Shelley, it's my fault Daddy left," Jules said, almost inaudibly. Her green gaze lowered to the floor. "He didn't know how to deal with a kid who saw ghosts. I woke up in the middle of the night and went to find him. I was scared and crying because I'd just seen his partner's spirit. I told Daddy what I

saw. He was so freaked out, he told me I was imagining things
and put me back in bed. The next day, I came home to find
Momma in the kitchen crying and Daddy gone."

Jules blinked back tears and Shelley's own eyes misted for
her sister. "Oh, Juliana, that's not why Daddy left. Didn't
Momma ever tell you?"

"Momma cried every time I mentioned him. After that,
everything happened so quick. The cancer, the hospital, the
funeral. She was gone before we knew it." Jules's head snapped
up. "What could she've told me?"

It was Shelley's turn to comfort her big sister. She hugged
her and shared a memory of the day she wished she could
forget. "Daddy had taken the car to the garage. It was always
breaking down, remember? Anyway, I was home sick from
school. I wasn't really sick anymore, but the school had a
twenty-four hour policy about fevers. Hannah was teething
and fussy, so Momma asked me to play with her while she
answered the door.

"Two very pregnant women were there. One woman had
deep olive skin and hair so black it was almost blue in the sunlight. She had twin boys on either side of her. They were
around twelve years old. The other one had white-blond hair.
I remember thinking she looked like a pregnant fairy. The
dark-haired woman asked if Momma was married to Jerimah
Scott."

Shelley paused, unsure how to continue.

"Who were they?" Jules asked, when Shelley let the silence
drag on too long.

"They said they were Mrs. Scott," Shelley said, remembering the way Momma crumbled that day. "They said Daddy
was married to all three of them."

Jules sat gaping for several long minutes. Shelley understood. She'd had nearly twenty years to adjust to the truth and
remembering that day still stung.

"How did I not know Daddy was a bigamist?" Jules whispered the last word. "Are you certain?"

Shelley nodded. "The blond one found some receipts that
didn't jive with something Daddy had told her about his business trips. Seems he liked to keep his real name when he married women, but he kept changing what he claimed was his

profession from one wife to the next. With us, he was a trucker. With the blonde, he was a land developer, and I don't remember what he said he did with the dark-haired one.

"They even brought photos with them. Some were of family vacations they'd taken with Daddy. Others were from some private investigator. I was so young at the time, I remember being excited to see Daddy in new pictures. Momma started crying and just didn't stop. She made the women promise never to contact her again and threw them out. Then she started throwing Daddy's stuff into the garbage cans out back.

"When he came home a couple hours later, they fought. Hannah and I hid under my bed while they yelled at each other. Hannah fell asleep—that girl could sleep through anything. I didn't. I listened to him tell her that if she'd been a better mother, she wouldn't have had freaks for kids. That if she'd been a better wife, he wouldn't have needed others. Then the door slammed. Momma started sobbing then. I crawled out from under the bed and found her in the kitchen. I hugged her. She made me promise not to tell anyone what had happened."

"Why?" Jules had tears streaming down her cheeks. "Why would he do that? Why wouldn't she want anyone to know? We have brothers out there somewhere?"

"At least two." Shelley shrugged. "Jules, Momma was a proud woman. If you had heard Daddy yelling, you'd have understood. He made it sound like his man-ho lifestyle was entirely her fault. And ours. He called us freaks. All. Of. Us. Then he left."

And damn it. That lump that always formed in her throat when she remembered that day came back. Her eyes stung and her vision turned blurry. God, she hated the man for destroying her mother. Hated him more for being the first in a long line of people to abandon her.

"Oh, Shelley." Jules pulled her into a fierce hug. "You were only five when that happened. I'm so sorry."

Her arms came up of their own accord, and for the first time in her life, Shelley let her sister comfort her about what their bastard of a father had done. "I'm sorry I didn't tell you. I didn't know you blamed yourself."

Jules squeezed tighter briefly, then sat back. "Well, the truth's out now. And there are more of us to find. After Hannah. We need to find her first. Then we'll be a family, like we should have been."

Dread made its way down her spine. "Jules, I'm glad you don't hate me for what I said when we were separated."

"What are you talking about? The screaming match? When I made you go with Nate and Jill. Please. I'm just glad you don't hate me. You're my sister. I love you."

And dang if that didn't make Shelley's eyes get all moist. Fear slid down her spine; this happy reunion couldn't last. Jules had to know that. And as much as it stank, Shelley had to make it clear. "Look, I'm happy to have found you again. And I'm glad you have such a good life, but I'm not staying here. I have a life back in Elkridge."

Jules frowned; she stared past Shelley at something near the open doorway. It was then that Shelley realized that the dread she'd felt slithering down her spine was actually the room temperature dropping.

She glanced back at her sister who'd gone pale.

"Are you sure?" Jules asked empty space.

Unsure whether speaking would break the connection Jules seemed to have with the specter, Shelley sat silent.

"Yes, I understand. But we're supposed to stay here," Jules said, just before the lights in the room flashed bright, then exploded.

Shelley ducked and threw her arms over Jules's head to protect her from the flying glass of the exploded light bulb on the bedside table.

And still Jules spoke. "Okay, I understand. I'll get her there, but you'd better guarantee that you'll stay with us. I don't want to walk into a trap without some way out of it."

The room went from freezing to saunalike within seconds. Jules fell backward across the bed, seemingly unconscious. Checking that her pulse was steady, Shelley hurried to the bathroom. Her shoes crunched across the broken glass. Grabbing a small wastebasket, she set it beside the bed. The room was stifling. She opened the slider and salty air wafted into the room.

Unsure what to do next, she reached for the phone to dial

Dev. She'd barely picked it up when Jules opened her eyes. She rubbed her head and slowly sat up, appearing disoriented. Dropping the cell onto the nightstand again, Shelley hurried over to her sister.

"Jules, how are you feeling?"

Her sister blinked twice before her eyes bulged in panic.

Shelley grabbed the bucket, but Jules shoved it away.

"Confused." Jules stumbled to her feet, swayed. "Tomás is really upset. He can't find Beau. He thinks something has happened to him."

Shelley caught her by the elbows and helped her remain upright, ignoring the fear skating down her back. "Why does he think that?"

"Because." Jules gulped air, as if to stave off the urge to vomit. "Because he can hear Beau calling for him, but he can't reach him. Tomás wants you to find Beau. Now. He says the child will only come to you."

CHAPTER 22

"I CALLED EVERYONE in," Captain Peterson said, walking into his office and taking a seat behind his large cherry-wood desk. "The sheriff of Elkridge is an old friend of mine. He's asked for our help with a couple of murder cases."

Dev struggled to keep silent. Normally, he didn't mind waiting. But he didn't typically have one very antsy vet at his house either.

The captain picked up his phone and dialed. Reynolds and O'Dell, the two homicide cops currently seated in the only two visitors' chairs in the captain's office, turned their attention to him.

"Eager to get back to your vacation?" O'Dell said out of the side of his mouth. He made a shooing motion. "Run along, kid. The real homicide cops can handle it from here."

"Thank you for that incredible offer," Dev replied, in an undertone. "The captain assigned me to this case. Don't you remember? I'd see a doctor about that memory issue you're having. They have meds for early-onset dementia."

"Good zinger, Jones. I didn't know you had it in you," Seth said, then turned back to O'Dell, whose face was turning as red as his ugly tie. "Why are you two here? I thought you were on the construction-site murder."

"Do I have everyone on the line?" The captain's question was louder than necessary and not directed at just the phone's speaker. Dev gave the captain his full attention.

Two voices, one male and one female, responded over the crackling airwaves.

"Great, let's get everyone up to speed." Captain Peterson glanced at the four men in his office. "Sheriff Webber, Dr. Clark, you're on speaker with four of my best detectives, Reynolds, O'Dell, English, and Jones. Gentlemen, Webber is with the Elkridge Sheriff's Office. You all know Dr. Charles Clark.

"Dr. Clark, let's start with you. Have you had a chance to examine the body found this morning in Elkridge?"

Dr. Clark, a woman in her mid-forties, despite her masculine first name, cleared her throat. "My findings are preliminary. I have examined the body identified as Tomás Rodriguez. I've also read the report the sheriff shared with me. His deputy's assertion that the victim had been stabbed through the neck with the screwdriver found in the apartment of one Dr. Shelley Grace Morgan was correct."

"We train them right in Elkridge," the sheriff said, pride in his voice.

"I'm sure you do, sir," she said, then paused. "However, the cause of death was not exsanguination. The victim was stabbed postmortem. There was very little blood in the trunk. The car in question also owned by Dr. Morgan appears to be a dump site rather than the kill site. The actual cause of death was due to dislocation of the C4 and C5 vertebrae in his spine." Dr. Clark, in true form, paused for effect, then added the layman's term, as if any of them needed it. "His neck was broken."

"His neck was snapped? You're sure?" the sheriff asked.

"Yes, quite positive. Someone broke it like the proverbial dry twig. Given the angle of the fracture, the killer approached the victim from the front, either subdued the victim, or moved too quickly for the victim to fight back. A single, very forceful snap, and the victim died within seconds," the M.E. announced. "I'd have to say, given the size of your victim, I would suspect the killer to be a male and at least six feet tall."

The sheriff exhaled a puff of air. "That's excellent news."

"Glad to be of service."

"Why is that good news, Sheriff?" the captain asked. "You seemed pleased with the M.E.'s report. But didn't that contradict your suspicions?"

"Yes, it did," the sheriff replied. No missing the relief in his tone. "That's the best damned news I've had in a week. If Tomás's killer is a man, then it absolutely rules out our prime suspect."

Dev had to admit, he was reassured to hear Sheriff Webber conceding the point so easily. Dev had already guessed the prime suspect was Shelley. He glanced at Seth who cast him a quick, barely imperceptible nod.

"You're happy to lose your prime suspect?" O'Dell leaned forward in his seat, speaking directly into the intercom. "Care to explain that bit of small-town logic to me?"

"Elkridge might be small, but it ain't run amok with stupid," Sheriff Webber retorted, his southern accent considerably more pronounced than it had been.

"O'Dell!" Captain Peterson snapped. "I apologize, Sheriff Webber. I believe my *detective* was trying to ask why you'd want your prime suspect ruled out."

Webber was silent for a moment, then replied in his normal voice. "Our prime suspect was Dr. Morgan. She's the town vet and one of the most respected people in Elkridge. The last thing I wanted to do was arrest the woman most folks in the Ridge have come to consider family. Doesn't go over too well going into an election year, to arrest someone who's well loved. So, yes, I'm pleased to have her ruled out."

Whoa. Shelley is that well regarded in Elkridge? Does she know this?

"Understood," Captain Peterson said. He leaned back in his leather chair and tapped his pen against his chin. Tap. Tap. Tap. He stopped, straightened, and asked, "Got any other suspects in mind?"

"Not really." Sheriff Webber's voice crackled through the speaker. "The only suspect we had was Dr. Morgan, but again that was only because the third victim was found in her car and the murder weapon in her apartment. It don't help that she's gone missing too. Although, Kenny, he's the local mechanic, says he'd heard from her just yesterday. Just no one's seen her. I'd like to know she was all right, myself."

Dev considered speaking up until his captain said, "Sheriff Webber, when you contacted me this morning, you mentioned that Tomás Rodriguez was the third member of your community to turn up dead in the last week?" Dev wasn't the only detective in the room to go on high alert. "Let's talk about the other two murders, Colbert Rush and John Wallace."

"Excuse me." Dr. Clark's feminine voice filtered through the air. "But as you already have my reports on those two cases, I'd like to get back to work."

"Of course. Thank you for your time, Dr. Clark." When she disconnected from the call, the captain asked, "Sheriff Webber, what can you tell us about the relationship between Wallace and Rush to Elkridge."

The sheriff didn't hesitate. "Their families have been here since the town was founded two hundred years ago. Rush didn't live in Elkridge anymore, but he kept a fishing cabin he used a couple times a year. We'd also see him once a month for his standing haircut with the barber. Rush's time in town was limited to a few hours a month, generally.

"Last week, Colbert Rush placed an order at the local antique store. He never picked it up. He also missed his appointment with the barber. Yesterday, his wife called us to report he'd been found murdered."

"You didn't hear about his body showing up all over Tidewater's beaches?"

"Not at the time." Sheriff Webber paused. "Last summer, another one of our local boys disappeared, John Wallace. Wallace . . . well, at the time of his death, he was still living in the house he grew up in. His body was found yesterday in the swamp by our town's mechanic, Kenny Parran."

"And now Tomás Rodriguez has been found dead," Dev said. Then he asked the question he really wanted answered, "Do you have anything tying the murders together?"

"Only Elkridge "

"Is it possible that this vet, Dr. Morgan, could be tied to all three men? That she knew them," Reynolds asked.

The sheriff barked a short laugh. "Son, it's Elkridge. Everyone knows everyone in this town."

"So it is possible that she could still be involved," O'Dell interjected.

"Except that Clark told us the Rodriguez killer is likely a man, at least six feet tall," Seth interjected and earned a narrow-eyed glare from O'Dell.

"She couldn't be Rush's killer," Sheriff Webber said emphatically. "Her alibi for his death is solid."

"How's that?" Dev asked, eager to hear just how solid her alibi was.

"Aside from the fact she's got no motive for killing Rodriguez, Rush, or Wallace?" the sheriff asked, but didn't wait for a response. "Rush was last seen at the antique store at five in the evening, by no less then four witnesses, on the night of his disappearance. And the M.E. puts the time of his murder somewhere between five p.m. and five a.m. the next day, when the first piece of his body was recovered. I know the doc is in the clear. She was helping my cat, Spider, give birth to her kittens. Spider was hit by a car and went into labor. Doc Morgan was with me from four in the afternoon until past four a.m. at the clinic the night of the murder."

Sheriff Webber has a cat named Spider?

Dev cast a quick glance to Seth, who smiled, but covered it with his hand.

"Is there anything else that ties the three victims together?" Dev asked.

"I can't think of anything." Sheriff Webber sighed. "Rodriguez is new to town. He's only lived here for about seven years."

"That's new?" Reynolds asked, a unibrow of confusion on his face. "What's considered local? Christ, live in Tidewater five years and you're considered a local."

"Not in Elkridge. Locals are folks whose parents were born and raised in the town. Not a lot of people move in or out. Dr. Morgan and Tomás are the first folks to move to the Ridge in years."

Reynolds visibly shuddered. "Thank God I live in the city."

The sheriff's voice turned cold. "Are you sayin' there's something wrong with small towns, *Detective?*"

"No, he's not." Captain Peterson ran a hand over his balding head and refocused the meeting. "You were saying Rodriguez wasn't a local?"

"Yes, but John Wallace and Colbert Rush were. Three

generations of Rushes worked in the sheriff's office. Most were the womenfolk. They worked in administration. Colbert was a deputy for a few years, until he decided he wanted more than small-town life. He quit law enforcement about twenty-five years ago and got into his wife's family business."

"Jewels," Seth said.

"Right." The sheriff agreed. "His wife had said that the Rushes still kept the family property but came for the summer to get away from the Tidewater tourists."

Dev's cell phone buzzed. He tugged it from his pocket and glanced at it. Shelley's name appeared on the caller I.D. He let it slide to voice mail, suspecting it was her asking, again, if it was safe for her to go back to Elkridge.

"What about John Wallace? Any ties to Rush?"

"Yeah, now that I think on it. Long time ago he and Rush went to school together. Grew up together. But where Rush went into law enforcement, Wallace became a lawyer. He's a retired assistant district attorney."

A current went through the room. Everyone straightened and turned eyes to the captain, who asked, "Did Wallace and Rush ever work on the same case?"

"I don't rightly know. If they did, it would have been more than twenty years ago. Most of the files from back then are in boxes in the basement of the station. I could have one of my deputies look—" The sheriff cut himself off, then whistled. "Wait a minute. I remember something about a case from when I was a kid. Something about a hit-and-run. Rush and Colbert were both assigned to the case. There was a lot of talk about it, but no one was ever arrested."

"Did they have a suspect?" Dev asked.

"Yeah. Eddy Jameson."

"The owner of the Elkridge Zoo?" Dev's pulse kicked up. Shelley might have been onto something much bigger than animal thefts.

"That's the guy." Webber paused. "How do you know the Jamesons?"

"Sheriff, I've got a better question than that," Seth said, drawing the attention away from Dev. "What do a retired D.A., a former deputy, and a dead zookeeper have in common?"

"That's for you and Jones to figure out," the captain said.

*   *   *

"DANG IT! SETH'S still not picking up."

Shelley tore her gaze from the road briefly and cast her sister a quick, sympathetic glance.

Jules apparently didn't notice. She slapped the button on her Bluetooth and tossed it into the cup holder of Seth's Honda. "Any luck with Dev?"

"Sorry, Jules. Dev's not answering either," Shelley said, gripping the steering wheel and fighting the urge to drive faster.

"What could they be doing?"

Shelley did look at her sister then. Jules had bags under her eyes and lines digging deep groves at the corners of her mouth. Shelley's heart squeezed, but she tried to cover it by lightening the mood. "Wait, I know this one. They're working a case and can't answer the phone."

"Ha. Very ha." But Jules's expression softened a bit. "Are you sure Callie will be all right by herself? You said she needs to eat every few hours."

"You said your assistant would take care of her."

Jules nodded reluctantly. "Yes, but I'm not sure how keen Dev's going to be on the idea of Diana having the run of his house. She does have a crush on him, after all."

Shelley shrugged. "He'll live. Besides, we couldn't exactly take a ferret and a nursing kitten with us, could we?"

"You've got a point, Tomás."

Shelley jerked her gaze to the rearview mirror again, half expecting to see the groundskeeper. All she saw was an empty back seat. "Tomás is in the car?"

"Yes. He's been back there for most of the trip." Jules mentioned the ghost as if she were discussing which kind of pet food to buy. "He said that Callie would do better in a warm bed than running around in the November night air."

Jules laughed lightly.

"What?"

"He also said that he was glad he didn't have to ride with the ferret. She doesn't like him."

"Lucy can see ghosts?" Shelley asked, stunned by the thought. "I've never had a single animal tell me they can see spirits."

"I don't know if they see them so much as sense them. And I don't know if all animals can do it. I've never had an animal talk to me. That's your crift," Jules said with a smirk. "But I know dogs can sense specters. More than once I've had Theresa's dog growl when a ghost appeared." An odd expression crossed Jules's face. She swiveled her upper body again, stared into the back seat and asked, "Were you outside my apartment building last night?"

"You know I was." *What was she talking about?*

"Not you, Silly Shelley." Jules waved a dismissive hand and grinned. "I was asking Tomás."

"What did he say?" Shelley asked after several minutes of silence. "And don't call me Silly Shelley. I always hated that nickname."

Jules winked at her when she straightened in her seat. "I know. Why do you think I used to say it?"

I came back for this? Shelley, wisely, kept her lips pressed tight rather than ask.

"Oh. Darn." Jules frowned. "Wasn't him. He saw you but was nowhere near you when the dog went nuts. He thinks it was a different ghost. Great, it was probably another lost soul who needed my help but will have to wait until I get home. Hope it wasn't a time-sensitive emergency in the mortal realm."

"Time-sensitive emergency in the mortal realm?" *Who talks like that?* "Can't you just call to the ghost? You said they can hear their names, right?"

"Yes, mortal realm. It's a lot easier to say than 'the land of the living.'"

Shelley exited off the interstate and the city melted away, replaced by a highway surrounded on both sides by thick forest.

"And I would call the ghost or ghosts if I knew their names, but Tomás didn't get close enough to find out."

It made Shelley wonder, "Is that the only way to reach the ghosts?"

Jules was quiet for so long, Shelley wasn't sure her sister would answer the question. "No, if a ghost sticks around the mortal realm, he or she looks for someone like me to talk to. Word gets around the ghost world when people like me exist. Usually I don't have to do anything, and they come to me.

Sometimes, like with that dead woman from Seth and Dev's jewelry theft, a ghost attaches itself to an object."

"The stolen diamonds?"

"Exactly."

"But I don't have anything of Tomás's."

"I think it's why he couldn't find you until you said his name. He was searching for you but had nothing to . . . I don't know, grab onto, I suppose. Am I making any sense?"

"In a weird way, yes." Shelley cast her sister a quick glance. "And you live with this all the time? I never realized how hard it must have been for you when we were kids."

"No harder than you talking to every squirrel, raccoon, and cat on the street," Jules countered with a grin. "It's not so bad anymore. Once I stopped fighting the crift, it's been getting easier. Plus, there are definitely benefits to being able to see things other folks can't."

A roadside sign read thirty miles to Elkridge. Shelley glanced at her watch. She didn't want to think about Beau, frightened and possibly in danger. The idea of anyone hurting that child made her queasy, and so angry she actually scared herself. So she pushed the thoughts away and focused on what Jules was saying.

". . . and Seth loves me for who I am. Just like Dev loves you." Jules smiled.

"Jules, I'm happy for you. I truly am. But I told you, Dev and I are just friends."

Jules gave her the "are you crazy?" look. "Right. And you *didn't* sleep together last night?" She paused and added, "Sorry."

"Oh God." A heat burned Shelley's cheeks. Even her ears went hot. "I have a life in Elkridge. I have a purpose there. Dev and I were just getting a college fantasy out of our systems." She clapped a hand over her mouth. "I can't believe I just said that in front of Tomás. Bad enough you heard it."

Jules shook her head. "Don't worry, he took off right after I apologized for mentioning that you and Dev slept together. I think if he could have blushed, he would have. Anyway, I think he was giving us some privacy."

"You were apologizing to him." Shelley's head was starting to ache. "I thought you were talking to me. How does Seth know whether or not you're talking to him?"

Jules gave her a wicked smile.

Instantly, Shelley regretted the question. "Never mind, I don't want to know."

All at once, the check engine light lit up and smoke began pouring from the car's hood.

DEV HADN'T LOOKED at his phone since Shelley called when he'd first stepped into the office. Now he could kick himself. Finally, the captain dismissed them to work on the case, and there were six texts from Shells; the last two read Can't wait and Worried about the boy. He was about to hit send when Seth, climbing into the passenger seat of Dev's car, said, "Fuck! The girls are gone."

Seth flashed his iPhone at Dev. The text from Jules said it all: Tomás thinks Beau is in danger. Come ASAP. "I can't believe they left after we specifically told them not to. What am I saying? It's Jules, of course I can believe it."

Dev was out of the parking lot and pulling onto the highway before Seth had fastened his seat belt. Snaking between cars, Dev kept the speed between eighty and ninety, all the while silently cursing Shelley and himself for not realizing sooner that she would feel obliged to race to the boy's rescue. Regardless of her own safety.

But damn! There was a killer on the loose. One who'd already likely drugged Shelley and had definitely been in her home. The idea of something happening to Shells . . . of her ending up like Wallace or Rush or Tomás made him want to puke. He'd be damned if he'd let that happen. She'd been hurt in college because he hadn't been there to protect her, but he'd protect her now.

They drove in silence for a half hour. Dev was lost in thoughts of his case, Shelley, and the meeting in the captain's office. He began to doubt his silence at the station.

"Seth, do you think I should have told the sheriff about suspecting that Shelley had been drugged?" Dev asked, gripping the steering wheel tighter and zipping around a car that pulled into his lane.

"Kid, plausible deniability. The moment you mention the drugs, you admit to knowing where she is. Even if the good sheriff thinks she's in the clear, you've just admitted to potentially hampering an investigation. You want to get yanked from this case? Tell the captain or the sheriff that you spent last night in bed with Shelley. I guarantee, you'll be off the case and on foot patrol faster than you can blink. Like it or not, you made the decision the moment you didn't call it in when you saw the news report." Seth made a disgusted sound in his throat. "Don't worry, kid, I'll be right there with you busting kids for jaywalking. Unless we can solve this first. So no, I don't think you should have said a damned word."

"Crap, we should have taken her to the hospital to be tested for the drugs in her system." Dev didn't want to think about what might have happened to her in her impaired state. Then it occurred to him. "I thought you were by the book. When did that change?"

"When I got engaged to a woman who sees ghosts."

Dev hit autodial on his phone and waited.

Ian answered on the first ring. "Glad you called, Cuz. Ryan and I have big news. We're headed your way. Should be at your place in about forty-five minutes."

"I hope it's good news. I need it right now."

Seth's phone rang. He answered it, then said, "Crap! The car broke down, where? Where the hell is Carson?"

"IT'S ABOUT THIRTY miles east of Elkridge," Jules said into the phone. "Seth, don't worry. There's a gas station with a little restaurant across the street called the Café and Gas."

Shelley stared through the steam, not smoke, rising from the hood at the shabby little diner on the other side of the gas pumps. Maybe they'd have someone inside who could look at the car?

"Ian and Ryan? Are you sure?" Jules sounded slightly exasperated. "Fine. I said, *fine*, Seth, dang. We'll meet you inside. Yes, she drove. I'd have gotten us lost before we left Tidewater." She paused, listening. "Yes, I know you said to add water to it before driving. We did that. I have no idea why it died. Maybe because the car's older than Theresa? Good-bye Seth." Jules pressed the button on her Bluetooth.

"Let's get the car off the road," Shelley said, putting Lucy in her carrier. Together they pushed the car the last few hundred feet off the mostly deserted road and into the parking lot of the gas station.

Hot and sweating, Shelley and Jules climbed back into the car. "Well, I won't need to go to the gym tomorrow," Jules said, wiping the back of her hand across her brow.

"You work out?" Shelley huffed, wondering if that would help her trim down.

Jules laughed. "Not ever. That was a joke."

"What now?"

"Dev, Seth, Ian, and Ryan are on their way. Dev and Seth are about forty minutes away, but Ian and Ryan were in Elkridge and on their way back. They should be here any minute with news."

"Has Tomás come back yet? Has he found Beau?" Shelley jiggled her knee, unable to sit completely still. "Maybe someone inside will give us a lift to Elkridge?"

Jules gave her a dubious look. "Look, Seth said Ian and Ryan will be here any minute. They just passed the café on their way back to Tidewater. We should wait for them."

"But Tomás said he thought Beau was in trouble, didn't he?"

Someone knocked on Shelley's window, making both women jump.

In the dim glow of the last vestiges of sunset, Ian smiled his usual Hollywood smile. "Pop the hood, then head inside for a bit while Ryan and I take a look. Dev and Seth will be here shortly. He said to wait."

"We don't have time to wait. Beau's missing."

"No, he's not." Ian gave a good-natured shrug. "He's fine."

"Really?" Shelley climbed out of the car and looked around for the boy. "Where is he?"

Ian's friendly expression turned to stone. "Ryan and I left him about an hour ago. At his foster mother's. She's a wicked-cold bitch. But the kid seemed okay, except for the bruises on his face that looked a couple days old."

"Someone needs to report her," Ryan said, reaching past where Shelley stood in the doorway of the car; he popped the hood. "We'd have brought him with us, but we couldn't get close to him. And he didn't look too excited to see two big men standing in the woman's doorway."

"But he did smile," Ian added, helping Jules out of the car. "When I promised her that I'd be back and there had better not be another mark on him."

* * *

IT HAD TAKEN ten minutes for Ian, Ryan, and Jules to convince Shelley to wait in the diner. Sitting in the booth next to the large picture window overlooking the road, she'd watched as Ian and Ryan poured antifreeze into Seth's engine, then took it for a test drive. The men pulled the car around the back of the café, out of sight.

Knowing that Beau was alive and unhurt, if not completely safe, at Mama Margaret's was a relief. The tension in her shoulders had begun to lessen.

Her cell phone rang and hoping it was Dev, she answered without looking. "Hello?"

"You've gotta help me! There's someone in here." Jacob's hushed voice sounded frantic. "Oh crap. Oh crap! He hit Dr. Kessler. The old man's not moving. I think he's dead!"

Shelley's heart catapulted into her throat, but she kept her voice even. "Jacob, where are you?"

"In the clinic. I'm in the dog spa." Jacob's whispered words were punctuated with sniffles. "He's going to kill me too. I know it."

"Jacob, call 9-1-1." Shelley started to sweat. He didn't answer. And he still didn't answer. "Jacob! Did you hear me? Call 9-1-1."

"I already did. The operator put me on hold." Jacob sobbed, his voice pitching higher with each word. "Oh, God! Oh, God! I can hear him moving around out front."

"Jacob, stay calm and quiet. Can you get out of there? Do you know who's in there with you?" Shelley tugged her sister's sleeve across the table to get Jules's attention, mouthing, "Call Seth now!"

"Christ, I don't want to die." Jacob started to cry. "He's gone crazy."

"Who's gone crazy, Jacob?" Shelley asked. "Talk to me, Jacob. Who killed Dr. Kessler?"

"It was—" Jacob's words were cut off with an ear-piercing scream.

Then the line went dead.

While Jules spoke quietly into her cell, Shelley dialed 9-1-1 and relayed everything Jacob had told her as calmly as possible. She explained about the phone call and the scream.

"And your name?" asked the operator, keys tapping in the background.

Shelley bit her lip. It's not like they couldn't figure out who was calling based on her cell phone. Elkridge was small, but it did utilize the advanced 9-1-1 system. She inhaled a deep breath and prayed she wasn't doing the wrong thing. "This is Dr. Shelley Morgan of the Elkridge Veterinary Clinic."

The tapping stopped and the operator went quiet. Across from her, Jules spoke earnestly into her cell. Her words hurried and hushed.

"Ma'am, did you say you're Dr. Morgan?" asked the 9-1-1 dispatcher, his voice unnaturally calm. "Are you at the clinic?"

"Yes, I'm Dr. Morgan, but no, I'm not at the clinic. I told you, my intern, Jacob Durand called me in a panic. He said someone is trying to kill him and the killer's still there."

"Ma'am, there are deputies on the scene. They would like to speak with you." He paused, then added in an even more casual tone, "Can you give me your current address?"

Shelley clicked end. She hugged the phone against her pounding chest. Almost numbly, she watched Dev's car pull into the parking lot. Jacob's words echoed in her ears.

I think he's dead.

CHAPTER 23

"TIME TO GET the sheriff involved," Dev said with regret the moment Shelley had filled him in on the call from Jacob. He turned to his cousins, who'd followed him into the café, saying in an undertone, "Stay with her."

He bent to kiss Shelley on the forehead, but she lifted her face to his and his lips found hers. It was soft and reassuring, and something warm flashed in her eyes. Then they misted again and she looked away saying, "I'll be here when you get back."

Seth followed him outside the café but gave Dev a bit of privacy. Still, Dev was grateful for the moral support. "I'll keep you out of it."

Seth gave a shrug but said, "Hurry up. Ryan mentioned they'd found something useful."

Dev nodded and dialed.

The sheriff answered the phone on the second ring. "Sheriff Webber."

"Sheriff, this is Detective Jones from Tidewater."

"I'm in the middle of an emergency here. Can I call you back?"

"Are you at the clinic?" Dev didn't miss the pregnant pause before the sheriff said, "How'd you know about that?"

God, this was going to suck when the captain heard Dev
had withheld his knowledge of Shelley. "Because Dr. Morgan
called me."

"She *called* you?" The sheriff's tone went sharp and cold.
"How in the hell did she do that?"

"Sir, we're old friends." *And if that wasn't an understate-
ment.*

"And you didn't think this was important enough to mention at any point in the past few hours?" The man's voice
edged closer to ice.

"I'm sorry, sir. You said yourself, she wasn't a suspect. I
didn't think my relationship with her mattered." Dev's phone
beeped. He glanced at the screen. It was Ian. "Sir, I do apologize,
but this is urgent. Dr. Morgan received a call from her intern. He
said there'd been a break-in and their boss had been murdered."

"Son, if you're planning to screw with my investigation—"

"I'm not, sir." Dev paused, then appealed to the man's com-
passionate side. "Sheriff, Dr. Morgan is very important to me.
I'd still like to join my partner and aid in the investigation.
Now more than ever. And, sir, you said yourself she couldn't
have committed the murders. I'm just making sure she's not
going to end up another victim."

Another long pause and the sheriff blew out a hard breath.
"I'm with Dr. Kessler in the ambulance right now. He was seriously injured. He went into cardiac arrest but was revived. When
my deputies arrived on the scene, he was the only one here. We
have a BOLO out for Jacob Durand. Where are you now?"

"We've stopped to get gas in Carson."

"Fine. I'll send one of my deputies to meet with you and
your partner."

"Thank you, Sheriff."

"Remember something, no matter how much I like Dr.
Morgan, if she's involved, you cannot protect her. And I will
be having a conversation with your captain about this. Keep in
mind, son, you and your partner are coming to Elkridge to
help. It's still *my* investigation."

Dev grimaced at the not-unexpected reprimand. "Yes, sir."

"I have to get off the line. I'll have one of my deputies contact you." The phone disconnected.

*   *   *

ADAM BARELY MADE it back to the zoo. For his plan to be successful, he needed the final executions to take place here. No exceptions. Seemed only fitting, considering why he'd started his righteous path in the first place.

Something was wrong. The zoo was unusually silent. No owls hooted. The leaves didn't rustle. Like the earth itself was waiting with bated breath, but for what?

A small snick of a twig snapping cut through the quiet.

Adam jerked his head to the right. Even in the dark, he could find his way around this place. He'd been doing it for years. Carefully, he moved through the woods, just to the right of the footpath leading to the tiger's cage.

Another snick. This time, followed by the sound of a chain-link gate squeaking open.

Not again.

He hopped onto the trail and raced to the tigress. He had maybe twenty feet of ground to cover before he could get into the safety of the trees. Adam would not fail again. He would see justice served.

THROUGH MISTY EYES, Shelley watched Dev kick at a rock in the parking lot while he spoke on his cell. When the car broke down, she'd been distracted. Now reality sank in.

"Oh, God! Poor Dr. Kessler. Jacob said he was dead. Someone had attacked them. Why is this happening?"

"I don't know, hon." Jules came around and scooted into the booth beside Shelley, wrapping her arms around her. Jules smelled like Momma.

Funny, Shelley hadn't thought of Momma's scent in years. And maybe Jules didn't so much smell like their mother as feel like her. Momma had held her just like this, the summer the baby birds fell out of the tree in the backyard during the thunderstorm. Shelley had wanted to run out in the middle of the lightning and hail, but Momma had stopped her and just held her until her tears were spent.

But Shelley wasn't four anymore. Momma was gone. She

couldn't do this to herself. She mustn't let herself need Jules, not even for temporary comfort.

Shelley pulled away from her sister's embrace and swiped angrily at her tears. "Why would someone kill Dr. Kessler? Is it the same person who murdered Tomás? And why bother to try to frame me, only to go and kill my boss?"

"I don't know, honey." Jules stroked a hand down Shelley's hair. "I don't know. We'll find out."

"Your boss isn't dead," Ryan said in his deep, rumbling voice. He'd returned from fixing Seth's car and squatted in front of them. Unlike Ian who made small talk an art form, Ryan hardly spoke. Despite his being a giant, there was a quiet grace about him. Soothing. Even squatting as he was now, he was so tall that he was eye level with Shelley.

"But Jacob said . . ." Angry tears burned behind her eyes. She'd already explained three times about the phone call from Jacob, she couldn't do it again.

Ryan gave his head a slow shake. "No, someone *tried*. Dev spoke with the sheriff. Dr. Kessler is in the hospital."

"Oh, thank God!" Relief made the tears she'd been fighting leak down her face. "What about Jacob? Is he all right?"

"The deputies found only the elderly doctor."

Shelley scrubbed her cheeks and forced herself to calm down. "What now?"

"We wait for Dev and Seth to come back inside."

Shelley opened her mouth to argue when Ian came to the table with six glasses of tea. *Are we having dinner here too?* Shelley's question must have shown on her face because Ian flashed his trademark grin and said, "We're taking up a booth, a table, and space in the parking lot. Least we can do is buy something. I ordered monster fries too."

He set the drinks down in front of her, while Ryan pulled a small square table flush against the one in the booth. Ian and Ryan flipped chairs backward and sat, leaving one bench in the booth empty. Jules, seeming to recognize that Shelley was better, moved back to the opposite bench just before Dev and Seth joined them.

To Shelly's surprise, she found she was still very thirsty.

"Ryan and I discovered some interesting facts in town

today," Ian said, spreading out photocopies of newspaper articles on the gray-laminate table.

"Talk fast, we've got a deputy headed this way," Dev said, his face grim.

"This was in the Historical Museum," Ryan said, pointing to a photocopy of an old newspaper article from the *Elkridge Edition,* dated May 10, 1989. In the center picture labeled DESCENDANTS OF OUR FOUNDING FATHERS: ELKRIDGE, VA., three young men, smiling for the camera, stood with arms wrapped around one another's shoulders. The one in the middle was familiar.

"That's Eddy Jameson, the zoo owner. He's wearing a deputy's uniform. Was it Halloween or something?" Shelley scanned the page, but no one else appeared to be in costume. What she did see startled her. She pointed to a man at Eddy's left. "Hey, I think that's a young John Wallace."

"And that's Colbert Rush." Seth pointed to another man several spaces over.

"McGivern's dead partner," Dev supplied.

"Wait, there's more. This article was continued on the back page." Ian slid over another sheet of the photocopied news article. "They were at their high school's five-year reunion. Listen to this: 'Best friends John Wallace, Colbert Rush, and Eddy Jameson are together celebrating the engagement of Jameson to the daughter of Elkridge veterinarian Dr. Herbert Kessler. Miss Rebecca Kessler and Mr. Edward Jameson are to be married on August 5, 1989.'"

"They were friends." Ian pointed farther down the page. "The three of them are mentioned several more times over the years, but never together again."

Recognition hit her like a bolt of lightning. "Oh, Frack! Colbert Rush. That's the guy with the bite on his hand. Now I know why that wound seemed familiar."

Ian and Ryan asked in unison, "Why?"

"It's a tiger bite." Shelley stared at the old image of Colbert Rush and tried to remember exactly what the bite had looked like. She couldn't quite see it. "Dev, do you have the photo with you?"

"Files are in my car." Dev started to rise, but Ryan was

faster, saying, "Toss me your keys—keep going." The key fob arced through the air. Ryan caught it easily and raced outside.

"Why didn't you mention it sooner?" Dev asked, his hand covering hers gently.

"I only glanced at it briefly when the news came on about a body being found in my trunk. I did tell you that he was local though."

"Fine," Dev said at the same time Seth asked, "What else do we know?"

Shelley glanced at the news article. "Something's not right." She reread the passage. "Eddy's wife wasn't named Rebecca. Her name was Leticia. She died in a car accident last year. The whole town still talks about her. She's the reason the zoo exists in the first place. Eddy built it for her."

"Maybe he divorced Rebecca?" Jules asked. The blue smudges of exhaustion under her eyes were more pronounced.

"I don't see how." Shelley started to ask Jules if she was okay, but then Seth put an arm around her. Jules rested her head against his shoulder. "Uh, Cristos, Eddy's son, told me that his parents fell in love at first sight and married just three months later. That was in 1989. How could Eddy have married Rebecca and Leticia the same year?"

"You know how," Jules said, eyes narrowed.

"Yeah, but Eddy's not like Daddy. Besides, something else is wrong. Dr. Kessler is my boss. He's said time and again his only children were his dogs. So who was Rebecca? And what happened to her?"

"Here's another article on Eddy marrying a Leticia Sandoval," Ian said, pointing at another page. "Whoa, looks like Leticia's family was the ruling class back in the day. How'd the owner of a broken-down zoo land her?"

"It wasn't broken down then. Eddy's family was well to do in their own right. From what I've heard, Eddy was devoted to Leticia. To this day, he hasn't been able to go near the road where she was killed."

Ian pulled out his cell phone and began to tap on it.

Ryan returned, dropped the files and key in front of Dev, reclaimed his seat, and asked, "What are you doing?"

"Searching for information on Rebecca Kessler." Ian frowned.

"Can you look up obituaries?" Shelley suggested. When

Ian cocked a brow at her in question, she added, "Dr. Kessler has never talked about having a daughter. And he's the type that won't talk about one of the dogs after it died. Could be the same thing for a daughter, couldn't it?"

Ian gave her a tight-lipped smile. "Impressive. You ever consider getting into security? You could make a helluva detective."

"Don't try to recruit my girlfriend, Ian," Dev said, putting an arm around Shelley's shoulders. "Shells has an important job. One that usually doesn't put her life in danger." He frowned, then turned his stormy gray gaze on her. "It doesn't, does it?"

"Um . . . no," Shelley replied, still stunned that Dev had claimed her. They'd had sex one night. Okay, she'd come several times that one night, but she'd slept in her own bed. It was crazy to assume they were anything other than friends.

But how many friends do you sleep with? There was that. Before she could argue with herself further, Dev kissed her.

His lips found hers and she melted. Not melted exactly. More like they went nuclear. Dear God, the man could kiss. It was so incredible she almost forgot they were in a restaurant full of people.

Ian snickered. "I'd say get a room, but we don't have that much time."

Shells broke the kiss and reached a slightly shaky hand toward Dev's file.

"Can I see the photo of the bite mark?"

"Romantic," Ian said at the same time Dev said, "Yes."

It only took a minute to find the picture she'd seen earlier. She pointed to it. "That's a tiger bite."

"You're sure?" he asked, hope lighting his eyes.

"Definitely. Specifically, it's Miah's bite." She pointed to the space in between two of the bite marks. "Miah is missing one of her incisors on the top. No one can tell me how she came to be like that. She's been missing that tooth since before I came to Elkridge."

"Shells, you're brilliant!" Dev kissed her again. A fast, rough kiss that was both scintillating and intoxicating. She wanted to kiss him again. Really wanted to. She might have, but at that moment, every glass on the table exploded.

The men all jumped up, snatching at the files in an effort to save them.

Shelley jumped too, but not for the files, for Jules, who'd slid sideways out of the booth and onto the floor.

"What the hell was that?" Ian asked, stepping aside for the waitress who bustled over with a tub and a cloth.

Dev met Seth's gaze and thought he knew. Last month, Seth had described a similar situation of lightbulbs exploding when Jules met with an angry ghost in the flower shop. But he couldn't tell Ian that. Instead he shrugged and hurried to save the files on the table.

Seth and Shelley walked Jules to the bathroom. Dev would have preferred to help too, but that option became impossible when Deputy Payne Munro stepped through the front door.

"*You* are the police detective from Tidewater?" Payne said.

Fucking perfect.

"I am. Glad to see you." Dev politely extended his hand. When Payne refused it, he said, "Sheriff Webber did send you to work with me?"

"Yes." Payne propped his hands on his hips and glared at Ryan and Ian drying off a couple of their files with paper towels. "Do you normally go around talking about your cases with civilians?"

"These men run Tidewater Security Specialists. They're private consultants here at my request." Dev said, casually.

"Security specialists that you hired." It wasn't a question. More of an accusation. Payne glanced around the table with suspicion and eyed the waitress who had rushed over to help sop up the mess. She wiped away the last of the mess, then hurried away. "Detective Jones, why didn't you identify yourself as an officer when we met on Wednesday?"

"It didn't seem relevant at the time." Dev shrugged. He didn't miss the way Ian's shoulders stiffened or Ryan's head cocked. They were listening too. "I was on a date. Not on duty."

"A date with a woman who turned out to be the prime suspect in multiple murders." Payne strolled toward Ian, who straightened and handed Dev the damp manila folder. Payne glared at the exchange and said, "I'd say that's very relevant."

"If you spoke with the sheriff, then you know Dr. Morgan is alibied." What was this guy's problem? Dev stepped closer to Payne and lowered his voice, "So I ask you, why do you care if I was with Dr. Morgan at the zoo?"

* * *

SHELLEY HAD BEEN about to step out of the bathroom to ask for a glass of ice water for Jules when she heard the commotion out front. Payne's nasal voice carried through the mostly empty diner.

Seth, who'd been cradling a semiconscious Jules, placed a hand on her shoulder. "Stay here," he whispered.

Still, she opened the door a crack and listened.

"We have a witness placing Dr. Morgan at the clinic tonight."

"That's preposterous," Ian replied at the same time Dev said, "They're lying."

"Really? We'll see. I'd like to speak with Dr. Morgan regarding tonight's attack on the clinic. You wouldn't happen to know where to find her, would you, *Detective?*"

Payne used the word *detective* as if it were interchangeable with *asshole. Jerk.*

"That witness placing Dr. Morgan at the scene wouldn't be one Reyna Jameson, would it?" Dev demanded.

Oh, Dev. No.

Dev had his back to the bathroom door, no doubt blocking the deputy from getting to it, but there was no missing the macho stance both men took. Dev's wide muscular shoulders seemed to expand as he folded his arms over his chest. He had that wide-legged, *don't fuck with me* stance that would make most men cower.

Not Payne. He might be thinner than Dev, and wiry, but he was just as tall. And Shelley had seen the deputy run a baseball diamond last summer. The man could put on some speed when he wanted.

"Are you claiming my fiancée would falsely accuse Dr. Morgan?" the deputy bellowed.

"Damn right, I am." Dev's voice was quieter, but no less menacing. "I've only met her once, but I've already caught her lying about Dr. Morgan in order to get her thrown out of the zoo. She was escorted out by you, as I recall."

"I escorted you out too." The deputy punctuated his words with a jab to Dev's chest. "It would be wise to remember you're a guest in my jurisdiction before you throw around more accusations."

Ian and Ryan moved to stand shoulder to shoulder with Dev. Shelley wasn't sure if it was to show solidarity or to keep their cousin from striking back.

Dev exhaled a snort of disgust. "First, we're not on your *turf* yet. Elkridge is still thirty miles west. Second, your sheriff asked for *my* help with your cases. Third, Sheriff Webber told me himself, Dr. Morgan was alibied for *all* of the murders. I know she couldn't have been at the scene of the attack on the clinic because she was in Tidewater when it happened. Now I don't know what game you're playing, but I won't help you railroad an innocent woman."

At those words, Seth stepped out of the bathroom and strode the short distance to stand by Dev. "What's going on?"

"Did you get your car fixed, Seth?" Dev asked, as if he and Payne hadn't just been doing the tough-guy standoff.

"Yes, it just needed coolant." He paused, then introduced himself to Payne. "I'm Detective English."

"Deputy Munro," Payne said, anger still darkening his voice. "Where'd you come from?"

Seth hiked a thumb over his shoulder, indicating the exit door across from the ladies room.

"Seth, it looks like we're not needed in Elkridge. I'm just going to call Sheriff Webber and confirm that our assistance is not required." He turned to Payne and asked, "Do you want to relay the information about the links between the murder cases?"

"Now, Detective Jones, don't go getting your boxers in a twist." Payne Munro's voice carried clearly through the diner. "I never said your assistance wasn't needed. What links?"

"SHELLEY," JULES CALLED out, her voice weak. Jules had been resting on the bathroom floor with Seth's suit jacket between her face and the cold white tile. She pushed to her knees.

Shelley rushed to her sister's side. Outside the bathroom door, the men's voices continued, but their words were garbled. "Are you feeling better?" she asked, touching Jules's clammy cheek.

Jules seemed to have difficulty keeping her eyes open but said, "Yes, a little. So cold."

Trying to warm Jules, Shelley zipped up her sister's jacket. Jules hadn't fully regained consciousness since the glasses had burst on the table. Was it normal for her to drift in and out this much?

"Seth?" Jules murmured.

"He'll be right back," Shelley said, stroking the damp hair away from her sister's forehead. In truth, she liked it better when Jules was talking. At least, she was alive. "Come on, Jules. Talk to me. Do you need anything else? Water?"

Jules's eyes flew open. Suddenly hyperalert, she grabbed Shelley's arms with both hands and said, "Tomás said someone is letting all the animals out of their cages. Beau's there too and he's hiding. Tomás is stirring up the animals, trying to give Beau time to run, but I think he's too scared."

Fear had her grabbing for her cell. She needed to get Dev in here. Or Seth. Or hell, even Payne.

"Shelley, the killer's in the zoo. Someone else has died." Jules shook her head, as if trying to clear the confusion. "I can't understand the new spirit. Too many voices."

"Beau. Is it Beau?" Fear squeezed Shelley's chest, but Jules managed to give her head a small shake.

"No. In danger. The killer. The animals running free."

Shelley jumped up. "Most of the animals in the cages are harmless, but not all. There's a Komodo dragon and . . . Oh my God! Where's Miah? Is she still locked up?" Shelley pushed down the image of a frightened Beau being hunted by a maniac in the zoo. But she couldn't keep her stomach from knotting. "Jules! Where's Miah?"

"Who?" Jules was fading again. "I don't know. Seth. Where's Seth? He needs to know the killer's there. Call the police."

"If Beau's in the zoo with the killer and the animals are running loose, he's in twice as much danger. I can get the animals back in their cages. I can save them."

"Go. Get Seth. So tired." Jules's eyes rolled back in her head and she went limp. Shelley gently lowered Jules back to Seth's jacket after patting it for his car key. Shelley pocketed it. Jules mumbled in her sleep.

She hated the idea of leaving Jules like that on the floor, but if she called out to Seth, everyone would come running. And there would be no one to help Beau or the animals in the zoo.

"I'll call Seth as soon as I'm on the road," she whispered, then stole out the door.

Dev and the others were steadily moving toward the front exit, so Shelley had to hurry. She slipped out the back door. Seth's car had been parked there after Ryan had added more antifreeze. Whether it was luck or planning, there were no other cars on this side of the parking lot. She backed out of the lot and headed to Elkridge. Guilt and determination warred inside her as she sent Dev a text: J had another V. B is at the zoo. Danger. Animals loose. Going to put them back. Tell S. that J. needs him now.

DEV HAD BEEN surprised when Seth volunteered to join the deputy on the ride to Elkridge. Especially when he'd turned to him and said, "Clean up that mess inside, kid. When you're done, meet us at the sheriff's office. We don't have time to wait for you."

Seth then gestured for Munro to lead the way to his squad car. The two men climbed in, Seth keeping up the conversation about the linked cases the entire time.

And just like that, Dev understood. Seth was playing the "kid" card to distract Payne, presumably so Dev could check on Shelley and Jules and get them headed back to Tidewater. He headed inside.

"Were all the chicks in your classes that hot?" Ian asked, popping a piece of grape bubblegum into his mouth. "Damn, I made a mistake joining the Marines. I should have gone to get my edumacation with you."

Dev made his way to the ladies-room door and knocked lightly. No one answered. He glanced at Ian who took it as an invitation to speak.

"Cary Devon Jones, you're being downright rude not answering me," Ian said in a perfect imitation of their Gram.

Dev laughed in spite of himself. "Shut up." He knocked again. "Jules? Shells? You in there?"

"What do you know? He does speak. I'm so shocked I don't know what to do with myself."

Dev was about to tell his cousin exactly what he could do,

when he heard Jules weakly call his name through the peeling white door.

He pushed it open and his heart sank. Jules sat, pale-faced and swaying slightly in the empty bathroom. Crossing to her, he squatted down. "Jules, where's Shelley?"

"The zoo." Jules's weak voice took on an urgent tone. "Shelley's going to the zoo. We got a tip that Beau is in danger. He's trapped in the zoo and someone is setting the animals free. But she left too soon. She doesn't know she's a target. Seth? Where's Seth?" She sank back onto her makeshift pallet of jackets as if her energy was suddenly depleted.

"Seth's with the deputy," Ryan said, appearing in the doorway behind them. Without being asked, he pulled his cell from his pocket and dialed. He stepped into the hallway saying, "Seth . . ."

Dev turned to see Ian's normally jovial expression harden. "Ryan can stay with her. Let's go," he said, as if Dev wasn't already bolting out the back door and into the empty parking lot.

They were in his car and on the darkening road in under a minute. Dev pushed away his fear and his fury at her leaving him as fiercely as he pushed the gas pedal to the floor.

The scent of Ian's grape gum mixed with the fumes of motor oil made Dev's stomach twist.

"You wanna tell me how your girlfriend and her sister got a tip *in a bathroom*?" Ian asked, rubbing his chin with one hand and pulling out his cell with the other. Without waiting for a response, he dialed. "Ryan, it's me. They back yet?" Ian paused, listening. "Good. That should put you only a few minutes behind us. Meet you at the zoo."

Ian shifted in his seat and said, "Want to explain why your little girlfriend went all Mary Jane Watson on us? We were there to help her, but no. She has to put herself in danger."

Dev considered not answering. Considered it long enough to let the silence in the car grow thick and heavy. God, he hated keeping secrets from his cousins. They were more than family. They were friends. As kids it had always been the McKinnon clan, back to back to back. It didn't surprise him that Ian and Ryan would do what was needed without explanation, but it burned at his gut keeping something from them that could potentially put them at risk.

Counting on his cousin's ability to see past the ordinary, he said, "It's not like that. She's not Mary Jane Watson."

Ian snorted. "Right. Your little chica didn't just jet off to the zoo, where a body was found in the trunk of her car *this morning*? She might be a hot piece of ass, but she has a proclivity for finding trouble. I say toss this one back."

"Ian, I'm only going to say this once. Call her a piece of anything again, and I'll make you eat your balls for breakfast."

"Fuck you, Cuz."

"Very mature. They teach you that phrase in the military?" Dev white-knuckled the steering wheel, pissed at Ian for being a dick. Pissed at himself more for losing his temper. Exhaling hard, he said, "Ian, it's complicated."

"Bullshit." Ian's normally easygoing personality evaporated. "You've dragged Ryan and me into this. We're withholding information from the police. Oh wait, I forgot, you are the fucking police! Tell me how it's *not like that*?"

Praying he was doing the right thing, Dev said, "You know Aunt Marlene? Shelley's kind of like her, only—"

"She's crazy?"

"No, she's gifted," Dev said and cringed. "Shelley can just do things other people can't."

"Like tell fortunes in bowls of vodka?"

"No, Shells uh . . . talks to animals." When Ian didn't do more than gape at him, Dev added, "It's why she's going to the zoo. She's going to get the animals to help her find Beau before she coaxes them back into their cages."

"You really believe this shit you're telling me?"

"It's not shit," Dev snapped. "Just keep your mouth shut and listen when we get there. You'll see for yourself. It's fucking amazing."

"Great, I'm probably going to get arrested or maybe even eaten by some wild animal because you're screwing Dr. Dolittle."

CHAPTER 24

A DAM CLAPPED HIS hands to his ears. Every fucking animal in the zoo was screeching, baying, roaring, bellowing, or shrieking. Who knew turtles made noises? Snakes slithered across the dark ground in front of him. The moonlight filtering between the trees barely lit the chilly paths.

Fall leaves showered around him as squirrels and golden lion tamarins hopped from branch to branch overhead. The forest surrounding the zoo was alive with animals awake when they should have been sleeping.

Up ahead, the tigress roared a warning. He recognized the sound. It was the same roar she had made when he'd shot her with the tranquilizer just before taking her cubs earlier in the week. But who would be shooting her now?

He ground his back teeth until his jaw popped. That fucking bitch was double-crossing him. She had sworn after he'd caught her stealing the first cub that she'd let him relocate the animals. She was going back on her word now? Did she have a death wish?

In a bolt of clarity, it made sense. She hadn't reset the cameras in the tiger cage by mistake as she'd claimed. She'd

planned to double-cross him all along. Fucking bitch was in
for a rude surprise if she thought that.

Adam raced to Miah's enclosure. With the dark all around
him protecting him from the cameras he hadn't had a chance
to disable, he searched for that traitorous bitch. His blood
surged as he found her, hovering just outside Miah's pen,
reloading the tranq gun.

He'd always heard of people seeing red, but he hadn't
believed it until now. Fuck. The moment he needed to tap into
his calm, it vanished, leaving only the empty raging machine
inside him.

Stalking closer to Reyna, he took in everything. The perimeter gate and barrier fence still secure. The bronze padlocks glinting in the moonlight. The single spotlight shining mercilessly
down on the tigress sprawled in the grass at the foot of the ramp
leading to her house. She roared another warning to her babies.

Adam swung his gaze left and right, searching for the three
remaining tiger cubs. The steam rising from the dewy grass
was the only movement out there, other than Miah herself.
The cubs must still be inside the house.

Reyna, that fucking coward, wouldn't dare approach them
yet. No, from the looks of things, the bitch was going to overdose the tigress by tranquilizing her again. Disgust and fear
bit Adam with razor-sharp teeth. Too fucking far. Too far
away to stop her.

He ran anyway. Headlong in her direction. She raised the
rifle. Took aim. The moment she would have pulled the trigger, something jumped up and knocked it from her hands.

The gun skittered across the dry leaves and into the woods,
not far from his feet. Adam picked it up and ducked back into
the shadow of the trees. Not to hide from the cameras. If
Reyna was brazen enough to stand in the middle of the trail
and shoot the tiger through the cage, she'd clearly already handled the security cameras. No, Adam wanted to know who'd
interfered with her plans. And why.

"It *was* you," a small voice accused. The boy. Beau was
here? "No, you can't do this."

"Go home, kid." Reyna pushed the boy aside, knocking
him to the ground. "This is none of your business." He hit the
ground with a flump.

"He'll kill you, just like he did Dr. Kessler."

Reyna blanched. "Dr. Kessler's dead?"

"Yes," his voice quaked, but he didn't back down. "And my papi told me someone was stealing the animals. I'm going to tell him it's you."

"You don't have a daddy. The whole town knows you're an orphaned freak." Reyna's haughty tone was edged with fear.

"That's not true." The boy jumped to his feet, his hands on his hips. "Tomás is my papi."

"Well, good luck telling him anything. He's dead too." Reyna snatched the kid's arm, wrenching it as she said, "You're not telling anyone anything."

Adam's chest tightened. Because of that crazy bitch, he was going to have to kill a kid. His stomach churned.

"What did you do with my gun?" Reyna's shriek brought Adam out of his musing. He hid the rifle beneath some leaves. He pulled his gun out of his waistband, then tugged his sleeve down over his right hand.

Reyna shook Beau violently. He appeared frightened but didn't back down. He kicked her in the shins in an effort to shake off her hold. The kid had guts.

Adam stepped from the shadows. Allowing himself to be seen, he called out, "Beau, close your eyes."

SHELLEY PARKED SETH'S car right next to the locked gate. Except it wasn't locked. It was closed, but the bronze-and-silver padlock lay on the ground. A cool wind slapped her hair in her face. She dug a hair tie out of her pocket and pulled her hair into a quick bun, then opened the gate.

Two steps inside and she nearly collided with a tortoise. While she was certain she could coax the animals back into their cages, she needed time to collect them all. Hurrying back to the gate, she pulled it tightly closed, then dialed Dev's number. He answered on the first ring.

"Dev, I'm at the zoo—"

"I know. Jules told me." He sounded out of breath, like he'd been running. "I'll be there in less than five."

A roar of pain and anguish erupted from deep inside the zoo grounds. Shelley jumped at the sound. "It's Miah. Dev,

I've got to go. Something's really wrong. Beau's in trouble, and the animals are running free. You can't come inside. I need time to put them away."

"Can't come inside? Are you nuts? I'm not leaving you in there alone."

Someone in the background made a comment that sounded remarkably like, "Mary Jane, you see?"

Shelley didn't have time to argue. "Dev, if the animals get out of the zoo, they risk being killed. Most of these guys are reptiles. People look at reptiles and think Godzilla." Another roar, this one weaker. "I gotta go. Guard the gate for me." She'd barely started up the trail when she heard the first gunshot.

A woman screamed, birds took flight, and the zoo itself seemed to explode with noise. But the animals took cover. Following their lead, Shelley slipped off the trail, still headed to the tiger house.

She was almost there when a raccoon darted across her path. She skidded to avoid colliding with it. Instead of running, the bandit-faced animal sat up on its hind legs and met her gaze levelly.

In an instant, images of Beau and Reyna flooded her mind. Shelley saw the woman shake him hard by the shoulders. A long shadow cast the boy in temporary darkness as someone joined them outside the tiger house. Reyna pushed Beau at the shadowy figure, only to jerk backward. Then Beau ran into the woods, where the raccoon had been watching from the tree.

The vision ended, and the raccoon scurried deeper into the woods. A hunch had Shelley following it. The raccoon climbed up a scrub pine and chattered at her.

Beau has to be here.

"Beau," she called in a stage whisper. "Beau, if you can hear me, it's Dr. Morgan. Come out."

The zoo still screamed with animals in a frenzy. Somewhere in the direction from which she'd come, a woman cried out in pain. Shelley cringed at the high-pitched scream. The killer had to be here, and she'd be fracking damned if he got to Beau now.

Using the tone her mother had used on her as a child, Shelley said, "Beau, I need you to come out right this minute."

Rustling erupted behind her. Shelley spun around to see the boy, sitting up, leaves cascading off him.

"Doc?" His voice was small, frightened. "Is it really you?"

Shelley dropped to her knees, so he could see her better in the moonlight. "It's me."

The child's left eye was still swollen. Silent tears tracked down the boy's dirty cheeks. He clung to her, his thin body shaking.

Shelley's heart ached and her eyes stung. She didn't bother to fight back the tears. "What are you doing here?"

"Two men came to see me today. They said they were your friends. Mama Margaret was so mad after they left, she hit me. I ran away. I looked for my papi, but . . ." he snuffled, "I couldn't find him. So I went to the clinic to find you. You weren't there. I hid in the storage shed until I heard yelling inside. I went in and . . ." Beau broke down completely; he pressed his face against her chest and shook. "He killed Dr. Kessler."

GUARD THE GATE, right. Dev was going to throttle one stubborn redhead the next time he saw her. Glancing at Ian, he said, "Did you get ahold of the sheriff's office?"

"Yeah, they're right behind us. Don't you hear the sirens?"

Dev hadn't, but he did now. He didn't answer as he sped into the zoo parking lot so fast, he swore two wheels left the ground. Cutting the engine, he popped the trunk of his car. As soon as he opened the trunk to reveal his gun box, Ian appeared on his right, stopping him.

"Cuz, the sheriff's on the way. Maybe the best thing we can do is wait out here. We don't know how much trouble she's in."

Dev jerked his arm free of Ian's grasp. "Are you fucking kidding me?"

Ian's serious face broke into a wide grin. "Fuck yeah, I'm kidding. Hurry up."

"Ian, don't be an asshole," Ryan said, appearing like a ninja from the mist on Dev's left. His bald head, covered with a dark skullcap—no doubt to hide the shine the moonlight would have cast—added to his already "don't fuck with me" look.

Dev opened the box, retrieved his Glock and two clips and

quietly lowered the trunk's lid. The three of them slipped through the gate, then carefully latched it into place.

The zoo was a riot of noise and action. A dozen snakes slithered past them but seemed to take no notice of the men in their quest. Overhead, monkeys shook branches and screamed as they hopped in the same direction the snakes slithered. Even the birds, normally quiet at this hour, called to one another before taking flight. Again, headed in the same direction as all the other animals.

Away from the gate.

Dev would have expected them to race toward freedom. Isn't that what wild or, hell, even tame, animals usually did when presented with the opportunity? None of these creatures were interested in that.

No, instead of freedom, they each slithered, hopped, and flew deeper into the belly of the zoo. At the fork of the three trails, Dev turned to his cousins. Ryan stared, his patent impassive expression giving nothing away.

Ian, however, gaped and hiked a thumb over his shoulder. "Shouldn't they all be fleeing that way?"

Every animal was headed up the Tiger Monkey Trail. Like the animals headed to Noah's Ark, they all seemed to have a single destination in mind.

Another roar went up. This one considerably weaker than the last two. Followed by a woman's scream. The shriek of pain made the fine hairs on Dev's arms rise.

All three men raced up the Tiger Monkey Trail, but the path was blocked by two tortoises having a slow motion war. Dev broke left and headed toward the monkey cages. Ryan broke right, heading into the woods. Ian leaped over the reptiles and disappeared up the trail.

Dev had only planned to skirt past the cages on his way to Miah and, hopefully Shells, but he tripped. Over the body of a woman. For one heart-seizing, blood-chilling moment, her slender fingers and voluptuous body appeared to be Shells.

The woman rolled over and blinked, blood pouring from a gash in her forehead. Reyna. She opened her mouth and screamed. Dev ducked to cover her mouth with his hand and something slapped the right side of his head.

The world started to spin, then faded as he collapsed face-first at the foot of the monkey cage.

"WAS THAT A gunshot?" Shelley whispered.

"Y-yes, I think so. He has a gun." Beau's teeth started to chatter.

Shelley pulled off her coat and wrapped it around his shoulders. She picked him up and walked carefully through the woods. Off the trail and hidden by the trees, Shelley pulled out her cell and dialed Dev. It went to voice mail.

She called Ian. More voice mail. Then Ryan. Still voice mail. Where were they? They were supposed to be guarding the gate, but if they heard the gunshot too, there's no way they'd have stayed outside, right?

In the distance, sirens wailed. The cavalry was coming. The relief made her almost giddy. Surely Dev couldn't be too far behind.

Then she heard it. Or rather, didn't hear anything at all. Every animal fell eerily silent, as if they too waited for the next attack.

She squinted in the darkness. The poorly lit trails revealed nothing. Not an animal, not a person. The ground beneath her feet was barely visible in the slivers of moonlight shafting between the trees.

Up ahead, a branch snapped. The sound ricocheted off her chest in the unearthly quiet. Beau whimpered then trembled in her arms, from cold or fear. Probably both. Shelley hugged him tighter, whispering into his ear, "Shh . . . stay quiet."

He nodded against her shoulder, his face buried in her blouse. Shelley's arms burned with the strain of holding him. He might be small, but Beau was heavy. Her palms started to sweat despite the chill in the air.

He slid.

She needed to shift or risk dropping him. Tightening her shoulders and bending her knees, she propped his feet on her thighs. Beau clutched at her neck, his small fingers tugging painfully at the hair at the nape of her neck.

Nearly straightening, she froze. A snake, thick and heavy,

slid across the toe of her shoe. It lifted its head, but she couldn't make eye contact in the dark. She didn't need to.

One of the zoo's three tortoises appeared and rammed its head against her leg. Urging her backward. Closer to the path, but still under cover of the trees. She stumbled into a solid wall of muscle. Two arms grabbed her from behind.

Shelley opened her mouth to scream, but a hand clapped across her lips. Silencing her. She wanted to fight, but she was at a distinct disadvantage with Beau in her arms. There was no way she was letting go of the child until he was safe. But she still had her feet.

If this bastard was going to kill her, she was going to leave him limping. Tightening her grip on Beau, she lifted her right leg and kicked back, hoping to God her aim landed somewhere near his groin.

CHAPTER 25

THE HUMAN WALL grunted, twisted his hips, and squeezed his arms tighter around Shelley and Beau. The child whimpered in pain, his face still buried against her shoulder.

"Shhhh . . ." a deep-timbred voice whispered against her ear. His hold slackened. She didn't need him to identify himself; she'd recognized the giant the moment her head didn't meet his shoulder. Only one person was that tall. "It's me, Ryan. Are you two hurt?"

"No." Her sweaty hands slid against Beau's back and he started to fall.

He clutched tighter at her neck, yanking her hair. Her back bowed, and she clutched at the child's wet shirt. *Why was his shirt wet?*

Ryan moved around them so quickly, she hadn't registered the action until his brown-eyed gaze collided with hers in the slivers of moonlight. Most of his face was hidden in shadows, but she sensed his urgency as he took Beau from her arms.

The boy started to cry and wriggle, grasping wildly for Shelley. Some instinct she couldn't deny or explain had her struggling to keep hold of him.

"Let me take him. He's bleeding." Ryan's words, although

whispered, carried a core of steel. And confidence. "I need to get him outside for help, but I'm turned around. How do we get out of here? Oh, shit! Are you bleeding too or is this all from him?"

He nodded to her shirt. She glanced down, surprised to find her blue sweatshirt stained brown with blood in the moonlight. Fear and fury whipped through her as she glanced at Beau's face. His big eyes were drooping and his mouth went slack as he shivered in Ryan's arms. The child had stopped struggling, cradled like an infant against the giant's body.

Shelley pointed left, in the direction of the exit. "Go, I'm right behind you."

Please God, don't let Beau die.

THE BITCH WAS coming around. He was going to make her suffer. Make that bastard watch. She'd actually held Beau in front of her like a fucking shield, when Adam had fired the first shot. His gut clutched. Boiled. Fuck, he was going to be sick again. He turned to the bushes and puked. Although he should have spewed on her. She'd have deserved it.

Inside the monkey cage, the old man finally stirred. The tranq had worn off. Eddy, that fat sadistic fuck, was going to finally get what was coming to him. Adam's only regret was that Beau was going to die too.

He'd gone back to find the kid after he'd shot that interfering cop, but he couldn't find him in the dark. Even if Beau had survived the gunshot, there was no way for Adam to take him to a hospital. He could never explain how the kid came to have a bullet in his chest.

Fuck!

Adam stomped over and kicked Reyna in the head. Something snapped and her head lolled awkwardly on her shoulders. A slow trickle of blood glinted like red silver in the moonlight.

Pinned across the chest by Dev's lifeless body, she didn't struggle or cry. Although someone whimpered.

Adam glanced into the monkey cage. The younger man still lay curled in the fetal position, out cold. But the old fuck, he was awake. Aware. There on the cold slab of concrete, fingers curled around the green and rusted chain-link fence, Eddy sat on his knees. His face, slick with sweat, red splotches darkening his cheeks, his bloodshot eyes stared fixedly at Reyna's unmoving body pinned beneath the cop.

Glassy, watery eyes lifted until they met Adam's gaze. Eddy opened his mouth, closed it. Licked his lips, then croaked out a single word, "Why?"

SHELLEY RACED WITH Ryan toward the exit. The moment he could see it, he shouldered his way in front of her and slowed their pace. It was infuriating. Why was he slowing *now*? Flashing blue and red lights swept between the wrought-iron bars of the front gate, illuminating the trees and ground, casting an eerie tinge to the foliage. Like an old faded photograph.

"There's too much open space between the woods and the gate," Ryan whispered, hugging a now-unconscious Beau closer to his chest. He shifted the boy to a quasi-fireman's hold. Beau's head on his shoulder, his limp body flush against the left side of his chest.

Ryan raised his right hand, bringing up a gun.

Jesus! Where'd he been hiding that?

"I need to get him outside. Stay close to me and when I give the signal, run as fast as you can for the gate."

"Where's Dev? Is he outside?"

Ryan didn't answer but moved stealthily, damned near silently, toward the edge of the trees.

Shelley took a step to follow, but something plunked her on the head. Hard. Clapping a hand to the sore spot, she glanced up and saw JoJo rearing back to throw another pinecone at her. The moment their gazes collided, a stream of terrifying images smashed into her mind hard enough to steal her breath and freeze her in place.

Eddy, dumped unceremoniously next to another lifeless body in the monkey cage. Reyna, using Beau as a human shield. Blood splattering in all directions as a bullet ripped through the boy's body. A man in a dark hooded sweatshirt with a gun chasing Reyna down the Tiger Monkey Trail. Reyna tripping, her face smashing against the cinderblocks and chain-link fence of the cage.

Reyna, lifeless, facedown on the path. Dev, mouthing Shelley's name, then rolling Reyna over. The momentary glimpse of relief on his handsome face an instant before he schooled his features. Reyna coming to and trying to scream. Something . . . gouging a furrow into the side of Dev's head. Blood spraying like a fountain from above his ear. Dev seeming to struggle for a moment, then collapsing.

The hooded man, moving closer, pointing the gun first at Dev, then at Eddy's stirring form before shifting back into the shadows. The images shifted to another part of the zoo. Another man—Ian—perceived as a threat by JoJo, pelted with acorns by BoBo while her mate snatched the gun from the man's hands.

The images stopped. Ian's gun dropped from the trees with a crunch onto the leaves at her feet.

Fear clogged her throat. Shelley couldn't breathe. Dev couldn't be dead. He just couldn't. Not now. She turned, breaking eye contact with JoJo, to call out to Ryan, but he was already slipping through the gate.

What could she do? She should run outside and tell them what she knew, but would they act fast enough? She had to help Dev. She was a vet, yes, but she knew more about the human anatomy than the average police officer. She could give Dev first aid until the cops could get inside.

Please, don't let Dev be dead. Please.

God couldn't hate her that much, could he? He'd already taken everyone else she'd ever loved—her mother, her adoptive parents, even her dog. He couldn't possibly be so cruel as to take Dev, the one man she'd ever truly loved.

Love. The realization brought hot tears stinging to her eyes. Her chest constricted with the fear that she might never be able to tell him. How could she not have said something sooner? And how could she not go to him now? When he needed her most.

Knees bent, she squatted and picked up the heavy, cold metal gun and clutched the grip tightly, careful to keep her finger off the trigger.

Slipping back up the trail, she moved as quickly and quietly as she could toward the monkey cage. She pulled her phone out of her pocket. She opened the list of recent calls. Her hands shook, but she managed to dial Ryan's number. He answered on the first ring. "Where are you?"

"He's hurt bad," Shelley said, ignoring his question. "I think that bastard shot Dev. He's not moving."

Ryan cursed, said something to someone else, then spoke into the cell again. "Shelley, do you see the killer? You've got to get out of there. The deputies are mobilizing to come in. Ian can help Dev. He's still in there. You've got to come out. Now."

She might have agreed. She should have. She would have, had a Komodo dragon not stepped out of the shadows and nudged her thigh.

A thrill of fear shot through her. These creatures were feral and capable of killing a man as big as Ryan. The moonlight shafting between the leaves gave the enormous lizard a nearly colorless façade. It lifted its head and rammed her knee, knocking her body backward and the phone from her hands.

The cell skittered on the crunchy leaves out of sight.

Then she saw them. All the animals—lizards, newts, monkeys, birds, and even the normal forest creatures, raccoons, squirrels, and a skunk were moving swiftly and with purpose up the Tiger Monkey Trail.

Shelley set off in the direction of the cages.

She followed the zoo creatures on their quest for a showdown with a madman.

SOMETHING SOFT TICKLED Dev's nose. Automatically, he reached with his right hand, only to hiss as pain burned from his shoulder, his fingers, and his throbbing head. His aching right arm hung, useless. The blinding heat made his vision swim seconds before a biting cold slid like melting ice down his right cheek.

He'd fallen asleep on top of Shells. Christ! He'd crush her like this. He started to move, but his whole body screamed with the stress of it and he stopped. His vision swam in and out of focus. What in the hell was going on?

Dev's memory came rushing back. He'd been in the zoo, searching for Shelley when he'd found her. No, not her. Reyna. Then someone slapped him in the head.

Not slapped. Shot. Someone fucking *shot* him. In the head! The person mostly missed, except damn, Dev must have reinjured his shoulder when he fell. Given the fact that the damn thing felt like a rooted redwood, and pain was shooting down his arm and into his fingertips, it had to be dislocated. Again.

Beneath him, Reyna moaned and tried to move.

"Shut up, you double-crossing bitch," the killer hissed.

Dev didn't have time to brace for the impact. The killer, who must have been aiming for Reyna's head, missed, and his booted foot connected with rib-cracking perfection to Dev's chest.

Dev didn't fight the force, just let himself be rolled onto his back with the blow. With his eyes opened to mere slits, he saw his attacker for the first time.

The moonlight shafted through the trees like a spotlight on Jacob as he tossed his head to the right, brushing the hair out of his eyes. In the dark hoodie and jeans, he could have been anyone out for a nighttime stroll through the zoo—the locked zoo currently being overrun by wild animals—but for the .22 clutched in his left hand.

Jacob swung the gun wildly between Dev and Reyna. His attention seemed riveted on something inside the monkey cage behind Dev's head.

"Wake up. Please, wake up," someone sobbed inside the cage.

Who's in there? Dev tried to clear his mind, but damn, it felt as if his skull were going to blow apart.

"Oops, must have killed him too soon. You were supposed to watch him die, you evil fuck," Jacob shouted. "But she's still here. Tiger-stealing, double-crossing bitch. Let me show you."

Reyna's body jerked as if he'd struck her, but she made no sound. Jacob ignored them and continued his tirade at the cage.

The man in the cage sobbed and begged, "Please. Why are you doing this, Jacob?"

"Shut. The. Fuck. Up." Jacob swung his .22 back toward Reyna, aiming for her head. "Adam! My name is Adam, not Jacob, not Eddy Junior. I'm Adam. Oh, you remember now, old man? Remember what you did twenty-two years ago? Or do I need to put a bullet in this bitch's head to jog your memory."

"No! Please!" The man in the cage squeaked in alarm, sobbed harder.

"I'm going to kill her slowly. Then I'm going to gut you and feed you to the animals you so judiciously protect. After all, they mean more to you than your own family. They've always meant more."

"No, please. Let my daughter go. I'll do anything, just don't hurt her."

Christ, it was Eddy in there.

Dev needed to get his head clear. Get his ass up and beat this bastard into the ground. But he couldn't make his arm move, and the sky still spun above him like a ride at the park after sundown.

His body wouldn't work, but he could still talk. Would it be more or less dangerous to talk? He could be shot—again—if he startled the asshole. Chances were, Jacob—Adam— whoever would probably kill him anyway. Clearing his throat, he attempted to reason with the insane would-be veterinarian.

"J-Jacob." Dev made his voice softer, weaker.

Jacob jumped and the gun swung into Dev's line of vision. "Adam."

Pretending he didn't see the weapon, Dev said, "Adam, you don't want to do this."

A crack of laughter split the quiet. "There you're wrong. I very much want to kill this motherfucker." The maniac swung the gun back toward Eddy. "Time for you to pay for your crimes, *Dad.*"

"Dad?" Dev asked, as much in shock as to distract the intern Shelley had trusted.

"Yeah, I'm his firstborn, isn't that right, fat man?" When Eddy didn't do more than wheeze a sob, Jacob went on. "Seems the old drunkard had his sights set on marrying the town hero's daughter. Didn't matter that he was engaged to my mother. Didn't matter that he'd already knocked her up. He shamed her and sent her packing. She returned to the Ridge to introduce us when I was four. Eddy here didn't want her interfering with his life. Didn't want no bastard risking all the money he'd get from his wealthy bitch wife. So he killed my mother."

"No," Eddy sobbed. "It was an accident. Ask anyone."

"I was there, you asshole." Adam paced back and forth,

cursing and waving his gun. In the clinic, he passed for a man in his early twenties, but right now, he looked older. Much older. Old enough to be who he claimed.

"Stupid motherfucker didn't know I was in the back seat sleeping when he ran her off the road. The car flipped and flipped. God, there was so much blood. I didn't know one woman could bleed so much. It coated me. My legs were sliced to ribbons, but she told me to crawl out. Run. She knew he'd kill me if he found out. So I ran and ran. But I watched the news. Heard my auntie talk about the half-assed job they'd done with his trial. How he'd gotten off with barely a slap on the wrists. How he'd kept his perfect little life while I lost everything. Then my auntie died and I was alone. Except for dear old grandpa who'd disowned his unwed daughter and wanted nothing to do with her bastard son.

"So I ran again. Forgot who I was. Where I'd come from. Until the day this fat asshole showed up on the news crying over the accidental death of his beloved wife. Drunk-driving accident my ass. He probably killed her just like he did my mother."

"No!" Eddy wailed the word. "I loved Leticia. She was my life. I'd never have risked her. Rebecca was an accident."

"Don't you say her name!" Adam raised the gun. Dev had a split second to throw his body in front of the weapon. The pain ripped through his shoulder, slapping him back against the bars. His head cracked against the metal. His hips scraped against cement through his jeans. Stars performed a Scottish country dance in front of his eyes.

Adam, unaware he'd just shot a cop or perhaps not caring, railed, "Do you hear? Do you hear how that fat fuck doesn't deny killing my mother? Calls it an accident. But I was there. I saw him stand at the guardrail and wave cars past, preventing help from getting there in time to save her."

"Oh, Jesus. Oh, Jesus. You can't remember that. You were four." Eddy whimpered. "I made a mistake. I thought she was already dead. You can't remember that."

Gray edged the corners of Dev's vision and he prayed he could hang on until help got there. A hand on his wrist and a whisper of Ian's voice let him know the cavalry had arrived.

"Stay still, Cuz. I need the bastard to come a little closer."

Ian's hushed words floated around Dev like a whirlpool. He paused, but Ian's next words made Dev wonder if he hadn't hallucinated his cousin's presence. "Don't ask me how, but a monkey stole my gun."

ALL THE ANIMALS scattered at the boom of the gunshot ricocheting off the trees. Birds took to the skies in a cacophony of squawks, reptiles slithered beneath bushes, rocks, and signs; even the fox, raccoons, and squirrels bolted for the trees.

Shelley blinked at the sudden emptiness around her. Without her companions racing to the scene with her and the echo of the gunshot ringing in her ears, terror arrowed straight through her chest, immobilizing her.

But only for a moment. Because up ahead, she saw a man lifting his arm and aiming at something on the ground. Shelley yelled, "Hey! Don't!" Then she ran a zigzag pattern, in case the killer started firing at her.

Everything happened at once. A swift-moving wraith leaped from the bushes. It was Ian and he dove headfirst, arms coming around the gunman's waist, knocking them both back and down.

A hail of acorns rained down from the trees like well-aimed torpedoes. The tamarins and squirrels and owls pelted the gunman. Ian's back took some of the attack, but it didn't slow him down. The gun skittered out of the killer's hands, toward Dev. He sat up, grabbed it, aimed and said, "Ian, stop playing with him."

One well-aimed punch and the attacker's head lolled back. He sank to the ground with all the grace of a drunk after a weekend bender.

Shelley's pulse thumped loudly in her ears. Her heart beat so loudly that, for a moment, she was deaf to everything but the sound of blood rushing to her head. Then someone yelped. It wasn't a scream, it was more a cry of shock. And it was enough to jolt her hearing back to normal.

Dev collapsed back onto the ground. His gun hand falling to his chest, where he clutched the toylike pistol to him, as if to keep it from being taken.

Shelley moved to Dev, glanced at Ian and . . .

"Jacob?" Shelley asked Ian and gestured to the unconscious man on the ground. "Is that *Jacob*?"

"Whoa," Ian said at the same time Dev groaned the words, "Gun, Shells."

Relief had an odd effect, sometimes. She'd seen him move. Had registered that Dev was still alive. But at the sound of his voice, she felt a rush of joy so profound that it made her eyes sting and her palms sweat. She turned to him, not forgetting about Jacob, just not caring.

She crossed to Dev, dropped to her knees, and swung her arms wide. Ian was tugging something from her hand. She jerked in alarm, when he said, "Just taking my gun back."

"Dev, please don't die," she said, surprised at the shakiness in her voice.

"I'm okay, Shells," Dev whispered, leaving his weapon on his chest and raising a hand to brush her cheek. His touch tender.

His head and shoulder bled freely. His breathing was steady, if somewhat labored. The sight of his injuries sent her emotions cresting until she was shaking. She stroked a hand down his clammy cheek. He was alive. He was still with her. Her throat was dry and her eyes brimming with tears, but she needed to say something. Her mind blanked and she said, "I-I thought I told you to wait at the gate."

Shaking and unable to stop, she did the only thing she could think to do. The thing she wanted, no needed, most of all. She lowered her head and pressed her lips to his.

Dev's lips were cold but welcoming.

The reassuring kiss was brief. Careful of his injuries, she hugged him close, her lips against his ear.

He trembled from pain or shock, maybe both. His voice weak and fading, he said, "Shells, I love you. I always have. I should have said it long ago . . ."

"Shhh . . ." she whispered. Tears tracked down her cheeks. Her own hands shook as she rocked him lightly in her arms. Deputies and paramedics raced to them. Hard hands clapped around her arms but before she was yanked away, Ian was there, shoving the hands off.

The reprieve couldn't last. And Dev, her beautiful cop. No longer the impossible fantasy she'd had since college, but a man, flesh and blood in her arms. His face gray with pain, his eyes hazed with the will to hang on, stared into her eyes imploringly.

And she was lost.

"I love you, Dev." She wasn't surprised when his eyes closed on those words. He'd barely clung to consciousness this long. He slipped now into the oblivion that offered an escape from his pain. The words ripped from her. "Don't leave me now. Please, don't leave."

CHAPTER 26

D EV TRIED TO sit up. Pain lanced up his right shoulder and made his already aching head throb. He hissed in pain.

"Whoa, sit still, Cuz." Ian's face bobbed in front of Dev's eyes. The normally happy-go-lucky Marine appeared worried, his face pale beneath his tan. Ian blinked his weary-looking eyes before he turned, calling over his shoulder, "Hey, can we get a nurse in here? He's awake."

Awake?

"Ian what the fu—" Dev cut himself off. An older woman with dark ebony skin, silver hair, and bright pink scrubs bustled into the room.

"Well, it's about time, sugar. How do you feel?" With a wide grin on her pleasantly plump face, she unlooped the pink stethoscope from around her neck and immediately pressed it to his chest.

Confused. But he thought better than to say that. His mind was rapidly beginning to clear and he deduced he was in a hospital. Which one, how long he'd been there, and what happened he figured he could get from Ian after Nurse Happy left the room. "I feel fine, thanks."

"No pain?" The grin slipped from her face, disbelief heavy in her voice.

As if to test her theory, she tugged at the bandages on his head and on his shoulder. Normally he would have held the pain in, but sensing her need to witness it, he let his breath out on a hiss.

She nodded. "You don't need to play tough guy with me. I got three grandsons as big as you. I know how you boys like to pretend you're all steel, but I can't help you if you don't let me." Nurse Happy grinned again, then winked at him. "Now you sit tight while I go get the doctor. Welcome back."

Waiting until she shuffled out the door, Dev turned to Ian. "What the fuck is going on?"

Ian ran both hands through his golden hair, sending it sticking up in odd directions, then tugged a piece of grape bubblegum from his pocket. He popped it into his mouth and chewed thoughtfully before sighing. "You're in Tidewater General. You were medevacked here after you decided it would be a good idea to keep a bullet in your broken collarbone."

"Christ." Dev touched his injured shoulder with his uninjured hand. "This was at the zoo last night?"

"Two nights ago," Ian corrected. He rose from his chair and clapped Dev's hand lightly. "The McKinnon clan has been camped out in the waiting room for news. Guess I'd better tell them."

Dev grabbed his cousin's wrist. "Wait, where's Shells? Is she okay? The last thing I remember is her bitching because I didn't wait outside. I think she was hit too. Is she okay?"

His fear rose as the memory of that night returned in rapid fire. Jacob, calling himself Adam, aiming the gun. Shelley running to Dev's rescue. The gun in her hands. The crash and pain exploding in his shoulder and head as he was hit. The sight of her pale face and quivering lips as she wrapped her arms around him. The heady scent of vanilla as her hair formed a curtain around them before she bent over and kissed him.

Ian glanced out the window into the dark night. His brows knit and lips compressed.

"Where . . ." He had to clear his suddenly dry throat. "Where is Shelley? Oh Christ, is she hurt? Take me to her."

Dev threw his feet over the side of the bed and tried to

stand. His vision swam and legs wobbled before Ian pressed a hand to his chest, forcing him back down.

"She's not hurt. Stay put." Ian pointed to the bed. "Lie back down and swear you'll stay there, and I'll tell you."

Under normal circumstances, Dev would have knocked his younger cousin to the floor and gone out the door, but right now a toddler could probably have beaten Dev in an arm-wrestling match, so he complied. "Fine, now tell me," he said, when he'd returned to the stiff and damned uncomfortable bed.

Ian sighed hard and said in one long breath, "Deputy Do-Wrong insisted on hauling her into the station for questioning. Don't look at me like that." Ian folded his arms over his chest and scowled. "Ryan and Seth went with her. She was released pretty quick. She's been downstairs with the family ever since. Except when she went to your place to check on her ferret. Who knew those ratlike things could be so damned cute?"

"Lucy's not a rat," Shells said, her voice floating in from the open doorway.

Monitors he didn't know he was attached to beeped like gunfire at her presence.

God, she was beautiful. In jeans and a pale blue T-shirt with her hair flowing in long red curls down to her shoulders, she could have been an angel framed in the doorway.

"Frack, Dev! I told you to wait at the gate. But, oh no, you had to rush in and save the day. If you had died, I would have killed you!"

Okay, so maybe not an angel. Still . . .

"Um . . . yeah." Ian rose to his feet and hustled to the doorway, turning sideways to slide past Shelley. "I'm just gonna give you two some privacy. I need to tell the clan you're back in the land of the living, so, uh, make up quick."

Dev hissed between his teeth at the scowl on Shelley's face as Ian all but left a vapor trail behind him.

For several long moments she remained in the doorway, twisting her fingers. Finally, she stormed—there really was no other word for it—over to the bed.

Dev braced himself for a tongue-lashing. She'd been frightened when he was shot. He'd seen the fear in her eyes just before he blacked out. Not a big jump from terror to anger.

But when she reached the bed, she bent over and pressed her lips gently against his. The touch was featherlight and so quick, he hadn't had time to wrap his good arm around her before she pulled back and put three feet between them.

"I-I'm glad you're all right." She cleared her throat and blinked rapidly. Dev's heart squeezed against his rib cage at the unshed tears in her eyes. "I'm not happy with you for getting shot, but you did everything I asked. You saved a lot of lives, animal and human, that night. I wanted to thank you before I went home to Elkridge."

"Home?" The monitors beeped wildly again. "Shells, you can't leave."

"I don't have a choice. I'm needed there." She shrugged. "Beau is being transferred from here to Elkridge General tomorrow morning. I've applied to be his emergency foster mother. My old social worker, Mrs. Harris, helped me. I can't stay here with Beau back in the Ridge."

"Oh." What could Dev say to that? Beau would need her. "What's his prognosis?"

Shelley smiled. "He should be fine. It was touch and go the first night, but the doctors are confident he'll make a full recovery."

But what about us? He wanted to ask, but before he could, Shelley said, "The zoo is being shut down. I've been offered an opportunity to help with the relocation of the animals. Dr. Kessler is a mess. Jacob was his grandson. Between finding out his daughter's child is a killer, being attacked, hospitalized, and learning he doesn't have Alzheimer's, he needs my help." She gave a half-hearted smile.

"He doesn't have Alzheimer's?"

"No. Turns out Jacob, who insists everyone call him Adam now"—she waved a dismissive hand in the air—"anyway, *Jacob* was drugging him with benzodiazepine. It's why he attacked my boss in the clinic that night. Dr. Kessler caught Jacob drugging his afternoon tea. I guess Jacob wanted to make his grandfather suffer for disowning his mother. He was trying to shut down the clinic. Only Jacob really does love animals. He wanted to protect them, even as he killed four people."

"An animal-loving, deranged killer? That's a new one on

me." Dev stretched, as much as the bed and wires would allow. "This has to be the strangest case I've ever worked, and it wasn't even in my jurisdiction."

Shelley's grin was brief. "I know what you mean. It gets weirder. Remember I told you about Miah's first cub? I was right. She really didn't hurt it. Reyna sold it. Jacob found out she was selling to private collectors and threatened to turn her in if she didn't make him her partner. Together, they stole animals, but Jacob relocated them to actual zoos and sanctuaries."

"What about the deputy? Did he know?"

Shelley sat on the edge of the bed and took Dev's hand into hers. "No, he had no idea. But he's in hot water with Sheriff Webber anyway. Sheriff figures he should have had a clue what his fiancée was doing."

Dev nodded. "I'm with the sheriff there." He paused, a flicker of something playing on the fringes of his memory. "Who was in the cage with Eddy?"

Shelley's expression grew somber and she pushed to her feet. "Cristos. Jacob had already killed him before we got there."

"I'm sorry, Shells." Dev interlaced his fingers with hers. "I know he was your friend."

Her red-rimmed blue eyes met his briefly, then she slid away from his touch. She put several feet between them before she said, "Anyway, I wanted to say good-bye. And thank you for everything you did."

"But what about us?" The words were barely out of his mouth when the sheen of tears in her eyes started to spill.

"I can't." She shook her head. "Dev, I-I'm sorry. I just can't do this. Tidewater is your home. You have a big family downstairs that needs you. Here. I don't belong here. I don't have anyone here."

"You have me." He gritted the words between his teeth, furious that he wasn't enough. Then it occurred to him. "You have Jules too. She's been searching for you forever. You're not just going to leave her again?"

Shelley shook her head and backed away. Tears tracked stains down her cheeks. Her blue eyes bright with agony and . . . fear.

The pain in her gaze was so overwhelming, he almost missed the fear. "Shells, wait."

Nurse Happy followed by a short doctor in blue scrubs and white lab coat hurried into the room. She called to Shelley over her shoulder, "Sugar, you'll need to wait outside while the doctor examines him. Don't worry, darlin'. Your man'll be just fine. Now go on outside and I'll come get you."

Shelley didn't run for the door.

But Dev wasn't surprised to learn she hadn't waited.

CHAPTER 27

T HE BELLS ON the door jangled. Shelley glanced through the square window in the door separating the back of the clinic from the lobby and spotted Lucy climbing onto the counter out front. Shelley couldn't see the front door, only Lucy.

The ferret daintily sniffed the air, then retreated to her hidey-hole back under the desk. Seconds later, the squeaks of Beau's new sneakers filled the unusually quiet space.

"I'm in the back, Beau. What are you doing here? You're supposed to be walking to school."

"Aww, Doc. How'd you know it was me?" He pushed open the door and entered the doggie spa. "What'd you do with all the dogs? You didn't, like, kill them, did you?" he asked in mock horror.

"Today's guests haven't arrived yet, smart guy." Shelley bent to sweep the last of the dust into the pan and dumped it into the garbage. Storing the broom and pan in the tiny closet, she worked to keep her voice even. "You know, the state only granted me temporary custody of you. If the social worker finds out you've been skipping school on my watch, she could take you away."

Beau's big brown eyes widened behind his new glasses. He straightened his shoulders, brushed his hands down his new shirt and jeans and gave her a solemn nod. "I'll go in just a minute. I won't be late, I promise, Doc. I just forgot to tell you something important this morning."

Shelley folded her arms over her chest and waited. This wasn't the first time in the past two weeks that Beau had shown up at the clinic before school. In the beginning, she'd accepted it because she understood better than anyone the fear of being alone in the world after the death of a parent. Like Shelley, Beau still had someone who loved him. But maybe his repeated excuses for breaking the rules were his way of pushing her away. Refusing her love.

The thought made her wince. Hadn't she done the same thing to Dev? Shoved him away? But she wasn't a child. She was a woman, full-grown with responsibilities, the clinic, the animals, and now a beautiful little boy.

A little boy who was noticeably stalling.

The bells on the front door jangled again.

Beau jumped, clapped his hands together once, then threw his arms around her waist. "I love you, Doc. Be back right after school!" Then he darted through the door and out of sight.

The lobby was silent, yet Shelley had the sneaking suspicion it wasn't empty.

It had to be Dev out there. She hadn't seen him in a month. And Beau had been asking almost nonstop about visiting him. Beau was convinced she and Dev belonged together and would be a family.

Her heart gave a funny little leap. If Dev was waiting for her, she couldn't show him how excited she was to see him again. She'd just have to keep her emotions under tight control. He was a city cop. She was a country vet. A country vet whose time in this particular clinic was coming to end. But that didn't matter. What mattered was that they didn't belong together, no matter what Beau thought. No matter how much her heart ached.

Schooling her face to a pleasant but distant grin, she pushed open the swinging door.

Her heart sank.

Jules stood in the middle of the floor. Her black winter

jacket hung lazily over her right arm. Her green eyes warm and hopeful. "Hi, Shelley. I hope this isn't a bad time."

Shelley forced herself to smile brighter, gesturing to the couch. "Not at all. I'm really glad you came. I'm sorry I couldn't drive out to meet you. Between closing up the zoo, helping here, and fostering Beau, I haven't had a free moment. Come in, have a seat." Once her sister arranged herself on the couch, draping the coat across her lap, Shelley sat too. Barely a foot separated them. It could have been oceans.

When Jules had called yesterday and asked to visit, Shelley had hoped Dev would come too. Her throat burned with disappointment.

Stupid. Why would he come? Hadn't she been the one to run away when he was in the hospital?

Except now she didn't want to run anymore. She wanted . . . no *needed* to see Dev, no matter how much that idea terrified her.

Fine. She'd just have to make time to drive to Tidewater and see him. And hope he didn't slam the door in her face for being such a freaking coward.

Tears stung the backs of her eyes. *Damn it. I'm not going to cry.* She quietly cleared her throat. "So, how've you been?"

"I could say fine. But the truth is, I barely started to get to know you again, and you left. I've missed you." Jules's lips curled at the edges slightly. She shifted her position, crossing her legs and resting a hand on Shelley's. "You've got Momma's hands."

Shelley glanced down at her unpainted nails, then at her sister's. Jules had dirt beneath her short fingernails. A testament to her life as a florist. "I don't remember her hands. I remember her eyes though. They were green, like yours," Shelley admitted, then tried to pull away.

Jules tightened her hold. "Momma's hands were always so sure and strong. Even at the end. That woman could stitch anything and it would look brand-new. I bet you get your surgical skills from her."

A blush heated Shelley's cheeks. She'd been told in school she had the steadiest hands her professors had ever seen. A familiar, uncomfortable sense of need, of longing, tugged at her heart. She pushed it away. "Yes, well, I got my study habits from Nate and Jill. They were both professors, and after they adopted me, they insisted I learn the proper way to study and not slide through school on grades that came easily to me."

She pulled away again.

Jules didn't stop her. She rose and paced the office.

"Tell me about them," Jules said, surprising her. "Your adoptive parents. I want to know what they were like. I want to know what your family life was like after . . . after . . ."

"After I went away?" Shelley finished for her. Then she saw it, the regret in Jules's eyes. And something old and hot gave way to something soft and comforting. "I figured out what you did. Sending me away like that. It took a while, but I got it. You were trying to save me from a life in the system."

"And save myself. I thought if I made you leave, you couldn't leave me first. Seems there's a lot of that going around." Tears glistened on Jules's lashes. Shelley nodded, amazed by how similar they were. Before she could comment, Jules went on, "I know I hurt you. I know I made you believe I abandoned you, but I didn't. You're my sister and I love you. I just wanted you to have a family that I didn't think I could have."

"But you did. Didn't you?" Shelley finally voiced the question she'd always carried. "You were adopted too. And by good people. Right?"

When she only nodded, Shelley said, "Then you did save yourself. You have a family now."

"Now that I've found you, Shelley, I have most of my family. Next up is finding Hannah. Ian says he might have a lead. The couple that adopted Hannah made the news a few years ago. He thinks he's close to finding her."

A thrill of hope went through her. Shelley pushed it aside. "Jules, we got lucky finding each other. We may never find Hannah, you have to face that."

Shelley's words were cut off when Jules crossed back to her, taking her by the shoulders. Love and sadness in her eyes. "No, I don't." Jules crossed her arms, her face a picture of determination. "And you can't tell me you don't hope she's out there looking for us. I saw the look on your face a minute ago."

"All right, yes. I want to find Hannah," Shelley admitted.

Saying it aloud made it real and, jeez, gave her hope. Hope sucked. "Jules, you already have a family. You don't need me—"

"My family isn't complete without you. I need you. Just like you need me."

God, she wanted to believe that. She might be twenty-four, but a woman always carries the girl she once was inside her. And the girl inside Shelley desperately wanted her older sister in her life. "I've been alone for so long."

"You're wrong, *Tiger Lily*."

Shelley froze. Her heart thumped wildly in her chest. "How do you know that name? No one's ever called me that but—"

"Nate and Jill, I know." Jules smiled gently. "They told me. They've been with you. Watching over you for years. Even Barty's been hanging around. He's the reason the other dogs go nuts."

Shelley shook her head. Her hands shook and her heart pounded. She had to stare, unblinking, to keep from letting even one tear escape. "Can they . . . ?" She paused, horrified by the way her voice shook. "Can they hear me now?"

Jules paused a moment, then glanced at something on the far wall. "Yeah, they can hear you."

"Can you tell them I'm sorry? I didn't mean it when I told them I was sick of them hovering over me. I wish I had gone to the cabin with them."

"Never say that," Jules snapped. She covered her mouth with a hand briefly, as if to restrain some emotion, then dropped it again. "Nate and Jill aren't the only ones who would be devastated if you had died that night. They said you have a gift, and they're so proud of you. Of what you've accomplished. What you will accomplish."

"Really?" Her voice wavered, but this time, she didn't try to fight the tears. "Thank you, Nate and Jill. I loved you both so much."

And for an instant, Shelley thought she heard a dog bark in the distance.

Jules let out a watery chuckle. "Barty didn't want you to forget him."

"Did he just bark?" Shelley's eyes widened when Jules nodded. "I think I heard him." Glancing in the direction of the sound, she added, "I love you too, Barty."

Jules's smile faded. "Shelley, it's time. They said they have to go. They've been with you all these years because they didn't want you to be alone. Now that they know you'll never be alone again, they need to move on."

For a moment, the clinic was bathed in a pure white light, so bright it made her eyes ache. Silhouetted in the glow stood a couple, holding hands and a gorgeous Bay retriever. The light grew blinding, then winked out.

In the silence, there was a lingering feeling of love in the air and the undeniable sensation of loss.

Jules's arms were around Shelley. She hadn't seen her sister move, but suddenly, her face was pressed against Jules's shoulder. Then all the pain and fear and guilt of the past flooded away, and she wept as she'd never wept before. For the mother who died of cancer, for the strangers who became her parents, for the sisters she thought she'd lost forever.

She wept until she was spent. Jules handed her the box of tissues Shelley kept on the bookcase by the couch. "Thanks," she said, soggily.

The front bells jangled. The door opened just enough to allow Dev to poke his head in. "Jules, Seth's on the phone. He says he thinks he's got something on your vision from last week."

Then Shelley saw him. His astonishing gray eyes flashed with concern and love before he blanked his gaze. He broke eye contact first. "I'll just tell him you'll call him back."

"No, wait," Jules said, rising. "Shelley, I need to take this." She leaned down and whispered, "And I think you need to talk to Dev. He's been a giant pain in the butt without you."

Gracefully, Jules plucked the cell from Dev's fingers and slipped out the door.

And there they stood, face to face in her office. Shelley wanted to tell Dev she loved him. She wanted to tell him she'd been a fool to run away. She wanted to kiss him.

Instead she blurted, "Hi, Dev. How's your shoulder?"

SHELLEY LOOKED SO vulnerable standing in the middle of the floor, chewing on her bottom lip. It took everything Dev had not to sweep her into his arms and kiss the worry out of her.

But he suspected she'd bolt again if he tried, so he flexed his toes inside his Ferragamos and held himself back. Except, damn, standing with his back ramrod straight made his shoulder ache.

"It's healing, thanks. How are the tiger cubs?"

A smile flashed across her face as she chewed her lip again. "They're fine. They're being relocated to the Tidewater Zoo next month. With the Elkridge Zoo closed down, I've been arranging for the animals to all find good homes. You know in a sick way, Adam was doing the same thing. While Reyna sold the first tiger cub to a private collector, Adam sent the other animals to actual zoos across the country."

"Real humanitarian."

Shells snorted. "Not really. He hates everyone. Even me. I can't think of him as Jacob anymore. Jacob was my friend. Adam is just a killer. Anyway, I went to see him in the jail and found out just how much he hated me. Seems our common love for the animals was the only thing we shared." Her smile faded to a look of complete despair. "He killed all those people, the jeweler, the D.A., and Tomás. God, poor Tomás. He died because he'd seen a tape from the night of Colbert's murder and figured out it was Adam. If you and your cousins hadn't stopped him, Adam would have killed Eddy, Reyna, Beau, and me too."

Dev did move now. Three steps was all it took. Then she walked into his arms. He couldn't keep from touching her face, her hair. He'd already known it all. And more. He'd made sure the sheriff's office shared the information with him.

"I couldn't lose you too," she whispered so softly against his chest that he doubted his hearing.

"But you left me."

She pulled back only far enough to meet his gaze. Her arms stayed securely wrapped around his waist. "Everyone I've ever loved left me. My mother. My sisters. My parents. Even Cam."

"I'm not them."

"No, but when you were lying there in that hospital bed unconscious, I knew if you'd died, I'd never get over it. It was hard enough losing all of them. I couldn't bear it if you had left me too."

"And you left me *first*." Realization had him hugging her tighter. "Shells, I can't promise I'll never die."

"I know that. I *know* that. I just . . . panicked."

"I can't promise I'll never die, but I can swear to never leave you." Dev hugged her tighter, comforting her and himself. "You are all that matters. I want you in my life. You and Beau. You're his mother. And you're my world. As long as I live, I'm yours, if you'll have me. I'll even quit the force and move to Elkridge. Whatever it takes."

"Oh, Dev. I don't want you to move to Elkridge." Tears brimmed on her lashes. "There's nothing for a city boy in this little country town."

"There's you."

She shook her head.

Dev's heart shriveled. She didn't want him. He'd come all this way, and she *still* didn't want him. He was an asshole. Well, he'd be an asshole with dignity. Releasing her, he put a foot between them. The confusion and hurt on her face almost had him reaching for her again, but he didn't. "I'd better go see if Jules is ready."

"But you just said you wouldn't leave me." Shelley grabbed his arm, halting his exit. "What did I do?"

"You told me not to stay." Now he was confused.

Shelley shook her head. "No, I said there's nothing here for you. When the tigers go to the Tidewater Zoo, I'm going with them. Beau and me. I thought you knew that."

Dev stared at her, hope ballooning in his chest. "You're coming to Tidewater?"

"Once I find a place to live," she said with a shrug.

"With me. You two can live with me." He pulled her to him again. "Damn, I thought you were giving me the heave-ho."

She squeezed him tighter. "No, I just suck at this. Give me a snake or a rabbit or cat or ferret, and I'm completely in my element. But people . . . they've always seemed so foreign to me." She pressed her hands against his chest until he reluctantly released her. Her hands dropped, then came together. She twisted her fingers. "Suddenly I have a family again. I'm a foster mother to the most amazing little boy. My sister is back in my life. I thought my life was going really well. I'd convinced myself I didn't need anything or anyone else. Then you poked your head in the door and I knew in that moment, my life would never be complete without you. I love you, Dev."

Dev's heart stopped and then galloped at her words. He stared into her beautiful face and was, as usual, dumbstruck. Shells didn't let his stoicism stop her. She stood on tiptoe and kissed him.

Thank you, sweet baby Jesus!

Dev kissed her back. And kissed her. Her hands were everywhere. In his hair, on his chest. Dear God! Down his pants.

Not that his own hands were empty. They were cupped happily around her lush ass as he lifted her from the floor. Crossing the room in two strides, he propped her on the counter. Her jean-clad legs wrapped around his hips as he laid her back, swiping the phone and papers out of his way as he moved. "No skirt today?"

"Dr. Kessler's not back yet. Still my rules for a little longer. Frack, I need to lock the door."

She'd barely said the words, when he dashed to the door, flipped the lock in place, and was back nestled between her sexy thighs. The top button of her blue shirt was open, revealing her long neck. He bent her over. Ran his tongue from her collarbone to her ear and smiled when she quivered. "Say it again," he whispered.

"Still my rules?"

He laughed and nipped her ear. "Tell me again that you love me. I want to hear you say it when you don't have tears in your eyes or are afraid I'll leave you."

Dev pulled back, stared into her sapphire-colored eyes and waited.

She kissed his chin. "I love you." She kissed his right cheek, said it again. Kissed his left cheek and said it a third time, "I love you, Dev."

"I love you too."

Then he jumped back and off of her, catching the ferret in midleap as she attempted to attack him. Again. "I swear, she keeps this up and I'm going to turn her into a toupee and give her to my Uncle Seamus."

Laughing, Shelley swept the ferret into her arms. "Lucy, why did you attack Dev this time?"

Shelley's eyes locked on the ferret's, then she let out a laugh so hard, she almost dropped Lucy. To Dev's shock, Shelley shoved the furry monster into his clumsy hands. Instead of biting him, as expected, Lucy curled up and went to sleep. All the while Shelley continued to laugh.

"What's so damned funny?"

"She was welcoming you into the family. She saw us *hugging* and wanted in on the action."

Dev frowned at the ferret, then at Shelley's delighted face. "Yeah, well. From now on, when we want to *hug,* she stays locked in her cage in another room."

EPILOGUE

⁓

T HE WHITE SEQUINED gown sparkled in the early evening sunlight. The June day had started off unbearably hot, but the evening cooled nicely. Just in time for the ocean-side wedding.

Shelley smiled at her sister and wasn't surprised to see tears glitter on Jules's lashes. Leaning in, Shelley kissed her older sister on the cheek and took her bouquet. Jules turned to face her groom. As the minister spoke of love and commitment, Shelley glanced at Dev.

Seated next to Beau in the front row, one hand thrown casually around the boy's shoulders, he looked completely content. Then he turned those storm-gray eyes on her, and her breath caught.

It shouldn't have surprised her to see his open adoration, but it did. And she reveled in it. This man loved *her*. Loved her so much, he'd been willing to sacrifice his career to stay with her in Elkridge, had she asked it of him.

She toyed with the wedding band on her left hand. And to think she'd been shocked when Jules had told her she and Seth got engaged after less than two months together. But it had been Shelley and Dev who had a quick, quiet ceremony on

Valentine's Day. They went from the courthouse to social services and applied to adopt Beau. They weren't legally a family
yet, but it wouldn't be long.

The minister spoke of love and family. Shelley listened, her
gaze drifting from her husband and child to her older sister.
Shelley's heart was so full of love and joy. Family was everything, and for once, Shelley wasn't afraid of losing them.

She doubted Jules would be the only one in tears before
long. Shelley had a secret she couldn't wait to share with Jules.
One she'd learned only hours earlier from a lovable if mangy-
looking stray dog. Beau had brought it home from the beach
with the intention of keeping it as a pet.

Something Shelley could hardly refuse when the dog Beau
had dubbed Snoopy winged an image into her head. A black-
and-white vision of a young woman sharing half her sandwich
with him outside the Boxing Cat Café. A woman who bore a
striking resemblance to her mother. And a distinctly unique
triple-rose tattoo on her wrist.

Hannah was in Tidewater.

Read on for a sneak peek at the first
Tidewater novel from Mary Behre

SPIRITED

Available now from
Berkley Sensation

JULIANA SCOTT LOOPED the strap of her black Prada clutch over her wrist and imagined scaling her apartment building in five-inch stiletto boots.

Where was a radioactive spider when you needed one?

The fire escape ladder dangled about seven feet up. She'd just have to jump for it. Or she could continue to stand there like some kind of crazily dressed prostitute turned damsel-in-distress at three in the morning. Someone might come along and help her; then again, the way her night was going, she'd probably end up a statistic. Or arrested.

But her heels were freaking five inches high. And she hated climbing, boots or not.

"Come on, Jules," she sang to herself as she plowed her hand through the contents of the bag for the third time. How could she not have her keys? She might be directionally challenged but she never forgot them. Ever.

A nearby streetlight flickered off, then on again, casting a dull yellow glow.

She shuddered; goose bumps rushed up her arms but it wasn't cold. That could only mean one thing: she wasn't alone.

She listened for whoever—or more likely, *what*ever—it was to make its presence known.

Nothing. Not a sound except the ocean waves washing against the sandy shore a block away. The gentle lapping water soothed her and a small, relieved sigh slipped from her lips.

"Who, whooooooo!" A barred owl swooped low and she let out a small yelp of alarm.

Crazy bird. Jules laughed softly at her own paranoia and rubbed her weary eyes. She hadn't seen a ghost in six months. Why did she think she'd see one in Tidewater now?

She refocused on finding her keys. She shoved aside the bags of dried lavender and oregano she'd picked up from the herbalist. Skipped over the Waitress Red lipstick she'd bought for tonight's party. Dug beneath her first prize blue ribbon. And came up empty.

She shook the purse. It felt oddly heavy, but it contained nothing else.

Even her cell phone was gone.

Dang it! Another fabulous blunder to add to an already freakish night.

How was she supposed to find her missing sisters if she couldn't even find her flipping keys? Finding lost things . . . now *that* would be a gift! Instead she'd inherited the freakish ability to talk to the dead. Unless a dead person could tell her where she'd left her keys, or help her find her lost sisters, she considered it more of a *crift*—cursed gift. She shook her purse one last time.

Stupid ghosts.

She glared at the ladder's twenty rusted stairs leading to her bedroom window. Hitching the purse strap up to her elbow, she heaved a sigh and jumped twice before her fingers connected with metal. The ladder lowered with a screech. The sound echoed against the brick as she stepped one precariously high-heeled foot on the first rung.

Man, tonight totally bites.

First, Mason Hart, that overgrown jock, tried to cop a feel at their college reunion. Now, she was wriggling up a fire escape in a skirt and bustier so tight, they squeezed all the breath from her body.

I'm burning this outfit tomorrow.

Finally on the second level, she pulled up the ladder behind her and latched it in place. Every other step, her boots snagged in the grooves of the metal deck. She started past her neighbor's partially opened window when the goose bumps returned.

An incredible sense of anger and sadness swept over her. Someone else's pain. The feelings smothered her sense of self and stole her breath. Bracing herself against the brick, she fought to erect the mental shields that she used to block out a spirit's projected emotions.

She visualized gray castle walls rising around her, the same mental image she'd used since childhood. Castles were strong and safe . . . impenetrable. With her mental shields in place, her breathing eased and she rested against the wall.

Below, the street sat eerily quiet and dark. Even the owl stopped hooting. As far as she could see she was alone, but her senses screamed she had company.

Minutes ticked past and nothing moved. A warm ocean breeze carried the sound of the rushing shore. Otherwise, silence.

Home and her bed waited less than a foot away.

"Help me . . . please . . ."

The high-pitched voice grated against her senses.

"Not now," Jules whispered, wishing she could just ignore the girly-sounding disembodied voice.

And a fresh one at that. New specters hadn't yet mastered the ability to communicate without rubbing against the corporeal plane. The effect on her body was like fingernails on a chalkboard. Unlike the dead, living people didn't make her skin crawl just by speaking.

Jules tried to lift her window. It didn't budge. She eyed the lock but it was open. Why wouldn't the darn thing move?

"I . . . need . . . you . . ."

Frustration tinged with a healthy dose of fear whipped through her. She shoved at the window again. It still didn't move. Rubbing at her goose bump–covered arms, she turned to her neighbor's window. It was open and dark inside. She dismissed the fleeting thought. She'd sooner scale down the building naked than . . .

Her mind muddled. She shook her head to clear it. The scent of sandalwood filled her. Warmth suffused her bones and she couldn't resist the pull to the open window.

The aroma intensified. Never before had anything smelled so wonderful. A warm, gooey, just-ate-the-best-caramel-brownies-ever feeling filled her. She had to get closer. The urge to get inside was overpowering.

The scent wafted through the open window and her body tingled, needing to get closer. The leather skirt hugged her thighs too tightly as she tried to step through. Instead, she shifted and pushed through headfirst. Each movement dream-like. Jules's belly on the sill and her booted feet still outside, the scent drew her in until she tumbled to the floor. Breaking the trance, the specter whispered one word.

"Finally."

WAS HE DREAMING? Detective Seth English of the Tidewater Police Department rubbed his eyes. Nope, no question about it. Someone *was* breaking into his apartment.

Criminals are just stupid.

Of all the nights to leave his window open, Seth had to pick tonight. He damned his recent bout of insomnia. Stress always did that to him. The sound of the ocean usually soothed him. Not tonight. His much-needed peace was shattered by a felony in progress.

He sat up. The blanket fell to his waist. Sliding noiselessly out of bed, he grabbed his gun and handcuffs from the night-stand. He slipped into the shadowed corner and waited.

Damn. The last thing he needed was a trip downtown and a night full of paperwork. Lately, it seemed to be one thing after another: his daughter's engagement, his new partner, their unsolvable case . . . and now this.

Could his life get any more complicated without his head actually imploding?

The window frame groaned then gave another inch.

The streetlamp outside cast her in silhouette. And she was definitely a she. Delicate feminine fingers slipped into the opening and wrapped around the frame, pushing the window slowly upward.

Seth watched, barely breathing, as she wriggled through the window. When she'd made it mostly through, her hands flew wide in front of her as if searching for leverage. Then she tumbled to the floor with a grunt.

"Stay down!" Lunging forward, he planted a knee in her back. He pressed the gun into the base of her skull. His other hand twisted each of her wrists behind her and cuffed them together.

"Ouch! Stop!" she screamed. "Help! Police!"

"I *am* the police." He ran his finger along her wrists to ensure he hadn't snapped the cuffs too tight. "You're fine."

In the dim light, Seth reached down to help her up. He couldn't very well leave her on the floor, regardless of the temptation. Fumbling in the dark, his hand brushed the warm satin skin of her bared midriff.

"Get your hands off me! Somebody! Help me!" She shrieked a banshee's wail next to his ear.

"What the hell are you yelling for?" He tugged her over to the bed and shoved her down.

She thrashed and screamed incomprehensibly.

"Enough! Or I'll charge you with disturbing the peace too." When she kept shrieking, he added, "*You* broke into my place, ruining the first night's sleep I've had in a week. I don't need you bursting my eardrum too. Now be quiet. I'm getting the light."

Her cries instantly died in the shock of blinding light.

When Seth's eyes focused, he pinched the bridge of his nose.

The hooker—she had to be a hooker—wore knee-high black patent leather stiletto boots, a black miniskirt that could have doubled as a headband, and a leather bustier. Her legs were long and lean and covered in fishnet stockings. And the swell of her breasts was, in a word . . . succulent. Her short, straight midnight-colored hair was too dark to be real. The woman personified sex, as was her obvious intention. But her green eyes made his pulse thrum.

They were astonishing, as if emeralds were cut and layered around the pupils. The most beautiful eyes he'd ever seen, in spite of the appallingly thick black eyeliner surrounding them.

And strawberries? God, she smelled like *strawberries*. His mouth actually watered.

Attracted to a hooker. I've sunk so low.

Chalking it up to his sexual drought, he focused on dealing with the handcuffed home invader thrashing around on his bed. He tried to shove his sidearm into his shoulder holster before remembering he was shirtless. Stomping over to the bedside table, he yanked open the drawer and dropped the gun in.

He hoped she'd think the heat creeping up his cheeks was from anger instead of embarrassment. Folding his arms across his chest, he asked, "Do you have any idea where you are?"

JULES SAT DUMBFOUNDED in the bedroom of a Greek god. He had espresso brown eyes, curly black hair, a long nose that had probably been broken a time or two, and a sexy, dimpled chin. His tan, muscular body was covered by a chest full of springy hair that begged to be touched. Dang! He even smelled good, like soap and the salty Tidewater air.

Ohmigawd, he's a walking condom commercial.

He scowled at her, waiting for an answer. Although to save her life she couldn't think of anything. Where *was* she? More important, what was she doing here? Then a mental switch flipped and it all became clear.

That freaking ghost! Jules couldn't very well tell a cop she stumbled into his apartment because a ghost made her do it. He'd haul her off to the loony bin.

"Well." Jules fidgeted against the cuffs and tried to adjust to a more dignified position on the bed. So not happening. "No, not really. I was trying to go home but, uh . . . locked myself out."

He arched an eyebrow at her but didn't say anything.

"I know this looks bad but just ask Big Jim. He'll vouch for me."

"And Big Jim? Who's that, your pimp?"

"What? No!" She laughed and shook her head at the absurd thought. "He's my dad."

"Is that what they're calling them these days?" He scoffed but didn't give her time to respond. "There's no one named Big Jim in this building. Try again, the truth this time."

"Ernie Ward! *Ernie* is my dad."

"I thought his name was Jim." He shook his head. He made a sound like a buzzer. "Wrong again. I've known Ernie for years but I've never seen you before. Want to try another name, honey?"

His biceps flexed, arms still folded across his chest, as if he wanted to move but barely restrained himself. The sight was distracting. He wasn't exactly muscle-bound, just finely honed. He stood fierce and masculine like an ancient warrior. Intimidating but ruthlessly sexy. It made her want to . . . She shook herself inwardly.

Why couldn't she think straight? This so wasn't like her. She didn't go gooey over any guy, regardless of how ruggedly handsome. But her heart pounded at an erratic pace and she'd once again lost the thread of the conversation. What had he just asked?

Think, Jules! Ignore the instant pull of pointless physical attraction. It had never done her any favors in the past anyway. *Something about him must be repellent. Find it!*

She looked at him again, this time skating her gaze past his naked chest and sexy arms and moving down.

Oh, it couldn't be.

She blinked, astonished.

He wore bright yellow pajama pants, covered in *lambs*.

Resisting the urge to laugh, she latched onto righteous indignation and straightened her shoulders. This condescending jerk treated her like a criminal, handcuffed her, and called her a liar. Oh, he was going down.

"My name's Jules. Not *honey*," she snapped. "And Big Jim—Ernie—*is* my father. He lives in this building and I live with him."

"I highly doubt it. Hookers don't live here," he said, tugging a red T-shirt over his head.

"Excuse me?" she yelled. "I'm not a hooker, and you owe me an apology!"

"Really?" he said, giving her an obvious once-over, his gaze settling on her bustier.

Her cheeks burned.

"Wait. I can explain."

"Enlighten me." He narrowed his eyes, doubt etched on his face.

"See, there was this costume party and . . ." Her words

trailed off. How to explain the theme of her college reunion without sounding like an imbecile for dressing in the ridiculous outfit just to win a blue ribbon? Now that she thought about it, *stupid* might aptly describe her decision-making skills tonight. "Well, there was a Pimp and Ho party earlier tonight. I was on my way home from it—"

"And you just happened to climb into my window?"

Jules opened her mouth to respond, but doubted he'd believe her anyway. So she settled on a half-truth. "It was a mistake. I meant to climb into Big Jim's window, but it was jammed and yours was . . . open."

"Ah ha!" His mouth twisted into a satisfied grin. "You admit to breaking and entering."

"Not breaking. Just entering. And who in his right mind sleeps in this city without a screen in his window anyway?" Oops! She hadn't meant to say that last part, but she pushed on. "If you'll just let me go find Big Jim—"

"Don't think so." With a grim expression on his face, he tugged her to her feet. "Time to go."

"Where are we going?" Jules dragged her heels, her stilettos scraping the wooden floorboards.

Still in his pajama bottoms, he jammed his feet into a pair of loafers.

Jules gaped. The gladiator image of him fizzled with each passing second. "Are you *really* planning to go out in public dressed like an overgrown four-year-old?"

"Shut. Up," he growled, jerking on a knee-length, brown leather coat. "Say another word and I'll charge you with resisting arrest."

"Wait, uh, I think there's been some mistake."

"You bet your sweet ass, there has."

"Where . . . where . . ." Jules swallowed in an effort to keep her voice from shaking. "Where are we going?"

"You're gonna spend the night in lockup."

"Please, not jail!" Her words ended on a squeak, but she couldn't help it.

Earth-bound ghosts, bent on driving the living crazy, seemed to love hanging out in graveyards and jails. When they realized she could actually hear them, she'd be defenseless.

The needy ones would annoy her, but the evil ghosts—who'd managed to elude the hell beasts that usually put them where they belonged—they could attack en masse.

Their vicious thoughts would seep into her consciousness like a staticky radio she couldn't turn off. They could strip her of her sanity. A single night in jail nearly drove her mad once before. She doubted she'd survive it a second time.

She pleaded, "If you'll just let me talk to Big Jim, he'll straighten this out, I promise."

He glared at her, wrenching open the front door. "You have the right to remain silent."

Guess again.

She rushed into the hallway, screaming at the top of her lungs. "Big Jim! Big Jim! Help me! Big Jim!"

"Quiet!" the cop shouted. He grabbed her from behind and clapped a hand over her mouth as the door slammed shut.

He pulled her against him. With her cuffed hands behind her back, she pushed against him, trying to twist away. Leveraging her weight, she clutched and got a fistful of coat leather in one hand and warm, cotton pajama bottoms in the other. She froze. Her hands were lined up with the apex of his thighs.

Could this get any worse?

Of course it could.

His body reacted to her unintended groping. Jules attempted to push away, but only succeeded in pressing harder against his tightening groin.

No, no, no.

Images of their naked bodies joined together slammed into her mind, stealing her breath. Never in her life had she experienced such vivid fantasies, only these weren't hers. Like the entrancing smell that drew her into his apartment, these images were coming from outside of her, manipulating her senses.

The sex scenes playing through her mind had to be courtesy of the cop holding her too close. Jules nearly swallowed her tongue at the onslaught of the explicit images he'd somehow sent winging into her mind. Before she had time to wonder how a living person managed to project his thoughts—and they *had* to be his—he'd spun her around to face him.

Her gaze dipped past his abdomen before zipping back to

his implacable expression. She hadn't intended to look, but in his fantasies he was huge. According to the sword tenting his pajama bottoms, that part of his fantasy was real.

And the gladiator image sprang to life again.

He cleared his throat, drawing her attention to his lethal gaze.

"I, uh . . ." Her cheeks heated as she stammered a muffled apology. His hand loosened, but remained pressed over her lips. "P-please—"

"Look, Happy Hooker, do you really want to add soliciting a police officer to your list of offenses tonight?"

"No," she whispered and shifted farther from him, pressing against the wall behind her. He crowded closer. At first it seemed threatening; except he emanated desire, not hostility.

A stream of heated images flitted through her mind, images of his lips exploring her . . . everywhere. Her breath skittered, her cheeks burned hotter, and her mouth went dry at the flare of attraction in his eyes.

"Mmm . . ." She tried to speak, inadvertently moistening his salty palm with her tongue.

The cop sucked in his breath. His darkening gaze flicked from her eyes to his hand on her mouth and back again. Then he drew his fingers across her lips in a manner so sensual, she shuddered.

"Don't push this any further," he whispered against her ear. He lightly traced her bottom lip with the tip of his index finger. Time stopped as his face lowered to hers.

Lost in his nearly obsidian gaze, she waited for him to kiss her.

And he was going to kiss her.

Somewhere in the back of her mind, she knew this was a bad idea.

But, God help her, she couldn't think of a single reason why she should stop him. His gaze lowered to her mouth and Jules licked her lips.

He leaned closer.

Her heart raced.

A rusty-hinged door squeaked open. Big Jim—who wasn't really big at all—appeared out of nowhere.

"Seth? What's with all the noise?" Big Jim yawned, stepping out into the hallway and closing the door behind him. "You're gonna wake April."

The cop leapt away from Jules but kept a firm grip on her upper arm. "Hi, Ernie. Sorry for the disturbance. Police business. I thought you and April were in Florida this week."

"Nah. We leave Monday." As if seeing her for the first time, Big Jim turned to her. "Jules? Is that you?"

She glanced at the man, barely twelve years her senior, who'd adopted her shortly after her thirteenth birthday, then back at Seth the Cop. Thanks to Big Jim's appearance, her illogical and ill-timed desire quickly morphed into anger.

Glaring at the cop with triumph in her eyes, she shook free of his hold. With as much pride as she could muster, which wasn't much considering she *was* dressed like a prostitute in handcuffs, she strode over to her rescuer.

"Hey, Big Jim." She planted a kiss on his cheek.

"Oh Lord, Jules! You look like a hooker." Big Jim's lips twitched.

"I won first prize in the Pimp and Ho contest."

"Oh God, you really did it! April said you were going to . . . but I never dreamed you'd actually have the guts to wear *that* in public." Big Jim laughed out loud. "I hope she took a picture."

The cop, who must have followed her, now stood so close his warm breath feathered across her ear. It sent electric tingles down her spine. *Oh boy!* She liked it. A lot.

This needed to stop. Jules slid from between the men.

"Do you know this girl?" the cop asked, oozing disbelief. "She climbed into my bedroom window tonight. She claims to live with someone named *Big Jim*. Then she tried to tell me she lives with you."

"I'm not a girl, I'm a woman." Jules bit off the words. She lifted her chin and added, "I do live here. I moved in this morning."

"She's my daughter. She—she calls me Big Jim. Family joke," Big Jim managed to say before lapsing into a guffaw.

"See?" Jules narrowed her eyes. "I told you so."

The cop took a step back. His eyebrows disappeared beneath the curly locks that fell over his forehead.

Big Jim's whooping laughs filled the hallway. Not seeing the humor in her situation, Jules glared defiantly at the cop.

He gaped, clearly bewildered, but made no effort to let her go.

With waning patience, she tapped her stiletto-clad foot on the linoleum and cleared her throat.

"Use your key next time, *Precious*," the cop growled in her ear, spinning her around. Then the cuffs were blessedly off. "You could have climbed into the window of a psycho. Good thing for you it was me. You got lucky."

Jules rubbed her sore wrists. "Gee, I never knew getting lucky could be so disappointing."

The cop opened his mouth, then snapped it closed. "Good night, *Big Jim*," he said, looking pointedly at Jules.

" 'Night, *Lambkins*!" she called out, wiggling her fingers in a mock wave as his door slammed shut.

Big Jim guffawed again. "Jules, for a woman determined to lead an ordinary life, you're off to an exciting start."

"Thanks a lot." Jules frowned at her salacious costume. Jeez, she needed to change into her own clothes.

With a sigh, she reached for the knob and twisted it. It didn't budge.

"Juliana . . ." Big Jim held open his front door.

Dang it! That cop had her so flustered she had tried to enter the wrong apartment again.

"You know," Big Jim said with a snicker when she finally crossed her own threshold, "you have a terrible sense of direction for a psychic."

STRETCHED OUT IN bed, she forced her mind to clear. Considering it was four in the morning, Jules should have been exhausted, but her mind raced. Across the room, her clothes and black wig lay in a pile on the dresser. The costume had been killer, but that wig itched all night. She scratched her head, capturing the coppery strands of hair between her fingers briefly and examining them with a grin.

Shock value. She won for that alone. After all, who would have suspected that she—a former preschool teacher, who never swore—would dare show up dressed as a member of the world's oldest profession?

Pride flooded through her. All through college she'd been the oddball. The one who was different. For a few hours tonight, she was normal. No one looked at her as if waiting for her to talk to a wall or an invisible person. Or a ghost.

Being crowned "First Ho" wasn't quite the same as being Homecoming Queen, but the general acceptance had been glorious.

Okay, so she had veered from her plan to be completely normal and boring, but it had been fun. After what she'd been through in the last two years with her divorce, she needed a little excitement. At least the party had nothing to do with ghosts or psychic abilities.

Tomorrow, she'd go back to being plain, ordinary Juliana.

For some reason, the neighbor-cop's face flashed through her mind at that moment. The man topped the charts on the sexy scale. He met her three *H* rule: hot, huge—the man had to be at least six foot two, not to mention where her hands had been earlier—and oh, so handsome. Yep, he could send a nun's hormones raging. And she wasn't a nun . . . she just felt like one.

Jules stared at the ceiling. She counted all the tiles three times before her eyes drooped closed. Just before succumbing to the exhaustion, Seth the Cop's face appeared again. This time his lips curled up in a roguish smile, making him more handsome than ever. She'd slipped into the state between dreaming and waking and drifted along with the fantasy.

His rich brown eyes grew black as he leaned in close, captured her mouth with his, and drank her in. He tasted like hazelnut coffee. Jules sighed with delight. He chuckled and buried his hands in her hair, pulling her closer. She breathed in the scent of sandalwood as he licked a path from her lips down to her collarbone before returning to her mouth. He swept his tongue inside and her senses exploded with the heady taste of him.

She opened her eyes but Seth had disappeared. Thick, gray fog blinded her.

Her world tilted and twirled, like a carnival ride, spinning faster and faster until it jarred to a halt. Lighting, sounds, colors—everything . . . changed. She was no longer herself but someone else. Jules had taken this particular type of trip too many times not to know when she'd fallen into someone else's gruesome reality.

"Pleeaaasssse," she cried in the darkness and shoved at

the walls crowding in around her. She scraped her fingernails down the metal walls, searching for a release latch that wasn't there. The stench of copper permeated the tight space. Blood oozed from her raw fingers. "Let me out!"

The car's trunk flew open. White light blinded her, then snuffed out. She lay still, unable to focus. She didn't need to see who had rescued her. Only he would have come. He'd promised he'd protect her. How could she have doubted him? Relief washed through her.

Hands wrapped around her wrists and tugged her from the Buick. Free from the vehicle, he released her wrists and caressed her shoulders. She slumped against him, then jumped at the sensation of the foreign planes of his chest.

This wasn't her lover. She tried to pull away but he manacled one of her wrists, refusing to allow her to escape.

She searched his face. Even masked by shadows, he exuded a lethal air. He might have cared for her once but not now. This man was a cold-blooded killer who meant to punish her for betraying him. His gloved fingers traced around her neck, while his thumbs stroked the hollow of her throat. She swallowed convulsively.

"Where are they?" The whispered words made her flinch.

"I don't know. Please, don't do this." She flinched and tears sprang to her eyes. "I did it for all of us."

"Where are they?" His grip tightened. "Give them back."

"I c-can't." She couldn't return them, even if she'd wanted to—he knew that.

His fingers dug deeper into her neck. She clawed at his leather-encased hands. Yellow spots blinked before her bulging eyes. Her ears buzzed. No! She'd only wanted to do the right thing. She couldn't die. Not yet. It wasn't fair! She had a future. Two lives depended on her.

She jerked her knee into his groin. He grunted but squeezed her throat harder. The buzzing in her head became a tidal wave of noise.

Her vision narrowed to a sliver of light then winked out to black.

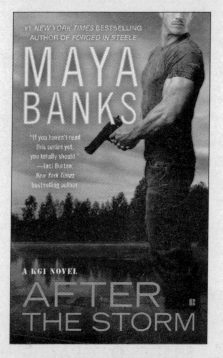